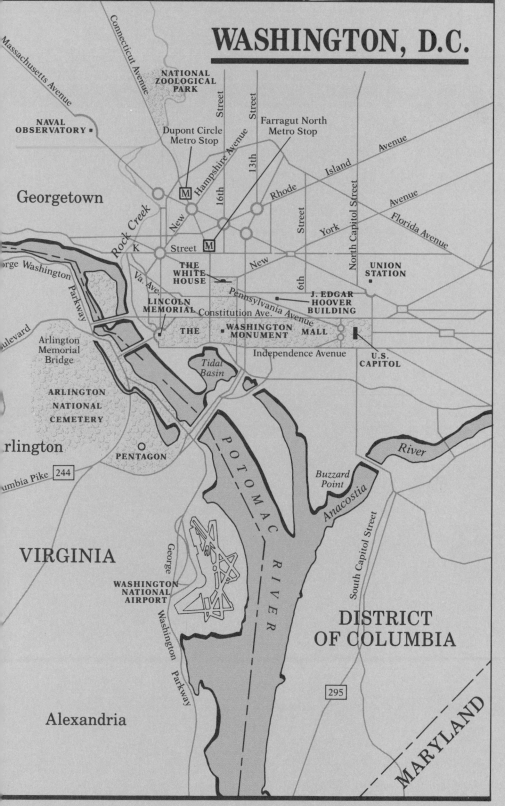

WASHINGTON, D.C.

Massachusetts Avenue

Connecticut Avenue

NATIONAL ZOOLOGICAL PARK

NAVAL OBSERVATORY

Dupont Circle Metro Stop

Farragut North Metro Stop

Hampshire Avenue

Street

13th

Street

16th

Avenue

Island

Rhode

Avenue

Georgetown

Rock Creek

New

York

Florida Avenue

North Capitol Street

Street

K

Street

THE WHITE HOUSE

New

6th

UNION STATION

orge Washington Parkway

Va. Ave.

LINCOLN MEMORIAL

Pennsylvania Avenue

J. EDGAR HOOVER BUILDING

Constitution Ave.

THE

WASHINGTON MONUMENT

MALL

ulevard

Arlington Memorial Bridge

Independence Avenue

U.S. CAPITOL

Tidal Basin

ARLINGTON NATIONAL CEMETERY

rlington

PENTAGON

Buzzard Point

River

umbia Pike 244

POTOMAC RIVER

Anacostia

South Capitol Street

VIRGINIA

George

WASHINGTON NATIONAL AIRPORT

Washington

DISTRICT OF COLUMBIA

Washington Parkway

295

MARYLAND

Alexandria

HARD
FALL

HARD FALL

RIDLEY PEARSON

Delacorte
Press

Published by
Delacorte Press
Bantam Doubleday Dell Publishing Group, Inc.
666 Fifth Avenue
New York, New York 10103

Library of Congress Cataloging in Publication Data

Pearson, Ridley.
    Hard fall : a novel / by Ridley Pearson.
        p.   cm.
    ISBN 0-385-30138-3 : $20.00
    I. Title.
    PS3566.E234H37   1992
    813'.54—dc20   91-15484   CIP

Manufactured in the United States of America

Published simultaneously in Canada

January 1992

10 9 8 7 6 5 4 3 2 1
FFG

For Colleen

ACKNOWLEDGMENTS

Cameron Daggett, Chief of Police, Sun Valley, Idaho

Seattle: Dr. Christian Harris, Psychiatrist; Dr. Donald Reay, King County Medical Examiner, the Seattle Police Department; John E. Hope, Simulator Projects/Training, Boeing Commercial Airplane Group; Jerry Femling, Senior Manager, Security, The Boeing Company

Los Angeles: Detective Dennis Payne, Robbery/Homicide, Los Angeles Police Department; various anonymous members of the LAPD substation, Los Angeles International Airport

Washington, D.C.: David Dodge Thompson, National Gallery. FBI: (Washington Metropolitan Field Office) Thomas E. Duhadway, Special Agent in Charge; James E. Mull; (Hoover Building) Stephen D. Gladis; David W. Wade, Chief Telecommunications Services; J. Christopher Ronay, Chief Explosives Unit; I. Ray McElhaney, Jr.; Robert B. Davenport; Dr. Rose Anne Fedorko; and to the many other Special Agents who could not be named. . . .

Thanks also to: Richard and Lynette Hart; Ollie Cossman; Louisa Jane Modisette; Jacques Bailhe; Franklin Heller; Ian Cumming; Darwin Ridd and Leucadia Film; Bruce Kaufman; Carolyn Johansen.

Office Management: Mary Peterson
Manuscript Preparation: Colleen Daly, Maida Spaulding

Special Thanks: Al Zuckerman, Writer's House; the Warden and Fellows of Wadham College, Oxford, England; the Fulbright Commission

NOTE: A glossary of acronyms can be found on the final page.

Some facts in this story (both in locale and of a technical nature) have been deliberately changed or altered for reasons of storytelling, or at the request of law enforcement or specific individuals who aided me in my research. Certain secrets remain intact, which is better for everyone. To the warm and generous people of Seattle, Los Angeles, and Washington, D.C., my advance apologies for any mistakes that could have been avoided.

1

CAM DAGGETT SHOOK his watch, questioning its accuracy, and glanced a quarter-mile ahead at the dirty, exhaust-encrusted sign that indicated the lane change for National Airport. Heat waves rose in fluid sheets from the pavement, distorting the distance, carrying gray exhaust into the canopy of smog. Given this traffic, they would never make it in time.

News radio explained that the congestion was the result of a three-car pileup with injury. Daggett checked the rearview mirror, wondering if he could pull some stunt with the car. He feared that if he didn't, there might be a hell of a lot more injury to come. And it wouldn't be a few cars on a highway; it would be the burning hulk of an airliner spread over several acres.

"What about a helicopter? We could call for a helicopter."

The big man on the seat next to him mopped his forehead and said nothing. Daggett's anxiety threatened again. He felt boxed in. By the traffic. By this obese man sitting next to him. He could feel his hair turning gray.

A yellow hamburger wrapper replete with golden arches fluttered like a bird with a broken wing and dove into traffic, adhering to the side of a Mercedes where it smeared catsup across the side panel doors like blood from an open wound.

He felt wounded, too, if pride could be wounded. Marcel Bernard had escaped FBI surveillance six days earlier in Los Angeles.

Now, through a fluke, a stroke of luck, they had the

man in their sights once more. Daggett had no intention of losing him again. Bernard built bombs for a living. He was one of the best, or one of the worst, depending on which side of the interrogation table you sat. The interrogation. Impatience gnawed at Daggett like a stray dog at the mailman's heel. A bulging file back in his office at Buzzard Point contained a grainy black-and-white photograph of what had proved to be a portion of Bernard's thumbprint. Laboratory evidence. As good as a noose around the neck. Hopefully, the gallows might be traded for information vital to Daggett's continuing investigation into the downing of EuroTours flight 1023. The man who built the bomb was one thing; but the man who planted the bomb—he was the real killer.

Up ahead, a driver climbed out of his car and popped the hood. The August heat and humidity had claimed another victim.

"Twenty-two minutes," he announced through clenched teeth to the overweight Bob Backman, enthroned in the seat next to him. Behind his back, they called him Falstaff because of his enormous gut. Coat off, wheezing like an asthmatic, Backman was soaked through in a sweat. "That plane goes in twenty-two minutes," Daggett repeated.

Backman attempted to appear calm. He was a bad actor. Perhaps he intended to part the traffic, a fat Moses at the George Washington Memorial Parkway.

Daggett had the leathery features of a major league first baseman. He had a hard brow, dark, intimidating eyes, and a prominent nose. His lips didn't move much when he spoke, a holdover from wearing braces during his adolescence. He was soft-spoken—a family trait—though by his build one might have expected more of a growl.

"Why exactly *did* you come along?" Daggett asked Backman.

"I wondered when we would get to that," Backman admitted, blotting a drip of sweat from his double chin. Backman was a bookish man, with a receding hairline and chapped lips. He tended toward shirt collars a size too big and suits a size too small. "You're not debriefing him. I am."

Backman conduct an interrogation? Impossible. It was like asking Ty Cobb back into the batter's box. Daggett gripped the wheel tightly in frustration. His Casio read: MON 8-13.

Backman said, "I suppose you think I'm trying to steal your thunder. You do all the legwork, I do the debriefing and take the credit. That's not how it is." He struck a pose, imagining himself a heavy, but this attempt also failed.

Daggett was thinking: To come all this way—to within a mile or two of finally interrogating Bernard—and now this loaf taps me on the shoulder and steals the dance. Again.

He and Backman had long since parted ways. Trust formed the cornerstone of any relationship, especially FBI agents working the same case; Daggett would never trust Backman again. A year earlier, Backman had pilfered a file from Daggett's desk, hand-carried it to the Special-Agent-in-Charge, and claimed credit for its authorship—a file that connected Bernard with the little-known West German terrorist group *Der Grund*. In that one move, he had effectively stolen eighteen months of Daggett's life. Afraid it might backfire on him, Daggett had not attempted to correct the injustice—authorship of such files was difficult, if not impossible, to prove.

As a direct result of this stolen credit, Backman had been promoted to chief of the foreign counterterrorism squad. The man was nothing but a lazy, unimaginative parasite who grew fat on the hard work of others. Over the past twelve months, he had developed this into something of an art. Everyone in the C-3 bullpen now took their files home with them out of habit.

When the chief of C-3 had climbed into his car thirty minutes earlier, Daggett had experienced an immediate déjà vu. The more things change, he thought. How many times had they ridden together like this? It seemed like ages ago. Despite his assertion to the contrary, Backman was here for only one reason: to claim credit for the apprehension of Bernard and any information gleaned through interrogation. Daggett plotted a way around this while Backman wheezed in the seat next to him, and lived up to his reputation as the human pork belly.

Backman knew little, if anything, about Bernard, and hadn't conducted an interrogation in at least a year, maybe longer.

"Nineteen minutes," Daggett said bluntly, wanting some action. "Neither of us is going to debrief him if we don't get him off that plane." He yanked on the door handle. He could run a mile in seven or eight minutes. He ran every morning of his life. He could escape on foot and conduct the interrogation himself. He had no intention of watching Bernard's plane take off overhead while he sat trapped in a car breathing in Backman's body odor.

"You wouldn't want to miss a chance to get Kort, would you?" the fat man asked.

Daggett pulled his foot back inside and shut the door. The dome light went off. He felt chilled.

"You're the one who gave us Bernard. You deserve to hear this." He nodded at Daggett with something like respect. The heat was obviously getting to him. Fat people had more trouble than most with the heat. "The Germans raided *Der Grund* last night." Daggett felt wounded: this was not the schedule he had hoped for. This had been his investigation, and now it was running away from him.

"They didn't get Kort," Backman added in a voice filled with regret and failure, yet tinged with a hint of apology.

Daggett nodded and coughed up nervous laughter, and along with it, a bitter taste at the back of his throat. Blood or bile; all the same. Nothing could hurt him now; he had gone numb. He tugged at his shirt collar. The button popped loose. It slid down his shirt and rolled down his leg. He grabbed for the button but missed, which held significance for him.

His pursuit of Bernard, his passing of information

about *Der Grund* on to the Germans—the last two years of his life—had all been directed at but one aim: to apprehend Anthony Kort. The carrot at the end of the stick that had kept him going. And now . . .

Backman interrupted his thoughts. Backman always interrupted. "Are you following this, Michigan?"

Daggett nodded, annoyed that Backman felt free to use the nickname. They called him that because of the college-letter jacket he lived in. It was a lucky jacket. If one looked real closely at the right-hand pocket, a small gather of thread about the size of a bullet stuck out there. There had been no Bible carried in Cam Daggett's pocket on the day he had been shot at, but instead an autographed baseball he had intended to present to his son on the boy's fifth birthday. The baseball now resided on Duncan's shelf, the hollow-point slug lodged deeply within it, and Duncan wore the jacket whenever possible. Daggett's *friends* called him Michigan, not people like Backman.

"If you think Bernard can get you Kort, you're dreaming," Daggett said. "The Germans shouldn't have gone ahead with the bust. How many times did we discuss that with them? Kort would have shown up sooner or later. . . . There would have been a lead of some sort. We're fucked. We'll never get him now."

"Bernard—"

"Bernard won't know squat about Kort. *We* don't know squat about Kort. A name, that's all. What else do we have? No face to attach to it, no file. Just the name from an untrustworthy squeal. We put too much faith in that in the first place. Who knows if there even is an Anthony Kort?" Depression caved in on him. The air in the car had gone impossibly stale.

"Of course Kort exists," Backman said angrily. "You know that as well as I." But you could hear in his voice that he didn't believe it.

"He's a starting point," Backman insisted, grasping at straws. "In all likelihood, Bernard built a detonator in his

Los Angeles hotel room. Right? And now, thanks to *you,* we have no idea where that detonator is! If we did, we might find Kort yet."

The Los Angeles Field Office had fouled up the Bernard surveillance, not Daggett. As the case-agent-in-charge, he was only indirectly responsible. It was a cheap shot and both men knew it.

Daggett argued, "We don't *know* that Bernard built a detonator. We don't know shit. And if you think he's just going to offer up the information—"

"It's *my* interrogation, Michigan. Mine, and mine alone. Got it?"

Bernard was Daggett's only hope. At all costs, Backman had to be prevented from conducting the interrogation. He reopened the car door, overwhelmed once again by the fumes. "Sixteen minutes." He still had a chance.

Attempting to sound calm, Backman said, "The Airport Police are on notice to keep that plane on the ground. The passengers will be told the delay is for mechanical reasons. Don't worry about it."

"You think a stunt like that will fool Bernard? You think the Airport Police can handle Bernard?" He slapped the car keys into Backman's damp, pudgy hand. "I'm going on foot."

"You're *what*?"

He hurried from the car before Backman could object.

To his complete surprise, only seconds into his run, he heard the heavy thump of a car door behind him, and knew without looking it was Backman. So it was going to be a race, was it? He lengthened his stride, lifted his chin, and pushed on toward the exit, far in the shimmering distance.

As Daggett ran, his body fell into the familiar rhythm, and his anger lifted. Running had a way of cleansing him, even in the heat and smog of Washington in August. Running to the airport, to an interrogation—how was *that* for dedication to the job? If the boys in the bullpen ever found out, he was sure to be razzed. At least he was running *away* from Backman—that much was in his favor.

His gun thumped at his waist annoyingly. A dozen sea gulls flew overhead, in search of landfill to plunder. Maybe one of them would shit on Backman.

Soaking wet with perspiration, Daggett reached the dingy Airport Police office on the ground floor of Terminal One, where he was greeted by two men in permanent-press suits who introduced themselves as detectives. Airport Police, a private company, had no legitimate connection to the metropolitan police force. These men were not detectives.

The security at any major airport consisted of a cruel assortment of various levels of authority. Metropolitan Police—real cops—had the power to arrest; their presence was typically small, confined to a half-dozen cars and twice that many men; city budgets didn't allow for the policing of airports on a large scale. That task was passed on to Airport Police, a private company that had the authority and necessary licenses for their patrolmen to carry arms, though these patrolmen could only detain individuals for later arrest by the proper metropolitan boys. Airport Police ran about a hundred men and women. Security, the people in blazers at X-ray machines, represented yet another private contract. They had virtually no authority, other than to search personal property; they passed their problem passengers into the hands of Airport Police, who then passed them on to Metropolitan Police. Communication between these various private and public organizations was as good as could be expected. That bad.

The FBI, the Federal Aviation Administration, and a half-dozen other investigative agencies fit into this command structure somewhere so difficult to define that they were viewed both suspiciously and often with a good deal of contempt by the private companies. Daggett felt this fully as he reached out his hand, and the two men facing him shook it reluctantly.

Following these uncomfortable introductions, they all

headed off at a brisk pace toward the gate. By the sound of his voice and the color of his teeth, the taller of the two was a smoker. He didn't offer a name. Daggett sensed immediately that these guys carried chips on their shoulders. They acted nervous and falsely overconfident. The Smoker was gravel-voiced and rough-skinned; he moved frantically, gesticulating wildly, the kind of man who probably ground his teeth in his sleep.

His sidekick—Daggett thought he heard the name as Henderson but wasn't sure—looked like an Italian version of the Leakey ape. He was hard-featured and stood firmly planted in well-worn shoes. He had almost no hair. Daggett saw him not as Henderson, but as Hairless. He had the look of a veteran field agent, stoic and inquisitive, the kind to ask questions, not answer them.

The airport was old. The basement corridor connecting the terminals was walled with a red carpet wainscoting. The ceiling was yellowing acoustical tile, the floor linoleum. A few brightly lit and recently remodeled concession areas seemed incongruous with their surroundings.

They climbed the unmoving steps of a broken escalator and approached the security check. "You're going to have to leave your piece with one of our boys at the security check. It takes a fucking mountain of paperwork to carry past the checks." The Smoker pointed to an armed cop in uniform who stood off to the side, intentionally distancing himself from the people who ran the X-ray machines and conveyor belt. "He's ours," the Smoker said, as if Daggett cared. All Daggett could think of was Bernard on that plane. "The blue coats are *Security*," he added distastefully. Daggett handed the cop his weapon, and the three hurried on.

The Smoker explained in his sandpaper voice, "We've got both the terminal and the plane covered. Six people in place: two women as flight attendants, a passenger in row nineteen, two maintenance guys, and a baggage handler." He paused. Daggett was thinking: And a partridge in a pear tree. This guy was full of self-importance. "Bernard's in eighteen-B—window exit to his left. We're told he bought both seats. I suppose that window exit is his way out if he needs one." He paused. "Don't worry; we got it covered."

The gate drew closer. Daggett's throat was dry and his heart was still pounding hard from the run. A commotion erupted behind them. It was Bob Backman. He looked as if he'd been swimming with his clothes on. He was refusing to surrender his gun.

Daggett said, "He's ours," mimicking the Smoker's expression, but in a tone of voice that disowned Backman.

The Smoker returned to Security to straighten it out.

Hairless spoke for the first time. "Security don't like us much. The feeling is mutual."

Backman reluctantly surrendered his weapon. Hairless, who didn't seem to miss much, was the first to spot Backman's wing tips. He nudged the Smoker and pointed out the shoes, which instantly reestablished the chain of command. Only desk jocks wore wing tips. Daggett wore a pair of scuffed Rockports. "Let's go," Backman said anxiously, taking the lead position. A fat duck in a drenched pinstripe.

The Smoker flashed his badge at the gate. They went down the hot jetway at something close to a run, Backman wheezing.

Daggett ducked through the plane's entry hatch, fourth in line behind Hairless. They hurried past a nervous steward. "We'll be out of your way in a minute," Backman said, trying to sound in control, but he was clearly uncomfortable here.

As a group, they quickly moved down the aisle. Inquisitive faces rose to greet them, some sensing excitement, others expressing a mixture of curiosity and sudden fright.

To Daggett they were the faces of the innocent, faces with lives behind them—and hopefully ahead of them. Faces of people like his parents and his boy.

With their approach, a man in row 19 rose and stepped into the aisle, blocking it. A flight attendant, a woman with hard eyes and gray-flecked hair, came up the aisle immediately behind him. Two of the Smoker's people, Daggett assumed. Bernard was now at the center of a well-executed squeeze play with nowhere to go. The emergency exit to the wing was effectively blocked by two "maintenance mechanics." Beautiful—like when the shortstop stepped up to take over second base in time to trap the steal. Daggett loved to see runners pinned; the "pickle" was one of his favorite plays of the game.

The Smoker's calm was impressive. Daggett heard some soft talking and saw Bernard's upraised palms as he was carefully drawn from the seat, patted down and advised to cooperate. Hairless quickly extricated his hardshell carry-on briefcase. Everyone's attention was fixed on the scene, heads craned.

Suddenly, Bernard's eyes caught Daggett's and their gazes locked. Daggett thought this must be the sensation a hunter feels as the animal lifts its head, suddenly alert to the hunter's presence.

Daggett knew this face all too well: he had lived with it for months. Bernard was dark-haired, with gray eyes, not quite handsome, just the kind of unremarkable countenance easily forgotten by even those who prided themselves on being observant. A vein pulsed strongly in his forehead. His occupation had cost him: His left hand was missing two fingers. But it wasn't the man's face, or his missing fingers that Daggett remembered. It was the black-and-white photographs of his work—the demolished restaurants, the aircraft, a half-dozen vehicles. A body count in the hundreds.

A monster.

The group filed out in professional silence. Daggett and Backman had their handguns returned to them at the security check.

The five men rode in the back of a Marriott food service van to a dull green building that seemed abandoned. A narrow hallway that smelled of grease and sweat led them to a windowless room that the Smoker had chosen for the interrogation. Daggett had a bad feeling about this room. Something terrible was about to happen.

Gunmetal desks in various states of disrepair, stacked three high, occupied most of the small room. A black, oily residue crusted the dysfunctional ventilation grate. The stale, dead air and the thick dust that rose with each footstep hazed the room in a curtain of gray, increasing Daggett's sense of claustrophobia. His throat went powder dry. The stifling heat prickled his skin and scalp, and he longed to be anywhere but here.

A handcuffed Bernard was seated in a chair in the center of the room. Hairless, the Smoker, and Daggett pulled a desk from the corner and used it as a bench, like fans in the bleachers. Backman wormed his sweaty hands together and glowered, pacing in front of Bernard like a man attempting a stage audition. He looked more suited for the role of headwaiter than cop.

"We've read you your rights. You're lucky to have them. Officially, you're being detained under the Terrorism Act of 1988. It gives us some rather broad powers, Bernard. Perhaps you're familiar with it?" He added, "You seem like a reasonable man."

Daggett cringed with the line. The Smoker lit a cigarette and exhaled toward the grate. The smoke mushroomed into an enormous cone and seemed to hang in the air. Hairless cleaned his impeccably clean nails with a penknife.

Backman tried again. "I can see what you're thinking. You're thinking that maybe it's not so bad you were caught here in the United States. After all, we guarantee due process even to international terrorists. You're thinking that on the federal level we haven't used the death penalty in decades, that if you remain silent and wait me out, some crafty attorney may take your case just for the publicity. What the fuck? Maybe somebody'll turn you into a TV movie, right?" It was true. Bernard displayed a disturbing confidence. Where did such monsters come from? Justice

for a man like Bernard came at the end of a weapon. No
jury. No trial. Two or three randomly placed shots and the
excuse the man had tried to escape.

"Don't even think about it," Hairless whispered. He
went back to his nails like an old lady at the hair salon.

Daggett realized that his hand was on his weapon. It
was as if that hand didn't belong to him. He withdrew it,
leaving the gun in the holster, and nodded as if he understood; but he didn't. Who was he becoming? What had this
investigation done to him?

Backman continued, "What you probably aren't aware
of is that two years ago Scotland Yard lifted a partial print
from EuroTours flight ten twenty-three. A piece of your
handiwork."

Daggett cringed. This was just the kind of technical information they should protectively guard at all costs. You
tell a person like Bernard this, and if he should get word to
his people, no one in *Der Grund* will ever make this same
mistake again. In point of fact, the tiny partial print in
question had required four weeks of sifting through rubble
to locate, another ten months to identify, an identification
that, because the print was only a partial, would not be
considered hard evidence by any court of law, but was
nonetheless one those in law enforcement felt could be
trusted. Backman had stupidly volunteered this information. "Sir," Daggett interrupted, quickly silenced by
Backman's harsh expression.

Backman continued, "We *know* what you were up to in
your Los Angeles hotel room."

That snapped Bernard's head. He was losing his confidence. His eyes began blinking quickly.

Backman paced. "One thing you don't know," he said,
"is that Daggett's parents and little boy were on flight ten
twenty-three." The Smoker and Hairless looked over and
stared at Daggett in disbelief.

Bernard also glanced at him, but showed no remorse whatsoever.

"I could leave you and Daggett alone for a few minutes," Backman suggested, his implication obvious but again ineffective. There would be no rough play in a dingy room at National Airport. It just wasn't done that way.

"You have an offer to make?" Bernard asked Backman a little too quickly, a little too hopefully.

Backman asked, "What if there is no deal? What if we're merely awaiting the papers to deport you? Ten-twenty-three was British. You realize that, don't you?"

The roar of a jet taking off made it feel hotter. Daggett loosened his tie further.

"You want that again?" Backman asked with an authority he had previously lacked. Daggett sensed the man's rebound. Backman, it suddenly seemed, was not weak but merely soft. Out of practice. He seized the moment effectively by asking the Smoker for a cigarette, as if he had all the time in the world. He didn't smoke, but Bernard didn't know this.

Bernard repeated, "There is or is not an offer?"

A sharp knock on the door shattered the resulting silence. The Smoker rose and opened it, spoke to an unseen person in a hushed voice, and then pulled the man's briefcase through. He closed the door. Daggett came off the table as the Smoker placed the briefcase at Bernard's feet. Backman said, "Your briefcase. Shall we have a look-see?"

They *knew* what was inside: deutsche marks. But to what purpose? A payoff? Financing? This briefcase had been a vital part of their investigation. What was Backman doing?

"You are *not* going to open that," Daggett stated. "Are you forgetting this man's occupation?"

"It was X-rayed," the Smoker said. "Twice. No sign of any wiring. No explosives. It's been cleared: we have nothing to worry about."

"Has it been sniffed? Has it been checked with ultra-sound? That bag should be handled by the bomb squad. That bag has been on the move since—" He caught himself before making the same mistakes Backman had made. He dried his palms on his pants legs. He was terrified. His eyes jumped between that bag and Bernard.

"Put yourself in *his* position," Daggett said, stepping close to Backman. "What if the suitcase *is* rigged? Unless he cuts himself one hell of a deal, he faces life imprisonment, at best. But what if he could take out the chief of C-three and the investigator responsible for ten twenty-three all in one move? What kind of a hero would *that* make him?"

"A dead hero," Backman said, unimpressed. "No one kills himself over principles anymore, Daggett. Use your head." He bent down toward the bag and released one of its two latches.

Daggett jumped forward and pushed him away from the bag. Backman slipped, reached for purchase, but fell to the dirty floor. His weight gave him trouble getting back to his feet. It was a pitiful attempt. Daggett offered his hand, but Backman refused any help. It took him several, embar-rassingly long, seconds to return to his feet. "Get out of here, both of you," Daggett shouted at the two others.

When the Smoker didn't move, Daggett added, "Now!" his focus still on the briefcase. Hairless pushed his friend quickly out the door.

Backman mopped his face with his handkerchief. "That was a *stupid* thing to do, Michigan. Really fucking stupid. That's going to cost you, big time."

Bernard said nothing. His attention remained fixed on the briefcase with its one open latch.

"You can order me to leave this room with you. Right? You can report me. Christ, you can probably get me fired."

"Damn right I can."

"So do it! Come on, let's go. Your only witnesses are getting away."

Backman pouted his lips and nodded. "Okay, I guess

you're right." He took a step toward the door. Then, abandoning his ruse, he threw his weight into Daggett and knocked him off his feet.

Daggett hit the floor hard, slid, and careened into the door.

Backman lumbered back to the briefcase and struggled with the other latch.

Bernard glanced up hotly and looked at Daggett with dark, wet eyes.

Daggett knew. "No!" he shouted as he reached for the door handle and dove into the hallway.

The door blew as a unit, straight across the hall, through the opposing wall, and out onto the tarmac. An orange ball of burning gas rolled down the hall like a tongue uncurling. The Smoker, Hairless, and the uniformed security guard they were escorting between them were all three knocked off their feet by the concussion. Fire licked out angrily and set the ceiling ablaze.

In a world of silence, Daggett belly-crawled for an exit door jarred open by the blast. Hairless appeared through the smoke, crawling on hands and knees. Partially blinded, he climbed right over Daggett. The two took shelter behind a cinderblock wall. The uniformed cop was on his feet, his pants on fire, running fast across the open field of blacktop, the Smoker trying to catch up with him. A surreal sight, punctuated by the slowly moving heaviness of a taxiing jet.

Daggett heard nothing; he'd gone deaf. He didn't want to hear; he didn't want to see. Bernard had won, even in death. He felt half crazy with frustration, the loss of life, the whole mess. He tried to scream. Still heard nothing. But the frightened expression he drew from Hairless told him his voice still worked. He wondered about his state of mind: maybe he wasn't half crazy, maybe he'd gone all the way. It certainly couldn't be snowing in August, but that was what he saw.

He extended his hand—there was no hair on the back

of it, he noticed—and awkwardly caught hold of some of the falling snow, like a child in his first winter storm.

Slowly, his fingers uncoiled. He still could not hear, but his eyes worked well enough. His hand was filled with confetti. He wasn't crazy after all.

Deutsche marks.

2

ANTHONY KORT SAT behind the wheel of the rental car carving a potato. He recalled his Bavarian grandmother doing the same thing. She wore thick cotton dresses, which covered her calves, and a tired white butcher's apron as she sat in a dark wicker chair on her back porch preparing a bucketful of potatoes to mash and later lather with butter, pepper, and generous chunks of pork bacon. Kort had no intention of eating this potato.

It was Tuesday, August 21. He had been anticipating this day for months. He needed detailed information on the behavior and performance of a Duhning 959 Skybus. A hundred yards away, on the other side of some cinderblock and glass, his chance to obtain that information, a Dr. Roger Ward, was in the throes of passion.

A pair of candles cast a yellow light on the windows beyond the small balcony of the third-story apartment on the corner of East Olive Street and Bellevue Avenue. It was the kind of light that flattered women, that witnessed whispers of affection with wine-sweetened breath, that failed to mask the distinctive, intoxicating smell of arousal. The building, a clean-lined, set-back, double-box structure of ivory stucco, had low-walled balconies enclosed by steel pipe banisters painted indigo blue. Its basement held two parking garages, both secured behind heavy metal gates. A placard sign on the sidewalk out front announced: SPACE AVAILABLE. The real estate agency used Seattle's Space Needle as part of its logo.

Kort continued his work on the potato, dividing his attention between Ward's Taurus, parked in the Pay-and-

Park, and the apartment window. The second game of the Mariners' doubleheader played softly from the car radio despite Kort's basic lack of understanding of the American game.

Kort wore stone-washed canvas pants, brown leather Italian walking shoes with rubber soles, a short-sleeved olive-green permanent-press shirt, and a navy-blue Nike windbreaker. For reasons of anonymity, his face was not entirely his, but instead the repository of theatrical cosmetics, pigmented contact lenses, a wig, and fake eyebrows. He was no expert at such things, but he got the job done.

Sarah Pritchet was obviously a good lover: Ward had been with her for hours. Kort couldn't help but imagine the sensations this man was experiencing. What he wouldn't give to be in the clutches of a willing woman instead of carving a potato in the front seat of a rent-a-car. But even so, his concentration remained fixed. With German efficiency, he compartmentalized the tasks before him: abduct Ward; gain access to the Duhning simulator. A mind cluttered with too much information, too many considerations, was incapable of quick reaction. Anthony Kort had the reactions of a cat.

As the sixth inning drew to a close behind the failed attempts of a Mariners' relief pitcher, the ember-red August sun sought the coolness of the Pacific, issuing a candy-pink glow to everything not in shadow. Kort left his rental and deposited the potato firmly into the exhaust pipe of the gray Ford Taurus. He slipped off into the corner of the Pay-and-Park lot, positioning himself behind a tow trailer bearing the weathered logo and address of Stoneway Asphalt and Paving. He lit a cigarette and waited.

Up the street a block, a group of six kids loitered outside the Malstrom's Market smoking cigarettes; 99¢ VIDEO, the sign read. He wished they would move on. Thankfully, a few moments later they did.

The relief pitcher must have found a second wind, or was himself relieved, for the arrival of the seventh-inning stretch took another three cigarettes. This was fine with Kort because the sunset blush and subsequent twilight had darkened into a starry summer night sky when three dimensions are reduced to silhouette and any measure of distance becomes unreliable.

Roger Ward appeared behind the polished bars of the security gate at the entrance to the apartment building. He paused to check the street carefully in order to protect his infidelity.

Like a lion in hiding before the kill, Kort watched him. He snuffed out the cigarette. He temporarily snuffed out his concerns as well: that he was now on his own; that Michael and the other members of *Der Grund* were, at this very moment, fighting the chill of Bonn jail cells; that many of his previously arranged contacts might now be compromised and/or conspiring with U.S. authorities to lay traps to catch him; that he now relied on a young woman whom he had neither seen nor worked with in over two years, a woman he had contacted less than twenty-four hours before, abruptly changing the timing and the degree of her involvement in this project; that this was the most ambitious undertaking *Der Grund* had ever attempted—fourteen months in planning.

He lightly brushed ashes from the front of his dark blue windbreaker, stepping completely out of sight of the Taurus, awaiting the sound of an uncooperative engine. That was his cue.

The Taurus ground away, refusing to catch. Kort waited patiently for the sound of the driver's door opening, which finally came, accompanied by a muttered curse of complaint. Now Kort approached, making sure to be seen so he wouldn't surprise the man. He needed the man to feel comfortable. He needed the man to feel rescued.

From a distance, Roger Ward seemed smaller than he actually was. He had hair the color of dead bamboo, a lantern jaw with a cleft chin, and gray-white sideburns improperly trimmed: the right a bit longer than the left. He wore a lime-green woven short-sleeved sport shirt and cuffed khaki trousers. His ankles were bare above shiny penny loafers. The left shoe had a new heel. Even peering angrily into the darkness of a raised hood at the uncoopera- tive engine, he gave Kort the impression of a man who had boundless energy and a great vitality. To spend a doubleheader with your mistress you needed great vitality, Kort supposed.

Too distracted by his engine problems, Ward took little notice of Kort, except to say "Damn thing" as Kort walked past.

"Problems?" Kort asked, stopping a few feet past the car.

"Know anything about ignition systems?"

"Not in those things. Computerized, aren't they?" Kort said. In a perfect world, he might have kept walking, but he couldn't play this too loose. He needed Ward to find it easier to go with him rather than bother his lovely Sarah Pritchet. If he elected to involve Pritchet, then the potato would be secretly removed, and the actual confrontation would have to wait until Ward was in his car and driving home. Kort had left himself options in either case. "Are you sure it isn't flooded?"

"Fuel injected," Ward replied. "I doubt it."

If the report on Ward was accurate, then he should be feeling rushed by now. The seventh-inning stretch left him only one inning to reach the Kingdome in order to catch the ninth, and make his appearance for a drink at his neigh- bor's balcony box. The drink was part of an insurance plan designed to support his alibi. He and Sarah Pritchet ran their own bases during home games, and if his wife hap- pened to ask, then the neighbor would unknowingly sup- port Ward's false claim to having been at the game. It was a neat little package that had been going on the better part of twelve months. With season tickets to the Mariners, Seahawks, and 'Sonics, it left only a few weeks a year where he had to come up with something more creative.

And again, according to the report, Ward was not as creative as predictable, which made him the perfect mark. He was reportedly pragmatic and terribly afraid of his wife: two key elements that made him attractive to Anthony Kort.

"I'm heading over on Denny Way," Kort said, bending the rules. Not quite an offer, but as close as he dare come.

"Are you?" Ward said. "Right now?"

"Yes. Right away." Kort watched as Ward lifted his head in the direction of the apartment. He was prepared to lose Ward at this juncture, and almost preferred that it happen this way: it would make their second encounter all the more powerful and therefore effective.

But the man asked, "Could I hitch a ride with you down to a gas station?"

Kort shrugged. "Sure."

Ward hurriedly lowered the hood and scurried around to the driver's door. Leaning in, he retrieved the keys and locked up.

Anthony Kort licked his chops—like shooting fish in a barrel.

Ward took the passenger seat. Having broken the seat belt's release mechanism, Kort suggested that Ward buckle up, waited for him to do so, and then started the car and drove off. The seat belt's ratchets took out the slack and Kort knew he had him—Ward could escape easily but not quickly. Time now favored Kort.

He knew the impact of immediacy, just as he knew the impact of claustrophobia, and so he hesitated only long enough to get the car up to speed. Hard to jump from a moving car. When he turned right on Olive Way, Ward spun his head curiously. "I thought you said Denny Way?"

Kort elected not to look at the man. "There's no need for your wife to find out about Sarah Pritchet, Dr. Ward." He wanted to look, to see the man crumble, his face drained of blood, his hands trembling. But he remained aloof.

"What?" Ward finally coughed out. "You're a private eye?" he asked after some thought. "Oh, my God. How long has she suspected?" And then, "Oh, my God" several more times. He concluded with the very astute "I can't believe this."

"You made a few mistakes. I won't bother you with all the details, but this thing you and Sarah Pritchet have for furniture . . . for positions . . . and your neglect, I suppose due to . . . excitement? . . . to close the blinds on several occasions. Well . . . what is it about a picture being worth a thousand words?" He tapped a manila envelope on the seat between them. Out of the corner of his eye he could see Ward's attention fix on the envelope.

He stopped at a red light. Ward seized the envelope, punched the seat belt release button, popped the door open, and got one leg out, only to find himself still strapped in the seat. Kort placed a firm hand on the man's left forearm and now looked over at him, waiting for eye contact. Ward continued to wrestle with the seat belt. "Close the door," the captor said sternly. Ward wheezed in defeat and obeyed. Then he looked into Kort's unflinching eyes.

Kort said with deliberate calmness, "We should talk for a minute before you go running off." The light changed, Kort accelerated strongly and threw Ward's head back. Disorientation was equally effective. "If you run out on me, I won't have any choice but to go to your wife, will I? And how would your supervisor over at Duhning feel about you snaking your assistant? Mm? My experience is that they tend to frown on affairs within the company. Mm? In a perfect world they'd let us snake whomever we damn well pleased, wouldn't they, Roger?" He waited a second and then added, "Mind if I call you Roger?"

Ward tentatively slipped the black-and-white photo out of the envelope. The shot wouldn't win any prizes for lighting or composition, but the two lovers had been caught in perfect profile in a particularly frantic moment: Sarah Pritchet's back arched, legs spread across him as Ward sat submissively in the chair. Their faces clear as day. "Picked that out myself," Kort said. "You can keep it if you like."

Ward breathed heavily as if about to cry. He asked, "Are you working for Karen?"

"Not working for anyone," Kort replied. "I need access to the 959-600 simulator. Thirty or forty minutes is all. I need you to put it through a few moves. Forty-eight hours from now you'll have the negatives."

"The simulator?" Ward asked, as if to say, "That's all?"

"Thirty minutes. The 959-600. I need you to run a few tests."

"Industrial espionage? You're blackmailing me?"

Kort hesitated a moment. He couldn't be certain how Ward would feel about industrial espionage, but he thought he could predict the reaction to blackmail, and so he said, "Yes, I am." When Ward failed to say anything, he added, "I'm interested in you putting the 959 through a few take-offs, that's all." He paused to give Ward a chance to think. He knew what happened to people in these situations: Their minds ran out of control; all the compartments popped open at once and the bottlenecked information tended to shut the system down; the ability to think slowed to a crawl. He thought Ward was probably lost back in that black-and-white photograph of him and Pritchet in the chair. Besides, he wanted Ward to understand the depth of his preparation; the more overwhelmed he could make the man feel, the higher his chance of success. After the pause he said, "We'll take your Taurus, because of the parking sticker. If we make good time, we may get you back for that drink at the Kingdome." With that he punched the radio's volume knob and the game came on. They listened while Ward collected his astonishment and repaved his face to a smoother surface. "Still the top of the eighth," Kort noted with the lilt of optimism in his voice. "Let's hope they make a game of it."

He gloated privately at Ward's reaction. Complete submission. Like a child with a parent. No objection. No questioning. One-on-one and he was outnumbered. Kort had written the script, and without the gift of improvisation, Ward found himself betrayed by his own inabilities. He turned to face Kort twice, as if about to say something, but apparently reconsidered or experienced a failed synapse, settling back in the seat with a dulled expression. Kort had to smile.

"This is a beautiful city," Kort said, admiring the lush vegetation in the headlights, the cool evening air. "I could live in a place like this." Ward wasn't listening. His privacy had been stripped to the bone in a matter of minutes. There was nothing quite as disturbing. He would never realize that someone had followed him to Sarah Pritchet's and on to the Kingdome, had pieced his alibi together by simply staying with him for a few short hours on only a few nights. But are any of us protected from such discoveries? Kort wondered. Without living in complete paranoia, is there any way to find true privacy? In his line of work one *existed* only through such privacy and anonymity. But this was not the result of paranoia; it came at the price of never repeating one's actions, never staying too long in the same place, never contacting anyone else. Staying ahead of those behind you. It came in the form of a solitary world of self-discipline and silence.

Kort wanted to lessen the chance of Sarah Pritchet seeing the two of them, so they made the switch from his rental to Ward's Taurus quickly. The Pay-and-Park, void of lights, provided a perfect spot to make the transfer. Ward was told to drive. Kort removed the potato from the exhaust pipe and tossed it into the bushes on the west edge of the lot. As he took the passenger seat he explained, "Causes enough back pressure that the car won't start. Muggers use the technique in parking garages. Always check your exhaust pipe *before* you get in the car. It may save you your wallet." Then he added, "Or your life." Kort mentally checked off another step from his itinerary, pleased with how well things were going. He needed his full attention and concentration for the minutes immediately ahead. They drove onto Aurora Avenue and headed south to where it would become East Marginal Way, with the worldwide headquarters of Duhning Aerospace only a few short miles ahead. There, the random elements of this operation would multiply like breeding rats. Kort prepared himself for it.

"Slow down," he instructed Ward, "you're driving too fast. If it's intentional, you're stupid; if it's not, you're nervous. I can't afford for you to be either. Understand, Roger? You're simply going to work. You've done this a thousand times. I'm a visitor in town from Europe who is interested in the 959-600. That's all that needs to be said. Now pull yourself together, friend, in case we have to speak to someone."

Ward glanced over at Kort from the driver's seat, a bit more wide-eyed than Kort had hoped. But then he nodded, exhaled, and seemed to settle down.

"That's good," Kort said a few seconds later. "Now let's go to work."

For the next few minutes they drove along a road bordered to the right with derricks and loading cranes. Kort rolled down his window and inhaled some of the pungent salt air of the wharfs. He wondered what it would be like to be a crane operator, a fisherman, a captain, or a deckhand. So different from his own life. He thought of the bizarre twists and turns that had led him to this particular place on this particular night. The air felt as if it might rain. In a perfect world the rain would hold off for another few hours.

When Ward signaled for a right turn, Kort mustered a sense of authority in his voice and said, "Where do you think you're going? Not here. Not yet. The badge room first."

"There's no security at Simulation," Ward protested.

"No security inside," Kort corrected. "I know that." In

fact, this blatant lack of security had led them to select a Duhning aircraft as their target. Simplification bred success; he knew it to be true. For unexplained reasons, the human mind tended toward complication. Chaos over order. Kort played the part of mathematician, constantly seeking the lowest common denominator; he continually reassessed the operation, searching out the lower ground in order to circumvent the foothills of potential problems. "But if you don't check in, then the patrol may question why you are parked over there. And anyway, all guests must be issued a pass." Ward's frightened eyes found Kort— knowledge often proved the most powerful tool of all. He continued on and turned the car left at a small guard booth. Seeing the sticker on the car, the guard waved him through. They drove through several large parking lots and stopped outside a well-lit office, all glass and steel.

"You needn't worry," Kort reminded before leaving the safety of the vehicle. He said it as much for himself as for Ward.

"They'll ask for identification," Ward worried aloud.

"And I will present identification." Then, in the clear voice of confidence, Kort told Ward, "Doctor, it is quite possible—probable even—that I know more about their jobs than they do. Yes? There will be no surprises." He dug into his pocket and came up with the fountain pen he sought. "You will remember as a child, disappearing ink?" He faked a smile, attempting to comfort the man. "We will use this pen in signing me in. Yes?" He handed it to Ward. So simple when you planned ahead; such disaster when you did not.

Two men in dark blue uniforms with arm patches showing an airplane silhouetted by a gibbous moon, sat behind the Formica counter. Kort heard the low-volume soundtrack of a movie, indicating a television kept out of sight below the counter. One of the men passed them a visitor's badge as Ward signed them in.

"You have some form of ID?" the bigger of the two asked.

Kort produced his shiny new wallet and opened it to the German driving license. As he offered it, the guard, apparently satisfied by the likeness of the photo, waved him off. "That's okay. Thanks."

Kort and Ward left them to the late show. As they reached the car, Kort asked for his pen back. He slipped it into his pocket. Everything in its place.

Ward set the turn signal and a red light pulsed across his face. He turned right onto Marginal Way and then negotiated a quick left onto a narrow road a block north of Duhning's main office. The car bumped over an obsolete railroad track. Huge corrugated steel buildings rose out of the darkness, their skylights lit brightly as the night shift continued the day's work. Ward turned left and left again, parking at the side of a smooth-metal building with curved corners and narrow glass windows that reminded Kort of an aquarium or a science center. It was labeled in bold black letters: E-17.

The interior of the building proved unimaginative. The center of the mustard-colored carpet was worn smooth by decades of foot traffic. The walls held the mandatory, self-indulgent color photographs of Duhning's history. The lighting was good, the air a bit stale. The place needed a face-lift.

Ward was walking too fast. "No hurry," Kort said quietly, both hands held in his pockets to hide the gloves. "Let's stop by your office. Yes?"

Kort shut the door. Piles of paperwork dominated both the desk and bulletin boards. A computer occupied the desk's return that fronted a window framing the dreary southern parking lot. On the far wall, a series of color photographs showed Ward alongside a variety of private aircraft. He looked much, much older at the moment: his eyes puffy with worry, his shoulders slumped forward in defeat. Ward consulted the simulator schedule. He confirmed that Kort's information was correct: the 959-600 was free until maintenance took over at two in the morning.

"Are we likely to run into anyone?" Kort asked.

"No. Not at this time of night."

"If we do, I'm nothing but another visitor. That won't be too difficult, will it?"

"I don't see why it should be. As you said in the car, we have hundreds of visitors a year, and at all hours. No. I don't see it as being any problem."

Kort noticed that the man's attention was fixed on the photograph of a middle-aged woman with waxy brown hair, and beside her a young girl of six or seven in a bathing suit, her face wreathed in a big smile for the camera. Kort said, "They needn't ever know about it. I'm a man of my word."

"Oh, I'm *sure* you are."

"You don't believe me . . ."

"Does it matter?" Ward asked. "I don't know what you're after, but if you intend to string me along, it won't work. Just so we *understand* one another." He was gaining his strength back, a result of his familiarity with his surroundings, no doubt. Kort needed him strong, but not to the point of rebelliousness. "Tonight is all you'll get from me," Ward said defiantly.

Kort couldn't risk giving the man any more time to pull himself together. "If need be, you'll introduce me as David Anthony, a pilot's representative of Belgian Airways. We've broken off negotiations with Air Bus and are considering buying four of Continental's 1996 options on 959s for our shorter routes. If we take the deal then we'll need a simulator and an instructor course. Easy enough?"

"You've thought it all out, haven't you?" Ward asked bitterly.

Kort said confidently, "I wouldn't be here if I hadn't."

They passed down a long hall, climbed a set of metal stairs, and stopped at the steel door, which had a keypad cipher lock requiring that a number be entered. Ward hesitated; it seemed to occur to him that he could still prevent this from happening. Kort said, "I'm aware of the non-security access on the first floor." He knew that the irony of this building was that where the second floor used the special locks, the first floor did not.

Ward entered the code without argument and opened the door to an enormous, brightly lit room with a high vaulted ceiling. Like a giant gymnasium.

They stepped out onto the catwalk that ran some forty feet straight ahead into the tremendous open space. To the right of the catwalk, rising on hydraulics from the cement floor like ambulatory space pods, were four enamel-white simulators. The space was immaculately clean. Each simulator had a large "elephant's trunk" carrying the mass of cables to a hole in the floor. Three of the pods moved silently, rising slightly up or down, careening left or right. The sophisticated hydraulics realistically duplicated the flight as unseen trainees worked the controls. Wrapped off the far face of each pod like opaque sunglasses, a series of flat metal surfaces indicated the screens for the computerized visual effects, so that once inside, trainees witnessed real-time moving images in a sweep of 190 degrees around them. These were among the most sophisticated flight simulators in the world.

"These are the runway specifics," Kort said, producing a folded piece of paper and handing it to Ward.

Ward accepted the note paper reluctantly. He located a pair of reading glasses and looked them over.

"Wait here," Ward said, crossing the aluminum bridge between catwalk and simulator. He stepped inside the machine, leaving the door open, and then came back out, passed Kort closely and indicated that he should join him.

The room marked *Simulator Computers* used filtered air, chilled to 64 degrees and pumped into the room with enough velocity that opening the door required a good strong push. The cold air slapped Kort in the face. He buckled under the surprise of the door's resistance, stepped through, and followed Ward as the door eased shut. The room had a false floor raised to allow space for computer cables. Windows looked out on the four simulators. Mainframes capable of crunching eighty million bytes of data thirty times a second purred as they went about their work. Ward spent five minutes programming the runway specifications.

Ward spoke softly as they left the room, "We have LAX in our database, you know. You should have just asked." The comment froze Kort, and a hot jolt of anger flushed through him despite the chill of the room—Ward's knowledge and his resulting confidence could become a problem. He hadn't realized Ward might recognize LAX just by some numbers. He had given him too much information, he decided. Would a man with this much background in avionics realize his purpose in conducting these tests? His intentions? Anxiety took hold.

Once Kort had crossed the drawbridge between the catwalk and the simulator, Ward raised it electronically, isolating the two and leaving the simulator independent and detached, able to move freely on its hydraulics.

The smell of the simulator was immediately electronic as Ward closed and locked the door behind them. The two men ducked and crossed into the flight deck, and Kort felt disoriented. The cockpit was ablaze with instrument lights. The windows looked out on an airfield—a simulated airfield, but one so impossibly close to reality that within seconds, Kort felt as if he were actually out on a runway. The parallel lights of the runway blinked in unison. "Amazing," he said, without meaning to.

Ward scowled as he worked a small-screen computer at the instructor's post. Then he moved into the pilot's seat.

Kort took the instructor's seat behind the pilot's chair. His stomach turned. He didn't want Ward to see him like this.

Anthony Kort suffered from acrophobia. Even the thought of taking off in a plane, much less from a position in the nose of the aircraft, knotted his stomach. Originally intended as part of this operation's preliminary research, and scheduled for another operative, this responsibility had fallen onto his shoulders. The situation required he avoid revealing his weakness. He had to maintain his domination over Ward. "What I want you to do is this: You will take off, fully loaded, and begin your ascent. When I say, you will release the controls."

"She'll crash if I do that," Ward replied, waiting for a different command. "And it'll be no fault of the plane," he added, defending his baby. "Thrust won't maintain the climb. She'll fall like a stone."

Kort said, "Just do as I say."

"You *want* it to crash? That's absurd."

"I want you to do as I say." He glanced away from the dizzying screen and studied his watch. He had to avoid looking at that screen at all costs; he had to avoid any sign of weakness. Besides, it was important he look at his watch: The timing had to be perfect.

Engineers working for *Der Grund* had spent months studying the specifications of the 959 to make this predictability as exact a science as possible. Kort was now to use the simulator to test their theories and discover their accuracy.

As the plane lifted off the runway, Kort counted off the seconds on his watch. When his watch read fifty-four seconds, Kort called out, "Now!"

Ward removed his hands from the controls and sat back as the speakers inside the simulator screamed loudly, the plane complaining violently, sliding toward impact, the combined effects horribly real. Louder and louder it grew until silenced by impact.

Even without watching, it took Kort a moment to recover after the crash. He checked several of the flight deck's instruments. The results of this first test were not right; he would have Ward repeat the simulation using a different duration of time between takeoff and loss of pilot control. He would try fifty-two seconds next.

Ward reset the simulator. The hydraulics leveled; the screen flickered and cleared. And there was the same runway again—LAX—stretching out before them.

Ward, as pilot, flew six takeoffs, each using a slightly different elapsed air time. On this sixth attempt, he got remarkably close to obtaining the data Kort sought. Dizzy with victory, and badly nauseated from his acrophobia, Kort ordered Ward to try exactly forty-seven seconds. This time would be perfect.

The flight deck's sixty-four-track stereo sound system duplicated everything from the sound of the jets and the wind to the grinding of the hydraulics and the thud of the wheels as they were drawn into the aircraft. The nose lifted dramatically from the runway, engines whining; Ward released the controls when instructed by Kort. Pilotless, the plane slipped helplessly and crashed. Kort leaned forward and again checked several of the instruments. He smiled triumphantly, and drew a box around the number 47. One last time—that was all he needed to be absolutely certain.

"You don't like flying," Ward suggested. "You haven't looked at the screens once."

Kort wanted one last run-through, but Ward's observation worried him. This last attempt had gone perfectly. The sense of achievement welled up in him, and had he been alone he might have cheered his own success. Perfection was everything to Anthony Kort. Forty-seven seconds. But he wanted desperately to repeat the test one final time—to duplicate his success precisely, to relive that success, to make absolutely certain his success *could* be duplicated. That was the point. His pursuit of perfection wouldn't allow it any other way. In a perfect world . . .

"Let's repeat that once more," he ordered.

"Forty-seven seconds again?"

"Exactly as we just did it."

"What is it that you're after? Who *are* you? This *isn't* corporate espionage, is it? It's something else." He turned around to face Kort.

"Just fly the plane," Kort instructed.

Ward had troubled eyes. He couldn't hide the anger on his face as his earlier fear gave way to a growing understanding of Kort's purpose. Kort thought about stopping here; he had what he needed. Ward's impatience was suddenly a liability. He was about to call it off when Ward encouraged the throttle forward and sent the plane charging down the runway. As the yoke came back, the hydraulics at the rear of the pod contracted, and the nose angled into the pale blue electronic sky. The jets screamed in stereo. The steep-pitched climb continued. This was wrong! Kort turned to chastise the pilot, and in doing so, made the mistake of looking into the hypnotic screen. He couldn't take his eyes off it. The ground faded below them; the nose aimed into the blue. The plane banked sharply left and right, up and down, as the pod physically responded to Ward's erratic piloting. Kort, who wore no restraining belt, fell from his seat. "Stop it," he demanded in a weak voice. The simulator continued to heave and jerk unpredictably on the hydraulics. "Stop it!" he tried again, but this time his food came up.

Ward spun around wild-eyed, and shouted above the roar, "You may ruin my marriage," he said in a menacing voice, "but there's not much left there anyway. You *will not* sabotage one of our planes, or whatever it is you have planned. I will not contribute to *that.*"

"Stop it!" Kort demanded, feeling slightly better from vomiting.

Ward came out of the pilot's chair, the plane slipping into a devastating dive, and laid a knee into the side of Kort's face—right into his bad tooth—as he pushed past. He was escaping!

Kort lunged forward and caught the man's ankle.

Ward went down hard.

The plane continued to dive. The sound grew to a fevered pitch. Kort climbed over him. Ward screamed for help. They wrestled. When Ward screamed again, Kort silenced him with a choke hold. He maintained the hold tightly until Ward lost consciousness.

The plane continued its long, eerie dive toward destruction. And although Kort knew he must release his hold, he could not. He took out his fear on the man's neck.

The 959 crashed. The sudden quiet was almost as deafening. Kort, regaining his senses, released his grip. Roger Ward fell away from him and rolled over, his eyes open and enlarged, his face a sickening blue. He was dead.

In the silence of the now motionless simulator, the stark reality of Kort's predicament slammed home. He had murdered Ward. An investigation would follow. There would be links to the simulator, to the 959—to everything he had hoped to prevent.

He was not a man to panic, but despite his training he did just that. He slapped the face of the warm corpse, repeatedly murmuring impossible demands that it return to life. He talked to himself trying to explain, to rationalize: he had wanted to gain control; to silence him; to scare him into behaving. Now this! He shook the man by the shirt. Come alive! The head flopped, ungainly, from side to side as if to say, "No."

Come to life, you bastard! Kort willed. But where he had the power to take the life away, he had none to restore it.

Slowly, he collected himself. Killing men was not something entirely new to him—he reminded himself. He released Ward for the second time. Ward fell heavily to the carpet, a soft thud. The man had made his contribution; Kort had what he was after. Kort threw the switch to lower the drawbridge, listening intently as it fell securely into place. He opened the door and peered around the edge at the three other simulators, all of which were still moving, their drawbridges up. He checked his watch: just under two hours before this four-hour shift ended.

It offered him a chance.

To leave the corpse inside the simulator module was unthinkable for it would undoubtedly be quickly discovered, bringing the police and reducing his lead time, which in turn would limit any chance of effective escape.

He collected Ward, throwing one of the man's arms over his own shoulders and supporting his weight by taking him below the ribs. He peered around the door once again. Seeing all was clear, he struggled across the drawbridge. Ward's feet dragged lifelessly. The catwalk seemed to grow longer with each step, but eventually he reached it and, just beyond, the door to the computer room. He shoved against the door, managed to open it, and lost his hold on Ward just as he stepped inside. Ward fell to the false floor. Kort had planned to hide the body amid the large computers, but the hollow sound of the false floor gave him a better idea.

He dragged him to the very back of the room, passing six rows of machinery in the process. He removed one of the false plates, revealing a network of tangled wire. He removed four more plates and was able to use the slack in the various wires to push them aside.

As he grabbed for Ward, the drawbridge to the third simulator began to lower. One of the crews was taking a break! Panic jolted through him like a live current. He grabbed Ward and stuffed him under the false floor as outside, the drawbridge continued its descent. Frantically, he replaced the floor sections, remembering at the last moment to search the man's pockets for the car keys. He grappled with the last sections of flooring—pieces to a puzzle. Finally, they went together.

He paused at the door, his mind racing ahead of him: He would have to call her from here; she would have to change her plans; he would have to trust her completely. So much to do.

The drawbridge lowered to within inches of clicking into place. Should he run for it, or bide his time and wait for the trainees to pass by before he attempted to leave unnoticed? No time existed for such thought; he had to act, to go with his instincts.

He tugged open the stiff door, and ran like hell.

Kort saw no way around returning to the hotel. He had to collect his things; he had to wipe down the room thoroughly and, as best as possible, remove any evidence of his having been there. He was practiced in such last-minute ordeals; they came as an accepted, though unwanted, part of his existence. The room had been paid in full through Friday morning, so that much he counted in his favor—a grace period. Enough time to train to Los Angeles and kill a couple of days in preparation. Yes, he still might pull it off.

He had a plane to bomb.

He left Ward's car parked on a residential street where he assumed it might take the police days, perhaps weeks, to locate, and removed his rental from the Pay-and-Park.

He had never intended to kill Ward. Now, for his actions, he paid the price in hasty departure preparations that put him at a much greater risk than he would have wished. In a perfect world, Ward would have lived, would have awakened the next day and gone about his business as usual, the secret of his affair, of his hour in the Duhning simulator, carefully preserved.

Inside the lobby, Kort watched a slightly hunchbacked woman continuously vacuum the same spot on the immense red throw rug that lay beneath the embroidered couches and marble-topped coffee table that formed the focal point of the lobby. She appeared to have fallen asleep. A young man with hard hair that appeared permanently wet, and a bow tie that showed elastic at the mouth of the collar, stood sentry behind the registration desk, his dark eyes glassy with fatigue, his cup of much-needed coffee tucked appropriately out of sight, its rising steam giving it away.

Kort didn't stop at the desk. No sense in giving this kid a chance to remember his face. He rode the elevator to his room and phoned instead.

"Front desk," this same young man said, chewing his words through a yawn. "How may I help you?"

"Could you scare me up a pair of pliers?" Kort asked.

"Pliers?" the front desk replied, somewhat surprised. "Is it anything housekeeping could help with, sir?"

"No. Just a pair of pliers. Can you get me a pair of pliers, please?"

"Maintenance would have a pair. Or housekeeping might. I'll check for you, sir. Should I send them up if I can locate some?"

"Yes, please. And call me if you can't. You'll remember to call me?"

"Yes, sir."

Kort waited by the phone expecting failure. It was his experience that problems ran in schools, like barracuda. No single problem was likely to kill you, but combined they could be deadly. Typically, when you least needed failure, it struck. For this reason, he always remained on alert.

To his surprise—and a good omen—a room service waitress delivered the pliers less than five minutes later. They were an aluminum alloy with green rubber handle grips. Kort sterilized them first by cooking them in the hot-water coffee maker provided for the room. After a ten-minute cook, he heated the mouth of the pliers with his butane lighter until the metal began to smoke. Then he allowed them to cool while he gathered his nerve.

The tooth had to come out. That was all there was to it. He had tried to make arrangements for it to be pulled professionally the following day, but he would no longer be here on the following day, so he had no choice. Rotten to the core, the tooth had to be extracted before he embarked on his train ride. The importance of the operation, and his relative isolation, forced the decision. Even so, he stood in front of the well-lit bathroom mirror, the pliers now cool and resting on a fresh towel, and stared at himself for several long minutes.

No one was asking him to do this, he reminded himself. Not anymore they weren't. *Der Grund* had been cut off at the knees. Out of a total of sixteen, only he and two or three others had escaped the bust. He had been disembarking an ocean liner in New York at the time he had heard about it. At that moment, he had realized both the jeopardy he faced and the freedom made suddenly available to him. Nonetheless, he had boarded the sleeper for Chicago, and on to Seattle, as planned. If he had his way, the operation would still succeed.

But that meant the tooth had to come out. Twice he picked up the pliers. Twice he placed them back down. He assumed there was a good possibility he might pass out during his attempt. He looked around. Hard objects everywhere. Not a good place to fall.

There would be blood as well. Perhaps a great amount, he wasn't sure. He cracked off the plastic wrap that sealed the cap to the bottle of hydrogen peroxide, wondering if he would find the strength to use it like mouthwash after the procedure. Infection remained his greatest enemy. Like it or not, the hydrogen peroxide seemed a necessity. Just the thought of it made him feel sick to his stomach. He and the pliers entered into a staring contest.

He carried them, the complimentary box of tissue, and the bottle of hydrogen peroxide into the empty bathtub, where he stretched himself out in a reclining position. He placed the bath mat behind his head as a cushion. He could pass out here. He could bleed here.

He hadn't noticed until that moment how ugly the shower curtain was. A very poor imitation of a pastel chintz, some of the color had apparently washed out of it, leaving only the worst of the orange and a morbid shade of purple fighting for visual dominance. To his eye, the purple won. It was just the kind of thing that belonged on the form letter left by the president of the hotel chain for customers' comments. He had to wonder if those things ever got read; he knew better than to think the president had ever seen the form itself, much less one properly filled out. He allowed himself several of these distractions. He spent a few minutes analyzing the work of the mason who had applied the shower's patterned tile, several more studying the bead of caulk that joined tub and tile. With the availability of such distractions diminishing, he faced up to the task before him.

The tooth had to come out.

Now.

He brought the pliers toward his mouth and stopped, remembering in an instant why he had begun before the mirror—he had to see what he was doing. He climbed out of the tub, moved his supplies back to the edge of the sink, and faced himself once again. Yes, this was better. Looking at himself. It made him feel stronger. He needed his strength. He could not allow himself to pass out—that was all there was to it. He had to maintain control.

He stretched his mouth open wide, adjusting his head so the greatest possible amount of light found its way to the impossibly red pulpy flesh at the back of his bottom row of teeth. The brown, rotted tooth there called to him in a pulsing, agonizing pain he had lived with for nearly two weeks.

He had bought the Anbesol for afterward, but now it occurred to him it might help beforehand as well. It was meant to kill the pain. He had plenty of that.

He opened this bottle, too, though its safety packaging was more contentious than that of the hydrogen peroxide. He planned the order of events carefully: Anbesol, extraction, peroxide, Anbesol. He repeated the words as a mantra, worried he might not think clearly once the deed was done.

Once and for all, the pliers rose to his mouth. The metal jaws still felt warm against his tongue. As they entered his mouth, he lost all sight of the beleaguered tooth, and resorted to a tactile exploration, where each wrong guess caused him enormous pain. The aluminum jaws nipped at his swollen gums. He forced his mouth open even wider, the pliers hard against his cheek, and gripped down onto the decay. His knees buckled as the pliers found purchase—he knew he had it now. Of this there was no doubt. His left hand went out to steady him. He pinched the jaws of the pliers tighter, counted quickly to three, and jerked straight up.

His scream, muffled by a diaphragm spasmodic from pain, and a hand stuffed into his mouth, died before penetrating the room's walls. The pliers, with their quarry, fell to the counter as he blindly found the hydrogen peroxide and tilted the bottle into his open mouth. This second scream had much more air behind it.

He spit out the pain into the sink and sagged down to his knees in agony, one hand groping for the Anbesol. He had to focus away from the pain. Away from his mouth.

The thought at work in his mind was whether or not the president of the company ever read those stupid forms.

3

CRUMBLING BRICK BUILDINGS of Washington, D.C.'s black ghetto crowded the potholed streets that ran down past gasworks and an electric substation to the polluted Anacostia River. Set back from the river's edge, looking like a twelve-story apartment complex, stood a government building, the upper floors of which housed the FBI's Washington Metropolitan Field Office. It was here, on the tenth floor, that Cam Daggett reported to work each day. Those who worked here called it Buzzard Point—the actual name of this spit of land.

The Hoover Building, on Pennsylvania Avenue, which the public had come to think of as the FBI, was, in reality, the administrative agency that set policy and oversaw the activities of 55 field offices, each with its own territory. Aside from a few laboratories, its function was almost entirely bureaucratic.

WMFO—or Buzzard Point—was one such field office. Because its territory included the "District" and surrounding suburbs, its investigations often assumed a national scope.

Six-foot-high gray-carpeted office baffles separated one squad from another, the contained office areas referred to by the agents as bullpens. C-3's bullpen contained nine desks—ten, including that of Gloria DeAngelo, secretary and den mother. Behind Gloria, another baffle worked to give privacy to C-3's squad chief. It was here that Bob Backman's desk sat empty.

A thin-boned woman of fifty-two, with straight black hair cut and curled at her shoulders, Gloria labored behind sad brown eyes and a rigid posture that helped knock a dozen years off the truth. She patted her hair self-consciously. At this hour of the morning, she and Daggett owned the place.

Gloria came over with a cup of coffee. "I can help you pack, if you want." He recognized the words she had spoken, but they lost form inside his head, the edges of the consonants made round and smooth by his ruptured eardrum. He had learned quickly to answer the phone with his left ear, to try to keep people to his left when he spoke to them, and to consciously avoid talking loudly. Not only was his newfound deafness an annoying and occasionally embarrassing disability, but it was unnerving and disconcerting as well. All sound to his right had died, as if he were suddenly only half a person.

He hesitated. "I'm not moving, Glo. I turned down the offer." Before she could object, he added, "Taking a promotion because of Backman's stupidity is not my idea of earning it. Pullman is next in command—he *has* to be bumped up. I don't." He leafed through a stack of pink memos. "I'm off to Seattle this afternoon. The field office out there invited me to have a look at something."

"Be reasonable, dearie."

"Reasonable? If I take the promotion, then I lose my field status, and this investigation along with it. I move into Pullman's old job. They park me permanently behind a desk, Glo. Me? Leather-soled shoes and three-hour meetings? No thanks."

"You're being selfish."

"Undoubtedly. I'm reminded of that often enough, without hearing it from you as well." He said it, and then regretted both the content and the tone. Not surprisingly, Gloria ignored the offense; she would not be swayed from her purpose. If Gloria was anything, she was determined. "You can't change what's happened."

Bitterness boiled over—repetition had a way of doing that to him. "If you put a melody behind that, you and Carrie could sing it in harmony." He tossed the memos onto his desk, suddenly more angry. Armchair psychology from an aging den mother he didn't need. The truth, he needed even less. "You'll be going through Backman's stuff. He was a secretive son of a bitch. If there's anything in there I could—"

"He isn't even in the ground yet, and you're picking at his bones."

"I'm *not* picking at his bones. I'm trying to find a detonator Bernard may have built." He checked his in-box and sorted through his memos. He tried a different subject. "What about Meecham's report?"

"There's a message here for you. He wants to meet with you at his office."

"Today?"

"Yes. Right away. He said he would be glad to get you out of his hair."

"He, and everyone else."

"Aren't we pleasant."

"Pleasant? I stay at home, I get the third degree; I come into work, it's déjà vu all over again." He hoped he might get a rise out of her, that a little humor—even borrowed humor—might provide an opportunity for a truce. But his attempt went right over her head, which wasn't hard, given her diminutive height.

"It's *safer* behind a desk."

"Do you and Carrie collaborate on these lines, or am I supposed to put this down to coincidence?"

"Can I help it if you're so damned consistent? So pigheaded? You're supposed to *listen*. You're supposed to learn something—not only from your mistakes but from other people's. Bob Backman didn't learn. If he had stayed behind that desk he'd still be alive."

"Bob Backman was a fool," he said soberly. Sadness, like the warmth from a strong drink, surged through him.

"Your son is in a wheelchair, I needn't remind you." She was red-faced.

She shut up then, but her expression acknowledged it came too late. The words hung in the air like fruit flies. There was no getting rid of them. "No, you needn't," he said, filling the resulting silence. The fruit flies flew into his eyes. He felt the welling of tears and attempted to fight them off.

It's not a dream, it's a memory, and though it comes down like a heavy curtain, it holds moving images like a projection screen. It's transparent enough that he can see through it to the boy beyond, the boy coming down the ramp; but substantial enough that he can't will it away. He knows that it's triggered by certain things: a smell in the air, a sound; for a while, just touching wool brought it on. But there seems no trick to get rid of it. No cure.

He's in the high school gymnasium the Germans have set aside for the identification of personal belongings. Most of it is now in clear plastic garbage bags marked with tags that indicate how far from the point of impact the item was found. The imperfection of the plastic clouds what's inside. After several minutes his eyes begin to hurt. The quantity of the belongings—the rows of clothes, bags, cameras, briefcases, papers, walking canes, baby strollers, golf clubs, computers—overwhelms him and he begins to cry. He's been crying off and on for the last three days. Sometimes it is simply the sight of a family that does it to him; sometimes it is something said at one of the briefings. He had seen a deer in a field the day before, and that had made him cry. He's vulnerable. He's not sure he'll hold up under the pressure. He worries he may start crying and not be able to stop.

Bag after bag; he pushes the plastic around to get a better view of what's inside. A doll, its head missing, holds his attention. Driving into town the morning after the disaster he had come across a dead woman in the very top of a tree, hanging by her feet. Her dress ripped off her, arms hanging down like she was diving into the water. Bloodless.

It was his first impression of the disaster in an otherwise pastoral and richly German countryside. Now he wondered if the child who had mothered this doll had been mothered by that woman. They would figure it out eventually. But for now, all he can do is wonder.

Total number of survivors: four. All children, one of whom was his now paralyzed son. Like the three hundred and twenty-seven who had perished, all four children had free-fallen from sixteen thousand feet. All four had hit a bog to the west of the village. Still, it was anyone's guess how or why they had survived. One, who was in critical condition from a staph infection, had become the focus of the media: to survive a sixteen-thousand-foot fall, only to die from an infection picked up in a hospital.

He moves beyond the doll, beyond the Samsonites, the Larks, the Land's Ends. Beyond the toilet kits with their exploded cans of shaving cream, beyond the blow dryers and the hair curlers, the cassette tapes and the magazines. It looks like a sanitary landfill.

He stops cold. He reaches out, but his right hand is shaking so badly he stuffs it back into his pocket. It's not in a plastic bag. Not yet. It will be as soon as he identifies it. Someone will tag it and scrawl a name onto the tag. It will be placed on a list, the list fed into a computer as it is every night. Eventually, the various, seemingly random items in the database will be connected with a particular passenger, and bit by bit a story will unfold.

It's Duncan's shoe, completely covered in caked mud and grass from the bog. A single shoe. A shoe that belongs on a foot that will never walk again. A shoe amid a pile of someone else's clothing: some bras, some panties, a blood-ied blouse. Duncan's shoe. His boy.

He signals one of the men wearing a camouflage uni-form and jump boots, a man who looks as tired as Daggett feels. Some of these men have gone without sleep for sev-enty-two hours now. Daggett sees the man approaching, tag in hand, and he begins to weep. Not because of the shoe.

Not for Duncan. Not for himself. But because he feels so deeply moved by the efforts of everyone involved, this exhausted uniformed boy among them, aware that none of the people here on the outskirts of this village, not one, will ever be the same again.

The LAFO explosives lab, located in the downtown Hoover Building, was cluttered with cardboard boxes, microscopes, and display cases housing every conceivable kind of explosive device. He wasn't comfortable around explosives.

Two technicians wearing white lab jackets continued working without looking up as Daggett entered the lab and crossed into Meecham's office.

Chaz Meecham had dark hair, intense blue eyes, and a thin, knowing smile. He talked fast. "Listen, we finally know a little something about what Bernard was up to in his hotel room. But with Backman getting it, the Bernard stuff is going to be moved down the list for a while. I thought you might want to hear some of this before it gets buried. Don't look at me like that, Michigan. It's just the way it is."

Daggett bit his tongue.

"Almost all of this stuff was caught by the vacuum filters, which shows you the tiny sizes we're dealing with. It's bits and pieces—microscopic, mostly—that fell from his working surface and were caught in the carpet. Bernard was thorough in his cleanup. We can tell that by how small the pieces are. But no one can clean up everything—not even a guy like Bernard.

"First, and of special interest, we've got some solder clippings with real high silver content. Quality stuff. That means one thing: He was building a sophisticated device, or devices. The biggest of what we've got," he continued, "are some plastic fragments." He slid a photograph in front of Daggett. The plastic fragments were set alongside a ruler in order to size them. To Daggett's untrained eye, they looked like nothing. "You see those when you're in my business, your pecker twitches. The surveillance schedule had Bernard going into an auto parts store, right? Our boys never did find out what he bought in there, but now I can tell you *exactly* what he bought. At least *some* of it. Dashboard altimeters. Barometric devices. *Two* of them, on account of the fact we've got six of these plastic nubs." He handed Daggett some graphs. Daggett glanced at them, not understanding a thing about them. These guys lived in another world.

"Two?"

He nodded enthusiastically. "There's the point of all of this: two. That's what makes all this so interesting." As Meecham continued his explanation, Daggett was imagining Bernard leaning over a hotel room table, constructing his detonator device in infinite detail, a soldering gun smoking at his side. "We've also got some platinum-plated silver wire. That's not good. It means he got hold of some mini-dets—miniature detonators. They're less than an inch long and pack one hell of a punch. They won't trip a metal detector, and they're very tough to pick up in X ray—a terrorist's dream. Hot enough to light any plastic explosive you can name. Hot enough to melt aluminum, bronze—any of your soft metals. Regular detonators are much more bulky and nowhere near as hot. What it means to us is that his devices are very, very small, or very complicated, or both. A mini-det is a lot more versatile than your standard detonator. You also have to go out of your way to obtain one, and that means he had a reason for wanting them."

"Where's it *leave* us?" Daggett asked. The room didn't have any windows. He felt claustrophobic.

"Now listen to me. Sometimes you put a pair of baro-switches in a row. Set them for different altitudes. That gives you a double-dipper. First time the air packs are charged, the first baro-switch opens. The plane takes off, goes higher, and the second baro-switch opens. That plane is guaranteed to be hell and gone from the ground. Depends what effect you're going for."

"But . . ." Daggett could hear it coming.

"But my instincts tell me differently. You get a feel for this kind of thing, Michigan. Probably the same in your line of work. What do I know? A guy like Bernard—he's a pro. He's efficient. Careful. He didn't leave a lot behind, but he left enough. Too much, in my opinion.

"We've got too many wire clippings for a single construction. Too much silicon, two altimeters. It all adds up." He flipped through a pile of black-and-white photographs shot through a microscope. "Too much for a guy as careful as Bernard," he repeated. "If I had to guess—and I'm only guessing—I'd say he built *two* detonators, Michigan. We know he had enough for *two* baro-switches, and as you just said, we know he bought *two* Casio watches. I'd say that makes the detonators nearly identical to one another as far as I can tell." Meecham paused, allowing it to sink in.

"Maybe he screwed the first one up, had to build another," Daggett suggested hopefully.

"Maybe. But then why did he buy two of everything *up front*? That doesn't jibe."

"So he made two bombs. Is that it?"

"Two *identical* detonators. Yeah. That's what I think the evidence tells us."

"And these baro-switches—"

"Mean they're both intended for planes," Meecham said, interrupting. "There's little doubt about that, I'm afraid. Whoever your operative is, he has enough hardware to drop two birds."

Daggett waited in the backyard for Duncan. The boy braked the wheelchair and rolled down the plywood ramp and came to a stop without a sound. A jay laughed from a nearby crabapple tree. The grass needed mowing. The ramp needed painting. The windows needed cleaning. Mrs. Kiyak poked her head out the door, looked at father and son, and smiled. She went back into the house, presumably to fix the boy some supper. Daggett worried the boy didn't spend enough time with kids his own age. There had to be something he could do about it.

Duncan was pouting. Daggett had promised long ago that, along with Carrie, they would rent a cottage on the Maryland shore and spend the upcoming weekend canoeing. A promise he was about to break because of Seattle and a plane he had to catch in ninety minutes.

Carrie was on her way over. He cringed at the thought. As much as he wanted to see her, as much as he loved her, and missed her, he didn't need a lecture. His devotion to the investigation—she called it worse than that—had caused them many a heated "discussion."

Here was a woman who had literally walked into his life, in the form of a property management representative, and had rescued him and Duncan from the difficult early days of starting over. A woman of tireless energies, she had taken immediately to Duncan. By the time the sexual relationship developed, Carrie had already been running their household and working with Duncan—easing him through the difficulties and obstacles that he faced daily. It only seemed to make sense that she would eventually become Daggett's lover. But now, looking back on it, it all seemed more of an arrangement, a convenience, than a relationship. With each passing week, Carrie assumed more control over their lives. By nature she was both fiery and domineering; the qualities that had initially made her so invaluable, and so attractive, now threatened to undo all that she had created.

He walked behind the chair to push the boy over to the chin-up bar, but Duncan didn't want his help, and hurriedly palmed the wheels, pulling away from Daggett, glancing furtively over his shoulder to assure his lead—his separation. He reached the low chin-up bar his father had built out of some old pipe and a pair of four-by-fours, slapped his small hands around the smooth metal, and struggled to lift the limp weight of his body.

"I'll help," Daggett said, walking more quickly to reach him.

"I can do it," the boy said. But he couldn't. He struggled, arms quivering, barely able to lift himself. He pulled, his face red from the effort, and shook his head violently as his father stepped forward. "No," he grunted, "let me." He tried again and then slowly sank from the minor success he had obtained and slumped back into the wheelchair.

Duncan wanted desperately to partake in an outdoor canoeing camp for the handicapped sponsored by ADD—Adventures for the Disadvantaged and Disabled—but a primary requirement, regardless of age, was upper body strength. Even at its lowest entry level, the weekend camp required five unassisted chin-ups. Duncan had yet to make more than two. Daggett wanted this camp for his son as badly as Duncan did.

"What's in Seattle?"

"A body. They found a body."

"I don't get it. I thought you were after that bomber."

"I am. But the body was found at an airplane manufacturer, and this guy's bombs go on airplanes. We want to see if the two might be connected."

"You think they are?"

"It's possible. I wouldn't be going if it wasn't super important."

"I know that."

"I mean it."

"I know you do. It's okay." He reached up again.

Daggett slipped his strong hands beneath the boy's arms, hoisted him, and said, "Let's try that again." But he hurt inside. He knew he was letting the boy down. Duncan lifted and, with his father's assistance, managed a chin-up. They had been working this way together for weeks now, Duncan's progress painstakingly slow. Daggett agonized over the process, pained to see his boy's lifeless legs dangling like a rag doll's. He had put on some weight during recovery and his arm strength had yet to develop. A few

weeks earlier, Duncan had begun using free weights after
months of Daggett's applying subtle pressure. Today, it
seemed to Daggett, the boy showed some new strength, and
he told him so.

Duncan said, "Again." Together they ran a series of five
chin-ups, and then Daggett eased him back to the chair.
"The only way there is through," he said, quoting what his
father had told him for many years. He figured a good fifty
percent of this was mental.

Carrie came around the side of the house, her chestnut
hair pulled up in a simple bun because of the heat, her
white Egyptian cotton sun dress revealing dark skin beneath. Sandals slapped on her heels. It bothered him when
she wore something like that, because she looked too damn
good. He knew she knew it, so he had to wonder why she
would come over looking like this. He decided it was just a
further extension of her recent independence. She had her
own agenda for where their lives should be, and Daggett's
FBI work—especially his dogged pursuit of those responsible for 1023—didn't fit into it. She wanted him to take his
talents into the private sector, where security management
offered two to three times the pay. She wanted them to
marry, have children, and leave Washington. She had made
all this quite clear on a warm moonlit night not three weeks
earlier. When her plan met with resistance, she stiffened,
and went off on this independence jag, determined to have
her way. In the last six days, she had spent the night but
once. They hadn't made love since the argument.

As she approached, confident and alluring, he noticed
but wasn't aroused by the lightness of her step, the summer
darkness of her skin. Her power over him, her control, di-
minished with each passing night. With less time together,
they had grown farther apart; Daggett was no closer to entering the private sector than he had been when all this had
begun. As she reached him, he actually feared her.

Duncan craned his head back, looked up at him, and

said, "Be nice to her, Dad." Daggett smelled a conspiracy. It mixed with her perfume.

"Hi there," she said to both of them. To Daggett, "What's this about Seattle? I thought we were going to the shore." Impatience gnawed behind her eyes.

"So did I," said Duncan.

It was a conspiracy. Now she was using his son against him.

"Duty calls," he said, fighting back his anger.

"No, it doesn't," she contradicted. "Each field office handles investigations in its own region. You've explained that a dozen times. Maybe duty *volunteers?*"

"Hey, yeah . . ." Duncan chimed in.

"Have you two been practicing?" Daggett asked. He recalled his encounter with Gloria earlier in the day. He felt cornered.

"You *promised* us this weekend. Doesn't that mean *anything?*"

"What would you like me to say?"

She went red in the face. "Keep practicing," she told Duncan. Clamping her strong fingers around Cam's elbow, she led him away. "You can't do this. You set up this weekend where he can *finally* get some time in on the water, you get him all worked up over it, and now you pull the rug out. What is it with you? You know what kind of damage that does to a kid?"

"Wait a second," he said, removing her hand. "You're telling me about my kid?"

"Somebody had better. He keeps company with a seventy-year-old who can barely keep her heart going with all the black tea in China. You think he's growing?"

"It's temporary."

"It's B.S. is what it is. Temporarily forever, right?"

"A man was murdered. It's important."

"You requested it, didn't you? You probably had to fight to be sent, didn't you? They don't need you out there, do they?"

"Yes, yes, and no, if you're scoring by inning." He hated being caught by her. He resented her attitude, her approach, everything—especially her being right.

"The shore, Cam. You don't want me along, that's okay. But skip Seattle. Please. Take Dunc to the shore and spend some time with him."

"I was spending some time with him before you arrived."

That accomplished what he was after. She shot across the backyard like a wildfire with a tailwind. He felt like running after her, but he stayed where he was; he took note of that.

"Nice going, Dad." It was Duncan, hanging from the bar.

"It's a murder, Dunc. It's important," he said from across the lawn.

"So go," the boy said to the father.

Only a few minutes later, he did.

4

ON SATURDAY MORNING, August 25—nearly two weeks after the Bernard explosion at National Airport—Daggett stood in the lobby of the Seattle Westin. He spotted the cop before any introduction was made. Lieutenant Phil Shoswitz's dark eyes looked out from a pale face, the result of long hours behind a desk. He wore a button-down white shirt and a wrinkled tie. His rubber-soled shoes showed the irregular heels of age and the scuffed toes of neglect. Shoswitz looked directly at Daggett; he, too, recognized an FBI agent when he saw one. They shook hands and made introductions.

Shoswitz had a drawn face and exaggerated, oversized brown eyes. He struck Daggett as a man who might have had a sense of humor once. In a voice unfamiliar with contest, he said, "I thought we'd head directly to Duhning. I have a car waiting."

Daggett welcomed the coolness of the Seattle air. He drank it in. The monorail passed overhead, tourists' faces framed in the windows. A street person draped in dirty burlap walked by, unsteadily holding a steaming plastic cup of coffee. His bloodshot eyes looked right through Daggett.

"You ever been out here?" Shoswitz asked, somewhat surprised.

Daggett maneuvered to keep the man on his left. "I was assigned here for a while. Back in the Bronze Age. Met my wife in this city. Met her in a bar. I even remember the name of the band that was playing—Duffy Bishop and the Rhythm Dogs." For a moment, no more than a blink of the eye, he was right back there. "You remember the little things."

Shoswitz nodded, but with sadness. "Still married?"

I must wear it on my shirt sleeve, Daggett thought. "No," he said.

"Me neither. Comes with the job, I suppose."

"More often than not, it seems."

"And now you're married to counterintelligence, huh?"

"Closer to the truth than I'd like to admit. Counterterrorism, actually. Foreign counterterrorism. My third year on this squad."

"Kids?"

"A son."

"I got two daughters. Somewhere. She get your boy?"

"No, I did."

"You're lucky. That's the worst part for me."

"How many years on the force?" Daggett asked. He felt uncomfortable sharing his life's story with a stranger, and yet—perhaps it was that they shared a badge, a way of life; perhaps it was their shared failure—he felt a bond between them. Shoswitz had apparently summed him up in a glance.

"Me? Too many, can't you tell?"

A beat-up car with black-walls and a bullet hole in the corner of the windshield pulled up, and they climbed in.

The driver, a sergeant named LaMoia, better dressed than most cops, had a strong hand, like grabbing on to a leg of lamb. He wore his black curly hair long, and carried an air of confidence that bordered on cockiness. Daggett and Shoswitz rode in the backseat. Daggett was struck by the changes in the city. "Some of 'em good, some of 'em bad," Shoswitz said. They took a left onto an elevated highway heading south. They discussed the first officer's report, and a preliminary conversation with Dr. Ronald Dixon, the King County medical examiner.

"Way it works at Duhning," Shoswitz said, "in case you're not familiar with it: If we want to talk to any of their employees, we do it off site, or else in a room their Security provides us. They arrange the interview, time and place, so there isn't a lot of fuss about someone being pulled away from their post. Now normally the sheriff would handle a homicide out at Duhning. Technically, it's his show, his turf —the Duhning site dates back so far that it's not within the city jurisdiction. But the Sheriff's Department asked for our help, which is just fine with us. LaMoia's on loan to them. I'm overseeing, which is why I left my desk to tag along." He paused, apparently leaving room for LaMoia to contribute. Then he continued, "Bottom line: Duhning doesn't like us on site. Period. But on a homicide, they don't have much choice. Thing about it is, we like good relations, so no shields, no heavy stuff. More than likely, we'll be shown around by their top guy, name of Ross Fleming. He's okay —one of your FBI boys Duhning snatched up after mandatory retirement. He'll take us in quietly. Simulation is an unsecured area, so we'll hardly be noticed."

"Unsecured? I read that in the report you faxed," Daggett said. "How's that possible with so much equipment in there?"

LaMoia answered, "Fleming is taking a lot of heat about that."

"I don't doubt it."

Shoswitz added, "You talk to him, it's understandable. He oversees security for a hundred and fifty thousand Duhning employees worldwide. A hundred-some-odd physical plants. He's working with a fixed budget, with his top priority the defense contracts, followed by aerospace and engineering. Simulation is essentially an advanced training facility for commercial pilots. Way Fleming tells it, until a few days ago—until *this*—it was a low-priority facility for him. They've got key codes on the doors—shit like that—but that's about it. I kinda feel for the guy; anywhere else, key codes and pass systems would be considered high security. One of their boys gets toe-tagged, and now everybody's pointing fingers. Truth-a-the-matter is—I mean *we* all know this—a guy wants to get in a place, he's gonna get in there. Plain and simple."

Shoswitz sucked some air between his teeth. "Fleming's not real happy about that either. You ask me, it just confirms it was professional. Like I said—they want it, they're gonna get it. This day and age, you just gotta start waving money around."

"Any evidence of that with Ward? Money, I mean."

LaMoia answered, "No. Nothing. No change in lifestyle, no sign of any hidden accounts that we can find. Wife says everything had been perfectly normal. But I'm not buying it. You ask me, he had a piece of pie on the side."

"Why do you say that?"

"John tends to think with his dick," Shoswitz replied, interrupting. "I'd consider the source, if I was you."

"Careful, I'm driving," LaMoia said. He jerked on the wheel to prove his point. The three of them laughed.

Shoswitz added, "A girl bends over at the water fountain . . . she better be on the pill."

"Whoa! Low blow, Lieutenant!"

"*Low blow* . . . See what I mean? Always sexual puns with this one."

"The *reason*," LaMoia said loudly, attempting to defend himself to Daggett, "that I say that about Ward, is because of this season ticket of his. I mean the guy lays out some major change for a regular seat at the Mariners—"

"Which, the way we're playing, shows some low-voltage intelligence in the first place," Shoswitz contributed. "Mind you, I'm guilty of the same offense. I got a season set as well."

"And then never shows up until the last inning," LaMoia concluded. "We checked that out, in attempting to confirm what his wife told us. She claims he *was* at the game. The person in the next seat over—also a season ticket holder—claims Ward seldom showed up before the ninth. On the night in question, he never showed up at all." He glanced into the mirror and searched out Daggett. "Conclusion—from one who thinks with his dick—he was handing his wife a wad of shit while he was handing some hair pie a wad of something else."

"Any clues who she might be?" Daggett asked.

"You're not buying into this?" Shoswitz protested.

Daggett shrugged.

LaMoia saved him by continuing. "Way it looks to me is she would have to be someone at work. This guy was a twelve-hour-a-day man, know what I mean? No outside interests. So unless it's a waitress, someone like that, I'm thinking it has to be someone in Simulation."

"Oh, Jesus!" Shoswitz barked.

"But no idea who?"

"If Fleming wasn't so tough on us about providing evidence before questioning his people, we might could quiz the pies out there and see if anyone blushed, or crossed their legs, or something. But the way it is—"

"I might be able to help there. If he used to be one of us, chances are he'll bend a little to help out."

"I wouldn't count on it," Shoswitz said. "This interrogation rule is policy; it comes down from above him. They've got their own little world going, over there. Same as all the multinationals around here. They make us jump through every paper hoop ever made for even the smallest of things. They cooperate, all right, but only if and when we've got a case dead to rights. Otherwise they'd rather take care of it themselves. Keep it in the family."

"So we think of some other way," Daggett suggested.

"Such as?"

"If Ward isn't at these ball games, then he's somewhere else. And," he said, addressing LaMoia, "I assume he's in his car."

"Far as we know."

"So we check the Duhning parking logs for the dates and times of the ball games. Maybe he was at work. Then we check DMV for any parking citations, going back maybe six months at a time. We pay strict attention to the dates and times of games. If we don't have enough hits there, we cross-check his credit card charges, see if he took hotel rooms or did some 'entertaining.' I don't like it much, but we dig this guy up out of the grave and we spread him around until we see what stinks."

"Shit," LaMoia said in a voice that bordered on respect, "for FBI, you're all right."

Daggett glanced out the car window. Ward's killer could be halfway around the world at the moment, or he could be in a Seattle hotel room drinking champagne, eating smoked salmon, and marveling at the picturesque litter of white sails on Elliott Bay and Puget Sound beyond.

"How about the car itself?" Daggett asked.

"Not yet," Shoswitz said. "We're assuming the killer drove it off site."

"So he didn't plan on killing Ward," Daggett said. "If we're right about him being a professional, he sure as hell wouldn't have taken a risk like that without being forced to."

"Agreed," Shoswitz said.

Steel cranes were busy stacking containers onto ships. Out on the water, a cumbersome ferry steamed for points unknown. The killer could be on that ferry. He could be on one of the container ships. He could be anywhere. He could have Bernard's handiwork in his possession. Maybe LaMoia could drive a little faster. Maybe they should skip over the tour of the simulator and get right down to tracing the movements of Ward's car.

Shoswitz read his thoughts. "We'll walk you through the simulator area, show you where the body was found, and let you speak to Fleming. Your Seattle office has been through all this once, but they said they asked you to come out here and have a look for yourself."

"That must make you some kind of expert or something," LaMoia said.

"Or something," Daggett said. He couldn't tell if he was being teased.

"What we know for sure," Shoswitz said, "is that one of them blew lunch—or dinner—inside the simulator."

LaMoia added, "Lab is checking the puke to see if there's any medical reason for this guy heaving. Microbes, that kind of shit. If not, then one of them had a bad case of the butterflies."

"Other than that we don't have squat, except that Fleming thinks it had to be based on inside information." Shoswitz picked at his ear. Daggett rolled down the window. His chest felt tight. The air smelled good. It reminded him of a restaurant out on the pier, and a time when he had been extremely happy. It suddenly seemed like a lifetime ago.

Daggett, Shoswitz, and Duhning's head of Security, Ross Fleming, completed a lengthy tour of the Simulation facility. Fleming, an energetic man in his late fifties, with short gray hair and hard blue eyes, wore the face of a man with a dozen secrets and chose his words carefully. He elected to observe, rather than speculate, chewing his thoughts behind an impassive face that revealed nothing. Daggett was shown the hiding place in the floorboards of the computer room, was given a "flight" in the 959-600 simulator, and spent twenty minutes in Ward's office with yet another Duhning executive, going through Ward's paperwork and hoping for a lead. Fleming suggested a tour of the badge room; Daggett felt he was being asked to leave.

That was when LaMoia, escorted by an attractive black woman under Fleming's command, arrived with a precocious grin pinned on his face. "Done," he said, handing a sheet of computer paper to Shoswitz.

"Already?" Shoswitz said in bewilderment. Even he seemed surprised by the efficiency of his own troops.

"What?" Daggett asked, attempting to interrupt, but wholly ignored.

LaMoia answered his lieutenant with a confidence that Daggett recognized as success. "I phoned DMV. Ward had three unpaid parking tickets, all in the last two months.

That, and six months ago we cited and towed his Taurus for blocking a hydrant. All citations issued within a block of each other." To Fleming he said, "What saved us was the way you fellas do everything on computer. Very impressive! They got this database, Lieutenant—"

"What exactly do we have?" Daggett asked.

Shoswitz handed him the green-and-white-striped computer paper.

LaMoia explained, "We searched the database for the addresses of Simulation employees first—based on my natural instincts. And there she was—bingo!—fifth one down. Lived right in the same block as *all* of Ward's citations. A thirty-one-year-old redhead; single; built to take a ride, or so I'm told."

"Sarah?" the Simulation man said in registered shock.

"See?" LaMoia said, popping a fresh stick of gum into his mouth. "Everyone knows her."

The conference room held a stainless steel and glass table with eight black leather chairs, a bulletin board, a projector screen, a phone, and a Mr. Coffee that had a fresh pot waiting. They each poured themselves a cup. Daggett noted the lack of a clock. No windows. A silk ficus with dust on its leaves. The only phone had a dozen incoming lines and a box attached to it that he assumed involved encryption. This is what the military would be like if it went private, he thought.

Sarah Pritchet was a little toothy. She was scared to death and it showed in her bright green eyes and her clammy palms, which Daggett felt as they shook hands. She wore a khaki suit with a pressed white T-shirt and black leather heels that stretched her calves tightly. Her hair was flame red, and she had so many freckles, it looked like she had been splattered with chestnut-brown paint, giving her face a kind of wounded look. Her brow was tight as she stood at the head of the table with her arms crossed tightly.

The suit hid her body, but not from the imagination.
LaMoia had made sure of that.

You hit people like Sarah Pritchet, he thought. You hit
them hard and see if they try to hit back. Daggett jumped
on the silence and said sternly, "Dr. Ward wasn't at the ball
game Tuesday night," while she was still standing. He didn't
offer her a seat because he didn't want her comfortable. He
explained that both LaMoia and Shoswitz were homicide
cops. That helped turn up the heat. She knew Fleming. With
both time and Ward's killer slipping away from him, Daggett felt the need for victory. He loosened his tie and unbuttoned his collar. It made him think of Backman; it was the
same shirt he had been wearing that day, and the button he
had sewn on didn't fit the hole well. "We thought perhaps
Dr. Ward had been approached at the ball game by the man
who killed him, but we know now that wasn't how it happened. He wasn't at the game, Miss Pritchet."

Tearing into the mind of a woman already upset by the
murder of her lover was not Daggett's idea of fun. Exposing
the secrets of the dead was even less so. The two had had an
affair. So what? If Ward had died in a traffic accident, no
investigation would have occurred—he could have died
with his secret intact. As it was, it had to come out, at least
to some degree, and if it had to come out, then the best
thing for the investigation was to use it to advantage. Shove
it into a crack and lean on it with all your weight. Eventually the crack would widen, and things would spill out.

"We could take you downtown. We could turn you over
to a policewoman and she could comb your hair. We could
try for other, more personal, evidence. The lab could then
tell us for certain whether or not you are the woman we're
after. But we're also after a killer, Miss Pritchet. He has a
head start on us. Quite frankly, we don't have the time for
all that lab business. So, what we're hoping for is some
cooperation." We're hoping for a miracle, he thought, but
didn't say it. "Without that cooperation, Miss Pritchet, the

courts, the press, and Duhning Aerospace will all become *actively* involved."

"No one wants that," Fleming added. She looked as frightened of him as a young girl might be of a father.

"May I sit down?" she asked.

He had to maintain his control. He didn't answer her. He asked in an unforgiving voice, "Dr. Ward was, or was not, with you on the evening of his murder?"

Anger forced her eyes wider. Beautiful green eyes, as hot as the color of her hair. "*Was!* All right? Yes, he was with me," she answered. "We were at my apartment. He left at the seventh-inning stretch."

"Have a seat, Miss Pritchet." Satisfaction pulsed through him. For the first time he felt the air-conditioning.

LaMoia removed a small tape recorder from his jacket, placed it on the table, spoke the date and time into it, named the people present, and then looked up at Daggett, who began the questioning.

Sarah Pritchet spent twenty minutes answering questions about her affair with Ward and the details of the night of Ward's murder. She was dismissed, and for the next hour and a half, Daggett, Shoswitz, and LaMoia reviewed the tape and established a more formal line of questioning for the upcoming lunch hour. Fleming checked in on them periodically and rejoined them for the second interrogation.

The initial search of Sarah Pritchet's apartment, conducted by both LaMoia and Daggett with a uniformed officer at the door, provided little of interest. Daggett looked over both her telephone bills and her canceled checks. LaMoia searched her personal belongings and toiletries. If Pritchet was lying about the extent of her involvement, it would require a team of experts to prove it. Nothing they found contradicted her story.

They moved their search outside to the Pay-and-Park she claimed Ward used whenever possible, and had most likely used on the night of his murder. Daggett thought of

himself as Dr. Roger Ward as he rode the apartment building's elevator down to ground level and walked to the front
gate. A pair of silver-windowed office buildings on the other
side of I-5 blocked any view of the Sound. A group of sea
gulls split the blue of the sky. Beyond, a commercial jet flew
silently over Puget Sound. Sight of the plane reminded Daggett of his purpose. However faint, he couldn't rule out the
possibility that Bernard's detonator might be intended for a
Duhning 959-600. Or was this merely coincidence? With
Bernard dead and few leads, any day now he might be
pulled from the investigation. He could keep it alive only by
connecting this murder to Bernard's detonators. The plane
he watched grew smaller and smaller. He felt his hopes of
taking the Pritchet connection one step farther diminish
just as quickly.

Daggett wandered the lot, studying the oil stains, the
cars, the drain, the bushes. If you're the killer, where do
you hide? He turned and studied the apartment building.
He studied the layout of the Pay-and-Park and its relation to
the building's front entrance. Slowly, like working with a
grid system, he backed up, keeping both the windows of the
apartment and the front door in view. He found his way to
the far corner, where a battered trailer provided decent
cover. He searched the area carefully.

"What are we looking for?" LaMoia asked, joining him.

"Who knows? Gum? Pocket change? Anything the killer
might have left behind."

LaMoia prowled the scrubby bushes.

Daggett found a crushed beer can—but it was clearly
weathered. He found an empty bottle of motor oil, and a
dead sparrow that appeared the victim of a cat kill. The
loose feathers had collected in a pile behind one of the trailer's deflated tires. A pair of charcoal marks on the lip of the
trailer's fender caught his eye. He touched one. The charcoal smudged his fingertip.

"When did you get your last rain?" Daggett shouted out
to LaMoia, who had disappeared in the bushes.

"I'll have to check, but I got a hunch it was Monday night. Might-a-been Sunday."

Daggett dropped to one knee, eyes sweeping the blacktop like searchlights. He used his ballpoint pen as a probe, exploring the gray-brown feathers piled behind the trailer's wheel. He found two cigarette butts. One in the feathers, the other lodged between the rubber and the blacktop. Not very old, by the look of them. Dropped by a man impatiently awaiting Roger Ward? The cigarette paper was black, the filter gold—expensive, by the look of them. Unusual. European? Excitement built inside him.

A few feathers at a time, he continued his excavation. Past the cigarette butts, behind a good deal of plumage, he discovered a small, crumpled package still wearing half of its coat of torn cellophane. More evidence? If they had had rain on Sunday, as LaMoia had said, then this box had been discarded recently. As recently as Tuesday night? Was he on to the person who had killed Ward, or some innocent by-stander who had killed nothing more than a few spare min-utes in a parking lot? You go with the evidence, he re-minded himself. You go with what they give you, and you make sense of it later.

He rolled the crushed box with his pen and read the print: *Anbesol—for temporary relief of toothache*. The pic-ture showed a tooth with lightning bolts coming out of it.

"Maybe our boy has a bum tooth," he called out to LaMoia.

LaMoia answered, "Tooth-dirty," trying to make it sound like *two-thirty*. "Time to call Chinese dentist."

"Time to call every dentist in town."

"You think?"

"He gives us something like this, right or wrong, we've got to follow it up, don't we? Could be he fucked up. This may be hard evidence."

"May be nothing."

"Agreed."

"Lieutenant's not going to like it. Too speculative. I think this is something more for you and your people."

LaMoia carried both paper and plastic bags with him, as Daggett was certain he would. Homicide cops carried this stuff around at all times. Together they bagged and labeled Daggett's discoveries. Then they widened their search area.

"How's this for bizarre?" LaMoia called out, emerging from the overgrown weeds holding the partially carved potato in his gloved hand. "Looks like a goddamned dildo, you ask me." It did, Daggett agreed. A phallus two inches in diameter and several inches long, emerging from the uncarved butt like a penis from a scrotum. "She likes 'em wide, but not too deep," LaMoia said, imitating a blues singer. He spun it around. "Idaho number one russet, maybe." He studied it. "I don't know, maybe it's some kind of gay blade. How would you like that up the old wazoo?" He made a motion with it that couldn't be mistaken. He tossed it to Daggett, who caught it.

Daggett spun it in his hand. The heart of the potato had blackened with air contact. "Someone spent some time on this," he said, puzzled by it.

"It ain't the meat, it's the motion."

He was about to toss it when he noticed that some of the black had come off on his hand. It wasn't just air-rot after all. He rubbed his fingers together and brought them to his nose. Inhaling, he experienced another sudden explosion of excitement in his chest, and he found himself wanting to believe that indeed this was hard evidence involving Ward's murderer. He said, "You ever heard that shit about when you lose your hearing, you can smell more?"

"No," LaMoia said. "I stay away from all that touchy-feely stuff."

"This is science, I'm talking about. Medical science."

"I never did well in science. Except anatomy," he added quickly. "But that was mostly extracurricular."

"Do you ever stop?" Daggett asked him.

"Only when she asks me to," LaMoia fired back. "And only then if I know she means it."

"Smell this," Daggett said, coming toward the man with pinched fingers.

LaMoia shied away.

"Smell it," Daggett insisted. He shoved his fingers under the man's nose. LaMoia's moustache twitched. Puzzlement creased his face.

"Exhaust?"

"Maybe it doesn't have anything to do with my hearing," Daggett replied.

He spent a good part of the late afternoon, early evening, on the phone with the Washington office and trying to reach Carrie. He drove up to Green Lake and went for a run. He had dinner at Ray's Boat House with the Bureau friend who had "invited" him out here to Seattle. They talked over old times and drank too much beer. They discussed Bernard and the German bust of *Der Grund*.

"You think this murder out at Duhning was Kort's doing?" his friend asked. "You think there's a chance he's over here?" It was the first time anyone had actually come out and said it, although both Backman and Pullman had inferred as much. Daggett wasn't sure how to answer. The man added, "I mean it seemed a pretty obvious possibility to me. That's why I invited you out here. Bernard is *Der Grund*, Kort is *Der Grund*. Bernard builds a detonator. Kort can't be found anywhere. I mean somebody's got to put the damn thing onto a plane or what's the use? And that's Kort's job, right?"

"We *think* it's Kort's job." In fact, the way things added up, he *knew* it was the work of Anthony Kort. Who else? But as the investigating officer, he couldn't vocalize such beliefs until he had the evidence to support them.

"That's all I'm saying."

"Part of me hopes it is; part of me hopes it isn't."

"I can understand that."

No one can completely understand that, Daggett thought. But why argue with a friend? Why argue at all, except for the beer and the fatigue? He wanted to argue. He wanted to lose some steam.

"You want to drive a bucket of balls?" his friend asked.

"I'd rather find a pitching machine and try a few line drives."

"I don't know of any pitching machines. But I know a driving range open till midnight."

"Sounds okay to me."

"They sell beer."

"Sounding better all the time."

"You playing the links much?"

"No. Haven't for a long time. Too expensive. I was playing first base on the WMFO fast-pitch team for a while. Same time I was coaching my son's Little League team. Hell of a good time." Something fell between them like a steel plate. Daggett felt completely alone. Memories flickered in the yellow and the bubbles of the beer.

"Right," his friend finally said. "What do you say we get going?"

It was a little after noon the next day when Shoswitz interrupted Daggett, who was in the middle of writing a report. LaMoia and five other sergeants had been calling dentists for the better part of three hours. Daggett was just giving up hope of connecting the Anbesol to a man with tooth trouble. That was the way it often worked: you had to give up completely before your luck would turn. Expectation was your worst enemy. Shoswitz had a restless energy about him. He had the nervous habit of massaging his elbow, and his eyes found it difficult to stay fixed on any one spot. "You may be right about the Anbesol," he told Daggett. "Four different dentists' offices all received calls on Tuesday from an out-of-towner who wanted some emergency attention."

Daggett said, "If the medical examiner is right about

that choke hold, then it's possible our killer didn't intend to kill Ward. If we play around with that, then he may have planned to still be in town on Wednesday or Thursday."

Shoswitz nodded. "Or Friday. Whoever it was, gave all four receptionists Wednesday through Friday to book him in. And they were all given a phone number and room number in case of an opening. Two of them left messages, but the guy never got back to them."

"A phone number?" Daggett asked. "You're telling me we have a phone number?"

"The Mayflower Park Hotel. It's a nice old place over on Olive Way."

"Can we move on this?" Daggett asked. "As far as the courts are concerned?"

Shoswitz said. "Have to check with your boys over in the Federal Building about that. I don't know shit about search and seizure on this kind of thing. But the way I figure it: They get creative, they'll think of something." Shoswitz handed Daggett the pad with the names of the dentists. Circled boldly in rings of intertwined ink so that it jumped off the page was: Mayflower Park Hotel, Room #311.

"We've had a couple pieces of good luck," Special Agent Frank Macalister told Daggett as they shook hands in the lobby of the Mayflower Park. Good luck ran in small schools, as far as Daggett could figure. Bad luck just plain ran out of control.

The man's deep voice sounded forced, as if without the effort it might be high and effeminate. Macalister was black, tall, and clean-shaven, a serious man with concerned eyes. He walked hurriedly, not checking to see if Daggett kept up. From the back, Daggett saw gray in the man's hair. "The guy in three-eleven left specific instructions with the front desk that he didn't want any maid service until he checked out. Said he was going to be keeping weird hours and that he didn't care about fresh towels. That request was

made real early Wednesday A.M.—Tuesday night, in reality."

"The time fits," Daggett said. "We guessing he didn't
want anyone knowing he had left? Something like that?"

"It plays."

"So we may have the right guy."

"If we do, he cut his own throat without knowing it.
His request meant that housekeeping didn't go through the
room until this morning," he said with a casual glance at
Daggett over his shoulder. They entered the elevator. The
doors closed and the car rose slowly. Macalister smelled of
after-shave. "Hotel trash isn't scheduled to be picked up until this afternoon. Whatever housekeeping cleaned out of
that room is in one of those trash bags. I've asked them to
hold off on pickup to give our people time to do some dig-
ging. We know from billing records that the suspect used
room service quite a bit. If I'm him, then I do a major clean
up before I split. I wipe the place down. I cover myself as
best as possible. But if he tossed out a receipt in his trash,
then that may ID it for us. His room number will be on the
receipt." He paused. "It's a long shot, but it's something."

Daggett didn't see it as a long shot. It made a hell of a
lot of sense. He suggested a couple other things they could
look for to ID the trash: gold and black cigarette butts, an
empty bottle of Anbesol, a grocery bag, or a grocery store
receipt that listed a potato. Macalister looked at him
strangely. Daggett explained, "He blocked Ward's exhaust
pipe with a potato."

"Right."

"What about a car? You can't get around this city without a car. The hotel must have some kind of parking arrangements for guests. They may be able to give us a license
plate number for this guy's car."

"That's good. I'll follow up on that. We got a license
plate number, we might get a rental agency."

"We should also talk to the maid."

Macalister nodded. "Already spoke to the front desk about that. They're going to send her up."

Macalister slipped a piece of plastic into a key slot and unlocked the door. "Electronic keys," he said in disgust. "When's this shit gonna end?"

It was a tiny but attractive room with a rose-and-teal chintz bedspread, almond drapes, and too much furniture: a couch, a desk, the bed and the bureau. It didn't leave much room for people. Macalister and Daggett both donned plastic gloves. The door thumped shut behind them. The claustrophobic space reinforced Daggett's sense of urgency. Ward's killer may have been inside this room. This was the bed he had slept in, the desk he had used. They were *that* close. No matter how small, it was a victory to be briefly savored.

Daggett walked over to the window and looked down at the cars, trucks, and buses below. "We want as many of the details as we can put together," he told Macalister, "what this guy ate, the quantity and especially the *brand* of cigarette he smoked, whether he showered or bathed—anything and everything that might shed some light on him." Macalister nodded, accustomed to such requests. The two men searched the room, wandering it slowly, heads craned down. The lab boys would find something—they always did. Whether or not it would help the investigation remained to be seen.

A knock came on the door and Macalister answered it. A shy Vietnamese woman introduced herself as Karen Xi. She was a tiny, flat-chested woman with callused hands, her hair held back by a white plastic clip with blue flowers. She had twisted teeth and flawless dark skin. Her frightened eyes seemed to occupy half her face.

"You're in no kind of trouble," Macalister explained.

"Yes."

"In fact, you may be able to be a tremendous help to us."

"Yes." Looking at him out of the corner of her eye, skeptically.

"You cleaned this room this morning."

"Yes. Check-out."

"You clean more thoroughly when it's a check-out?"

"Yes."

Daggett wondered, was it too much to ask that this woman remember this room in particular?

"You clean a lot of rooms," Macalister said, reading his mind.

"Many rooms."

"You probably don't pay much attention, one room to another. Is that right?"

She nodded, shrugged her shoulders, and offered them both an innocent expression. She still seemed scared.

"*I* wouldn't pay much attention, I can tell you that," Macalister encouraged.

She smiled, but raised her hand to cover her mouth, not allowing those awful teeth to show.

"You wouldn't happen to remember anything in particular about this room?"

"Yeah, sure I do."

"The guest?" Daggett blurted out, interrupting, drawing a look of annoyance from Macalister.

"Did you see him?" Macalister asked. "Do you remember the guest?"

"Not him. Don't remember *him*. Remember *room* . . . clean room. Very neat and tidy. Easy to clean."

"Neat?" Daggett asked. This was just the kind of information he had hoped for—it shed some light on the man's personality.

"You notice when you clean rooms."

"I'm sure you do," Macalister said. His eyes asked Daggett to stop, but Daggett couldn't. "He smoked," Daggett said.

"Yes."

Now Macalister glared, but Daggett was unrelenting.

"Do you, by any chance, remember what the cigarettes looked like? What color?" Daggett asked.

"No. Don't remember. He smoked. He left the window cracked open."

Daggett walked over to the window and studied the building and its fire escapes more closely. If pressed, could a person escape from that window? Yes, he thought it possible. Edge your way over there, drop down to the overhang. Possible. Leave the window cracked open to speed up your exit. "We'll want the latent-print team to pay special attention here."

"Did you ever see a gun, a knife, anything like that?" Daggett asked her.

"No. Nothing like that."

"Did he speak to you?" Macalister interrupted.

"No. I never even saw him. He done something, this man?"

The killer's invisibility bothered Daggett. First at Duhning, now here.

"*Anything* unusual? Anything at all?" Daggett blurted out in frustration, further annoying Macalister.

"Oh, yes," she said, drawing their attention with her sharp voice and suddenly bright, anxious eyes. "The tooth!" She beamed. "Not every day you find a tooth."

5

ANTHONY KORT CRINGED as he explored the gaping wound at the back of his gums with the rubber tip of the toothbrush. It was ugly back there. His jaw was so swollen on that side that he had taken to stuffing an enormous wad of tissue between his opposite cheek and gums in an attempt to balance the look of his face. If ever there was a chipmunk, he thought, it's me. He didn't mind it so much: he looked like a different person, and that had its advantages.

He felt exhausted from the train ride; he had been unable to sleep, too preoccupied with the repercussions and subsequent preparations resulting from Roger Ward's unintended murder. The last several days had been hectic; he didn't like Los Angeles.

He rechecked his watch for the date: August 27. Two weeks to the day since the explosion that killed Bernard. Hopefully, by late this afternoon the unfortunate loss would mean something. Bernard had made himself briefly immortal: he still lived in the form of the detonators he had left behind.

Monique Cheysson arrived at the door of his Los Angeles hotel room precisely at nine-thirty. It had been nearly two years since he had last seen her but he recognized her face immediately, even when distorted by the door's fish-eye security peephole.

He opened the door for her.

She entered in behind a waft of musky perfume and the rustle of fine fabric. She carried a black briefcase.

Kort slipped the DO NOT DISTURB sign over the knob and

closed the door firmly. The dead bolt insured privacy. She spun around dramatically to face him, the well-practiced turn of a fashion model at the end of the runway. Monique was always onstage.

A curtain of fine black hair fell to just above her shoulders and then curled under stylishly. Low bangs shortened her forehead and framed a face that was all brown eyes, cheekbones, and red lips. She had perfected the demure expression of appearing half asleep—or ready for bed. Her self-confidence drew attention from across a room—it bordered on arrogance. She had square shoulders, high breasts, and a waist so tiny that he thought he might be able to reach around it with both hands.

He had been fantasizing about her for weeks.

"Any problems?" he asked her.

"It is right there," she said, pointing to the briefcase. She had less of an accent than he remembered. If she tried hard, she might even pass for American. Her voice rang with disappointment.

"What's wrong?" His fantasy collapsed. He had imagined her seducing him. He had imagined a reenactment of Frankfurt.

He recalls that first time he saw her with crisp clarity. He remembers the cold, his breath white, his nose running. So cold that her face is hidden by the mask of frost on the windscreen. It's a silver Mercedes—stolen, of course, with stolen plates. His passport is a forgery, and therefore his identity; everything about him is a forgery. The door sticks with the cold as he attempts to open it. She leans across the front seat and bangs it open for him. He sees her for the first time through the frost-glazed glass, the determination on her face, the rouge on her cheeks, a silk scarf, dark sunglasses. Typical of these operations, they haven't met until this moment the door complains open. How Michael manages this is anybody's guess. The training, the logistics. . . .

A dozen or so people, all orbiting around him regularly, but not so much as a shadow shared between them.

"The fucking car wouldn't start," she says angrily, and he likes her right away.

"The suitcase?" he asks.

"In the trunk." He offers an expression that questions the intelligence of that and she interrupts him before he speaks. "Where a suitcase belongs. Especially *that* suitcase. You think I was going to keep it on the backseat?" Yes, he likes her. Despite her obvious good looks, he is not physically attracted to her. It has been two years since his wife took her own life, and in that time not once has he felt anything like lust for another woman. Only despair. He feeds on the despair, like a tick feeds on the blood of a stray dog. It motivates him. It forces him toward purpose. It is this despair that has turned a grieving widower into a killer. He doesn't know this killer—he doesn't stop to know him—but he doesn't know the other man either, the man of a wife and a child and a workaday life he left behind. He doesn't want to know. He has purpose. That is enough. It will suffice.

"I'm Monique," she says.

He finds himself staring at her.

"Something wrong?"

"No, nothing."

"You're French," he observes.

She ignores this. "I do not know why I should feel so nervous, but I do. It is not so very hard what we are going to do, is it?"

"The bag will match?"

"Of course it will, but I warn you that hotel is impossible. I have never seen so many people."

"And the schedule?"

"Yes. I double-checked."

"Then it's done. There's nothing to be nervous about."

"My insides say differently." The car stalls at a light.

The engine grinds and slows behind the efforts of a drained battery. He knows exactly how that battery feels.

"Wait," he tells her. He switches off the radio, which she had turned down but not off. He turns off the fan. Like closing off compartments. "Okay. Try again." Someone honks at them.

"Fuck off," she says, glaring into the rearview mirror.

"Pay no attention to that."

At last the engine flutters to life. "This fucking car!" she says. "This fucking cold. I hate Frankfurt. I hate this place."

"Pull in behind that bus," he instructs.

"Oh, my God, we are here! And look, the bus is early. Oh, my God." She glances at him with an expression of horror, as if this were her fault.

"No it's not," he tells her, finding his watch beneath his glove. "It's right on time. Pull over here."

As she drives around the block, he carries the suitcase into the lobby, jammed with a hundred pieces of luggage. You can barely move for the luggage. An older couple, clearly late, sets their bags among the others and goes to join the tour for the final free breakfast. One thing you can count on with the Americans, he thinks, is that they will never turn down a free breakfast.

He carries the suitcase across the lobby. Monique has done her job well. There, in the sea of hundreds of bags, are ten, maybe fifteen, identical black Samsonites. Just like the one he's carrying. He cuts his way into the throng and sets his bag next to one of its twins. With his back to the registration desk, which is frantic with check-outs, he slips the personal identification tag off the one bag and on to his. It takes him less than ten seconds. There, it is done. All of these bags will be loaded by the bus driver, his substitute among them. At the airport, at check-in, the bags will be matched with passengers. By switching tags, he has insured this bag of his will be claimed. There will be one extra Samsonite that will not be claimed. Because of rules, it will not be loaded onto the plane. On large tours, such mistakes occur regularly. Nothing will be made of it. The bag will be returned to the hotel or destroyed by airport Security. His replacement will be boarded onto the plane in its place, Bernard's bomb inside.

He pulls the scarf up around his face and flexes his gloved hands, a person preparing for the bitter cold. Only his eyes show above the scarf, like an outlaw in a western.

The Mercedes is waiting. She is bent over the hood, stretched out, scraping the windscreen clear of ice. He feels a twinge of lust stir his loin. So foreign an experience is this that he only faintly recognizes it for what it is. He gets in the car. She climbs behind the wheel.

They drive for three hours to a Bavarian-style chalet hotel where they are to stay for three days. She talks for the entire trip. But he likes it, welcomes it as a blind man welcomes back his sight. It's the most time he has spent with any one person in over a year. As she is parking the car she says, "There has been a slight change of plans. We are to stay together."

"What?"

"Michael insisted."

"Impossible. We'll take two rooms."

"It *is* two rooms. It is a suite. We are registered as a married couple. Do you find the idea so offensive?"

"It's not that at all."

"What then?"

"Two rooms."

"Listen, my passport has the same name as yours. So we share the same suite. So what?"

"Three days. We're here for *three* days with nothing to do!"

"He is right about you."

"Right about what?"

"He said you are wound up as tight as a spring. He said you could use the rest."

"What does he know?"

"Plenty. And you are wrong. About the three days, I mean. About nothing to do."

"Am I?"

"It is three *nights*. Only two days. And do not worry about being bored. I can be very entertaining."

"This is Michael's doing," he says, smelling a conspiracy.

"Of course it is. It is *all* Michael's doing. No? Relax, you are in good hands." She smiles. "Wonderful hands."

He follows her like an obedient pet to the registration desk, signs them in, and accepts the key.

"Only the one bag?" asks the cherub-faced girl behind the counter. She has blond braids and enormous breasts. Red lipstick on her teeth.

Monique answers before Kort can get out a word. "Yes, only the one. We won't be needing a lot of clothes," she says, winking as she adds, "It is our anniversary." She hooks her arm into his and leads him toward the lift. He feels a flood of heat in his cheeks. Embarrassment is as foreign to him as the earlier stirring in his loins. This is new ground. He's uncomfortable.

They are only in the room a matter of minutes when a bottle of champagne is delivered.

"We didn't order this," he tells the delivery boy. Always suspicious.

"Compliments of the manager, sir," the boy says, pushing his way past and setting the champagne down. He makes a fuss, buying time for the tip. Kort obliges him and the boy leaves.

Monique whirls in from the bedroom and picks up the small note card alongside the glasses. "How thoughtful," she says.

She hands him the card. She already has the foil off and the cage open. She's twisting the cork. It explodes from the bottle with a bang and his hand instinctively goes for his gun.

He's standing there with his hand inside his coat—she's

shaking her head at him—and he thinks, maybe she's right, maybe I am wound up a little tight.

"Read the card," she says, pouring two glasses of the wine.

He does. *Happy anniversary,* it reads. *Enjoy your stay with us.*

She walks over to the television and turns it on to CNN. They watch for a minute. Nothing yet.

Kort checks his watch.

"Relax," she says, handing him a glass. "We have nothing but time."

She lifts her glass to his, and there's that smile again. And he knows what she has in mind. And he knows he will enjoy it.

He was thinking that nothing repeats itself; nothing is ever the same. Time doesn't heal all wounds, it causes them.

She placed her hands on her hips defiantly. "Any problems?" she repeated. "We have nothing but problems! It is *over,*" she said. "Do you not see that? Do you not *feel* it? They have arrested him. Placed him in jail! My God, the sense of relief when I heard that."

His face burned. "Relief? How can you say such a thing? Michael is in *jail.* He'll go to prison—probably for the rest of his life. And you . . . you act as if it's a holiday."

"It *is* a holiday. We're free! He *used* us. Me, for the better part of three years; you, for how long? Five years? How many has it been for you? Or has it been *too* many? Maybe *that* is the problem."

"And *Der Grund*—The Cause—what of the cause?" He saw a flicker of guilt cross her eyes, and in that instant knew she could be won over. "You've become like all the rest of them—you give up before accomplishing anything." He was shouting. He crossed the room and turned up the volume on CNN. He ran CNN every waking hour.

"He has brainwashed you. Have you somehow forgotten that he blackmailed us? How can you forgive him that?

I cannot. Will not. He is paying for it now. He deserves it. Why should I throw away these last two years? Give me one good reason."

He thought for a moment and replied in terms he knew she would accept. "Because he will see us hunted down if this operation doesn't come off." He gave this time to sink in. "Even from jail." He watched as understanding registered on her face. He said, "The *only* way to break free of this—if that's what you want—is to see this operation through. No more *Der Grund,* no more operations. It's that simple. You can *buy* your freedom, Monique. We can both buy our freedom. Think it through."

She paced the small room, hands in her pockets. There was more in this for him than for her. One of the men he intended to kill, the present chairman of EisherWorks Chemicals, was the man he held responsible for his child's birth defects and the destruction of his family. He needed Monique in order to accomplish this operation. Tackling an operation this size, alone, was nearly unthinkable.

"What operation? You must be kidding? We are crippled. We are nothing but a three-legged dog." She glanced over at him suspiciously.

"We may be a three-legged dog, but we still can bite!" He tapped the briefcase, indicating the detonator, and stepped toward her. He felt a wonderful sense of power. Was it the result of the briefcase and its contents, or her? He wanted to take her. Right here. Right now. It had nothing to do with love. Nothing to do with feelings. It was power. He wanted her to submit to him fully, to open herself for him, to surrender. She had the face of a little girl when she climaxed—almost as if her pleasure was pain. He remembered that clearly. God, how he wanted her.

"A *two*-legged dog," she corrected. "It is just the two of us now. No?" She collapsed to the edge of the bed. He sat next to her.

"A two-legged dog can still drag itself. A one-legged dog

can only lie down and die. I won't do that. I refuse to do that."

She leaned herself against him fully. "So what now?"

He felt triumphant. "Now, we have some time to kill." He reached over and unbuttoned her top button. She slapped his hand away but he knew she didn't mean it.

"Tell me," she said.

He unfastened the next button. "I'm going to drop a couple of planes. First here, and later, one in Washington. EisherWorks is finished."

"You said the same thing at Frankfurt."

"True."

"And just exactly how do you intend to do this? You killed Eisher; they replaced him—"

"With Hans Mosner," he interrupted. But whereas this name meant everything to him, it could never mean as much to her. Mosner had been in charge of the Duisberg factory at the time of the contamination emissions that had poisoned his community and his wife's pregnancy. Mosner was now chairman of EisherWorks. "Mosner is going to be in Washington. He is one of our prime targets."

She looked at him skeptically. "More than one target?"

A pigeon landed at the window. Its wings were discolored by the polluted air. You couldn't see a half mile, it was so bad out there. He felt tempted to point out the pollution to her. It's what Michael would have done. "It's complicated. You'll see. In good time, you'll see."

"See what?" she asked.

The less she knew, the better, and yet he was anxious to tell her because the plan was complex. Its complexity added to his sense of power, of superiority. He was anxious to tell *anyone*. The loneliness of the past month—his weeks in hiding prior to the operation—nearly fell prey to the comfort of her company. "It's better you don't know everything. What I can tell you is this: The plane we are dropping today is carrying key ingredients in the manufacturing of pesticides that can't be sold in the U.S. because of Food and

Drug regulations. So, to get around the law, an EisherWorks American subsidiary makes the ingredients here and flies them to Mexico where they are combined to make the exact same pesticide that is outlawed. That pesticide is then used on Mexican food crops that are later harvested and eventually shipped back for consumption in the U.S. Around and around it goes. It stops today, this hypocrisy. And this is only the prelude."

"Meaning?"

He hadn't meant to explain this much, but he was started now, and it felt good. "There's to be a meeting in Washington. Heavies. Mosner will be at this meeting, William Sandhurst of BiGeneer, Matthew Grady of ChemTronics, Douglas Fitzmaurice, Elizabeth Savile, Howard Goldenbaum. The heads of the biggest companies. I'm sick of cutting off fingers and limbs. It's time we cut off the head."

Her voice filled with excitement. She recognized all the names, just as he knew she would. "Kill them all? What . . . they are all going to be on the same plane or something?"

"Or something. *Anything* is possible if you put your mind to it. Didn't your parents ever tell you that? You'll see." He had the third button undone. Anything possible indeed. She hardly noticed. He reached in and cupped her breast. She filled his hand fully with a warmth that he felt in his groin. "With something like this, you take your time."

"You are making fun of me. I hate you."

"I'm making love with you."

"Not until you tell me what it is we are going to do."

"I can't. I've already told you more than I should."

"No you haven't." She looked him over and her eyes reconsidered. "Then again, there are other ways to make you talk." She smiled. He skimmed his fingers lightly over her breast and felt her respond.

He wondered if his erection was the result of touching her, or the enormous sense of power he now experienced.

He pointed to the television. "The television is the only thing that talks to the people. The only thing they listen to. So we're going to fill their screens with a little truth for a change. A few flames on the runway is always good for prime time. CNN is going to love us."

She was grinning. She had a beautiful smile, alluring and cunning; a woman filled with sexual secrets. One of these secrets he already knew from personal experience: All you needed to do was tease her lips and it was like lighting her fuse. He had never met a woman so sexually charged—so addicted to it.

"I've missed you."

"You are a liar."

"It comes with the territory," he said, his finger circling her creamy red lips until she kissed it and then drew it into her mouth and sucked on it, wrapping it in her tongue.

The talking was over. He slipped his wet finger out of her mouth and, working down her body, found her nipples now fully erect. He felt triumphant—like setting the timer on a detonator. His next chore after this. Forty-seven seconds, he recalled.

She tugged at his belt buckle. But this was not to be her show. He teased her legs open slightly with his slick fingertip, and spun tiny circles there until she willingly surrendered to her own pleasure.

Everything was in its place now. Despite the drumming in his heart, the pain in his jaw, he felt himself relax. Things were going just fine. Actually, much better than he had hoped.

Thirty minutes later, the bed sheets lay in a heap, and the air smelled of her. It had been the frantic lovemaking of two people in a bomb shelter, the lovemaking of no tomorrow. They were bonded. They were a team again.

"How is it you can remember those things?" she asked, her voice dreamy. "Are women so much the same?"

Did he dare to tell her that between Frankfurt and now there had been only one woman, and that it had been a complete disaster? Did he dare give her that kind of power over him? He thought not. Once you've gained the higher ground, you don't voluntarily surrender it.

"You wouldn't kiss me," she said, touching his swollen cheek.

"Be glad I didn't. I need a dentist. Badly. It's infected. But it will have to wait. There isn't time."

"It must hurt."

"I will live."

"You don't know that," she said. And they fell silent for a time.

"We survived Frankfurt," he reminded.

"That was different," she contended.

"Not really so different."

"We were but two of a team in Frankfurt. We had the support of the entire team. Now . . . It is not the same at all."

"Not so different as all that." He felt good. She had put him in a good mood.

"Where will you go after this?"

"Arrangements have been made—for *both* of us, if need be."

"I like it where I am," she said. "Will I have to leave?"

"Maybe not," he lied. "We'll see."

There wasn't time for him to shower. He toweled off and reapplied some deodorant.

"You had better dress," he said, checking his watch. He dabbed some Anbesol into the hole left by the pulled tooth, cringed and waited for it to take effect. When the open sore began to numb, he said, "It's time we get started."

The Los Angeles suburban sprawl swallowed them in blocks of matching three-bedroom homes with attached garages. Many of the lawns had gone brown, the result of the prolonged drought. Two young blond boys, shirtless and tanned, raced by on roller blades. Kort was pleased to be in the comfort of the air-conditioned van. "It was a good choice for a rental," he said.

"You said it should be big."

He nodded. He hated small cars.

"Are you going to tell me what it is we're doing, or am I expected to be clairvoyant? Who is this Dougherty?"

"A mechanic for AmAirXpress. Being part of the cargo group, the AmAirXpress flights use a different runway. That's important to me."

"But *I* can get you onto the field, Anthony. It's all been arranged for weeks. You've hired us as consultants. Why did we bother establishing all that if we're not going to use it?"

"We *are* going to use it."

"But why Dougherty then? I don't understand."

"The new security measures they've enacted."

"The head-counting?" she asked.

"Exactly. You can get me onto the field, but I still need a properly coded ID badge to enter the AmAirXpress maintenance yard from the field side. I could *never* get into AmAirXpress through their worker entrance. Not carrying what I'm carrying. Besides, the AmAirXpress security guards must know Dougherty by face. So it has to be from the field side. It's only machines on the field side. Computerized entrances. With his ID card they can be tricked into thinking I'm Dougherty."

"We're going to steal his ID badge?"

"Providing the Greek's information is correct—and it was in Seattle—then Dougherty is a drinker. Recently widowed. So we're going to borrow his ID badge and leave him with a hangover."

"I think you've overestimated their abilities. During any given shift, there are literally *thousands* of airport and airline personnel on the field side. Have you ever looked out the window of an airplane?" She grinned. "Oh, that's right, you don't like to fly." When he didn't say anything she started talking again. Her constant talking bothered him now; it meant she was nervous. "Sure, they have this new head-counting rule, but no one's paid much attention to it. I know we haven't. Airport Police know they're vulnerable from the field, but their security is very tight from the passenger side, which is their greater concern. There's very little anticipation of a plan as thought out as this. They just aren't ready for it."

"That may be but I'm not taking any chances."

"And how do I fit in at Dougherty's?"

"You are my assistant," he informed her. "A man and a woman together are much less intimidating than a man alone."

He stopped talking and went about preparing the syringe, hoping she would be quiet. He had to tell her twice to keep her eyes on the road. He had been alone for far too long. It was unnerving the way her mouth went on.

"What is it you're giving him?" she asked, once he had the syringe filled and the plastic cap back over the needle.

"Grain alcohol. One hundred and eighty proof."

"It looks like a lot."

"If I've correctly guessed his weight it won't kill him."

"And are you so good at guessing weight?" she asked, tugging on her blouse.

He looked her over. "One hundred and six," he answered.

She placed both hands on the wheel and looked straight ahead. She was blushing. "You won't kill him," she said.

After that, she was quiet.

They drove past a group of children clad in Day-Glo swimsuits dancing in the roaring plume of hydrant water. As Monique steered clear of them, Kort raised his hand to block his face. He worried about Monique's apparent lack of these instincts. The van bounced over trenches of hard-packed dirt and mud that cut across the road. Sewer work. Kort's sun visor fell down, and he pushed it back into place.

As they passed the number 11345 stenciled in yellow paint on the curb, he signaled Monique to pull over.

The tract house had all the charm of a shoe box with windows. The postage-stamp lawn and the property's sole bush were victims of neglect. A rusted television antenna leaned rakishly on the roof.

Monique tied a white chiffon scarf in place and donned a pair of sunglasses.

"Okay," he said, feeling his own excitement in his chest. "Here we go."

He opened the van's door, and stepped into an oven. His throat burned. His eyes stung. The air was toxic. It only served to reinforce his allegiance to *Der Grund.* The people and the politicians treated the environmental issues as if they could be solved without effort—as if twenty or thirty years were available to think up solutions. It was time for action.

They approached the front door side by side. A garden snail had smeared its trail of slime across the width of the cement stairs that rose to the front door. Kort applied his toe to the snail and ground it to a paste. As Dougherty answered the door, Monique was still staring down at the brown goo.

Dougherty had the hard, crusty hands of a fisherman. He had bloodshot blue eyes and looked as if he was either battling or working on a hangover. His T-shirt advertised Dos Equis beer. Because he was wearing blue jeans, Kort guessed he had not yet been outside in the heat. Kort addressed him in a bored and impatient voice. "Kevin Dougherty?"

"Yes?"

Kort said, "Bill Rembler, SCI—Security Consulting International—Mr. Dougherty. This is Linda Martin," he said, cocking his head toward Monique, who offered a half-hearted smile. "Business, I'm afraid. I wonder if we could have a few words with you a moment? Inside—out of this heat—if you don't mind."

Dougherty half shrugged and stepped aside, clearly caught off guard and uncertain. Just the way Kort wanted him. The inside of the house was gloomy. Drawn drapes closed out the neighborhood and closed in a sense of desperation. It smelled damp, like an old piece of discarded clothing found in the bushes. The living room was littered with dirty dishes. The television was tuned to a game show in which unhappy-looking has-been celebrities were grilling a buxom housewife who wore too much makeup and spoke in a high, grating southern twang. Dougherty's eyes drifted to the television and his interrupted program. He asked, "What's this about?"

Kort reached inside his breast pocket and pretended to read from a paper he found there. "You work on the Duhnings for AmAirXpress. Maintenance," he stated.

"That's right," Dougherty confirmed.

"You and too many others," Kort continued, playing out his role. "What we got going here is a possible breach of security, Mr. Dougherty. Our agency was called in because Airport Police believes some maintenance identification cards from LAX may have been counterfeited. What we gotta do," he said, again indicating himself and Monique, "is pick up all the IDs for maintenance personnel. Your people will either have a temporary card for you when you report in, or will return your existing card to you. We gotta make sure that none of the cards have been counterfeited. All right?"

"My card ain't been touched," said Dougherty in a wet voice. "I can save ya the time."

"Just the same," Kort said in a determined tone. "This is the procedure. You can appreciate that." Kort's hand found the syringe in his pocket.

"You better give me your name again—names again," he corrected, including Monique, "and let me make a call." He looked Kort in the eye.

Monique said sharply, "Let me tell you something, Mr. Dougherty. You can make all the phone calls you want, okay? But the bottom line is going to be the same for Rembler and me, no matter what." She stepped in front of Kort. "We've got twenty-seven more of these to do today. It's a million degrees out there," she said, circling now, and holding Dougherty's attention. Kort readied the syringe inside his pocket. This wasn't exactly the way he had planned it. "Feels like a million degrees," she added. "And this is my time of month, if you get the message, and I'm not feeling too charitable. So why don't you skip the phone call and get us the ID tag, okay?"

Kort reached from behind to deliver his choke hold—not to kill Dougherty as he had mistakenly done with Ward, but to silence him and render him unconscious. At the same time, his right hand withdrew the syringe from his pocket.

Dougherty sensed him. With a loud roar, the heavy man spun and caught Kort with a forearm, knocking him off his feet. The syringe flew out of his hand and fell to the carpet.

Dougherty lunged toward the front door. Kort sprang to his feet, intercepting him and delivering a vicious kidney punch. Dougherty stumbled with the blow. Kort drove him down. Dougherty crashed beneath Kort's weight and sucked for air. Monique passed the syringe to Kort, who stabbed it into Dougherty's pudgy neck, injecting the contents. Dougherty blinked behind glassy eyes, drooling as he tried to speak. He grew progressively incoherent and lost consciousness a few minutes later. They were long minutes for Anthony Kort.

"Jesus," Monique said. She was trembling.

Kort heaved a sigh of relief. She had done well. He lifted the heavy head by its hair and then let it thump to the carpet, nose first. "He's out," he said. "Gloves," he added, pulling two pair of latex surgical gloves from a pocket and handing a pair to Monique. He gave her his handkerchief. "The door," he instructed. "His clothing, the skin on his neck. Don't miss anything."

"His skin?"

"I touched his neck. They can develop prints on human skin. They can develop prints on clothing. On practically *anything*. Don't wipe, scrub him down like you're doing laundry."

"I don't *do* laundry," she snapped.

Monique negotiated the van off the San Diego Freeway and came to a full stop at a traffic light on Century Boulevard.

"Talk me through it," he instructed her.

"Don't *worry* about it, Anthony," she said condescendingly. "I can get us in, drop you, and get myself out without a bit of trouble. This is something I do nearly every day of the week."

"But it's usually in Washington," he reminded.

"LAX is old hat to me. I'm out here all the time. You're on my turf now. Relax, I know what I'm doing." She continued through the next few green lights and drove past the signs indicating LAX's arrivals and departures. After a few more blocks the number and quality of the buildings decreased and then, with barren acreage to their left, they passed the various offices, warehouses, and hangars for the subcontracting companies, including several of the major air-freight carriers, all enclosed within perimeters of chain link fence topped with razor wire.

The van slowed.

Kort's heartbeat increased.

She steered the vehicle into a crowded parking area and shut off the engine. "You have his overalls in there?" she asked, pointing to Kort's carryall.

"Yes."

"At the bottom?"

"Yes."

"Good. If they happen to search that bag—something I have *never* seen done—then I will make up some excuse about our needing the fire extinguisher on one of our trucks. Don't you say anything."

"We won't pass through a metal detector?"

"Here? Heavens, no. I'm telling you, you're overestimating the security. All we care about is that the people coming through our facility are our employees. We're not about to search all their lunch pails. Remember this is a private security subcontractor hired by AmAirXpress. They work for *me,* not the other way around. I'm a big shot out here—the benefits of being a home office executive."

He had studied the layout of the facility on paper. Now he watched it come to life as they left the parked van on foot. From this unsecured, street-side parking lot, they were to pass through the privately operated security check she had mentioned and into the secured area that housed the facilities and field-side parking lots for In-Flite Foods. Adjacent to the security check was a gate that provided vehicle access to the secure area, though this was locked and rarely used. Field-side vehicles were fueled and maintained within the secure compound to avoid the lengthy process of vehicle searches. The food delivery trucks passed through one of the three Airport Police checkpoints, where they were randomly subjected to intense scrutiny. For this reason, Monique had elected to walk Kort onto the field through In-Flite.

As planned, they arrived when the parking lot teemed with employees changing shift. To Kort's relief, he saw that nearly everyone carried some kind of backpack, bag, or lunch pail, just as Monique had said they would. He followed a confident Monique toward the long line at the gate, which moved surprisingly quickly. As Monique had reported, the guards were simply making sure each employee wore an ID tag. It appeared they weren't even taking the time to match faces with photos.

They stopped in front of the guards. She said, "Monique Paine," and fingered the ID badge she had clipped to her blouse. "I'm with the Washington office. You have a pass for my guest."

The guard checked a list, ran a finger across it, and then reached out of sight and came up with the white plastic visitor's tag. "This is Mr. Anthony," she said.

"Yeah, yeah," the guard replied, eyeing the line as it backed up behind them.

Monique handed Kort the tag. He clipped it to his pocket and the two passed through. They quickly broke away from the others and walked by themselves, approaching a group of parked vehicles.

"El Al it isn't," he said softly to her. She grinned.

"Over here," she instructed, gesturing toward a green sedan with a white In-Flite logo painted on the driver's door. "Climb in. I'll get the keys."

Kort obeyed her, uncomfortable following orders.

The window frames of the unremarkable building she entered were pitted and corroded brown. The building itself was a large, one-story cake box sided with corrugated steel, painted an old beige. Where the drains emptied from the flat roof, the paint was streaked and stained. The chain link fence that surrounded this inner parking lot looked rusted enough to come apart by just yanking hard on it. His makeup and wig made the already uncomfortable heat nearly unbearable. He did his best to push this discomfort back into an unused compartment and shut it away.

"All set," she said as she climbed into the driver's seat alongside him.

"I was recalling your nickname," he told her in a sentimental tone he didn't recognize. Just looking at her face, the name had popped into his head—like spontaneously remembering the words of a song when hearing the melody played.

"Unique," she said. "I liked that. I thought perhaps you had forgotten."

"No, of course not."

She drove onto the field and along the designated traffic

corridor. She took the long way around in order to reach the far side of the AmAirXpress maintenance area.

"You know what to do?" he asked.

She didn't answer. Instead she said, "You'll contact me when you've reached Washington?"

He removed the visitor's pass and clipped Dougherty's badge to his overalls. The magnetic strip on the back was his key to the electronic gate only yards away. He grabbed the flight bag that contained the fire extinguisher. He handed her the visitor's pass. "You'll take care of returning this?" he asked rhetorically.

"I'll take care of *everything*, Anthony." Her eyes wished him good luck.

" 'Unique,' " he said, opening the door. "It suits you."

6

THE SEARCH TEAM found the tooth on Sunday morning. As Murphy's Law would have it, the trash bag that contained the tooth was one of the last to be checked. But the contents proved to be a lab technician's gold mine: the extracted tooth, bloodied tissues, a spent bottle of Anbesol, and two bars of hotel soap. It had been rushed by special courier to the forensics lab in the Hoover Building in Washington.

Monday noon, Daggett was in the offices of the Seattle Field Office, in the midst of sending a secure fax to Paul Pullman, when someone called him to the phone. He hoped it might be the anticipated lab report. Below, on Puget Sound, one of many huge white ferries cut a wide wake away from shore. Sea gulls followed at its stern. Traffic moved sluggishly on the elevated section of roadway paralleling the shore. The pulse of the city continued indifferent to his concerns.

When he heard LaMoia's voice, he immediately knew what this call was about. The Mayflower Hotel had provided them with a license plate number for the car belonging to the guest in Room 311. Motor Vehicle had been able to trace the license number to a leasing company; through the leasing company, they had then traced the car to an obscure off-airport car rental agency that did most of its paperwork by hand. It was typical of this kind of police work that the deck often seemed stacked against you—for every step forward, two steps back. Now, finally, another step forward.

"The rental agency has a client for us," LaMoia said. "I thought you would want to talk to them."

"I'm on my way."

Mrs. Lori Slaughter, the rental company's second in command, had walnut-colored skin, straightened hair pulled back tightly and held in a ponytail by a metallic band. Her silver earrings, in the shape of flying geese, reflected the overhead fluorescent light, distracting Daggett. Her jawline ran into her neck, and she wore loose clothing, giving her a square figure. She wormed her tongue nervously inside her upper lip with its soft brown lipstick. People had a way of coming undone when being questioned by the FBI. Daggett had thought the letter jacket might remove some of this pressure, but it didn't seem to help.

She was reading a computer screen. "Mr. Antony"—she didn't pronounce a *th*—"rented from our downtown agency, which is actually a parking garage, 'cross from the Westin. The reservation for the car was made on the seventh of July for an August twenty-first rental. A midsized four-door. We upgraded that to our premium line because of availability. He declined insurance. He held the reservation with a Visa—"

"A credit card!" Daggett interrupted enthusiastically. "A *valid* credit card?"

"That's what's interesting about this, Mr. Daggett. When he failed to return the car on the twenty-second, we notified the police the car had been stolen, which is customary. They asked us the same thing. Now usually when a car is stolen, the credit card turns out to *also* be stolen. But not this one. It's a perfectly valid card."

"I'll need that number," Daggett said anxiously.

"It's right on the form."

Daggett wrote it down in his notebook. "And I'd like to interview the person who rented him the vehicle, if that's possible."

She raised a finger, placed a brief phone call, and then

hung up. Her faux fingernails, long enough to be claws, were painted an iridescent pink. To Daggett she said, "James Channing is the boy you want. And he's presently on duty. Goes off at four. He's expecting you."

"Fine."

"But I must caution you that these boys see dozens and dozens of customers per week. That he'll remember Mr. Antony is highly unlikely."

He didn't appreciate the pessimism. "We'll see," he said.

Two hours later, he was forced to admit she was right: The young man who had rented the car remembered nothing about the man. He remained invisible wherever he went, and Daggett's frustration built with each dead end. Now that Visa card meant everything—a credit trail was often as valuable as a "smoking gun."

Shoswitz picked him up at the hotel a half hour before the ball game. The lieutenant had not changed clothes. "I like the letter jacket," he said immediately.

"First base," Daggett said proudly. "Lettered my last two years." It stirred up memories he would just as soon have forgotten. Different people. Different dreams. He glanced out at a sky confused between cloudy and clear. Partly sunny, they called it. Partly cloudy. Depended on what percentages you saw when you looked up there. A judgment call.

"You should be happy," Shoswitz said. "Right? You made some good headway today."

Another judgment call, Daggett thought. The man saw blue instead of clouds. "Should I?"

"We've got a valid Visa card and they've flagged it for us. This guy uses that card again, we'll know it within minutes. I'd say that's some major headway." Shoswitz bunched his thin, colorless lips and nodded in self-agreement. "That's a hell of a starting point. A lot of cases wouldn't get *that* far."

"We lost a possible witness. That hurts." Another day,

another investigation, Daggett might have felt okay about
how the day had turned out. No day went without some
setbacks. As it was, Pullman was anxious to get his report
on the Backman bombing. That could take a week or two.
If that happened, then all the Bernard work would end up
in a file somewhere going yellow. The thought of that infuriated him.

The Kingdome, looking like an enormous flying saucer
perched in a sea of blacktop, lay ahead of them. Thousands
of people poured into it. Balloons. Pins. Caps. Daggett
wasn't thinking in terms of baseball or the ball game. He
was thinking: So many people, so many eyes in a city this
size. How many of these people saw him and never knew it?
How many of these people could help if they only knew
what they had seen?

"You always so cheery?" Shoswitz asked.

"Sorry. Tired, I guess," Daggett admitted.

Shoswitz parked the car. Seemed like they walked for
ten minutes before reaching the Dome. The game hadn't
started, but the fans had. They were wound up.

"You gonna be okay?" Shoswitz asked as they sat down
in seats a mile from nowhere.

"Yeah, fine thanks."

Daggett hated the lying most of all.

The rain struck the hotel room windows like handfuls
of pebbles. Special Agent Macalister's deep voice sounded
even more forced over a phone line: "Visa's mainframe
went down or we would have had it sooner," the man began, apparently recognizing Daggett's voice and not bothering with any sort of greeting. "David Anthony bought a one-
way Amtrak ticket from Portland to Los Angeles. He paid
cash for the actual ticket, but according to reservations
records, he phoned in a last-minute request for a sleeper.
The sleepers require a credit card to hold a reservation, so
his card had to be preapproved for the total amount. We got
the flag because of the authorization request. He was on

that train, Daggett. It arrived in Los Angeles yesterday afternoon. If he took a hotel room in L.A., he didn't pay for it by credit card."

Daggett dragged the phone off the nightstand as he headed to the closet to start packing. The pounding in his chest had nothing to do with blood pressure, nothing to do with moving quickly; it was the drumming of excitement.

As Macalister continued talking, Daggett was thinking: Just like a European to order a sleeper compartment—they hate the coaches on our trains.

". . . which means we may have lost him," Macalister concluded.

"Lost him?" Daggett asked, struggled with the buttons on yesterday's shirt. "Reissue the warning to all commercial carriers at LAX: All Duhning 959s should be triple-checked for possible bombs. Luggage and carry-ons should follow El Al international rules. Fax the L.A. office anything we have. Mention the tooth; that may still be giving him trouble." When Macalister failed to say anything, Daggett asked, "You still there?"

"Still here. I'm writing it all down."

"And do me a favor," Daggett said, his arm finding its way down the sleeve of his letter jacket.

"Go ahead."

"Have someone book me a seat on the next flight to LAX."

From five thousand feet, the coiling black tendril of smoke looked to Daggett at first like the unwarranted emission from a factory so typical of the urban sprawl. Or maybe, on closer inspection, it was an entire city block afire. Only its proximity to LAX and the steady stream of fire trucks racing toward it—toylike trucks from this altitude—gave it away.

He didn't know for certain until his pager began beeping from his belt. He was carrying a special pager capable of reaching him anywhere in the continental United States,

Europe, and a limited section of Asia. Its twelve-character alpha-numeric readout enabled the Bureau to pass field agents cryptic messages as well as phone numbers.

Daggett moved his coat out of the way and silenced the pager. He read its message, though the smoke below had already told him what had happened. HARD FALL

A plane was down.

He knew it was a Duhning 959; he even knew something about the man who had caused it. His throat constricted and his eyes stung. An elderly woman in the seat next to him demanded in a grating voice, "Lean back so I can see. . . . What is it? What is it?"

Daggett leaned back, and she stretched herself across him, pressing her pale face against the glass. "I can't see. I can't see," she said. "Was it an aeroplane?" she asked, close enough to kiss him.

But Daggett didn't answer. Thought of another crash drew him back.

The Christmas tree is nice: no tinsel, lots of handmade ornaments. It reminds him of Christmas with his grandparents outside of Bend, Oregon, snow over his head and ice so thick, you have to saw through it to fish. He remembers. He feels awkward being here and being single, but it's the holidays, and despite Peggy's abandonment, despite Duncan's being overseas with his parents, he feels a need to be with people. Friends. It's not terribly Christmasy. Rain. Wind. Carols on the stereo, but it doesn't seem right. Nothing seems right. Except the tree. The tree is right.

He is still drying out from being caught in the rain as he is dragged to circulate the crowd. He is looking for someone to attach himself to. He is looking to get drunk. Tonight is no night to be alone. His first Christmas without Peggy in recent memory, a hollow, empty feeling, and the pain is as immeasurable as his love. The trouble with Bureau parties, he realizes, is that agents, by nature, are a sarcastic bunch; they hide their emotions beneath an impenetrable veneer of bravado. There is no sentimentality. No one singing. It's shop talk and bawdy jokes everywhere he turns.

Always the jokes. Too often racial. Always the pasted-on smiles and slaps on the back. The winks. Within a few minutes he longs to be elsewhere, anywhere, but the die is cast: he's stuck. Clay Primrose spots him and waves him over to talk to some redhead in a green sweater and a short skirt. Doesn't know her that well. Feels nervous. Knows it's not what he wants, but he wants even less to make a scene.

The television is an annoyance in the adjoining room where some of the kids are focused on an animated special involving the Grinch. It's something completely out of place at a Christmas party, he thinks. As the introduction to the redhead is made, as he's watching her lips but suddenly picturing her in bed with him, the news breaks in on the Grinch.

The eggnog is carefully balanced, tightly gripped, for this group tends to gesticulate wildly while reconstructing stories, fabricating stories; he's not about to let his fly. Daggett misses her name. His mind is in a knot of moist lips and this woman—this body with its wild red hair—spread out before him, when he loses her completely. Loses Primrose too. His head jerks toward the door, toward the whining kids whose show has been interrupted, toward the television with the talking head and the flashing graphics announcing a Live News Update.

It's the number that grabs him, that slams into him with such a force, it knocks all the wind from him. He teeters. He's going to go down.

The number.

He wills his knees to support him. Locks them.

"Ten twenty-three," the talking head says in a dreadful, unemotional monotone. "EuroTours flight ten twenty-three."

Eggnog sloshes across his fingers. He's spilling his drink. The video that fills the screen is shot at night. Ugly orange flames spread across an entire town. "Frankfurt to Heathrow," the man says, repeating the number. Daggett knows the itinerary; a photocopy is presently folded in his breast pocket. Flames. Bright orange flames. The remains of the plane scattered in little bonfires for miles.

Miles.

Duncan . . . His parents.

There's no more sound, like someone turned everything and everyone off. Nothing. A blank hole where he had been standing.

The plastic glass of eggnog slips to the floor, its contents spilled. "All those aboard the commercial jetliner are presently presumed dead," the anchorman says, almost straining to make reference to Lockerbie. He's comparing numbers as if it's a contest. Daggett hears, "It's not as bad as Lockerbie."

At the piano, a group of vodka drinkers—unaware of the television, of the children, of Daggett's spilled drink, of the redhead—form a group. A department accountant, a good-looking woman named Suzie, begins to sing along with the stereo in a surprisingly beautiful voice. The sound turns Daggett's head, it seems so incongruous, given the sight on the television. Suzie is looking right at him.

> *Silent night, holy night*
> *All is calm, all is bright*

The scene on the television is anything but silent, anything but holy. The panic in the face of the talking head, the beads of sweat on his forehead as he vamps to keep his station on the air with a live report: anything but calm. And the only brightness is from the leaping orange flames and the pulsing incendiary flashes from the blue lights atop the rescue vehicles.

Daggett slumps and kneels into the puddle of eggnog, his attention fixed on the television. One of the kids hits the remote hoping to lose this guy, but he is replaced by a dozen others, all with the same message, nearly the same words, all apparently reading from the same script.

Primrose calls out to him, "No great loss." He is referring to the spilled drink, but that's not the way Daggett hears it.

On the darkened, flickering screen the roaming camera surveys the images of the tragedy. Daggett crawls toward the television, Suzie still singing.

There, not six inches from his face, beamed via satellite in living color—dying color—he sees and then thinks he recognizes his very own light gray Samsonite suitcase he had loaned Duncan. It lies there in the field among similar personal belongings and crash debris.

His suitcase.

His only child.

His parents.

Dead? Or crying out somewhere in the flames?

Silent night, holy night, she begins again.

Twenty-two minutes, four phone calls, and a one-mile taxi ride later, Daggett stood on the outskirts of the wreckage.

A hundred yards off, black, oily smoke rose in towering pillars. The carcass of the disemboweled jet lay broken and twisted. The plane had crashed in the back half of Hollywood Park, home to a horse track and a hotel, an enormous expanse of land, a half-mile square cut out of suburbia. Like so much of Southern California, Hollywood Park had been drilled for oil. Several of the behemoth pumps had been sheared off at ground level by the plane and were now burning out of control. With the fuselage and the half-dozen wellheads all flaring orange plumes into a thick black sky, it looked to Daggett like an image of hell. The rising smoke blocked out the sun.

Patrol cars continued to roll in from nearly every L.A. division. CHP had sealed the exit and entrance ramps to the San Diego Freeway. Inglewood cars had already shut down several streets, isolating a huge crime scene into which passed only rescue vehicles and other cops. Daggett paid the cab and walked, his badge hanging open from his shirt pocket. Had to be a hundred cops already. Impressive. They had created a press area that had a good view of the wreckage and the rescue efforts; it was already teeming with cameras and bright lights.

"Officer!" one of the reporters called out. But a man in a suit, whom Daggett took for the press relations sergeant, waved this man back, allowing Daggett to proceed.

When such devastation is reduced to the size of a television screen, he thought, all effect is lost in translation. The fire trucks—there were dozens of them—seemed tiny next to the torn and flaming fuselage. From his window seat on the plane, the disfiguring of the landscape caused by the crash had taken the appearance of an exaggerated teardrop. But on the ground, at eye level, the wreckage seemed to stretch from where Daggett stood clear to the horizon.

It was only upon closer inspection that Daggett realized the clutter was not suitcases and baggage, but cardboard boxes of every shape and size, their contents spread about like litter. Air freight? Not passengers? Daggett, carried away by a flood of relief, ran toward the debris. A fireman caught up to him and turned him around, briefly confused as he saw Daggett's FBI shield.

"Bodies?" Daggett inquired.

"Only two, so far as I've heard. But we haven't been able to get close enough to confirm that." He pointed out a number of twisted fifty-five-gallon drums strewn about the burning landscape. From this distance, they looked like crushed aluminum beer cans. "One of our boys got too close to one of those drums. He's on his way to the hospital at the moment. Some kind of chemical in those things. It's all over the place."

"Chemicals?" Daggett couldn't keep the excitement out of his voice. The possible linkage to *Der Grund* seemed blatantly obvious.

The man looked at him oddly and said, "We're holding everyone back until we know what the hell we're dealing with."

In the birthplace of Disneyland and Close Encounters, this must have seemed like a free show. Daggett walked toward a group of men standing near detective cars. These would be the guys in charge. A mud-brown four-door Chrysler pulled to a stop at this same moment. The first person out of the car's backseat was Phil Huff. Daggett cringed. Now the fun began.

Huff was Daggett's age but looked a few years older because of a receding hairline and too much time in the sun.

Huff's round face kept his brown eyes wide apart, leaving some hairy acreage above a sharp nose that had seen enough knuckles to carry ring scars, and giving him the calculating look of a meat inspector. He had lost some weight in the last few weeks, taking the clumsiness out of him. He wore a new poplin suit and a brown bow tie embroidered with forest-green fleurs-de-lis. He carried a cigarette caught between his fingers that went unlit. When his hands were busy, he stuck the weed away behind his fuzzy-haired right ear. The two men had met on a refresher course at the FBI center in Quantico, Virginia. Huff had been a former homicide cop from Baltimore.

The hardness in Huff's eyes and his erect posture told Daggett it was the same Phil Huff: aggressive, intuitive, with the instincts and timing of a cornered snake. The wind shifted, carrying traces of the billowing smoke. The smell stopped Daggett, for it had the whiff of death in it.

Huff's voice came over his shoulder. "Hey there, Cameron," he said, knowing Daggett preferred Cam to Cameron.

Daggett offered his hand; Huff switched the unlit cigarette to his left and the two men shook. Huff had the handshake of a butcher—he needed to prove something. Huff tucked the cigarette away. "No need for them to send someone, Daggett. Especially you." He smiled the practiced smile of an insurance agent about to talk you into additional, unnecessary coverage.

"Guess Pullman sees it a little differently," Daggett fired back. In fact, Pullman hadn't known about this incident until a few minutes earlier.

"You're looking a little gray around the gills. You handled Bernard real well, I hear. Wha'd you do, send flowers to Backman's widow or what?"

"Is this the way it's going to be, Phil? I could be asking you how your guys lost Bernard in the first place." Huff blanched, and didn't have a quick retort. Daggett asked, "Have you heard anything about chemicals being on board?"

Huff shook his head. "Nothing."

"That's what one of the firemen told me. See those cans out there?"

"Haven't heard a thing about it." Huff didn't seem a bit interested.

Understanding the importance of this investigation to his own, Daggett asked, "What about the NTSB? Where do we stand?" The National Transportation Safety Board was responsible for the investigation of all commercial aircraft incidents, and, as such, oversaw the orchestration of the various investigative agencies involved, including the FBI. In nearly any other kind of investigation, the FBI took and maintained control. But not here. Not today. The fact that Huff would act as liaison and representative for the agency seemed dangerous to Daggett. The Bureau's reputation was about to slip a notch. Huff only knew how to be concertmaster; to him, the second chair was a foreign country.

"If we can give them proof of criminal intent, then it's ours," Huff said, returning the unlit cigarette to his lips, where it bobbed as he spoke. "And I suppose that's where you come in, right? A guy wouldn't come all the way out here from Buzzard Point and stick his nose in one of *my* investigations unless there was damn good reason, now would he? Buzzard Point being so busy and so secret and all."

Buzzard Point *was* busy, but no more so than any other major metropolitan field office.

"How many of us will there be?" Daggett asked. The only crash site he'd been part of had been EuroTours 1023, and then, arriving more than seventy-two hours late, and only as a civilian in a foreign country. A complete outsider. He knew the general procedure of such investigations, the hierarchy and basic structure of command, because of his association with and training for service with C-3 at Buzzard Point, but now found himself hungry for details.

"A trailer is being brought on site," Huff explained. "NTSB and Inglewood Police will operate out of it for the next several days. Right now we got every police division represented from West Hollywood to the Sheriff's Department. It's mostly uniforms for crowd control. FAA is sending a team, so is AmAirXpress, a General Electric engine team, a Duhning team, Alcohol Tobacco will send us a bomb sniffing group, Airport Police are loaning us some dogs in the meantime. County coroner, maybe a couple of fire marshals. I'd say we can expect a half-dozen insurance investigators. All told, sixty-some investigators minimum, maybe reach that by late tomorrow. As long as it remains an 'accident,'" he said, drawing the quotes, "then I'm supposed to sit in the back row and suck my thumb—"

"Or your cigarette," Daggett said, watching the thing tick in the man's lips as he spoke.

"But if you got something right now tying this to Bernard, or one of his contacts—something hard we can hand these guys—then we tap their shoulder and do the dance."

Which is exactly what you would love, Daggett thought, but kept from saying.

"Your being here means terrorism is involved. A plane goes down . . . You fall out of the sky at about the same minute . . . You're not here by coincidence, are you?"

"You're lightning fast, Phil. I'll say that."

Huff's lips puckered like the end of a string bag coming closed as he took a drag on the unlit cigarette. "So are we talking *suspect,* or what? Is that why you're so interested in these chemicals?"

Daggett savored the moment by speaking exceptionally slowly. "What I'm allowed to tell you . . . is nothing. Zero." And then he smiled.

The L.A. uniforms did a better job than he had expected of clearing the curious, keeping traffic out, confining the press in their assigned area and giving the firefighters room to work. "It's because of this neighborhood," one of the cops explained to him. "Guys out here are probably the best street cops in the state. Closing off a block, they do two three times a week. We are *constantly* chasing down a shooter or a dealer. And I mean constantly. Same thing with the crowds and ditto with the traffic. It's a war zone out here. . . . Not this exact neighborhood—these are your middle-class blacks right around here—but only a few blocks away is real trouble. Far as we're concerned, this is just another night in the City of Angels. Fuckin' Pebble Beach this is not."

A plain vanilla car pulled in behind Huff's and something made Daggett look. Huff glanced over his shoulder, "That'll be the FAA."

As Daggett saw the face through the faintly tinted glass of the rear window, he looked around quickly for a place to hide—a foolish reaction, but unavoidable. At the sight of her, he could almost feel the hot sun baking his skin, could smell the distinctive perfume of suntan lotion. When he checked one more time—just to make sure—she was looking back at him, eyes hopeful and full of excitement. Lynn Greene opened her door and slid her legs out first, holding her skirt and then coming out of the car like an actress curbside at the Oscars.

Huff explained unnecessarily, *"That* is their explosives expert, if you can believe it."

"I can believe it," Daggett answered.

■

He is sitting in the sixth row, a couple seats in from the aisle. The man at the podium is in the midst of a lecture on Progress in Plastics, which ends up a history of plastic explosives. A bone-thin man with virtually no hair and an aging voice that's impossible to hear, he quickly loses the attention of those in attendance.

Daggett spots a profile in the third row that he finds much more interesting than the lecture. She has high cheekbones, a Roman nose, and a funny little smile. She's dark and bashful, blushing over something the woman in the seat next to her has whispered. And when she glances over her shoulder at him, like a teenager in Algebra II, he understands they are talking about him and he feels a warm flash of embarrassment and lust pulse through him. They both quickly look away.

The lecture continues and he wonders how he can introduce himself. This is the last course of the three-day seminar and he can't believe he didn't notice her until now. He experiences a brief flirtation with guilt; he's been with Carrie only six months and here he is plotting a way to meet this total stranger. Mentally undressing her. He convinces himself it's a healthy reaction to a boring lecture, and when they are finally dismissed he sticks to his own aisle and intentionally avoids any chance of contact. He doesn't need that kind of temptation.

Three months later he sees her again, and this time it's on the Maryland shore while out for a walk on one of those hot summer afternoons where you think if you're ever going to die, now's the time, things are so perfect. But they're made more perfect with the sight of her. The sand burns his feet, so he stays on water's edge, chasing a group of feeding sandpipers along in front of him. They scurry furiously to avoid him, then take to flight, landing twenty yards in front, only to run again as he draws closer. An endless chase. He doesn't recognize her at first, perhaps because of the large sunglasses she's wearing, or perhaps because his attention is more fixed to her stretched form and the tight single-piece suit that molds to her like body paint. He walks past, she up the beach toward the small clapboard cottage, he ankle-deep in the foaming reach of the low waves as they come to shore.

It's on his way back, as he's trying hard not to stare, that he hears a clear voice call out with a false German accent, "Zee ahhd-vent of plassteeks brought purr-fek-shun oont power-ta-bill-it-tee." Sitting up, glasses pulled down that Roman nose, squinting eyes staring over the rim, she smiles coyly, her raised brow asking, "Remember?"

He does remember—how could he forget?—and he leaves the safety of the cool water and heads toward her, not noticing the hot sand beneath his feet. "Third row," he says.

"That's me," she admits. "And as I remember, you took out of there like it was a house afire."

"I was running late," he said.

"You were running. I was aware of that."

He can't think of how to reply. They introduce themselves. She's Lynn Greene, at the FAA now. Explosives. He's prepared to turn that into a joke, but thinks better of it. He's already flirting. Carrie and Duncan are back at the cottage only a few hundred yards down the beach. He doesn't need this kind of complication, but he can't seem to pull himself away. She's pretty, there's no denying it, but that's not the attraction. It has something to do with her inquisitive expression and the humor that waits behind her eyes.

They make small talk. He remains standing. She shields her exposed eyes from the sun, but can't stop squinting. Sand clings to the backs of her arms like glitter. Her dark hair is ribbed from a wide-tooth comb that she uses between swims. The comb is spilling out of her overturned straw beach bag, along with a bottle of lotion and several hardcover novels, one with a bookmark. They talk authors. She avoids best sellers. He eats them up. Then they talk movies and jointly come to agreement on the brilliance of *Annie Hall* and Woody Allen in general. "You talk shellfish?" Daggett asks, quoting from a favorite scene. They laugh, she with her head back, her red lips open wide, the lowered sunglasses pushed back up her creamy nose.

Daggett says good-bye and hurries off.

"Running again?" she calls after him. It stops him and he turns to look back at her. She waits a moment before smiling and lying back down, with a tug on her suit.

He'd like to tug the suit right off her, and she knows it.

It's several more days of long walks before Daggett finds himself pacing the water line outside her cottage. She's in a terry cloth robe, the same ribbed hair, when she appears through the screen door and calls out, "High tide will eventually bring you closer to the steps," and waits for him to approach the cottage. The way she wears the robe it's easy to fantasize that she's not wearing anything underneath it. Her leg jumps out as she's standing, peering inside the ancient refrigerator, calling out the contents to him: iced tea, beer, diet Coke, an orange, an apple. It's a deep brown leg and it tucks itself back inside as she closes the refrigerator and hands him an iced tea in an aluminum can. She takes a beer for herself. He doesn't remember having made any request.

She sits down across from him. The kitchen table is tiny, the recipient of dozens of coats of paint, the latest a marine green. There are clean dishes stacked to the right of the sink, a cantaloupe in the window. The room smells of salt water, and suntan lotion, of violet bath soap and coffee. The door is open to the bathroom. Its fixtures are old, the shelves littered with women's things. A bra hangs from the shower curtain rod. He feels like he's lived here for weeks.

Five minutes stretch into ten, ten into twenty. She drinks another beer. She hands him one and he doesn't refuse. It's easier than any conversation he's ever had. Thoughts swirl around in tangles. Knots. He tells her about Duncan, but leaves out the paralysis. He tells her that he's divorced, and finally explains his relationship with Carrie, that the three of them are in a cottage just down the beach, though as he hears himself tell it, he doesn't quite know the author. Lynn Greene doesn't seem the least bit bothered by any of it. The humor remains, the closeness. She doesn't pull back and start building walls. She doesn't threaten, though she certainly flirts, which after a while strikes him as part of her personality. She's the hot-blooded variety, and she's comfortable with that. The closest she gets to a come-on is "We all need distractions," but it's said in a way that confuses him and leaves the interpretation up to him, and he decides to let it go.

Two hours pass. It's her beer going flat that tells him how long it has been. He excuses himself. "I'm not running this time," he says. He's trying to tell her something, but he's not sure why. She's amused.

"I enjoyed it," she tells him. To him, her comments sounds as if they've made love. And he realizes they have been making love for two hours. Making love with their clothes on.

When they're out on the porch and he says good-bye for the second time, it's Lynn Greene who spots Carrie first. Carrie is standing down by the receding water of low tide, looking up at them. Misunderstanding. Assuming. Burning. Carrie turns abruptly and in stiff-legged strides splashes her way first at a fast walk, then at a run, back down the rose-colored beach.

Daggett wants to say something, to apologize, but he's not sure whom to apologize to, or what to apologize for. He's back on the beach, in no particular hurry, well aware that Lynn Greene is not just a passing acquaintance, and that Carrie is not far off in her assumptions.

Standing there in a parking lot filled with the haze of petroleum smoke and the chaos of the firefighters, Lynn Greene smiled at Daggett privately, her eyes sparkling. "Cam Daggett!" she shouted, as only long-lost friends shout.

Huff rocked his head in disbelief. Daggett felt his face warm and his stomach turn. She came toward him excitedly, in long strides. He wasn't sure how to receive her. He wanted to swallow her in his arms—but not in front of Huff.

A sudden and thunderous explosion caused a hundred people to dive to the ground simultaneously. Daggett and Lynn Greene ended up close to each other. Only a few feet apart, it was not the explosion that stunned Daggett, it was how beautiful she looked, even in fear. Even these many months later.

"It always was fireworks with you, Michigan," she said from the corner of her mouth. "How the hell you been?"

She didn't give him time to answer. The explosion threw a piece of the plane's wing onto the horse stables, and as its flaming fuel drained onto the roof, a sheet of fire wrapped itself around the building. The scream of the trapped horses pierced the fading rumble of the explosion. Firemen fled in a hasty retreat coming straight at Daggett and Lynn, who were already back on their feet.

Lynn stopped one of them with a blunt straight-arm. "What about the horses?" she asked, incredulous.

"You fuckin' kiddin' me?" the fireman replied, a quick glance to Daggett for support. "Dog food, as far as I'm concerned."

"Bullshit," said Lynn Greene.

She took off at a full sprint toward the stables. Without fully understanding his own actions, Daggett found himself only a few steps behind her. "Lynn!" he called out. But she ran on, pretending not to hear.

The inside of the stables, thick with the black, oily smoke, was filled with the deafening panic of the horses as they cried and kicked for freedom. Lynn turned to Daggett —she *knew* he was there—and hollered over the cacophony, "You take that side!" She sprang a stall door open and was nearly stampeded by the fleeing horse. Daggett body-blocked her off her feet as the horse hooves fell within inches of them.

"Lynn!" he shouted in protest. The roof burned, a ceiling of orange flame. A large section of wall collapsed. Several horses escaped through the resulting hole. She pushed him off.

"You take *that* side," she repeated, coming to her feet and continuing down the line of stalls. One by one they liberated the Thoroughbreds, who raced out of the building with white eyes and frantic hooves.

He glanced overhead to see a full third of the burning roof about to fall in. Again he shouted to get her attention. He pointed. She looked to the roof but then shook her head in defiance. She freed two more horses. Daggett realized the quickest way—the *only* way—to get her out of here was to save every last horse.

Water began to rain down on them—the firemen had turned their hoses on this building. Two men in oxygen masks and orange rubber suits, with black boots and thick gloves, appeared out of the billowing smoke. One of them shouted angrily, his voice muffled by the mask: "Get the fuck out of here!"

The piece of the roof caved in, but it was at the other end and it fell into empty stalls. Lynn and Daggett ignored the fireman. They opened the two remaining stall doors simultaneously and the escaping horses knocked the fireman off his feet. With his heavy protective clothing and oxygen tank, he came clumsily to his knees. Lynn offered him her hand but he waved her off furiously.

Daggett and Lynn ran from the smoke into the welcome air, followed only seconds later by both firemen. They turned in time to see the stables fully aflame. Loose horses, their eyes bright with fear, chaotically sprinted for freedom, scattering people in their way.

The remaining section of roof gave way, and seconds later, the walls folded in. The building lay almost flat.

Flames leapt fifty feet into the air chasing a billowing spiral of thick smoke.

"You could have been killed!" he said angrily. It was at that moment he realized the depth of his feelings for her.

"No," she said confidently, shaking her head, eyes tracking the flames. Her face glowed in the orange light. "It isn't my time."

"Your *time?*" he asked, now more furious than ever. Next thing she'd be reciting horoscopes.

She looked over at him, taking her eyes off the fire. "You know these things, Michigan." Then she took his hands into hers and squeezed. He forgot all about the fire. "Sometimes you just know."

7

PERCHED ON THE thin lip of the hotel bathtub, Daggett's feet hung down into the steaming hot bath water. Every so often his feet protested like this, stiffening like boards. A good long soak was the only solution.

"It's not right," he said in a voice that resonated loudly in the small, tiled bathroom. He had a thing about rightness. "We need to keep going on this."

A moment later, over the drone of a television commercial for a bamboo steamer on the ubiquitous CNN, Lynn Greene declared encouragingly, "It's dark. We'll start up again at first light."

"It has nothing to do with darkness—it has to do with the report of chemicals being on board the plane. Did you see those people in those space suits? Jesus, what a sight! That's what cleared everyone out of there. You see how the TV crews ate that up?"

"And for good reason. What if the site *is* contaminated?"

"All the more reason to suspect sabotage, if you ask me. Chemicals? That's *Der Grund*'s calling card. Not that I can prove it."

"Who?"

"Never mind. The point is—"

She interrupted him. "The point is that we got very lucky. The fire neutralized the chemicals. That's the report I got. Without those wellheads burning as they did, we would have had a *real* disaster on our hands."

"From my end, that's all the more reason to keep up the

investigation. Waiting around for guys in space suits to ana-
lyze spoor samples—"

"You're disgusting! One night is not going to hurt anything. We'll get a fresh start tomorrow. If there's something
there we'll find it." She handed him one of the vodka-and-
Rose's she had mixed using the supplies from the mini-bar.

"I need proof of criminal intent. I need some good,
solid linkage in order to keep my investigation alive." He
took a deep swallow and balanced the glass on the edge of
the tub. Lynn supported the doorjamb with a shoulder. "I've
spent nearly two years on this case. I don't come up with
something and I'm history. They want my report on this
other thing—this bombing out at National. Can you believe
that? They would pull me from a case like this to have me
write a goddamned report on a dead man?" He looked to
her for sympathy, but found none.

"We don't call it 'criminal intent,'" she said, correcting
him. "We call it *suspicious causes.* But so far there's nothing
like that. Nothing at all." She added, "Besides, maybe a new
assignment would do you some good. You don't look so
good."

He pretended to ignore her last comment. "The NTSB
press guy is already talking it up like it was an accident.
CNN, all the papers—everyone is calling it an *accident,* for
God's sake. The NTSB is selling a line of bullshit. That news
conference was way off."

"It was accurate. We all pride ourselves on accuracy,
don't we? It's the NTSB's show. It remains their investigation until evidence allows you guys to take over. Listen, if it
were up to me, I'd give you anything you want. But you
know that—and you don't seem to want." She took a sip of
her drink. She wasn't talking investigation. He hid himself
in his drink. "And the fact is we've seen *nothing* on site to
indicate suspicious causes. We have the air traffic controller
reporting that one of the flight crew called out a cockpit
fire. The plane went down within seconds. Not one eyewitness has described anything like an explosion. Nothing in

the wreckage yet to indicate explosives. The NTSB doesn't have a lot of choice here."

"A Duhning 959–600 at LAX—maybe loaded with chemicals? I have a dead body coming out of a 959 simulator set to an LAX runway. I've got a known terrorist building altimeter detonators in his Los Angeles hotel room. Los Angeles, LAX . . . get it? You're going to tell me it's coincidence?" He continued before she could interrupt. She had a penchant for interrupting, for getting her own way. "Don't go soft on me, damn it all. Someone has to maintain their objectivity."

"Objectivity? Is that what you're preaching?"

"Am I preaching?" he asked, reaching for the drink and draining a fair amount of it.

"Yes, you are."

He looked at her distorted image through the irregularity of the glass. She stretched as he spun it. "You're the air accident investigator," he said. "The explosives expert. You're leading the FAA's investigation on this thing."

"Damn right," she agreed, tilting her drink up in a way that stretched her long neck. "And don't get so personal. You're not making this any easier."

"It *is* personal. You should be helping me on this."

"I'm trying."

"Are you?"

"Yes."

He watched her in profile as her throat tightened as she swallowed, and he found it provocative. It had probably been a bad idea to invite her up here.

"These go down too easy," she said, studying the small glass, "but why don't I make us another?"

He finished his and handed it to her.

"How are they doing?" she asked, nodding toward his feet.

"I'll tell you after the second drink."

She left him alone to his thoughts. Like his voice, they tended to bounce around in the small room. As she seemed to be taking too long, he called to her, "It has got to be the work of the same guy. There are far too many overlaps. Doesn't that count for anything?"

"No," she said, joining him again. "Not to Lynn Greene the investigator. I shouldn't even be aware of that side of your investigation. I'm paid for my objectivity—something I lost the minute I saw you on site." She sat on the closed toilet. They were close to each other. She lifted her glass; the rims chimed. "Here's to working together," she said. "At last."

"I need your support on this."

"Even though I'd rather be playing, than working."

"Please help me."

"One step at a time. There's a system in place here. Give it a chance to work."

"I can't. What if Bernard made more than one trigger?"

"Who's Bernard?"

He didn't answer. He tried the drink. It was stronger and he wondered: by design? She was right, they did go down easy. His feet looked bigger because of the magnifying powers of the water. Big, pale, wrinkled feet with crooked toes. Very romantic.

She said, "I'm supposed to be objective. Don't worry: no one is going to whitewash this. I won't allow that. What would be the point? Between the lot of us, we'll be looking at every conceivable explanation for that crash. Believe it."

"I can't wait six months," he said. "These things always take six months."

"I understand that." She adjusted herself and it brought her closer to him. She ran her fingers through his hair and he felt it down to his toes. "I'll do what I can. Promise." She was at his back where he couldn't see her and he found it disarming.

"Lynn," he said so deliberately, it was like a referee blowing a whistle. He heard her ice rattle, and then the gentle pump of her swallowing.

"Okay," she said without any hurt in her voice. "But

unless you fill that thing with ice water and dunk me in it, I had better be going. I have other ideas about how this night should be spent." She kissed him on his neck below his ear. It ran a few thousand volts down his left side. His body hair stood at attention.

"How's Duncan doing?" she asked. That cooled him down. When he failed to answer she added, "That phone call you just made sounded more like a business call than a man calling his son."

"Sometimes that's how it is between us."

"It shouldn't be."

"I know that."

"You're mad."

"Yes."

"At me?"

"No. At myself. The truth hurts."

"He has a sitter?" she inquired. "Or is it *her*?"

"A sitter tonight. Old enough to be his grandmother. She's become sort of part of the family."

"The sitter or Carrie?" Lynn asked. "Strike that from the record," she added. "I'm not a very good loser."

"Who says you've lost?" he asked as she handed him her empty drink. At the moment he knew everything there was to know about emptiness.

"You're with her, aren't you? I had hoped my dazzling personality and bathing suit silhouette might change that arrangement. Some things you learn to accept. Some things you don't," she warned.

More tempted than ever to stop her, he ran an arm out and she dragged her fingers along it until their hands swept over one another and the very tips of their fingers kissed.

She found her purse, stopped in the narrow passage-way to look in on him. She smiled at him long enough to convey a message. She wanted to stay; she wanted him to ask her. He smiled back. She nodded and shrugged. The door closed behind her, and a second later Daggett was

standing where she had been standing, his wet feet on the
carpet, hand gripping the doorknob. But he didn't turn it.

The next morning the phone rang him awake in the
middle of a room service breakfast. His morning run had
been hampered by his vodka of the night before.

The voice of Phil Huff said, "We're in the clear here, so
I'm going to keep it brief. There's something going down
that you'll want to be part of. I'll pick you up outside the
lobby in about ten, twelve minutes." He paused. "Any problems with that?"

"I'll be there," Daggett said.

Huff wore the same poplin suit, his shoulders square
with arrogance. Daggett caught himself staring at the scars
on the man's nose, wondering if women were attracted to
scars. Huff had plenty of both. He drove the same mud-
brown Chrysler Daggett had seen him in at the crash site.
The front seat had a ratty slipcover, and Huff's heel had
worn a hole in the floor mat in front of the accelerator
pedal. The radio was crusted with dust and spilled coffee.
The vinyl of the sun visor was split open from the years,
like a piece of fruit left too long on the windowsill. Huff
steered them into traffic, slipped the police light onto the
dash, turned it on, and, as traffic parted slowly, said, "Our
boys got a call from the LAPD substation out here at the
airport, telling us about a call one of their downtown
squads got. A mechanic for AmAirXpress claims he was
jumped and drugged yesterday by a man and woman at his
home. Says his airport ID and overalls were stolen. They
rolled a detective on it a minute ago. We hurry, we may
catch most of the show."

Daggett considered all of this briefly. "If it holds, this
could give us authority over the crash investigation," he
said anxiously.

"Something better than that," Huff said, teasing Daggett
with the long pause that followed. "You're gonna fuckin'
love this."

Daggett wouldn't beg. He waited him out.

"The chemicals on board this airplane?" he stated as a question, forcing Daggett to reply, "Yeah?" "Made by a company called ChemTronics with refineries—or whatever the fuck you call them—in twenty-some states." Huff left another long pause, pretending to be busy with the car, though the car seemed to be driving itself on a road completely straight. "ChemTronics, come to find out, is a defense contractor—wink, wink; nudge, nudge—and is in bed with none other than EisherWorks Chemicals."

Daggett's pulse doubled and he tried not to give Huff the pleasure of seeing or hearing his enthusiasm, which required a substantial effort. "In bed?" he asked.

"EisherWorks owns controlling interest in ChemTronics. It amounts to an American subsidiary."

"So this *could* be *Der Grund.*"

"I thought you'd like it."

Daggett mulled over the possibilities. Would a financial connection between the two be enough to convince Pullman or his superior, Richard Mumford, of *Der Grund*'s suspected involvement? He doubted it. It wasn't hard enough evidence. And even if they had received a threat, Chem-Tronics was unlikely to share it with the FBI. Ignoring terrorist threats angered stockholders and drew unfavorable publicity; both affected share price. Major corporations received threats all the time, and for the most part, they used their own security departments to handle them. But even without a "hard" connection, it boosted Daggett's confidence that he was still on the trail of Bernard's detonators. And where the hell did it lead from here? What was next?

Phil Huff said, "Thermos at your feet is black with sugar. You look like you could use a cup."

They drove for nearly twenty minutes, at which point he had lost track of where they were. The curbs, sidewalks, planting, even the houses, all looked the same. "I'm a real estate bigot," he said. "To me this all looks the same. Where the hell are we?"

"Dougherty's place is right up here," Huff said, obviously amused.

Daggett spotted the detective's unmarked car. Four-door, black-walls. "Stop!" he demanded, and the driver responded immediately by hitting the brakes. They both rocked forward toward the dash and settled back.

"What?" Huff asked angrily, eyes searching. "Christ, the way you said that, I thought I was about to hit something."

"You were," Daggett said, indicating the street in front of them. "Take a look." Pointing.

"Yeah?" Huff asked, not seeing.

"The tire tracks," Daggett explained. "The mud . . . the tire tracks there by the curb, see? But none behind the wheels of the unmarked." He glanced over his shoulder and sipped the coffee. "Fresh ditches. Sewer work, right? But what about the mud?"

Huff looked too. "Kids musta had the hydrant on yesterday."

"Yeah. Exactly. A lot of tracks down the middle of the street, but only this pair over here by the curb."

"Son of a bitch," Huff said excitedly. He backed up the car to stay out of the tracks. He parked it. "I'll get the dick's keys. I got a Polaroid under the seat." He reached down and located it, and handed it to Daggett. "You leave it in the trunk and the film bakes."

"Measuring tape?" Daggett asked.

"Should be in the kit in the trunk." He handed Daggett the keys. He said, "This dick wasn't thinking about the crime scene."

"No, he wasn't. So why don't you ask him politely to cool his heels a minute." He made it a statement. "Talk to him. See if we can have this guy to ourselves for a while. There's nothing in this for LAPD. Nothing but paperwork for this badge. Tell him we'll take it off his hands."

"He won't like it," Huff cautioned. "Just us being here means there's something to it."

"That's why we do this alone. Right, Phil?" Daggett said. "We don't need any tongues wagging."

"No shit."

"And while you're in there call your lab boys. Tell them to bring stuff to cast these ditches . . . vacuums for inside the house . . . the whole nine yards." He added, "We treat it like a major crime scene."

"The lab? I can't do that. We don't even know for sure your guy was here," Huff protested. "Right? Let's not get ahead of ourselves."

"A mechanic's ID stolen the afternoon of a crash?" Daggett asked, incredulous. "Make the call, Phil. I'll take my chances on this one."

By the time Daggett and Huff returned from the nearly three-hour interrogation of Kevin Dougherty, the crash site at Hollywood Park looked completely different than the night before. The strewn packages and overnight mail envelopes of various colors, shapes, and sizes were gone, carted off to a nearby high school gym for inspection by FBI and FAA explosives experts. With the fires now extinguished, the ominous, other-planet quality of the previous night gave way to the feeling of a battlefield on the morning after: every object spread over five acres was either carbon black or mud brown. The disemboweled tail section of the fallen aircraft stuck out of the ground like a piece of modern sculpture. It was near this tail section that Daggett spotted a small group of investigators that included Lynn Greene. There were forty to fifty investigators roaming the debris, stooped like shell seekers on a Florida beach, many carrying clipboards, cameras, or clear plastic bags containing grotesquely unrecognizable items. One crew, near the detached nose, was running debris and mud over a sifter; others searched the screen like archaeologists after pieces of history.

The entire effort seemed somehow removed, as if acted out on a stage so large he couldn't see the edges. Again, he thought of the doomed flight 1023 and found himself thankful he had been several days late to that site. To add hundreds of dead bodies to this horror was unthinkable. He marveled at how efficiently, how effortlessly, the several dozen investigators managed to work side by side, each performing a specific function, many of which no doubt overlapped. If only law enforcement ran so smoothly.

Huff emerged from the command center trailer a few minutes later. "For what it's worth," he said, "this investigation may soon be ours."

"How soon?" Daggett questioned.

"It can't be turned over to us without *suspicious causes.*"

"What about Dougherty? What about his ID tag being ripped off? Doesn't that give us *suspicious causes?*"

"Us maybe, but not the NTSB. They need some hard evidence. Crash site evidence." Huff added optimistically, "At the noon meeting the team leader will announce that all the search teams should give evidence of criminal intent top priority. We've canceled the noon press conference. We can get a better handle on all of this by the evening meeting. We're moving some of the teams so that all of us will be staying over at the Marriott. NTSB cut a deal for the main conference room, and two of the smaller ones. All in all, it's going well."

"Going well? What kind of hard evidence do they need, Phil?"

"More than tire tracks and the testimony of a mechanic. I don't like it either, but we're not going to change it. They work *inclusive* to the crash site. They can't allow off-site threats or security violations, or even supporting theories, to influence or bias their objectivity at the site itself."

"Objectivity?"

"Listen, they understand our position, okay? The way they laid it out is that they'll jump on the slightest bit of evidence, and that they're more than willing to give any and all of our requests top priority. We're not butting heads here." He glanced out toward the team at the tail of the aircraft. "Cross your fingers those guys can put Humpty Dumpty back together again."

"Meaning?"

"The voice-recorder tape is a mess. I'm told they're dealing with half a mile of spaghetti."

"But we need that."

"We need a lot of things."

"What about the data recorder? The DFDR," Daggett asked.

"They say it looks fine. It's being flown back to Washington on their private plane later this afternoon. Once they untangle the tape from the CVR, it'll be flown back so they can be synced up."

"I'd like to listen in on that."

"It may be a week or two, from what I hear."

"Even so."

"I'll mention it. Listen," he added somewhat tentatively, "my SAC has directed my squad chief to make this crash investigation my ticket. They don't understand your being here. Told them I invited you to help out. So, technically, we're both following up the Bernard ticket. That didn't exactly cut it for them, but there's not much they can do about it. You're my guest. That means we've got to give you access to the investigation."

Was this the same Phil Huff? "I appreciate it."

"It didn't help much. They won't let me give you any people."

"I'm on my own?"

"LAFO has three counterterrorism squads all told. As of ten minutes ago, all three are assigned to this case. That gives me about thirty guys. You run any requests through me, I'll make sure they're handled. Plenty of guys to go around. Maybe I can swing something."

"What am I hearing?" Daggett asked.

"Listen. WFO is the Office of Origin on Bernard. We're the O.O. on this crash."

"And Dougherty?" Daggett asked. "Where the hell does Dougherty fit into this?"

"Bring me something. Okay? You like the Dougherty connection, so do I. Bring me something my squad supervisor can get hard over and we'll take over this crash investigation in one phone call."

"You're helping me?"

"I'll help where I can."

"Why the sudden change of heart?"

Huff took a moment before replying. "I didn't sleep last night. Not because of this crash, but because of Backman. I fucked up the Bernard surveillance, Daggett. I admit that. I see that now, okay? I let it get away from me. I let *that briefcase* get away from me. Where did he make the drop? In the men's room? The coat check? Shit, I don't know what went wrong, but it went about as wrong as it can go. First Backman; now this. What the fuck? You reach a certain point, you realize it's time to change your act." He studied his unlit cigarette and then threw it into the mud. "Where are you going, in case I need to reach you?"

Daggett could hardly find the words. Huff apologizing. *You reach a certain point, you realize it's time to change your act.* The words echoed inside him like the last penny in a piggy bank. They could have come out of his mouth just as easily.

Huff repeated, "Where you going?"

Daggett answered, "To find us some evidence."

The tire tracks outside the home of Kevin Dougherty produced quick results. Measurement of the wheelbase, as defined by the two opposing tire tracks, identified the vehicle as a Chrysler—either a Dodge Caravan or a Plymouth Voyager. Betting on a rental, Daggett turned his attention to the local agencies. The killer's rental car in Seattle had given him a credit card to flag and trace; maybe this rental car would be worth something as well.

A phone call placed early Wednesday morning revealed that Chrysler had an exclusive rental agreement for Caravans in the L.A. area with Overland Car Rentals. Overland kept only eight Caravans at its airport agency. Of the eight, two had been returned the day of the crash—one a few hours before the crash, and one only minutes after. In a city where forty-five-minute drives were common, Daggett was grateful to be working out of the airport Marriott, which was all of five minutes from LAX and the Overland agency there.

Daggett bumped over the security spikes at the entrance, passing the gatehouse on his left. Ahead of him a sea of returned cars awaited cleaning. A Vietnamese boy of about eighteen, leaning awkwardly over two pieces of electronic gear that hung from his belt, approached a returning car and began punching numbers into one of the heavy boxes.

Daggett found the supervisor, Milton Butts, in a small office through a door behind the main counter. The room reeked of aftershave, reminding Daggett of Backman. Butts was a black man with graying temples, a dead front tooth, and the stump neck of a former wrestler or lineman. He had wide-set brown eyes that flashed between vacancy and annoyance as Daggett made his requests. He wore a company blazer and a shirt that couldn't button around that thick neck, the knot of the company tie attempting to hide its shortcoming. The left lens of his reading glasses was thumbprinted. He had missed a spot below his nose in this morning's shave, leaving a triangle of black stubble on his upper lip.

He typed slowly, but with accuracy. As he read from the screen he said in a deceptively tranquil voice, "Both of them vehicles rented to women, if that matters any."

"But one of them paid cash," Daggett said, feigning confidence. Worry written on his face. "Will the computer show that?"

Milton Butts reexamined the screen and asked, "Now just how did you know that?"

"A lucky guess." He closed his eyes and thanked whoever was watching over him.

Butts puckered his lips, not liking the answer. "Her name is Lyttle, with a *y*. Maryanne Lyttle. A one-day rental. Reserved it with a card but paid cash. She kept the car for about six hours—that's fairly common with our business customers," he added editorially. After studying the screen a moment longer he added, "Nothing out of the ordinary here."

Daggett requested a copy of the agreement, and Butts printed one out for both of them.

Daggett read the agreement over.

"Has the van been cleaned?"

"Sure it's clean," Butts said angrily. Then adding, "You don't look too pleased about that."

"How clean? Inside, I mean."

"Truthfully? This time of year, as busy as it is, probably not perfect. You seen that parking lot out there. Packed with returns. Every day it's like that," he complained. "And between you and me, our employees are not exactly highly motivated. Know what I mean?"

Daggett placed a phone call and ordered the van be towed to a garage where field office personnel could go over it immediately.

"This got something to do with the crash, don't it?" Butts asked when Daggett hung up. "Shitty thing, that crash. Hurts all of us. You should have seen our cancellations this morning. I wanna tell you, even a goddamned accident hurts business. People is very superstitious when it comes to flying." Then his eyes rolled and he exclaimed, "You telling me it wasn't no accident? *That* what you doing here?"

Daggett sized him up and answered, "Officially, I can't comment. Unofficially I can use all the help I can get."

"I be *goddamned,*" Butts said brightly. "Goddamn Arabs or what?"

Daggett asked, "What do these letters in the return box refer to, Mr. Butts? Can you tell me that?"

Butts looked his own copy over and nodded. "We rent and return right from Baggage Claim. The majority of our return business is done out here, off-airport, where we clean and service the fleet. But our Express customers are handled on-airport. Both pickup and return. That's all that's saying. This van was rented and returned on-airport." In boyish enthusiasm he added, "Say! You know what I bet would interest you?" He checked his watch. "But shit, we had better move quick."

Daggett didn't like the sound of *we.* "What's that?" he asked. "What might interest me, Mr. Butts?"

"We had a whole series of holdup problems down there on-airport. Put in a hidden video system not six months ago."

"Video?" Daggett asked, his mind racing ahead to the possibilities.

"Thing of it is," Butts said, obviously worried, checking his watch again. "It's a twenty-four-hour loop system. Endless tape, or something. You know. Same as they do in the terminals."

"The terminals?" And now Daggett exploded out of his chair, frantically waving for Butts to hurry, for it suddenly occurred to him how to catch this Maryanne Lyttle.

On Thursday morning, August 30, Daggett entered the Los Angeles County Federal Building—an innocuous white structure surrounded by suspiciously green grass. The Feds apparently weren't paying much attention to the drought.

The audio-visual technical services lab of the Los Angeles Field Office of the FBI used a small windowless office on the sixth floor. Daggett knew the video techs here in L.A.

were among the best in the country. Not only was L.A. at the heart of such technology, but LAFO saw more than its fair share of practice: the drug squad used video surveillance extensively. Drugs in L.A. were big business and a central focus for the LAFO. The room was crowded with every kind of video and television equipment, some recognizable to Daggett, some not. Daggett buttoned his sport coat to hold off the added chill, reminded of the computer room at Duhning. He'd left the letter jacket in the hotel room.

Cynthia Ramirez steered her wheelchair over to Daggett and shook his hand strongly. She had fire in her glassy eyes and a sly little smile. Daggett saw the chair and thought of Duncan. Ramirez was rail thin, wearing a cable-knit sweater with a plaid blanket covering her legs. Her dark hair was held off her bony face by a red plastic clip in the shape of a bow. Her fingers were ice cold and as long and slim as chopsticks. "They call me Fragile," she said, still maintaining the smile.

"Michigan," he said, careful not to crush that hand.

"It suits you. Don't ask me why."

He withheld any similar comment.

"What's this?" she asked, eyeing the cardboard box of videotapes he had brought with him.

"I'm told you're the best we have in video enhancement."

"Compliments will get you everywhere."

"Black and white, endless loops. One tape shot in an airport garage. The other fifteen are on loan from a private firm that runs the video work out at LAX."

She grinned. "That's Bernie Shanks's company. He came out of this office, you know?"

He nodded. "Yes. That is, I found out. It's how I was able to walk right out of there with these things. Without Mr. Shanks I have a feeling it would have taken a few weeks in court."

She reached for the box and pulled it down into her

lap, where it landed hard. Enough to break bones that small, if indeed there were any bones under the blanket. It was hard to tell. "Endless loops don't offer very good quality. Oxide wears right off 'em."

"That's why I asked for you. For the enhancement."

Propelling herself over to one of the machines, she glanced back at him. "I'm no miracle worker," she said.

"That's not what I hear."

She caught his eye then and held it. "We could use more around here like you." She smiled. He returned it.

"That top tape . . . it's cued up for you. There's a woman standing at the rental counter. Scarf. Sunglasses. Can barely make her out. If we could enlarge her face, build it back to something we can use . . . I'm hoping she went inside the terminal right after returning the car. I'm hoping we can follow her movements from one video to the next. Each of the other fifteen tapes is from a particular set of camera stations inside the terminal. Each overlaps a piece of the other's territory—for the sake of coverage. But picking her out of the crowd . . . I don't know. It looked pretty hopeless to me. People's faces aren't very big on those tapes. But if you've ever seen a crash site . . . This woman may be responsible. I figured it was worth a try."

Her face hardened, and she briefly looked like a different woman altogether. Then her features relaxed. "My crash site was on La Cienega. A VW bug and an ambulance, Michigan. I was driving the bug, unfortunately. I didn't hear the ambulance siren. We're still in court over that, and it's been six years. It ran the light and struck me here," she said, rubbing her right side as if she could still feel the pain. "Now why don't you chase us down a couple cups of coffee —mine's black. We're gonna need it."

Daggett brought two more cups of coffee over the next two hours and then two plates of fried chicken and mashed potatoes from the cafeteria. Fragile, as she insisted on being called, had transformed a nondescript oval sitting atop a woman's body into a grainy but recognizable digital portrait on a high-resolution computer screen. With each progressive electronic enlargement, the computer redrew the face, compensating for the lack of definition. She then shaded and filled with a wand she referred to as the airbrush. Many enlargements later, the face of Maryanne Lyttle stared back at them. To Daggett, this was nothing short of a miracle.

Fragile saved her efforts to disk and printed out a hard copy onto paper. While she began searching the airport terminal security tapes, a sketch artist named Willard used the airbrush and the better part of an hour to erase the woman's sunglasses and, using the width of the bridge of the woman's nose as a reference, drew in a pair of eyes, complete with eyebrows and hairline. "It's as close as we'll get," Willard said proudly as he stiffly rose out of his chair.

"No it's not," contradicted Fragile Ramirez. "She took off her glasses inside the terminal."

Daggett looked over at the screen, his heart jumping from the combined effects of excitement and boiled coffee. Fragile had a white box framed around a small head in a random sea of air travelers. It was much more defined than the earlier image. As Daggett watched, the frame grew increasingly larger, driving the other images off the screen. With each enlargement the computer redrew the face. Fragile waved the wand, making up for where the computer missed. Again the face grew more visible. Again, Daggett's heart jumped. So close now!

Willard grabbed the hard copy of his efforts and held it side by side with the new face on the screen.

"What do you think of that?" he asked loudly, a full-tooth grin opening his face.

The two images were identical.

Daggett came out of his seat and shook the man's hand. He bent down and kissed Fragile on the cheek. "You're magicians, both of you."

"It was the earrings," said an excited Fragile. "That other shot didn't give us any clothes, didn't give us any sig-

nature to follow her with." Daggett hadn't noticed the earrings until that moment. They were big black ovals. Easily
identified, if you thought to look. Fragile had thought to
look. She was blushing from the kiss. She continued, "We'll
be able to follow her now, Michigan, one camera to the
next. Guaranteed. If she boarded a plane, you'll know
where she was headed. If she left the terminal, you'll know
by which exit. Those earrings were her downfall. She
should have thought twice before wearing those earrings."

"Yes, she should have," said Daggett, realizing suddenly
that was just the point: A professional wouldn't make such
a mistake. Was he dealing with an amateur?

Willard left the small office. Fragile said, "You look a
little white, Michigan. You all right?"

Daggett, staring at the face on the screen, nodded
slightly. Doubt had wormed its way into his head. An amateur. Was it possible?

Or, after all this, did he have the wrong woman?

Daggett attended the nine o'clock meeting at the Marriott, amazed both by the smoothness with which it ran and
by the huge number of people taking part in the AmAirX-
press investigation. Well over a hundred were in attendance, covering both sexes and as wide a variety of races as
there were specialties. It reminded him of a political con-
vention, the way delegates group together. Over there was
the crew of investigators for General Electric; and there, a
team representing the airline pilots' union. With each comment from the dais another series of heads would fall as
eyes were cast to the accompanying reports; small inter-
group discussions would supersede the present report, and
then another group of experts would lower their heads and
begin a similar routine. On the dais, Huff sat third from
center, next to Lynn Greene. During his report, Huff reem-
phasized the criminal intent angle, keeping details vague,
and once again encouraged everyone to dig for hard evidence.

When the meeting ended, after nearly ninety minutes, Daggett felt well briefed on the progress at the crash site but depressed and discouraged with the results.

The flight recorder data—the DFDR—had been sent to the FAA lab in Washington for analysis. The damaged voice recorder—the CVR—was still being worked on here. Parts of the broken aircraft were already being tagged and transported to a hangar at LAX, where an attempt at reconstruction would be made if any suspicious causes surfaced. To date, none had, and this weighed heavily on Daggett. His only hope to continue his investigation lay in the debris of the crash; both, at the moment, were in pieces.

He had to maintain his optimism, had to maintain a broad base to the investigation to give it every possibility. As tempting a suspect as Maryanne Lyttle seemed, Daggett couldn't allow himself to be obsessed with her. He still believed a *male* operative, using Dougherty's identity card, had gained access to AmAirXpress 64 while on the ground. Maryanne Lyttle, at best, was this man's accomplice. A driver? A scout?

Daggett telephoned his WMFO voice-mail mailbox, where an impersonal woman's voice told him he had six messages. He stepped through the process of retrieving them. Only the last had to do with this case: "We have a blood type and we have a thumb print." The voice belonged to a man who introduced himself as Barge Kolowski, a fingerprint expert at the Washington State Forensic Science Laboratory. "Blood type came off that tooth. The print was developed off the bar of soap. It's a beauty, by the by. He was smart enough to throw away the bar of soap—a shower is somewhere you don't often wear gloves—but we found *his* trash because of that tooth, and that's something he didn't plan on. We've forwarded the print to your people here, and I assume they'll pass it on to Washington. More of those same cigarettes, as well. We think they're a Russian brand called Sobranie, for what it's worth. If you have any

questions, give me a call during office hours or at home."
The man left his home number.

Daggett, alone in his hotel room, drink in hand, hung
up and shouted, "Yes!" into the empty room. Evidence had a
way of doing that to him.

The phone rang. He set the drink down and checked
the clock: 11:30. Late. He answered it brightly.

"Washington, D.C.," the tired, frail voice stated.

"Fragile, is that you?" he asked.

"The gate. Your mystery woman, Maryanne Lyttle? I
just watched her on videotape as she boarded a flight for
Washington, D.C. The gate's destination sign is as clear as
day."

"Washington?" His voice cracked. An operative still at
large. Kort? An unaccounted-for detonator. Washington,
D.C., WMFO's territory. His ticket. He was both excited and
afraid.

He breathed into the receiver, saying nothing, stunned
by the thought of a second target somewhere in his home-
town. He stared at the small ice cubes on the carpet as his
glass rolled under the end table and disappeared. The
phone had knocked the drink off the end table.

"Michigan?" she asked. "Did you get that?"

It made sense. Bernard had built the detonators in Los
Angeles. Flight 64 had been bombed in Los Angeles. Bernard had then turned up in Washington . . .

His stockinged toes searched beneath the end table and
located the spilled glass, rolling it back out.

"I got it," he said into the phone.

Carrie watched as the plane from Los Angeles slowed
to a stop out on the airfield and the boxlike shuttle vehicle
used at Dulles International drew alongside to board the
passengers and deliver them to the terminal. She hoped for
his sake that the vehicle was air-conditioned. She had lived
through some unbearably hot, humid summers while growing up outside New Haven, but nothing to compare with

this. This heat made her impatient and irritable. She was mad at him before she even got a chance to say hello. This heat was *his* fault.

She lifted a finger toward her mouth, prepared to nibble at her nail, and then thought better of it. More than anything, she wanted a cigarette.

On the way to the car, she attempted several times to engage him in conversation, but he didn't respond. Nothing new there. He carried his briefcase—he never went anywhere without that thing; she carried his hanging bag.

"You're mad about something? Is that it?" he asked, sounding bored with the subject before it began. This infuriated her.

"First, the three of us were supposed to go to the shore *last* weekend. Then you promised Duncan it would be this weekend. It's Labor Day weekend. It's a holiday. I know you couldn't have gone to either Seattle or L.A. without *wanting* to, without pulling some strings. So you're making choices, and those choices are pretty clear."

He took a long time before saying, "Rather unusual circumstances, Carrie. I explained that before I left. Duncan understood." The implication was that she didn't.

She spoke softly. "I need to be more than a pair of legs and a you-know-what." Cam gave her one of those looks. She could feel him pull away. "We're losing each other."

"We haven't lost anything, Carrie. Misplaced maybe. Not lost." They walked along in silence.

"That's it? That's all you're going to say?"

He glanced at her.

"I hang my heart out on my sleeve and your sole contribution to this discussion is to correct my syntax?"

"Carrie—"

"What the hell is going on here?" She felt like an idiot. But as he blushed, she understood. She stopped cold and set the hanging bag down. "You saw her, didn't you?" Lynn Greene lay at the core of all her fears. To Carrie, this stranger represented her biggest threat. Cam fantasized about her—imagined her better for him; she *knew* he did, without their ever having discussed it. She wanted security from this relationship. Love? yes. A mate? certainly. But more than anything, she wanted to *belong* to someone, to have them belong to her. She and Duncan and Cam had quickly formed a team, and the safety she felt as a result of this had become everything to her. On a beach one afternoon, over a year ago now, Lynn Greene had changed all that. Now she lived in the darkened shadows of fear, afraid to look out, afraid to be seen. The hope of permanent companionship grew weaker with every argument.

"She just showed up. Sixty-four—the crash—is her assignment. It was *nothing.*"

"Did you *sleep* with her?" Tears threatened. She felt foolish. She took a deliberate step away from him, arms crossed tightly. People were watching now. A stream of dispassionate humanity parted and poured around them like water around a rock.

Who was this jealous woman? It sounded like her voice, but she didn't create scenes; she didn't explode in jealous fits, especially not in the middle of Dulles International.

"I'm not going to give that the dignity of a response." He took up his hanging bag. His expression said *Are you coming?* His expression said even more.

"You thought about it," she said in a defeated, completely sober voice. He didn't deny it. It seemed as if several minutes passed. She reached down deeply within herself and spoke just as he was about to walk away from her. "No crime in that, is there?"

He turned and viewed her cautiously. What did he want from her? A surrogate mother for his son? Someone to wash the dishes and take out the trash? Someone to lie down for him? What had happened to the months of laughter? What had happened to the inquisitive questions and hours of talk? Gone. What had happened to the surprise flowers and the dinners out and the hours of petting before a single button was loosened? Gone.

She said bravely, "Hell, if fantasy is a crime, we're all indictable." She didn't fantasize about anyone except him, but she wasn't about to admit it. The thing now was to give him a way out.

"I asked you to pick me up because I missed you," he said.

She forced a wide smile onto her face; he didn't seem to know when she forced it. "I thought it was to save cab fare."

"That, too."

She walked over and buried her face in his collar where it smelled so much like him, she almost wept. He dropped the hanging bag and wrapped a tentative arm around her—he wasn't big on showing his emotions in public. A moment later they joined the mainstream.

"Hell of a welcome back, eh, Cam?"

"I can handle it."

"You can, can't you?"

"That bothers you?"

"I think it does." She added, "Threatens, maybe."

"Inside, Carrie, I don't handle it very well."

"So when are you going to let me in? I was in there once."

Daggett said nothing. His puzzled expression and the sudden distancing she felt again told her he didn't have an answer, and that it bothered him.

But it bothered her more. And she was keeping score.

8

ANTHONY KORT STEPPED off the train and onto the platform at Washington's Union Station. The air around him weighed a few hundred pounds and was so hot, he broke into an immediate sweat. It smelled of steam and darkness down here. He liked it.

He traveled by train, not only because of his fear of flying but because there was no security screening whatsoever. You could board a train with any kind of weapon or bomb, any drug, any disguise. If absolutely pressed, you could even jump from a train.

Trains had their drawbacks as well. They were tediously slow, and in America, poorly serviced and uncomfortable. Disenchanted black people waited on you with complete contempt. The sleepers were inadequately small and poorly ventilated. The food tasted like warmed-up wet cardboard.

Kort had spent three days on the train, an opportunity to plan and rest. Despite this down time, or perhaps because of it, he had grown progressively more tense as the days had dragged on, a runner before the marathon.

Kort rode a taxi several miles from Washington's Union Station train terminal and then disembarked near, but not at, a Metro subway entrance. He reached the Metro, rode it two stops, changed to the other side and rode one stop back, alert all the while for surveillance of any sort. He took a room in a former colonial mansion, now a bed-and-breakfast, a room that had been reserved in the name of Kevin Anthony. David Anthony was a thing of the past. His room offered an unobstructed view of the two streets on the building's perimeter, and three avenues of escape. The proprietor's wife, who ran the desk, was a handsome woman in her fifties, graying hair, glasses, and a rigid posture. She explained the rules in a sweet but businesslike voice: breakfast served from seven to nine; alcohol was available in the evening hours, five to ten o'clock, at an extra charge; no unregistered overnight guests; two keys, one for the front door, one for the room. Lost keys cost twenty-five dollars. No music after ten; room phones would not allow direct-dial long-distance calls, but phone company credit card calls were possible through the telephone company operator; towels were changed daily, sheets every other day unless otherwise requested; all the rooms had window air conditioners and guests were requested to switch them to the Energy Efficient mode during the daytime hours when the room was not occupied. "Let's see," she said, checking her red leather–bound book with its tabular columns, "we received a wire transfer for the deposit. Thank you," she added, looking up. "And the balance will be paid by . . . credit card?"

"Cash," replied Mr. Kevin Anthony, producing a series of crisp one-hundred-dollar bills. One of the beauties of automatic tellers and international cash systems was that a single plastic card gave one instant access to funds. His red Cirrus card—a dedicated ATM card—allowed him to withdraw up to one thousand dollars in cash a day, six days a week. His remaining three Visa cards each had twenty-thousand-dollar credit limits. Now in phase three of his operation, the David Anthony card would be retired. Michael had seen to the accounts—thankfully *before* his arrest. Money was the least of Kort's problems.

He spent the holiday weekend familiarizing himself with the empty city and its impressive Metro subway system. Tuesday at noon, wearing his own face and his own short hair, he stood on the corner of K and 21st, awaiting her. Perhaps it was his fatigue that made him remember, perhaps the sound of the police siren as it passed, perhaps the nagging realization that it could happen again—he could be arrested anywhere, at any time. Such was the nature of his life. It bred paranoia and suspicion in him. Whatever its cause, he found his memories as unavoidable as the truth; glimpses of his own history, they were bound to repeat themselves. He had relived this a hundred times in the last five years, like the recurring nightmare it was.

It is five years earlier, his wife and child barely cold in the ground.

He returns to his home—his sanctuary—in a state of numbness, not bothering to switch on the lights. He imagines blood on his hands, though there is none. He thinks of Lady Macbeth. His movements seem slowed and dreamlike—a castaway's vision of love. He passes a table that holds a photograph of his wife taken only weeks before the birth, while she was still in the glow of pregnancy.

He carries his deed as a beast of burden carries his load: painful but resigned to his calling. The police will come for him any minute. He is as certain of this as he is that he murdered the man. He holds no remorse. The space within him that remorse might occupy is instead filled with both a keen sense of justice and the hollow ache of loneliness. Being all alone in the world is the real hell. He is neither proud nor ashamed of the murder. He is satisfied. Pouring the vodka into the glass, he briefly perceives himself as the hooded executioner, the man who learns to accept his actions.

After many hours and many drinks the morning light comes. It paints itself in harsh geometric patterns. Fears, like shadows, play on the walls of his thoughts.

Briefly, he relives the event.

"An error!" his victim had dared to claim, his eyes begging forgiveness as Kort towered over him where he lay in his bed. Forced to drink the very waste his factory discharged, this time in full concentration, he vomited twice before a yellowish foam cemented at the corners of his lips and his nose began to run like a child's. Kort forced a third glass down him, and then it had been only a matter of minutes before it burned through his internal organs. He groped for air; his face turned a disturbing blue; his eyes enlarged. When he clearly had no fight left in him, no hope, Kort had left him—for death is only truly frightening when it appears you might yet escape it. Let the doctors come. Let the seed of hope be planted as an ambulance rushes the man away to stomach pumps and blood tests and toxicology reports. Let him hope, and let that hope be denied. Let him drink from the cup of hope only to vomit again.

The radio had confirmed it: The founding chairman of EisherWorks Chemicals was dead before Kort had completed the long drive home.

He thinks of the knock that will come to the door any minute and the years of darkness and confinement: the payment that is expected of him for this deed.

The rising sun just brushes the windowsill in a bright rectangle of mustard orange. After a few hours it becomes a trapezoid, and then the opposing jamb is flooded in a late afternoon brilliance that forces him to look away. At this same moment he also looks away from the deed for the first time. He flirts with the dangerous thought, the possibility, that the police may not come. It is at once both heady and intoxicating. He finds himself delirious with hope.

He does not avoid the guilt, he confronts it. An act born of premeditation, there is no choice but to accept responsibility for the murder. The last glint of sunlight leaves the smooth surface of the window frame, a spark snuffed out. An entire day has passed. The haze in the room gives way to darkness, and once again the consequences of his deed overwhelm him. The vodka bottle goes empty. So does his stomach. These fleeting hours seem an unexpected dividend. Certainly the knock will soon come, just as the sun will return to the windows.

He has been reared to believe they will come. He *ex-*

pects it. But what if they should not? What if by some divine act this murder went unaccounted for? What then?

The heels of the first day are nipped by the budding of the second, and so again with the third. By the dawning of the fourth day the pit of fear gives way to hunger and he eats quietly and alone. The phone has not rung. No knock has come upon the door. He is no longer frightened by his isolation, his loneliness, but quelled by it. These hours are as peaceful a time as he can recollect. He eats precious little, but he eats, finding sustenance.

By the fifth day he is cleaning up after himself. His act of only days earlier is now much more unreal than he ever imagined possible, as if someone else had committed the deed while he was but a witness. Order returns to a life where none was imagined possible, so convinced was he of his arrest. The shower water goes cold, but is not noticed. He takes a seventy-minute shower, devoted entirely to the sensation of the pressure streaming down upon his scalp, to the numbness of his head and the quieting of his thoughts. It is in the shower he finds his sanctuary within his sanctuary, and where, over the next two days, he devotes a majority of his time, no consideration of water temperature. His thoughts and his guilt are carried away down the drain.

Sleep does not come. He tries warm milk, earplugs, blindfolds, and music. He tries reading, counting, praying, and masturbation. Then it's back to the cold shower water that rains down on his head carrying his fears along with it. He justifies his deed. He dares to allow himself a glimpse of freedom. Every waking moment is perceived as freedom and therefore too sacred to sleep through.

He no longer takes food for it requires preparation and he can't think that far in advance. There is only the recent past—the murder—and this immediate moment for him. His hunger goes unnoticed, except for the insomnia; he fails to connect the two. His sustenance comes from alcohol, though try as he might—and he *does* try—he can't find intoxication. He finds headaches, he finds himself urinating often, he finds his bowels loose and violent. He finds another crack of light seeping through one of the pulled blinds and corrects the situation. He pins blankets over the windows, and when he runs out of blankets, he seals off several rooms, blocking them with furniture so he won't make the mistake of going inside and disturbing himself with sunlight. It is as if by blocking out the light, he has stopped time, has blocked out the world, has hidden away where They can't find him.

His beard grows, and his hair becomes oily and filthy despite the endless showers. He takes to cleaning his fingernails with a green plastic party toothpick. He can barely see his nails in the dark, but he cleans them all the same, cleans them until the skin beneath them bleeds.

It is the end of the alcohol that leads him to her medicine cabinet and the treasures he finds within. Never had he known what resources lurked behind her hinged mirror. In the dim light of the bath, it is her face he sees in the glass, not his; his tears on her face. Behind the mirror are a variety of recent medications for a woman unable to confront her situation, a new mother unable to cope with the deformed child that has come from her womb. A child deformed by the chemical discharge of an EisherWorks factory some three miles away. Seeing this array of prescriptions, he flirts with the thought that these took her life, not her. That these were in control, not her. But it is impossible to escape the truth: She killed their child with these drugs, and then she killed herself. They are never coming back, either of them. Kort goes off to visit them.

He greedily consumes the pills in varying combinations, delighted by the bone-dry throats, quivering limbs, and various stages of numbness they inspire. He embarks on voyages of introspection so dark that he wonders if he has gone blind, only to find it is a form of induced sleep so deep and distant that he cannot claw his way out. The small, disfigured, asexual infant is disgorged from her womb and caught by the trembling, gloved hands of a doctor at once afraid, but pretending to be otherwise.

It gets so that he cannot pass by the medicine cabinet without a handful. And so it is that he is alternately in the chair, shivering cold from his nightmares, and in the shower, shivering cold from the water.

The only warmth comes from deep within him as he recollects with some pride his deed.

He sleeps, off and on, for the better part of the next seventy-two hours. He awakens and takes a ten-minute shower, stopping when the water runs cold. Control has miraculously returned to his life. He cleans house and prepares himself a hot, nourishing meal from frozen foods. This meal won't stay down, but the next one does, and the one after that. Slowly, the blankets come down from the windows. Light returns into his life. The furniture is moved from the blocked doors. He shaves. He presses his trousers, dons a coat, and ventures outside to clear the stoop of the newspapers and mail that have collected. Then, frightened, he returns inside and locks the door like a paranoid old woman.

The frozen food is the next supply he drains. He exhausts it, still too frightened—of what he's not exactly sure —to venture out past the porch. Freedom has come, and somehow the area beyond his own door represents a test of that freedom he now has no desire to lose. It is a cherished, treasured entity, this freedom. They still haven't come for him! Has it been a week, two, three? He has lost track.

Days later, a knock comes on the front door.

Heat flashes up his spine and the hairs on the nape of his neck stand erect. His hands go clammy. His right hand is shaking and his knees feel weak.

Then he thinks: It's just a delivery, a solicitor of some sort. It's nothing. But secretly he knows who it is; who it must be.

"Police, Mr. Kort. Please answer the door. It will spare us both. I don't wish to make a scene and kick your door in,

and you don't wish to repair it." The voice waits. Kort looks
around. There must be someplace to hide. He can't think
straight. His feet won't move. Some spittle runs from the
corner of his mouth. He wipes it off on his sleeve and thinks
what a pitiful murderer he is. He should be plotting a way
out, not trembling like an idiot. "Please," comes the voice.

That's all it takes: Kort reaches out and turns the doorknob.

The man is big. He is alone. He holds the doorway like
a sentry. Sunlight flames from his shoulders. He speaks. He
even shows his identification, but Kort hears only the one
word, a word mixed in with all the others: *Inspector.*

Kort considers what it would take to kill the man.
There's only one of him. Invite him in. Make it happen. Get
far, far away. Is it possible.

"It is not what you're thinking," the man says. "Believe
me, I know what you are thinking. I have done this before,
Mr. Kort. You have not. To every problem there is a solution, to every solution, negotiation. At least in my business."
He steps through the door and presses close to Kort as he
swings the door closed. "Open some windows, please. It
stinks in here." When Kort doesn't move, the man repeats,
"Open some windows, please." He walks past Kort and does
it himself. Kort is standing, staring at the front door. Just
on the other side of that door . . .

"I am conducting the investigation into the murder of
Joseph Eisher. Would you like a cigarette?" Kort reaches
out and accepts one from the man, who then lights it for
him. It is this taste he always remembers. "I am here to
arrest you for that murder."

These are the words Kort has heard in his mind a hundred times over. They are so familiar to him that he isn't
sure if this man, this cigarette, this moment, are real or
imagined. Perhaps he's still intoxicated by the alcohol or
the drugs. There's no telling. The cigarette tastes good—
wonderful—and that's when he realizes it's no dream.

"It does not necessarily mean I *will* arrest you for that

murder," the man teases, a perverse grin on his face. The face is hard at the edges. The skin of his left cheek is rough. A bristled moustache on his upper lip juts out like a shelf. He's cut his chin shaving. But it's his eyes that hold Kort. Blue eyes—gentle, humorous, knowing. They are smiling at Kort. "I am not going to arrest you, Mr. Kort. Not necessarily. You can be of value to me. We can be of value to each other. We have much to discuss. You may call me Michael. Sit down please, Mr. Kort. You have a very important decision to make."

She drove a red BMW with a cellular phone and a compact disk stereo. The luncheon was take-out. Turkey croissant sandwiches with cream cheese and sun-dried tomatoes. Kort drank an espresso; Monique, decaf au lait. They ate on a plaid blanket by the shore of the Potomac with a distant view of National Airport. Joggers, dragging from the heat, passed in front of them.

"I read about it," she said. He looked over at her, something tugged at his heartstrings, and he flirted with a dozen thoughts—everything from running away with her to making love with her here on the blanket—before managing to shut out such ideas. "We did not take credit for it. I do not understand the *point* if we do not take credit. There was a *reason* behind it, was there not?" She shifted uneasily, tugging at her skirt. "Have we resorted to indiscriminate killing—like the Arab barbarians? Is that the path down which Michael has led us?"

"We don't take credit. That's just the point. That's the real genius of the plan. 'Let them be accidents,'" he said, directly quoting Michael but not letting her know this. "If they knew it was terrorism, they would focus on us instead of Mosner and EisherWorks. Let the public figure it out for themselves. This kind of thing: There will be endless investigations, everything from the FBI to congressional subcommittees. By now they've already begun. If necessary, some key reporters will receive important documentation from 'anonymous' sources. With our help, they will flush out the 'truth' about EisherWorks's duplicity. It will fill the papers for months. Years perhaps. Two major air accidents within a few weeks of each other. And what do we accomplish?" He counted off on his long fingers, "Mosner and the others dead; EisherWorks bankrupted; the unveiling of what amounts to an antienvironmental conspiracy between the largest chemical producers and the U.S. government agencies. Who knows what else? It's beautiful."

"And this meeting is next?"

"Yes."

"How is it to be done? You still have not explained this."

"I told you: I can't explain everything. You must understand that." He said, sipping from his coffee, "It's too hot for coffee. I should have had an iced drink. This heat is oppressive; no wonder Washington empties in August." He set the espresso down and took another bite of the sandwich. He wiped cream cheese from his lips.

"Tell me," she said in a demanding tone.

He snapped his head toward her. "I'll tell you *nothing*. Do you understand? Nothing more than you need to be told. Nothing more than *I decide* you need to be told. There's such a thing as trust, isn't there?"

"Is there?"

"Would I be eating here with you if I did not trust you?" he asked. "Completely exposed. Nowhere, no way to escape." He waited. "Well?"

She didn't look at him. She spoke to the blanket, "Sometimes I hate you for the way you are."

He was thinking: That makes two of us.

She folded the wax paper around her sandwich. A small, colorless bird bathed itself at river's edge, the splashing of its wings foaming the polluted water. Again, he felt tempted to point out the pollution to her. Instead he said, "I need you."

"I hate you."

"No you don't."

"Yes. Yes, I hate you."

"Okay. So that's it then: You hate me."

"No I don't."

"You're confused."

"Yes."

"Angry."

"Yes."

"With me?"

"With everything." A pause. Then she continued, "The meeting. When is it?"

"You need to contact the Greek. He knows the date. He can tell us."

"And that is all? That is all I do?"

"For the time being, yes. That's all."

"And later?" she asked.

He couldn't take any more of this. They could train him to keep his cool in the midst of gunfire, in handling bombs, but no one had prepared him for her. He couldn't do this without her, and she seemed to know that. "You mustn't keep asking me that. I can't tell you everything. It would be foolish to do so. But your time will come. Believe me: Your time will come." She was squirming. It bothered him. "I *need* you," he said, still believing this was what she wanted to hear. "I can't do it without you." Her eyes lit up.

He hid his smile of confidence from her by trying the coffee again.

"I thought you didn't want any more of that," she said.

"It's not so bad."

"I'll never understand you," she said in disappointment.

No you won't, he was thinking, though he didn't say so.

He reached over and drew his finger slowly on her soft, pouty lips. She licked out at it and caught it briefly. "It tastes sweet," she said quietly.

"It's you that is sweet," he countered. He felt himself respond to her. It was some kind of chemistry with them.

Around and around his finger went, slippery and warm, her tongue darting out after it.

"Let's get out of here," she said breathlessly, eyes closed.

"Yes," he agreed. "Let's."

9

WITH HER SAD brown eyes and broomstick posture, Gloria's demanding expression stopped Daggett cold. She was still angry about his refusing the promotion. It was the first time it had occurred to him that her jet black hair might be covering the truth. He felt tempted to ask her if she dyed it—it was one sure way to silence her before she spoke.

He placed his briefcase down heavily onto his desktop, and with a few nods said hello to a couple of the gang who had beaten him into work, already busy on the phones. CNN ran with the sound down low from a battered set in the corner. It ran twenty-four hours a day. The remaining desks went empty. Some of the guys had stretched the holiday weekend into a week's vacation. Others were on field assignments, a few on opposing shifts.

He said hello to her. She was playing it smug. "We get a new agent today. He'll be in any minute."

"Glo," he said, "this is important to me."

"I don't want to talk about it." She handed him a fax. "Here, this is for you."

It was the flight manifest, listing passengers who had flown from Los Angeles to Washington on the plane that the mystery woman, Maryanne Lyttle, had boarded after dropping off the rented minivan. Daggett scanned the list for her name, but it wasn't there. He couldn't allow this to discourage him. An operative would change aliases at every opportunity. They would change looks, driver's licenses, credit cards, everything. It didn't give him the kind of hard evidence Pullman was demanding to see. It left him in the familiar no-man's-land of suspicion without proof. Investigative Purgatory. He wanted to believe that Lyttle—by whatever name—was involved, but he couldn't be certain.

The new man's name was Bradley Levin. He was thirty-two, fiercely handsome, and a good deal taller than Daggett, maybe six-two, two hundred or two-ten. Strong upper body. Long, black curly hair with a shock of premature gray in the front. Gentle dark eyes, but chiseled lines to his face, his cheeks shaded by an insistent five o'clock shadow. Daggett greeted him enthusiastically, but it was an act: Although he needed help badly, the idea of working with a transfer was less than appealing. They got to know each other over more burned coffee. This time in the first-floor cafeteria. Levin had started out at the Denver field office, where he had worked kidnappings. "Miami after that. Drugs," he explained in a low, warm voice. "We took up some slack for the DEA. Surprise inspections of commercial aircraft."

"The AirEast bust?" Daggett inquired.

"That was mine," he admitted reluctantly. He blushed. Daggett was glad for the humility. It was less and less common around WMFO.

"Now Counterterrorism here with you guys. I gotta tell you: driving up here, what a neighborhood! I can see why they treat the garage like a jail for cars."

"Wait till you work the night shift. You end up carrying your piece with one in the chamber."

"I believe it."

"We're in some deep shit here. I need an independent thinker, Brad, not a yes-man. I need someone to bounce ideas off of. Work with. I need someone to do a lot of the shit work and smile through it. Your experience with the commercial airlines will come in handy. But, honestly, this is probably the worst time to come aboard here. We're frantic. We've got a live one on the run. Dangerous, as in bombs. You have less than no time to catch up on all this. You have your reading cut out for you. Tempers are on hair triggers around here, so beware. I'm working on a deadline: I've been given one more week to prove that a murder in Seattle and the crash of flight sixty-four are both connected to Bernard. So beware . . . office hours are anytime you're not sitting on the can."

"Like Miami."

"Good," Daggett said, relieved. "Then you're used to it."

"Very."

"If we're lucky, we slam-dunk this guy. If we're not so lucky . . . well, there's nothing worse than wandering a burning field littered with body parts, especially knowing it was your job to prevent it from happening. There's pressure, and then there's this kind of pressure." He paused and lost his concentration. "Anyway, welcome aboard."

"Thanks."

"They call me Michigan around here—you don't have to, but everyone else does." He took hold of the letter jacket.

"I get the idea," Levin said.

"I did some reading of my own before you got here. Your SAC in Miami wrote good things about you. Says you think first and talk later. You're single. I won't ask."

"Good, 'cause it's none of your business."

Daggett paused while the two challenged each other with stares. "It *is* my business. We're open books around here. All of us. Just so you know. Counterterrorism . . . it *has* to be that way. We've never been penetrated from the outside. Not that we *know* of anyway. You understand?"

"It's worse when you're in Drugs in Miami."

"I can believe it."

"You should. I'm not in the habit of lying."

"Well, that answers the point about your being insolent."

"As Popeye said to the potato farmer: 'I yam what I yam.' "

"That's good. I'll try to remember that." It won a smile. Daggett said, "Pity about your schooling. But if I'm Michigan, then you're Ohio. Is that okay with you?"

"Fine, as long as we both know which is the superior school," Levin said.

Daggett wasn't going to allow himself to be led into that. It was an argument that could last days. Lifetimes, maybe. Not now anyway. "An A student right through college. That's impressive."

"My parents pushed."

"What do they think of the Bureau?"

"Next question."

"They don't approve," Daggett said.

"They had me picked for an attorney, like my father. From the age of about six months."

"So now you're an overachiever. Is that supposed to explain your record? Is that what you're telling me?"

"I'm not telling you anything. You're asking. If you ask, I answer, okay?"

"You'll like it here; you'll fit in. One thing nice about Counterterrorism is you're left alone a lot. It makes for more freedom, but comes at the cost of more reports."

"What's the squad chief like?"

"Pullman? He's new to it."

"So I hear."

"He's okay. The last guy was a bounty hunter. Wanted credit for anything that happened to go right. Can't tell yet what Pullman will be like. Guys change when they get the corner office."

"I heard you turned down a promotion. Any truth to that?"

Daggett wondered if this was Gloria's doing, or just an office rumor. "I've got my reasons."

"I thought we were open books around here."

They locked eyes and Daggett sensed he had made a friend. He asked, "Any friends in the area?"

"You're my first," Levin said, testing the waters. Daggett nodded. Levin added, "Couple of people I know from Quantico should be around here someplace."

"You want to discuss assignments?"

"Why not?"

"I don't know whether you've had a chance yet to review the *Der Grund* file—"

"I have."

"Good. Then you know that in Europe they're considered a radical Green group, that they target the petrochemical/pharmaceutical industries."

"What about ten twenty-three?"

"Including ten twenty-three. It was carrying commercial chemicals in the cargo hold. They made a threat and it was ignored. One thing we know about them: They seem to have some sort of collective conscience, as perverse as that may sound. In *every* case they have issued a threat prior to committing their act of terrorism. They do this to a flaw. And their signature is that they kill using a product, or by-product, of the company they've targeted. The Semtex derivative that was used to blow up ten twenty-three was manufactured by the same company whose chemicals were in the cargo hold. A German company called EisherWorks Chemicals. Now, come to find out, the stuff on flight sixty-four was manufactured by an EisherWorks subsidiary. That's not good enough evidence for the desk jocks like Pullman, but it is for me.

"I'm convinced the murder at Duhning and flight sixty-four are connected, although I have yet to prove it. I can't even prove sixty-four was sabotaged. We have our work cut out for us. Pullman—and Mumford above him—requires more than coincidence. To make matters worse, he's under some intense pressure to sideline me long enough to write a comprehensive report on Backman's killing. All I've given him so far is a one-pager. That kind of report would take me a couple weeks—some in-house review, maybe even testimony on the Hill. You get started on something like that and suddenly it's a couple months later."

"Tell me about it. Same thing in Miami."

"I've been on the Bernard case a long time. The only way I'm going to stay on it is to deliver something of substance. I figure I've got two chances: one, I come up with hard evidence that puts Bernard's device on board flight sixty-four; two, I link a threat to a major chemical company with my suspicion that whoever's behind this is now in Washington."

"And which do I get?"

"Number two." Daggett turned in his chair to face his good ear toward Levin. With them both talking softly, he was having trouble hearing.

"Your assignment is to find their next target."

"Oh, is that all?" The oily skin between his dark eyebrows knitted with intensity. He squinted across the desk at Daggett like a nearsighted man without glasses. "Who says there *is* a next target?"

"The lab believes Bernard built *two* detonators. I think the first was on flight sixty-four, though I'm not sure we'll ever prove it. They're both barometric, so it's got to involve an aircraft. Commercial? Cargo? Who knows? You've read the file: the only real lead we have is that a woman who rented the van that was parked out front of the AmAirXpress mechanic's house in L.A., boarded a plane bound for here. That much we *can* prove. Bernard built the detonators in L.A.—sixty-four goes down in L.A. Next time we caught up with him, he was here in Washington. This woman flies to Washington. Coincidence?"

"So we play the odds," Levin said.

"I don't know what else to do. We could, and should, try asking the various chemical giants about recent threats to their operations, but the sad truth is, they get way too many of those, and they handle them themselves. They don't like the publicity that often comes with our involvement." Daggett leaned back, "You look a little overwhelmed. Too much?"

"Not at all. Just trying to see the various angles. In Miami you have the drugs and you have the money. This has a lot more angles to it, that's all. I don't want to miss any."

"Mind you, it's all hypothetical. Maybe it's not *Der Grund,* maybe there isn't a second target."

"Okay, I'm buying. So what's next?"

"Der Grund targets chemical companies. Often, the executives. Flight sixty-four fits with that—there were chemicals on board. It seems to me the first place we start.

"I think we explore every avenue we can think of," Daggett continued. "They've targeted chemical company executives in the past. So the first thing we do is get the travel itineraries for the executives—say from VP up—in every major chemical company. We see who, if anyone, is coming to town in the near future. Just to cover our bases, we should request notification of any recent threats received. If we turn up any, these should be compared by Linguistics to earlier *Der Grund* threats for overlaps."

"Will they give out itineraries that easily?"

"One thing you'll find in this squad that may be different than Drugs. All you do is mention the word *terrorism,* and people will give you damn near anything you want."

Thirty minutes later, Gloria entered the bullpen carefully balancing a plastic bowl of lentil soup along with a tuna sandwich and a large OJ. She treated him better than she treated Pullman. "You don't look so good," she told him. She placed the food squarely before him. "You should marry that girl of yours. You need someone to look after you." She attempted to straighten the papers on his desk.

Daggett playfully tapped her on the hand. "I'm not through with those."

"Even *you* can't read six files at once, dearie." She continued her cleanup, undaunted, creating space for his food. "Be nice to me, Cam Daggett, or I won't tell you that Duhning called while you were downstairs."

Daggett reached for his pink message slips.

"Fifth one down," she said, isolating it, extracting it from the others and dangling it out of his reach. "If you would remember to put your extension on voice-mail, then

little old ladies wouldn't have to answer the phone for you."
Then she handed it to him.

Reading the slip, he reached for the phone and she
said, "No, sir. You eat this food first. Doctor's orders. And
I'm standing right here until you do."

"Glo."

"Eat."

She continued fussing with his desktop while he ate,
making order out of the chaos. She rambled, as Gloria
tended to do, lecturing him on a variety of personal subjects ranging from an observation that Carrie wouldn't
"hang around forever," to the fact that "all work and no
play makes Jake a dull boy." She never quoted perfectly.

Daggett was reaching for the phone when Levin strode
into the bullpen with an ebullient expression on his face.
Daggett replaced the receiver, not wanting to quash the
younger man's enthusiasm.

Levin pulled over a chair and at Daggett's invitation,
accepted half the sandwich.

With a mouthful of food, Levin said, "This may be the
only time you'll be happy to know that one of your co-workers—namely, me—is the proud son of a dental hygienist."

Daggett looked at him peculiarly.

"I came across the lab report on that tooth we turned
up in the hotel trash."

He handed Daggett a photograph Daggett would have
preferred not to see a second time. Especially not while
eating. Daggett pushed it back at him.

"It's the *way* the tooth fragmented," Levin explained,
interpreting the gesture as an invitation to illustrate his
point. "Right here," he said, pointing. "See? Just one root
showing. Our man *may* have the other left in his jaw. If he
does, the thing will probably go south on him and he'll need
some serious attention in a hurry."

Daggett felt a wave of excitement shoot through him.
"How certain is this?"

"If that root is in there, he's in trouble. He can't fix *that* himself. So I thought we should alert all the dentists both in L.A., to see if it was done there, and here in Washington too. We'll put the word out to watch for an out-of-towner who needs work on that particular tooth. Number seventeen."

"We can't bust Kort for having a tooth repaired," Daggett pointed out, "but we can put him under surveillance. The dentist could keep a blood sample; we might even get a DNA match."

"*Two* major metropolitan areas. It's going to mean a hell of a lot of phone calls," Levin said.

"It can be done by computer. We have a phone system all set up for this kind of thing—like the phone solicitations you get. You record the verbal message, scan the numbers you want called right out of the phone book, and the computer does the rest. It dials the various numbers until a line is answered and the query responded to. The query can be as complicated or as simple as you like. Talk to Tech Services; they'll set it up."

Levin left in a hurry, taking the photograph of the tooth with him.

Daggett returned the call to Duhning and spoke to a woman named Fedorko. She had a slight midwestern accent and chose her words carefully. "We have had our work cut out for ourselves, Mr. Daggett, but we are a diligent bunch here at Duhning, as I am sure you will appreciate when you speak to Dr. Barnes tomorrow. He's an engineer on our investigation team."

"Tomorrow?" Daggett asked.

"He's on his way to Washington as we speak. I'm to set up a meeting with you or one of your associates at your earliest convenience. My understanding is that it's a matter of the utmost urgency. The message is that the simulator session with Dr. Ward was backed up to disk. Dr. Barnes will explain it further when he arrives."

For Daggett, his imagination running away with him, the next twelve hours passed slowly.

■

His meeting with Barnes began precisely at three o'clock, Wednesday afternoon, with Brad Levin in attendance. With the permission of Barnes, it was tape-recorded. Barnes, a narrow-faced man with a brush moustache and long, wispy hair, reminded Daggett of a college professor from the sixties. He knew his stuff when it came to simulators and computers, but had trouble communicating. His accent was either German or Swedish. Each time he explained a point, Daggett felt compelled to repeat his impression of what had been said to make sure he had it all straight. This consumed a lot of extra time and created extra strain. By the two-hour break, the back of his shirt was soaking wet. He kept the letter jacket on to hide it.

"I think I'm confused by all of this," he admitted when Barnes seemed to be running down.

"Go ahead," Barnes suggested.

As Levin sat quietly, Daggett said, "You said that the one thing all the simulations had in common was that they involved lack of pilot control?"

"Yes. Dr. Ward simulated release of pilot control of the aircraft at a number of different altitudes, all quite low, and *immediately* after takeoff."

"And you also said that this agrees with what we know about the AmAirXpress crash?"

"Precisely so. Yes. Loss of pilot control would help explain the behavior of flight sixty-four. We need the voice information from the Cockpit Voice Recorder to know for sure."

"We still don't have that?" Daggett turned to ask Levin.

Levin answered, "They don't want to ship it back here for examination until all the repairs are complete."

"I thought those things were indestructible," Daggett said.

Barnes corrected, "*Nothing* is indestructible. But it may

not matter. The audiotape recorded by flight control supports a cockpit fire, as I'm sure you're aware."

Daggett felt frustrated. He hadn't heard *anything* about
flight control tapes. He didn't want Barnes to know that.
"What would that prove?"

"It might explain the loss of pilot control. Toxic fumes
perhaps."

Daggett made a note of it. Toxic fumes would show up
in the autopsy report. He asked, "Why wouldn't the autopilot be on?"

"A general misconception, I am afraid. Autopilot—
auto-thrust, it's called at takeoff—is available but rarely
used because it takes the plane entirely out of the pilot's
control. Disengagement, if needed, requires several seconds, and even a single second during takeoff is an eternity.
Autopilot *is* used, but would not typically be engaged until,
say, eighteen thousand feet or so—quite a few minutes into
flight."

"It's available, but they don't use it?"

"Most accidents occur during, or just after, takeoff.
You'll find ninety-nine percent of pilots prefer to have manual control over the bird during this period."

"So you're saying—your theory is—that there was no
one at the controls? Essentially there was no pilot flying the
plane?"

"Theory?" Barnes responded. "It is physics, sir. Plain
and simple physics." He referred Daggett to his notebook
and pointed to a diagram of 64's projected flight route in
the few short minutes it was airborne. "Flight sixty-four left
the runway at this point. It crashed . . . here," he said,
pointing to Hollywood Park. "Well, you see—as I've already
shown you—it's the same with the simulation." He unrolled
a map obviously drawn by a computer. "If you remove all
control of the aircraft here," he said, pointing to his map,
"forty-seven seconds into flight, then given the appropriate
data, the simulated 959 impacts here," he said, punching his
computerized map. "If you scaled it correctly and overlaid

this map onto a map of the L.A. area, you would see that the area of impact is also Hollywood Park."

Breaking a long silence that followed, Daggett, still very much confused, asked, "What about wind speed, ground temperature, that sort of thing? It can't be an *exact* science, can it?"

"With smaller aircraft, the light winds we're talking about would certainly have made a difference. Not so with something this size. It all comes down to thrust, gravity, ground speed, and flaps. It's entirely predictable. Avionics *is* an exact science—that's what I'm telling you. If we can land an unmanned space probe on the dark side of Mars—a project Duhning was proud to be part of—we had better be able to predict the flight pattern of a commercial carrier one minute into flight!"

"But why?" Daggett asked. Barnes stared at him. How was he going to sell Pullman—and worse, Mumford—something like this? This was the type of thing you kept to yourself until you understood it. He broke his silence. "What about Ward? I know he was in Simulation—I understand that much. But what end of things? With a new aircraft like the 959, someone would have to train the new pilots, wouldn't they?"

"That's correct. The pilots have to be recertified for the 959 before they fly it. It's the same with any new aircraft."

"And if they all learn from the same guy, then essentially, during takeoff let's say, they're all going to perform about the same way as whoever taught them, aren't they?"

"That follows logically, yes. I can see that."

"And Ward—I know he was trained an engineer, but the pictures on his office walls—he was a pilot, too, wasn't he?"

"Many of us are pilots."

"But he flew jets."

"That's not unusual either. Jets are what Duhning builds."

"But my point is: There have only been what, twenty,

twenty-five pilots through the program so far—I read that in one of the reports. You haven't sold all that many planes yet."

"Twenty-seven aircraft," Barnes said, interrupting and correcting the number, "is a significant production, I can assure you."

Daggett ignored it. "Who was in charge of training those people who then trained the pilots? That would be one of the engineers, wouldn't it be? That would be some-one familiar with the new aircraft. Someone like Roger Ward. Ward was in charge of training," he stated. "Ward was Duhning's expert on flying the 959."

Barnes adjusted his glasses and flipped through some papers. A moment later, reading, he shook his head and then looked up.

He offered Daggett a puzzled, ironic expression, and then his first smile of the day. "And just exactly how did you know *that*, Mr. Dagger?"

10

MONIQUE DOWNSHIFTED AND followed the signs for the Beltway. It was the safest place for a meeting. The car purred so softly and sensually that Anthony Kort, who sat stoically in the seat beside her smoking a nonfilter, wasn't sure if it was the car or the woman making that titillating sound. She wore a sleeveless, soft pink cotton cable-knit suit with matching flats, glossy pink lipstick, and no other makeup that he could see. She glowed in her pink, the brilliant sunlight washing her in a smoky mist. She was radiant and composed. Strong and confident. He wanted her now. Right here.

Kort set the cigarette down, unfastened his seat belt, and slipped his hand under her pullover.

She hummed contentedly and reached over to stroke him.

His hand roamed the soft warm skin of her chest and then wandered lower, finding her knee, the edge of the skirt, and finally sneaking up underneath. He knew he was on safe ground. Monique liked it wild. She grinned and parted her legs. His fingers reached the top of her silk hose where he encountered a garter belt—he *loved* garter belts—and just beyond, her intense warmth, like a furnace.

"Later," she said, gently closing her legs and trapping his hand. It was a tease. Typical of her.

He freed his hand and worked on the cigarette. "So what about the Greek," he asked. "Tell me."

His efforts were useless without the Greek, a complete stranger, whose motives came into question. The Greek's front as a restaurateur/caterer covered his true business of corporate espionage. He was believed to have an extensive network of people on his payroll, some pressured into supplying information, some, like the Greek himself, motivated by money. For a fee, he could procure the architecture of Intel's latest chip circuitry, or the number of plant closures and layoffs anticipated by General Motors in the fourth quarter. He could tell you which Big Swinging Dick on Wall Street had a drug problem, or the voting patterns of a particular board of directors. He was in the information business; it had been the Greek who provided them with Roger Ward and Kevin Dougherty. Kort now relied on him for the exact date of the "secret" meeting. He found his reliance on an outsider repugnant, but at this late date saw little way around it.

In this regard, Monique served a useful purpose as a go-between. A buffer in case the Greek intended to sell Kort to the authorities. Also, communicating with the Greek involved a computer bulletin board and most of that technology had passed him by. Monique had her place as a pawn.

Still, he had to wonder: Was the fall of *Der Grund* coincidence, or had the Greek found a way to double his profits?

He could feel her reluctance to tell him whatever it was she had to tell him, and it annoyed him. "Well?"

She drove a little faster. He wasn't used to having no destination. It unsettled him. She said, "The message was that he does not have the date. The name you want, but not the date. The date has been changed, and he has no way to find out what it is."

"Impossible!" Kort hollered.

"I am only telling you what the message said."

"Impossible," he repeated. "We paid him." The date of the meeting was critical to his success. Without it . . . "I must speak with him. It must be as soon as possible. You will arrange it." Then he reconsidered. "No, no. That's no good. He must not know. He might sell me off to someone." He couldn't keep his thoughts clear. Compartments came open without his consent, flooding him with mental noise. He rolled down the window. It helped.

Several minutes passed. Kort smoked a cigarette, and then another. He tried to clear his head. "I've just had an idea," she said from behind the wheel. He didn't want to hear her ideas; he wanted time to think.

He glanced over at her; her eyes sparkled with excitement. He misunderstood it, thinking she was going to talk sex. The way she lost focus on what really mattered infuriated him. She said in a low, fierce half-whisper, "There is to be a reception next week hosted by the airline lobbyists. It is to celebrate tougher security standards at airports. Not *your* favorite cause, but, of course, as vice-president of In-Flite, I am invited. Everyone in the industry will be there. And, if you desire, so will the Greek," she stated. "I can arrange it."

He looked puzzled and she added, "A very good friend is organizing the event. It is an elaborate international cuisine. The Greek is not only a restaurateur, but also a caterer, is that not so?"

He nodded, intrigued by the suggestion. Risky, he thought, but perhaps worth the try.

"I can arrange for him to cater the Greek food at the reception. It will be no problem. We will attend—you as my guest. You get your surprise meeting with him on neutral ground. What do you think? Are you up to it?" Her face was glowing. He could smell her perfume, even over the cigarette smoke. He had underestimated her.

"I love Greek food," he said.

11

"WHERE'S CARRIE?" DUNCAN asked his father, wheeling his way to the kitchen table. The question interrupted Daggett's current train of thought, which didn't involve Carrie.

It bothered him that in this era of moon shots and microchips, bullet trains and automatic tellers, there were so few wheelchair-accessible dwellings available within commuting distance of the nation's capital. He didn't like this house much. The floor plan was strangely cut up—"for heating reasons," Carrie had explained when leasing him the place—the rooms too small, the floor plan a rat's maze. The house had been remodeled by an elderly couple, the wife chair-bound with arthritis, a pair who evidently found it difficult to stay warm and to pay the electric bills, thus the small rooms. But the light switches were set appropriately low, as were the room thermostats; the halls and passageways were four feet wide, the doors three feet six, and there were ramps where needed. It made life easier for Duncan— of primary importance to his father.

The outside of the house was white aluminum siding with fake black shutters that, if you came too close, looked cheap. The fake chimney, a poorly built chase of faux-brick vinyl and wallboard, really irritated him. Of all things! Why such pretense? The only explanation seemed to be that every other house on the block had a chimney. Despite his problems with the place, he knew Carrie was right: a house is made a home by the people in it, its personality determined by the inhabitants.

"She didn't stay over," Daggett answered.

"How come?"

"You want to know why?" Daggett asked. He and Duncan were always honest with each other. "Because she's mad at me for working so much. For promising I'll do things and then not following through. For leaving you alone so much of the time."

"Like Mom," the son said. It was an observation for him—a memory—nothing more, but it devastated his father.

Daggett suddenly saw himself as a man doomed to repeat his mistakes, despite his better intentions. He wanted to blame fate, but knew better. He admitted, "She thinks you spend too much time with Mrs. Kiyak and not enough with me—or actually the other way around, that *I* don't spend enough time with you."

"Sometimes you do," Duncan said, and the truth again stung Daggett. Carrie was right. That hurt him even more.

"Mrs. Kiyak's okay," his son said lamely, his lack of enthusiasm driving yet another spike through Daggett's heart. "Sometimes she smells really weird. Old people smell weird."

"You like her, don't you?" Daggett asked in a tone that forced the boy to agree. Patterns. He used the same technique with Carrie, though with less effect. He was thinking about Lynn, again. Wondering how much she had to do with Carrie's absence. Wondering why she dominated his thoughts. Could he use the investigation as an excuse to call? Did he dare tell her that since their reunion he had heard her voice behind him, had seen a piece of her in every woman he passed on the street? That he was haunted by the memory of a few fleeting hours of happiness, and that he laughed aloud when he recalled the image of the fireman being knocked down by the horse?

"School starts in a couple days," Duncan said, avoiding an answer.

When they had both finished breakfast, Duncan backed up the chair—Daggett's cue to open the back door. The two went outside into the small backyard and the chin-up bar.

Duncan urged, "All you have to do is sign the form. Couldn't you lie, just once?"

"You're making headway, Dunc. You're doing just fine."

Duncan clasped the bar tightly and pulled with all his strength, arms quivering. He made two pull-ups easily, but trembled at the third. He needed five to qualify for the canoe trip. Daggett wanted to shove his hands beneath the boy's arms and cheat him up. But only if requested—that was the rule. After several long seconds, Duncan said, "Okay."

Daggett felt the warmth of his son between his hands. He assisted, but avoided doing the work for him, feeding him the cold steel bar gradually until it graced the fine hairs of his chin. It would not be too many years before those hairs would be whiskers. Time, the common enemy. The last tryout for the Indian summer canoe trip would be held in just three weeks. By then they needed all five pull-ups. It wasn't much time. Daggett hoisted the boy again, and again. He'd give anything to see the boy qualify. Duncan's arms shook like rubber but he managed six in a row—assisted.

"That's good work," Daggett said.

Duncan slapped down into the chair, smiling.

Daggett wanted to hug him. He said, "Weights and push-ups will help."

"We're getting there, Dad. I *know* I can do this."

"Damn right."

"Have another cup of coffee," the boy instructed. "I'll try some on my own."

"Just holler," Daggett said, hesitating before heading inside, preparing himself to sit by the window and pray for miracles.

The same every morning.

Just before lunch, Daggett and Bradley Levin took the FBI shuttle van to the Hoover Building, where they were briefed by a lab technician on the variety of trace evidence discovered inside the Dodge Caravan that had been rented by Maryanne Lyttle in Los Angeles on the day of the crash. As occasionally happened, the results of that work had been erroneously sent to the lab at the Hoover Building rather than directly to Daggett at Buzzard Point. This time the error happened to yield some benefits. Daggett and Levin received a full, expert briefing. As predicted, the van had not been cleaned very thoroughly, which meant that the scientific scrutiny undergone by the LAFO forensics squad had reaped a good deal of microscopic evidence. "You play racquetball, Ohio?" Daggett asked as the two entered the basement corridor in the Hoover Building that led to the loading bay where they would wait for the return shuttle.

"You bet."

"You doing anything for lunch?"

"Whipping your ass."

Twenty minutes later they were suited up. Daggett stuffed his briefcase into a crammed locker and forced the door closed, then locked it.

Levin said, "You sleep with that thing, Michigan?"

"Backman had a slight problem of confusing authorship of good ideas. He seemed to think they were all his." He pointed to the locker. "Conditioning, I'm afraid."

The back wall of the court facing the viewing seats was sealed in heavy Plexiglas, which Daggett appreciated because you could talk in here without concern of being overheard. Early on in the game, as his blood began to circulate, his brain came alive again. Meetings tended to numb him.

Levin proved a good player. The shots came fast and hard. Levin served the first game and was winning four to one when Daggett reviewed the case, hoping to distract him. "We're assuming Ward's killer took a *train* from Portland to L.A. Not a plane. What's it tell us about him?"

Levin played out the point, winning it, and then answered. "He's probably carrying a piece. Maybe an entire arsenal. Trains are safer."

Daggett jumped all over the next serve and won the point. As he approached the box he said, "I mean about the *man*. What about *him?* I don't know about you, Ohio, but the way I work . . . I could give a shit what kind of gun a guy's carrying. My concern is what kind of mind is controlling the finger that's on the trigger of that gun. See? This guy orders a pair of pliers from room service and yanks his own wisdom tooth in his hotel room. Now *that* tells me something. The blood type on the tooth, that's pertinent to the case, sure it is; it may prove useful at some point. But that's not really what interests *me.* You see what I'm saying?"

Levin didn't answer. Daggett served. Levin swung and missed. Good. Three, four. He served again; they had a tremendous rally and Levin won the point. Oh well.

"Maybe he doesn't like flying," Levin said, midpoint, a point he subsequently won. "Maybe that's why he puked inside the simulator."

"Good!" Daggett shouted loudly inside the small court. "That's *exactly* what I mean."

"If I were in his line of business, I might have a fear of flying myself."

"Anything more?" he encouraged. Levin won a string of points. Daggett tried to concentrate on the ball. Levin was proving a little *too* good.

"He's patient," Levin said between serves.

Daggett allowed the serve to bounce away from the corner without even swinging for it, which won Levin's attention. "Patient to the point of being cool. Even chilly. Fucking stone cold, is more like it."

"Brass balls."

Daggett added, "That's a long time stuck on a train, well aware the body you left behind has probably been found. It would drive *me* crazy, I can tell you that. If I thought someone might be after me, a train is the last place I would want to be."

"Maybe he didn't have any choice. Maybe his acrophobia is so bad he can't fly at all."

"Maybe." The next few points went to Levin as well. Daggett won one finally and then served several winners. "What do you make of all the trace evidence we just heard about?"

"Make of it?" Levin asked, looking for some guidance.

"Yes," Daggett replied, giving none.

After the point Levin answered. "The brown hair on the driver's headrest was from a healthy woman. Oil content indicates it's real hair which is nice for us because our Miss Lyttle is a brunette, and that fits. Red hairs in the back were from a wig. Probably him. Dougherty remembered him as a redhead. Because smart operatives seldom do the driving, she'd be in the driver's seat, and the operative in the shotgun or in the back. We have the cigarette ash in the seat fabric to support that. Same chemical composition as the ash from the cigarette butts you found in that parking lot. Pullman wants evidence . . . there's a match. No pun intended."

"And there's the Anbesol," Daggett reminded. "The fact that those were fresh spills helps us."

"Which further supports *my* theory that he made a mess of the extraction and that tooth is still bothering him."

"Agreed. Score a point for you."

At the mention of points they went back to the game. Levin won by a considerable margin. "Chalk up one for Ohio State," he crowed. Goaded to a frenzy, Daggett jumped to an early and commanding lead in the following game. For the glory of Big Blue. He fought hard, but to his dismay Levin staged an exasperating comeback and won.

"Another?" Daggett asked.

"I'll play if that's what you want. What is it about you Michigan guys? You never know when to quit."

Just right. Cocky. Defiant. Independent within the framework of loyalty. Daggett handed Levin the ball, raised his racquet, and stepped into the corner ready for the younger man's best shot.

Daggett won the next three games straight.

Monday noon, he was summoned to Mumford's office. "What exactly are you after, Michigan? Maybe I can help you." It was an unusual but not unexpected opening to a meeting, given that it came from the mouth of Richard Mumford, Special-Agent-in-Charge of the Washington Metropolitan Field Office. The SAC lorded over 640 special agents, second in size only to New York City. Much of WMFO's work extended into the territory of the FBI's other fifty-five field offices, and so Mumford's power and authority was in some ways like that of the Director's. Daggett thought of him more as a general than a director, perhaps because of his substantial size, or the way he kept himself in shape; perhaps because of his intimidating confidence, or his strong voice, or his habit of looking inside you as he spoke. His eyes were a relentless Mediterranean blue. His face had the hard bones of a boxer. He carried a golfer's deep tan and a full head of hair, belying his fifty-odd years.

"I'm after Bernard's detonators, sir," Daggett replied carefully. "That's my present ticket."

Mumford's corner office was large enough for a three-hole chip-and-putt and looked out over the Anacostia River. It held two large brown leather couches, a dark wood coffee table, and an enormous nineteenth-century desk that dominated the center of the room like an island in a sea of carpet. Photos and old dark oil paintings in gilded frames adorned the walls. It didn't fit with the rest of Buzzard Point's bleakness, but it fit Mumford. He was comfortable here, arms spread wide on the couch behind him, making it look more like an oversized chair. Mumford had a favorite-uncle quality about him. Daggett knew most of the stories about the man were true, though guys like this took on mythical proportions after a while and you had to be careful what you believed. What was important to Daggett was that Mumford would stand up for anyone, anything, he believed in; would confront anyone. If he had fears, he never showed them. The rumors were that he was loud and opinionated, whether in the Director's office or in a closed-door meeting of a Senate subcommittee. He was famous for once telling the president that his fly was down by saying: "You're about to lose some votes, sir."

Mumford could grant him carte blanche or pull him from this assignment with a snap of his fingers. Daggett kept that thought foremost in his mind.

"This new guy, Levin, has been making a bunch of phone calls," Mumford stated. "He's working with you, isn't he? Tell me about these itineraries you've requested."

"We're looking for linkage to sixty-four. That's all."

"The vote on the AmAirXpress crash isn't in yet. Am I right? The investigation isn't ours; it belongs to the NTSB. Besides, you shouldn't be working on sixty-four anyway. It's not your ticket and, to my knowledge, there has been no positive linkage to *Der Grund.* The Office of Origin on that one is Los Angeles. Don't fuck around with me, Michigan. I'm told the tenth-floor fax machine has been spitting out itineraries all afternoon. Just what exactly is your—*our*—interest there? I *am* supposed to know what's going on around here. I asked Paul Pullman; he didn't know. So now I'm asking you."

"Because of *Der Grund's* possible involvement, and because a lot of circumstantial evidence points here to Washington, we're looking for a possible chemical industry target that might be coming here to Washington."

"But no *hard* evidence linking *Der Grund.* Am I right?"

"The evidence is limited to circumstantial at the moment," Daggett acknowledged. "But there's a growing amount of it and it points here, so it only followed, logically, to determine which executives of which companies have trips planned here to Washington."

Silence. Mumford, deep in thought, lifted himself out of the couch, approached his desk, yanked open a drawer

and fished out a half-empty bag of potato chips. He didn't
offer any to Daggett. He sunk his hand into the bag as he sat
back down. After eating for a minute he said, "What happens in our line of work, Michigan, with as many investigative agencies as there are here in Washington, is we end up
opening the other guy's can of worms by mistake. When
this happens, it usually only requires a couple of phone
calls to straighten it out." He ate a few more chips. "If there
are priority or national security considerations at play,
then—depending on circumstances—secrets will, or will
not, be shared."

Daggett said, "And in this case?"

"There was a meeting to be held here in Washington.
Top-level people. We weren't supposed to know about it.
But I'm told it's going to be pretty damn clear from those
itineraries what's going on, and the people who called don't
want *anyone* knowing about this meeting, so they've had to
change the date. All because of you."

"All we did—"

"Without knowing it, by going after these itineraries,
you pointed out a chink in the armor. It has people worried
that someone else could have done the same thing, and they
don't like the thought of that. This thing was—*is*—supposed
to be very quiet," he said, whispering for effect. He finished
the bag of chips, crumpled it up, and tossed it across the
room, missing the wastebasket, which clearly disappointed
him.

"Now, because you stepped in it, it's ours. Cute, huh?
No one wants responsibility for the safety of these executives, and since we're counterterrorism for this city, guess
who gets it? There are six bigwigs coming to this thing.
Coming *and* going. Some by private carrier, some by commercial. We have a detonator that remains unaccounted
for. Yes," he said, answering Daggett's surprised look, "I
read my agents' memos." He huffed. "It's a fucking security
nightmare, and now, thanks to this itinerary business,
thanks to *you,* it's all ours. *Yours.* We're the ones now re-

sponsible for the safety of those executives while they're in transit. I'm giving it to you, partly because of the secrecy involved, partly because I suspect Bernard's detonators are involved. Mostly because I don't want anything to do with it. Technically it's domestic, it should be C-one, not C-three, but I'm overlooking that. You're the one who opened the can of worms; you're the one who gets to eat its contents.

"You're one of the best agents who has ever worked for me, Michigan. I'm not fucking kidding. That's why I overlook that stupid letter jacket, and half the other rules you break. Linking Bernard to *Der Grund* took nothing short of genius. You should have had a medal for that one. I've let you ride on that success for longer than I should have because you have a nose for this shit. I've left you alone. You think I didn't know Backman stole that file from you?" Daggett sat there stunned, unable to answer. "Fact is, Backman —and I liked the man—was safer for all of us behind a desk. I gave Bob the promotion and I told him to leave you alone. And alone you have been left. Now the goons on the Hill want me to stick you behind a desk for a couple weeks so you can explain how it was that Bob opened that suitcase and blew himself and our prime suspect to hell and gone. I've held them off because I've wanted you in the field. But this time, because of who is involved, I'm out of luck. *You're* out of luck.

"The safety of these business people is now your prime responsibility, your absolute *first priority*." He cautioned, "Don't mix up your priorities."

"No, sir."

"Bernard, the crash of flight sixty-four, this stiff in Seattle—forget about them all. You've got bigger fish to fry. And let me pass along a little insight of my own: The people I'm talking about don't give something like this away. It's their meeting—Top Secret—and yet they get me on the horn and hand this thing off to me before I can think how to duck it. You got to ask yourself why.

"It's because they're afraid of it, Michigan. That's the

only explanation. Now, if this thing goes south, if they lose one of these guys to whoever has Bernard's other trigger, they can point the finger over at us.

"You brought us into this by requesting those itineraries. Now it's *my* ass on the line, and I don't like that. Stay focused. Those planes—the well-being of those executives—come *first.*"

The SAC stood and walked Daggett to the door where he handed him a red file folder and waited as Daggett signed off for it. "For God's sake, keep this on you at all times," he said. "These are the *new* itineraries. Who's coming to town, how they're getting here, how they're getting home. As long as they're in the air or on the runway, they're your ticket. You can't do this alone. Take the new guy from Drugs—I'll do the paperwork. But no one else. That," he said, pointing to the folder, "is our only copy of the specifics. No photocopying. No eyes, other than yours. Understood?"

Daggett nodded.

Mumford eased his office door shut, closing out Daggett, who looked up to see one of the executive suite's three secretaries staring at him. He had that strange sensation she had violated his privacy. He wondered if that was how women felt when he imagined them without their clothes on. She forced a smile and went back to her work. She wasn't all that bad-looking and he realized he had never seen her before.

Holding on to the red file, Daggett felt naked himself. He broke into a quick walk, headed straight to the bullpen, and locked the file away in his briefcase, where it belonged.

12

HE HAD LIVED in agony for the last eighteen hours; he had no choice but to seek the help of a professional.

The dentist's office, chosen at random from the Yellow Pages, occupied the second story of a contemporary red brick building off N Street. Kort approached the officious-looking receptionist and introduced himself as Albert Kotch. He touched his jaw where it glowed an infectious red, apologized for not phoning ahead, and in the same breath explained that he was more than willing to wait out the entire day if necessary, if there was any hope—any hope at all—of seeing Dr. Rosen. After a quick check in the back room, the receptionist smiled and pointed to the waiting room. Kort sat back with the copy of *People* magazine he had bought at a newsstand. How could he resist a cover story on the downing of AmAirXpress flight 64?

The article was titled "Sifting Through the Wreckage." It focused on Lynn Greene, a good-looking explosives expert running the FAA's investigation. And whereas the eyes of the average reader would certainly have remained on the shapely Ms. Greene, his did not. Instead, he studied the bits and pieces of 64's debris scattered over the smoking background. Other magazines had carried other pictures, but she was standing right among the wreckage; this was good stuff. He saw the wires, the bulkhead, the scraps of fuselage, and, only incidentally, the paramedics, the firemen, the stretchers, and the ambulances.

The article itself was a letdown—it concentrated too much on her and too little on the crash. Over the course of his cross-country train ride, Kort had read several newspa-

per pieces on the crash. These had been long on content,
but short on visuals. This *People* piece proved much the
opposite. As he reached the end, one photograph stood out.
He knew the face because there had been a one-hour television special comparing Lockerbie to 1023. During this
show, Special Agent Cameron Daggett had been pointed out
to Kort by Michael Sharpe, who knew him by face because
of his own police work, and Daggett's close association with
the Frankfurt bomb squad during the 1023 investigation.
Now, here, at the end of Kort's well-filed and exceptionally
clean fingernail, the same face looked out from the pages.
He stood well in the background, slightly blurred but
clearly visible, turning to avert his face from the camera.
Caught, nonetheless.

Hostility surged through Kort like a drug. Enemies. So
Daggett was on this investigation as well. Did it mean he
had made the connection to Bernard's detonator? A hot bolt
of pain gripped his head. They had gone to great lengths to
use a device that could fool the investigators. Had they
failed?

"Mr. Kotch?"

It took a moment for Kort to identify with the alias, he
had not used it in so long. To the receptionist he said,
"Sorry, infection must have hurt my hearing." He smiled at
her politely and she smiled back.

"There's been a cancellation," she said.

Rosen, a balding man with a prominent nose, a cleft
chin, and a tiny scar by his left eye, wore a white doctor's
jacket over an Oxford button down and beltless trousers
with a stretch waist. He wore leather shoes with thick rubber soles and had the breathy voice of a conspirator. A
poster, Scotch-taped to the ceiling, depicted the Chesapeake
in autumn. New Age music played quietly from a speaker
mounted by the window.

There were three stalls. A hygienist in each of the first
two, and Rosen with his plump Chinese assistant at the end.

Kort, aka Kotch, sat and then lay back in the padded dental chair, thanking Rosen for seeing him. He explained, "The tooth came out a few days ago while chewing a caramel, but I think some of it may still be in there."

Rosen snapped a pair of latex gloves on his hands, and, already inspecting, said, "It was your wisdom tooth, Mr. Kotch." He glanced up at his assistant. *"Seventeen,"* he said strongly to her. To Kort he then explained, "Nasty-looking infection. We'll get you on a course of Amoxicillin following this, to take care of that infection." The assistant dropped a group of stainless steel tools, scattering them loudly onto the floor. "Li," he said harshly, "why don't you call that in *now* while I'm exploring, and that way we won't keep Mr. Kotch waiting. Do you have a favorite pharmacy, Mr. Kotch?" he asked the man in the chair.

Kort, caught by the question, was relieved when Rosen added, "There's a place on Twenty-third we use quite a bit. It's not far." Kort nodded, his mouth occupied by two of Rosen's fingers. The assistant still sat on Kort's left staring at his misfortune, red-faced. Rosen snapped at her: "Well, Li, clean it up, and make that call." She did so.

Rosen clucked his tongue sympathetically and said, "It's messy in there, Mr. Kotch." He turned to his left, opened a drawer, and withdrew a plastic gas mask enclosed in a clear plastic bag.

Kort saw this and said, "No gas, Doctor. Thank you anyway. I'll sit still."

"Impossible. It's too infected. I'll have to cut. It may require a stitch or two."

"Novocain then. No gas," Kort said emphatically.

"I can't make any promises," the doctor said. "I suggest the gas."

"I understand. Thank you. Novocain will be just fine."

The doctor seemed nervous. Kort attributed this skittishness to the dilemma of gas versus Novocain, or a professional's concern for a patient's well-being, but as he rolled his head and caught sight of the man's eyes, a pang of alarm cut through him.

Kort's defensive, almost paranoid, nature took over. He compartmentalized the experiences of the last few minutes and reviewed them individually. Rosen had overemphasized the tooth number. *"Seventeen,"* he had said to his assistant. "Why don't you call that in *now,*" he had ordered. On the other hand, because he had selected this office at random, no one could have been expecting him. Just as he was convincing himself he was oversuspicious, he noticed the X-ray machine. Why suggest anesthesia *before* taking X rays? Something wasn't right.

"Mouth open, please?" Rosen said, hovering over Kort like a raven over carrion: in his talons, the hypodermic with its glistening needle.

The Chinese assistant returned to Kort's side in too much of a hurry and stared at Rosen intently. The doctor refused to look in her direction. "Head back," Rosen instructed, placing one hand gently on Kort's shoulder. The needle continued its approach. Kort's eyes danced between the two, doctor and assistant, back and forth. And there it was: a last-second silent reproach from doctor to assistant.

Kort knew.

His reaction occurred as if rehearsed a hundred times. In one deft motion Kort's hands secured the wrist of the assistant, snatched the hypodermic from the doctor's fingers, and then, smoothly, delivered the full contents into the soft flesh of the assistant's pinned forearm. The assistant screamed as the needle pricked her skin and Kort plunged the drug into her. She broke loose, took three steps, and collapsed heavily to the floor. She had fainted in fear. Rosen, on the other hand, flailed about in complete panic.

Kort flew out of the chair, knocked Rosen's arms aside, spun him around and pulled him into a choke hold. He tightened the hold. Kort produced his Beretta and used its threat to contain the hygienist, who had appeared from the next booth. Her eyes bugged out with fear. Seconds later, Rosen's body went slack. Kort let him fall to the floor. He backed through the door into the reception area. The mother and child had gone, no one else was waiting. The receptionist, half paralyzed with fear, clung to the phone. Kort rushed her, grabbed the receiver, and replaced it in the cradle. He dragged her to the office door, which he locked, and took her into the back where the cowering hygienist had slumped to the floor with her arms above her head. Kort pushed the receptionist toward the hygienist. She stepped over the body of Rosen's assistant.

He had to assume Rosen's assistant had phoned the police, or worse, the FBI. Too much time had elapsed. He needed a disguise if he hoped to leave the building. Of the two women before him, the hygienist was by far the larger.

Eyes darting about the area, his attention fell on the mask Rosen had intended to use on him. "You!" he said, to the hygienist. "Gas." He waved the gun at the receptionist. "Quickly!"

"Thank God," the receptionist said. The hygienist fumbled with her equipment, all thumbs, but managed to get a mask over the cooperative receptionist and put her under.

"Now, out of your clothes," Kort said.

"I have money!" the woman blurted out.

"Now!" he hollered.

Crying, the hygienist shed her dress in seconds. "Pl-please," she muttered, awkwardly stepping out of the dress as if she had never done this.

"The slip, tights, and bra," he instructed, starting to undress. He could have forced her to take the gas first, but undressing an unconscious woman would be too difficult and time-consuming. Frightened, this woman moved very quickly. She lowered the slip to the floor, and peeled herself out of her hose, revealing white bikini underpants. "God, no," she mumbled again.

She was finished protesting. Her teeth chattered with fear as she unhooked the bra. She removed it tentatively,

hiding her breasts in folded arms. She sobbed uncontrolla-
bly, head hung.

"The gas!" he demanded. "Quick!"

She obeyed, juggling his orders with her modesty. She
sat down, legs held fast together. "Don't hurt me," she
begged. She turned on the gas, placed the mask over her
face, and moments later fell motionless.

Bradley Levin came down the hall at a full run. He
pulled Daggett out of earshot of passersby and whispered in
broken breath, "We just got a call from a dentist's office on
N Street. Wisdom tooth—number seventeen. He's in the
chair *right now.*"

There was no time to alert Pullman. "We'll need
backup," Daggett said as the two of them ran toward the
waiting elevator, their effort attracting attention. Levin got
a hand in the elevator and held it. "We'll phone it in from
the car," Daggett said as the doors shut.

Daggett drove. Levin placed the flashing light on the
dash and handled the car's cellular phone. The desolate
ghetto of Buzzard Point blurred past. When Levin finished
with the phone he reported, "They've dispatched two cars.
One is backup for us—they'll handle ground level. The
other is for surveillance on the pharmacy in case we miss
him."

"Pharmacy?"

"The girl who called it in gave us the name of a pharmacy on Twenty-third."

"Call the dentist. See if he's still there." Daggett glanced
over. "What's wrong?" Levin had turned a scarlet red.

"I don't have the number. It's a Rosen—Dr. Rosen."
Levin snatched up the cellular and dialed information. Daggett scowled from behind the wheel. He fished an antacid
from his pocket and chewed it.

"It's ringing," Levin announced.

Daggett stopped chewing; white pieces of chalk adhered to his lower lip. He ran a red light, dodging the traffic. Levin clutched the dash.

"Still ringing," Levin said, in a constricted voice. "No answer."

Anthony Kort, stuffing the bra with his own dirty socks, froze as the phone began to ring.

He fought for self-control, efficiency his only hope for escape. He pulled the panty hose as high as they would go. The dress wouldn't zip closed over his wide shoulders, so he donned a lab jacket. He tied a pink scarf over his head and under his chin, covering his sideburns, put on a pair of large sunglasses and slung a purse over his shoulder. They could be out there by now, watching the building; they could be stopping every man they saw. But a woman?

Carrying a shopping bag filled with his own clothes, he took a deep breath, unlocked and opened the office's outer door, and stepped into the empty hallway. He headed for the stairs but then changed his mind to return to the elevator. Who would use stairs in this heat? When the elevator finally arrived it was empty, and he heaved a sigh of relief. He wouldn't pass too close an inspection.

As the heavy doors shut, he instinctively touched the weapon hidden just beneath the surface of clothing in the top of the bag.

As Levin and Daggett entered the office building's crowded lobby, Daggett waved Levin toward the fire stairs and headed straight for the elevator, fearing he was too late, hoping he might be wrong. The two most likely explanations for the unanswered phone were that the suspect had disconnected the phone and fled or that he had killed everyone. There was only an outside chance the man was still here.

In this building devoted to medical professionals, the lobby churned with activity. People from all walks of life stood clustered by the two elevators, which came open at nearly the same moment. Daggett, only a few yards off, stopped short and tried to get a good look at those disembarking, keeping his suspect's vague description foremost in his mind: fortyish, male, average height, average build, possible red hair, possible swollen jaw . . .

As the impatient group in front of him merged into those leaving the elevators, he felt overwhelmed by the variety of faces that blurred past him: this man was bald, this one too short. Too many.

An unexpected push came from behind as a fat lady made for the open elevators. Daggett lost his balance and bumped a nurse coming at him.

Daggett! Kort thought as a fat lady pushed the man into him. A few minutes earlier, a blurred magazine photograph, now the man in the flesh. Head down! he reminded himself as he feigned attention on the contents of the shopping bag: never look back. FBI agents were like rodents, if you caught sight of one, then there were scores unseen. He kept his hips pumping ever so slightly, making certain not to overplay the part, his nerves raw, his skin prickling beneath the dress.

He had no trouble spotting the nervous young man with the dark hair who stood by the fire stairs. He kept an eye on him as he approached the doors. If there was to be trouble, it would come from that direction. Any others? Were they outside in their officious unmarked cars, eyes trained on the entrances? Kort moved up to a noisy group of professional-looking types that bunched at the outer doors. The topic of conversation was the hot weather. As they pushed through the doors, he stayed with them. The man holding the door sparked at the sight of a nurse's uniform and said with a British accent, "I don't believe we've met. Are you coming along to—" and caught himself when he recognized an obvious transvestite. "So sorry," he demurred, side-stepping away from the silent Anthony Kort.

At the corner, Kort turned right and headed off alone.

■

Daggett covered his left hand with his handkerchief and pinched the doorknob tightly to avoid smearing any possible prints; his right hand remained stuffed inside his letter jacket ready with his weapon.

Locked!

He tried it again, to no avail.

An evil foreboding overpowered him. Had he gone too far in alerting the city's dentist offices? He had knowingly involved the inexperienced, the innocent. He wanted out of here. Let somebody else discover the carnage. Not him. Not again. He had had enough for one lifetime.

Ten minutes later, the building superintendent opened the door. Gun down, Daggett slipped inside. The medicinal smell of a dentist's office was something he associated with pain.

The reception area was empty. He hesitated briefly, took the gun in both hands, trained it at the floor in front of him and quickly rounded the corner into the suite. Dead bodies. All female. Three of them. One, naked. To his right, the doctor . . . He felt his eyes sting, his stomach knot.

He jumped around the partition, ready to shoot, and progressively searched what turned out to be a file room, a bathroom, and a storage closet. It was only as he dared to look at the bodies once more that he noticed the naked one breathing. Relief came stubbornly. Could they be alive? Later, he would think how odd it was that he should accept death more readily than life, tragedy more readily than survival.

As he inspected the fallen bodies he found all with a solid pulse, only the dentist had a visible injury, and superficial at that. This discovery was at once both disturbing and unsettling, unexpected and appreciated.

His defenses relaxed, he suddenly understood the meaning of this one woman's nakedness. He rushed into the hall. Not waiting for the elevators, he bounded down the fire stairs in leaps and jumps, hand singing on the rail. As he burst through the door, he found Levin's semiautomatic trained on him.

"A woman!" Daggett said too loudly. "We're looking for a *woman.*"

"Aren't we all!" came the voice of a man mopping the floor not ten feet away.

Daggett would have called for paramedics, but the paramedics in Washington were notoriously late, if they ever arrived at all. Instead, he called in a medic who belonged to WMFO's tactical response squad, the FBI version of a SWAT team.

On this man's advice, paramedics were called in anyway, responding at about the time the women came around. All but Li, Rosen's assistant, who remained under from a high dosage of anesthetic.

The victims were suffering from shock, and in the sweltering August heat and humidity all four were driven away fully wrapped in blankets.

The police issued a Be On Lookout for a man wearing a nurse's uniform, but not surprising to Daggett, nothing came of it. The afternoon dragged on, Daggett impatient to interview those involved.

He phoned Carrie, who was out—was she ever in?—and left a message. Mrs. Kiyak promised to stay with Duncan until Daggett made it home, which, he acknowledged, might be quite late. Personal matters handled, he and Levin found a burger and beer at a local bar and ate in relative silence, the cloud of failure hanging over them. They returned to Buzzard Point by seven, which was the previously arranged hour for Rosen's interview. His assistants, all but Li, who had finally awakened at the hospital, were to follow.

To Daggett's disgust, Rosen's employees arrived with husbands and attorneys in tow, bent on self-protection and suing Rosen. This, in turn, required Daggett to solicit one of the Bureau's on-call attorneys, a middle-aged woman who had to commute in from Alexandria. The attorneys combined to delay matters for several more hours and dilute their clients' testimony down to nothing.

At one o'clock in the morning, Daggett headed for home knowing nothing more than when he had started, angry enough to kick a hole in a wall. He sent Mrs. Kiyak home, poured himself a deep drink, and drank it on the small flagstone patio off the kitchen. The drink only served to depress him. The only objects in the night sky, other than a few brave stars, were jet aircraft. He took his second drink in front of CNN. He was chewing two antacids when his pager and phone sounded simultaneously.

"Dad?" he heard his son's groggy voice call from his bedroom.

"I've got it, Son," Daggett called out, lifting the receiver. He closed his eyes tightly, hoping that for once it was a wrong number.

It was the right number.

Pullman's weary voice said, "It's been a long one for you, Michigan, and I could put someone else on it, but I thought you'd want it first."

"Paul?" Daggett suddenly felt the drinks. He didn't appreciate the preamble. He'd had a day of it.

"They woke *me* up on this one, Michigan, but it's your ticket. This dentist. This Dr. Rosen. He never made it home, Michigan. His wife's worried sick. I thought *we* had better go looking for him rather than put city uniforms on it."

Dr. John Rosen is the first to leave the FBI following the interviews. He is still shaken from his experience of that afternoon, rattled by the hours of interrogation, desperate for a stiff drink, some dinner, and a long night's sleep.

All afternoon he has been thinking about his children and about his wife. You go through something like this and you learn where your priorities lie. If he hadn't had obligations to his patients, he would have booked a flight for two to Flagstaff and spent a week with his parents at their home just outside Cottonwood. He would have drowned himself in gin and tonics and made love as many times as his sex organ could handle it. The tentative nature of life had reared its ugly head. He feels old and vulnerable.

After a block, he gets lucky and flags a cab. It smells like cigarettes. The radio blares news of the Middle East. A day earlier he might have been interested, but not tonight. He wants to hold her. He wants to get home and hold her and tell her how much he loves her. God, how he loves her.

"Here?" the cabbie asks.

"Fine," he answers, paying too much for such a short ride. The world is full of criminals.

To reach his parked car—the reason for his return—he can either enter the building and take the elevator or simply walk around back. At this late hour he chooses to walk it. The private parking garage is well lit. Only a few cars remain parked at this hour. As he's heading toward his, he notices her. She's squatting by the front tire of the car next to his. The tire is completely flat. She's tugging on the rim of the wheel thinking it's a hubcap.

"You can't do it with your hands," he tells her. "There's a tool you use for that." He fishes for his keys. "I have a cellular. I could call a service station."

She looks up at him. A pretty face beneath a curtain of fine dark hair curled at the shoulders. Bangs. Huge brown eyes. Startling in the way they dominate her face. High cheekbones. Wet red lips that sparkle as she smiles. "Would you mind?"

It's her French accent that throws him. She's too pretty and it's too late at night. He knows nearly everyone in this building by sight, but he doesn't know her. As his mind attempts to remain rational, to seek an explanation, he senses the man standing behind him. He hears the familiar voice before he can think of what to do. "Lightning *does* strike twice," it says. His knees go all watery; he can barely stand. His vision shrinks as if someone has strapped blinders onto him. He's lost his breath.

"He is going to pass out," the woman says in a panicked voice, and that brings him around.

"No," says the man who belongs to the gloved hand that sticks to his neck as it grabs him. "He's going to be fine."

The ride in the elevator takes forever. It is he who breaks the police seal, he who keys in the security code, he who locks the door behind them.

"You will finish what you started," the one with the infected 17 says. "She's here to make sure you do just that." The gloved hand pats him on the shoulder. "She'll kill you if you fuck it up."

She smiles at him. She doesn't look like a killer, but he believes every word. His heart hasn't worked this fast since the hundred-yard dash in high school. That was 1966.

"You'll use Novocain this time. No tricks."

"Why?" he asks.

"Because my tooth hurts," this horrible man answers.

"I mean why me?" he restates.

"Where's the last place on earth I would be tonight?" the man asks before answering himself, "Right in this chair." The grin is forced but effective. It's the eyes that are evil. Cold blue eyes that he suddenly realizes are some kind of contact lens. His legs forsake him again.

The woman lowers the blinds before producing a weapon that seems inappropriately large.

"I can't work with that aimed at me," he protests.

The man answers. "I suggest you try."

The work is difficult without an assistant. He realizes how dependent he's become on his assistants, how slowly it goes without them. He grows nostalgic for all the years he has spent in private practice. Melancholy. Several times he loses his concentration, teased away by both painful and rewarding memories. He can sense that this is the last work he will ever do, his final performance. He has always thought of his work as a performance. He knows that because of this, logically, there is no reason to do this at all. He debates stabbing his stainless grabber into one of this man's dead eyes and tearing it from the socket. But he doesn't have the strength for such things. He is a dentist, a damn good dentist, and goes about his work to prove it.

When he's finished—and it's damn good work—he steps back and signals the man to get up.

"I will need some antibiotics and some painkillers," the patient informs him. He's never liked patients telling him his job.

"I don't have any," he lies poorly.

"Of course you do. You are flooded with samples. Mistakes are costly in this game, Doctor. Have a seat," the man says, waving him into the chair. Then he is pushed down into the chair, and he can sense the violence, the intense anger, lurking within this man. He has to bite down hard to keep his teeth from chattering. He's strangely cold and more frightened than ever before. He feels dizzy and disconnected. "Tell me where the pharmaceutical samples are kept."

He can't answer. He tries to speak but his voice won't cooperate. He sees more of that anger surface in the man's face and he points as quickly as he can. The woman passes the man that gun—it looks smaller now—and runs off in the direction of his own pointed finger. She comes out of the office a few seconds later waving a box of Amoxicillin samples.

"Good," the angry one says. The one with the stitch in 17. Really a very good job, all things considered.

His arms are taped to the arms of the chair and he is briefly light-headed with joy. Why bother to strap him down if they're going to kill him?—it's his first glimpse of hope and he welcomes it by closing his eyes.

The panic fills him once again, and his eyes come open as he hears the paper wrapper being torn from the syringe. He knows that sound. The man with the ice-blue eyes fills the syringe with the mercury that has always been kept in the back with the plaster molds and plastic resins. The mercury doesn't belong out here. It certainly doesn't belong in a syringe.

When had they taped his mouth? It's only now he realizes he passed out, that much has happened in the last few minutes. It's only now he regrets his life spent under a hot light in the throes of other peoples' bad breath, of failing to communicate his true feelings to his dear, sweet wife and children, of making a mess of things without any one incident he can point to. The mercury dances at the tip of the needle and he hears it hit the floor. Those eyes are awful. Like a mask. Inhuman and severe.

He feels that needle prick his skin. He hears the woman gasp and he turns his head to plead with her, but his tears blur his vision, and justice is served in a blinding stab of pain in the center of his chest.

Levin was roused at his apartment by telephone, as was Mrs. Kiyak, who took an inordinately long time to return to sit Duncan. She mumbled something in passing about having her own room, and trundled off to Daggett's bed to sleep, as per their arrangement.

Levin contacted the superintendent of Rosen's office building and Daggett met the two of them inside the N Street entrance. A few minutes later, they reached Rosen's office door. Their bright red police crime scene seal had been torn, indicating the door had been opened without authority. Daggett knew what they would find. He hated himself for it. This was *his* fault. He had not thought the situation through: interrupted, the killer had never received his dental work.

Daggett disliked the smell of a dentist's office. Always the same blend of alcohol-based medicine and old toothpaste. He walked through the reception area, noticing the chest of toys in the corner, and the abundance of dog-eared, out-of-date magazines. He had never seen a dead body up close. He had seen hundreds, perhaps thousands, of photographs; he had seen a few corpses at the crash site of 1023, but only at a great distance. He had seen body bags, caskets, and his grandmother at her funeral. It surprised him to realize this—all these years at the Bureau, and this his first body. He thought he had it wrong, and for several seconds, as he stared into the lifeless eyes of Dr. John Rosen, he tried to correct himself. It made him feel chaste, and he found this as distasteful as the sight of the poor man in the chair. He had not believed an ounce of innocence remained in him, given the harsh realities of the past few years. And yet this discovery was not unlike the loss of his virginity—it was clearly a moment in his life he would never forget.

This man was not breathing. His eyes were dry, his pupils fixed. He smelled of excrement. Where had he been looking with those eyes? Where was he looking now? What had he been thinking at that moment? What would Daggett be thinking when his time came?

He heard Levin at the door. If he was ever going to do it, it would have to be now. It was childish, really, this desire. Strange and macabre. Not at all the sort of thing he would see himself doing. But the temptation proved too great. Levin would be here any second. This was his only moment of privacy.

He reached out and touched the man's skin, the tentative caress of a child petting a horse for the first time. He jerked back with the sensation, and on reflection he thought it was partly from fear of being caught, partly because of the surprising coolness. Partly because he knew this feeling, and he couldn't, for the life of him, remember from where.

13

OUTSIDE HER OPEN bedroom window, the leaves of the rhododendron bushes clattered like thin slats of wood. A breeze! Thank God, wind. Perhaps the heat wave would finally pass and stop stunting the cycle of every flower in her garden. The tulips had long since passed, of course, but oh, what a sight they had been. A riot of color intricately woven like the threads of an Asian silk, patches of yellow, salmon, and a cherry rose the likes of which she had never seen. She lived for her garden, both vegetable and flower alike, and resented the destructive heat.

Carrie uncoiled the delicately patterned floral sheet from her naked body and lay in bed with the delicious breeze streaming across her. It was like something sent from heaven. She rolled up onto an elbow and faced it head-on, drinking in the scents and perfumes. The breeze lifted some hair from her face, and she thought that if it would only rain, and rain hard, this heat would pass. All would be well again.

Almost all.

Before donning a stitch of clothing, the heavenly breeze still rushing over her, she lay back, reached for the phone and dialed her sister, who answered loudly above the chaos of children at the breakfast table.

"It's me," Carrie said.

The children's voices faded. Carrie could picture her sister, the portable phone pinched on her shoulder, heading across the African hardwood floor toward the study with its red leather chairs and sofa, and walls of alphabetized books. Her husband was the type to alphabetize their books and keep a card catalogue of Christmas card addresses that included the names of any children and notes of the last time they had gotten together.

"You're calling late."

"It's a lazy morning. I have to get going. I can't find the energy."

"You see," her sister said. "There's the difference. There's exactly what I was talking about yesterday."

Carrie was wondering why she put herself through this every morning, for she knew what was coming long before the sound reached her ears.

"I'm telling you: When you have other *interests* you can't wait to get going in the morning. You dress differently, you eat differently."

"He's *eighteen* years old! How fair is that to Eric?"

"He's twenty-one. And who said anything about Eric? It's fair to *me*. I'm alive again. I love Eric. I love the children—"

"Do you love . . . *him*? Whatever his name is . . ."

"Love? Love is not the issue here. I'm infatuated. My heart beats quickly when he touches me. My skin goes completely electric at just the sound of his voice."

"That's guilt."

"It isn't either."

"It might be."

"It's physical attraction. It's natural. It's multiple orgasms, for God's sake! When was the last time Cam did *that* to you?"

"Don't bring Cam into this."

"Not in recent memory, was it? I can hear it in your voice. That's because you've lost the infatuation. I'm telling you, nothing has been better for Eric and me than this . . . distraction. It makes you appreciate what you've got, and it makes you realize what you're missing."

"You make it sound like therapy."

"That's it! That's exactly what it is."

"But that means you're *using* whatever-his-name-is."

"Don't call him that. You know damn well what his name is. You're jealous. I can hear it in your voice. I may be your younger sister, but you should listen to me. I'm *experienced* in these things. Cam is treating you poopy. You know it, and I know it. You've been bitching around about it for the past six months. If it wasn't for his son you would have left him by now—"

"That's not—"

"Don't interrupt. Admit it: You're more in love with the son than you are with the father! You think that's something new? It's because you would make such a *good* mother. You come to it naturally—unlike some of us. Maybe you should take over with Eric and the kids and I'll go back to being single. I *like* it out there. I *like* it when someone notices what I'm wearing and how I smell. Can I help it?"

Carrie wanted to protest, but who could protest the truth?

Anne filled any silence handed her, including this. "Listen, even if you don't *do* anything, if you just got someone interested, you wouldn't believe how much better you would feel about yourself. I *know* that sounds backward, but it's true. And you could *use* that with Cam. Believe me, you could. You let it slip. You drop a few hints. And then you find out what he's made of. If it's real between you two, then you're going to see a major attitude change. If it isn't, well, then it isn't. Right?"

"I hate talking to you."

"Then why do we do it every morning?"

"Because I love it."

"I thought so."

"Damn. Then I suppose I'll call again tomorrow."

"No you won't. I'll call you. It's my turn."

"I thought Eric was upset about the phone bills."

"He *was*. He was upset about *everything*. But I'm happy. And when I'm happy, I put out. And when I put out, Eric's happy. And when Eric's happy he doesn't mention anything about phone bills or milk going sour or the kid's school plays. I'm telling you, kiddo—make yourself happy. It's extremely contagious."

"So you'll call me."

"Absolutely. Besides, I want to hear how this flashy dress works out."

"The reception! Oh, God, I'd forgotten about it."

"No you hadn't. You couldn't possibly have. You spent a week picking out that dress."

"What are you, my conscience?"

"I try. I'd give a million bucks to see you in that dress. To see him see you. If I were you, I'd play it up all the way. And don't talk yourself out of the high heels. They're half the outfit. And you shouldn't stop there, for that matter. What goes on, comes off—it's a rule of physics like what goes up, comes down. You've got to be thinking ahead, to *later* in the evening. Do you have a garter belt? A nice frilly teddy and a garter belt? That works every time."

"Are you happy?" Carrie asked, interrupting. "I mean, do you think you're really happy, or is this all some kind of justification thing?"

"Don't criticize that which you have not tried."

"Now you sound like Mom."

"Speaking of whom? You think she's all lily white? Don't tell me you never saw through that bridge-club-on-Thursday-afternoons business . . ."

"You're awful! That's disgusting! I don't believe that for a minute!" She heard laughing at the other end, as only Anne could laugh, and Carrie wondered what she would do without these daily calls. "Don't get pregnant," she said into the receiver, and Anne laughed all the louder. "I love you," she added as she gently placed the phone down.

She studied the way the sunshine played on her nakedness, the way the tiny hairs caught the light, giving her skin a kind of glow. It had been ages since Cam had said anything nice about her body. Ages, since she had been honestly happy. Tears blurred her vision. She felt a hopeless bundle of confusion. Anne, with answers for everything. What to do about it? How to get there from here?

She stuffed her face into the pillow and sobbed. For her, answers came hardest of all.

On his desk, in the bullpen, a small stack of pink message slips awaited Daggett. On the top was Lynn Greene's name and a Washington number. He didn't look at any of the others. He had hoped for a call, just as he thought about making a call, but had never expected to find her here in Washington. He dialed. This had trouble written all over it, and yet he felt the excitement of anticipation as the phone at the other end rang. Seconds later, he heard her voice. "Lynn?"

"Speaking."

"It's me. What are you—"

"We need to talk," she said harshly, cutting him off. "In *private*. Can you come downtown?"

The urgency in her voice intrigued him. Everything about her intrigued him. "Where?" he asked. "When?"

"You know the cafeteria at the National Gallery?"

"I thought you said *private*."

"About an hour?"

"I'll be there."

Daggett sat in the dining area of the National Gallery's subterranean cafeteria, facing the waterfall that flowed from outside in, mesmerized by it, hypnotized by its relentless song. A thin sheet of silver water flowed over the corrugated cement and collected in a small rectangular pool no wider than a flower box. It was at this moment he realized that his hearing was indeed improving, for it seemed to him he could hear all the frequencies, the percussive drumming of the body of water, the sparkling delicacy of the tiny droplets as they danced to their death. Three overhead triangular skylights admitted natural light, which explained the thriving existence of the abundance of potted plants. He pulled out his date book to make some notes, astonished to see it had been four weeks since Bernard and Backman had been killed in the explosion at National Airport. He shut the book just as quickly. Day after tomorrow was his last day to bring Pullman and Mumford evidence, or lose the case. He didn't need any reminders.

He drank some iced tea and watched the parade of tourists with their squeaky-clean running shoes and dog-eared guidebooks. She was right: For such a public place, this was indeed a private spot. Like so much to do with Lynn, it seemed an excellent choice.

He saw her then: a lot of leg, linen, and a bouncing white cotton blouse. She acknowledged him with a wave and joined the beverage line. He rose for her when she approached a few minutes later, but she signaled him back into his chair. He wanted to kiss her hello, but she failed to offer him the chance. She took the chair opposite him and sat down.

"You look upset," she said.

"Surprised, is more like it."

"With my being here in Washington," she stated. She was like that: She knew what he was thinking before he did.

"You look good to me."

"Stick to the subject."

"What is the subject?"

"AmAirXpress flight sixty-four."

"What *are* you doing in Washington?"

"That's not the subject."

"It is to me," he said.

"You think I'm chasing you."

"Only in my wildest fantasies," he said.

She dismissed this with an oblique expression. "Ostensibly, I came as a delivery boy—*person,*" she corrected. "In fact, I think I was called out here because my superiors didn't like seeing my face plastered all over *People*. Did you see it? They wanted it to be their faces instead. We've already had a little talk about administration policy concerning publicity."

"And what's this all about? Why this?"

"This was *my* reason for coming. We turned up something in our sifting."

"Sifting?"

"The ashes. Hollywood Park."

He couldn't focus on her words. He was stuck on her face, and the sincerity in her eyes. On memories. Sifting the ashes, indeed. There was an energy to this woman. Sexual, intelligent, curious—difficult to separate one from the other. Driven by her job, or by something just beneath the surface that she labored to control. He had felt that same eagerness toward his work once, that same sincerity. No longer. Now he wanted results. He wanted the people—the person—who had done this to his son. Kort? The truth—if any existed out there—had become a by-product along the way, a means to reach his end. Truth and justice were luxuries for people who had nothing personal at stake. They had faded from his vocabulary like a second language once learned but long forgotten. "Ashes," he echoed.

"Our investigators sift the ashes, grid by grid, square foot by square foot. Square inch by square inch. It's one of the reasons we take so long at crash sites. Fortunately for you, they started at the nose of the plane. They have an area roughly three acres to cover. You know how many square feet that is? How many square inches? You know how long that takes?" He didn't answer. "They started near the cockpit, which, as I say, was a lucky thing. Yesterday their sifting screens caught a tiny piece of glass. To the untrained eye, it looks like nothing more than a broken Christmas light—one of those little white twinkling ones."

"But to the trained eye?" His eyes had not left her face. They were trained eyes as well. He, too, was examining grid by grid. She had been spared both worry and time. What few lines appeared at the edges of her eyes with her expressions, characterized her as thoughtful and sincere. They caught the light like an artist's shading, adding depth and contrast, enhancing her intentions.

"Depends on who you ask. *I* think it may be part of a mercury switch," she said, deliberately attempting to rattle him. He refused to give in that easily. He continued to search her face. "Mercury switch as in sabotage." She waited for him to say something, but he continued to stare. He was beginning to think in terms of hotel rooms. "On hearing this, I suggested we notify you—the FBI—immediately. I hit resistance. 'Not yet,' I was told. 'Let's wait for the lab report, shall we?' I didn't want to wait that long."

Neither did he. It seemed clear to him now. They had missed their chance back on that beach a few summers ago. The chemistry had been there—obviously—but the opportunity had been denied. An injustice.

She continued in her businesslike tone. He wanted this woman gone and the real Lynn back. He wanted the woman in the sunglasses and the terry cloth robe. "To date, we have *no* proof of explosives on sixty-four. No suggestion of sabotage. Not by eyewitness reports, not by any of the lab work." She paused, allowing him to say something. When he failed to contribute, she continued, "The NTSB will continue to control this investigation until there is conclusive proof of suspicious causes. My people will continue to control the crash evidence as long as possible. The more agencies involved, the more paperwork, the more meetings, the more hassle. But ever since you told me about that guy getting killed at Duhning—"

Daggett sat up squarely. Back to reality. "It's worse. We now know there were two detonators made. Everything points here to Washington for the next target."

"You put me in a hell of a bind, by telling me all this, you know that?"

"That's the idea, isn't it? I'm working against the clock here." He checked his watch. "This same time two days from now, I'm off this case. That is, unless I bring the brass something convincing and win an extension. Tell me about this mercury switch. How certain are you?"

"Me or my *superiors*? and I use that term loosely. That's just the point. Not certain enough to give up the investigation and turn it over to you guys. That's what would happen if we were certain. This evidence was on the way to our lab. I was arguing for a priority rating, meaning it would be advanced to the top of the pile. To give you an idea, so far we've tagged one hundred and twenty-one items for lab tests. That's another reason these crash reports take so long. But they didn't agree with my request. The priority request was denied. They're pissed off at me because of the *People* article. We're talking bruised egos here."

"Was?" he asked. "You said it 'was' on the way to the lab. What did you mean by that?"

"We'll get to that." She looked around cautiously.

"Tell me about mercury switches. Anything special, other than what I already know?"

"No. I doubt it. You tip the bulb; the mercury moves; an electronic connection is made. A crude detonating device. In the case of sixty-four."

Daggett interrupted. Moving his hand to demonstrate, he said, "We're talking takeoff. Nose goes up. *Boom.*"

"Exactly."

"But no sign of an explosion. You just said so. Isn't that right?"

"No explosion, that's right."

"Something else then?"

"Maybe. First I'd like to know if this glass bulb is a mercury switch or not."

"And if it is?"

"There are other ways—other than explosions—to bring down a plane."

"Name one."

"Gas. I was thinking about gas."

"Zia?" he said.

"Yes."

"Oh, Christ."

On August 17, 1988, the president of Pakistan, Muhammad Zia ul-Haq, his chief of staff; the army's vice-chief of staff; the American ambassador, Arnold L. Raphel; and General Herbert M. Wassom, head of U.S. military aid to Pakistan, all died in the crash of Zia's C-130 Hercules transport plane. It had been a nightmare for Daggett and the FBI's foreign counterterrorism group, who, along with other criminal investigators and sabotage experts, had been excluded from the investigation. With such a prestigious passenger list, motive for murder abounded.

Based on Islamic religious law requiring burial within twenty-four hours of death, the bodies of the flight crew were cremated only hours after the crash. This eliminated the chance to autopsy the flight crew. As a result, speculation remained as to the actual cause of the crash. Lacking any evidence from the autopsies of the flight crew, nothing could be proven. After eighteen months of inquiry, after much supporting evidence, the most likely explanation for the crash was that poison gas hidden somewhere on the flight deck, or introduced into its air supply, had killed the flight crew, and perhaps the passengers as well. With no flight crew in control, the plane had gone down. The fatal crash remained listed as "likely sabotage."

Daggett said, "Gas? We would have caught that in the autopsies."

"Would we have? That's out of my expertise."

"We *should* have. I've seen the autopsy protocols—there's no mention of toxic gases in the blood or lungs. Now you make me wonder how reliable that is. With the oil wells burning and all that jet fuel going up . . . well, there wasn't much left of the two in the cockpit. I wonder how reliable those autopsies are?"

"Way beyond my expertise," Lynn said, blanching.

"We'll know a lot more once we've listened to the voice recorder."

"The voice recorder? It's here?"

"That's what I'm doing here. That's what I meant by me being a delivery boy. Our lab has it as we speak. We'll listen to it either late tonight or tomorrow. Depends on everyone's schedules."

"What about my schedule?"

"You're invited, of course. Have you ever been to one?"

"No," he admitted reluctantly.

"It's emotional. It's hard."

"I can imagine."

"No, you can't. Not really . . ." She said this softly, but he felt her pain as clearly as a strong gust of wind hitting his chest. He identified the emotion immediately: It was the same as when he told others about Duncan's disability. "No, I can't," he acknowledged. Then he remembered he had to be by Mumford's side this evening. "I have an obligation tonight. If it's going to be tonight, I'll need to be pulled away. Physically pulled away. My boss won't have it any other way."

"The reception?" she asked. "I'm going too. I'll be on a pager."

"If you hear anything—"

"I'll come rescue you," she said.

He nodded, still looking at her, believing she was right in more ways than she intended. She was capable of rescuing him. He wanted to tell her. But then he saw a change in her expression, and he realized perhaps he already had.

She looked around nervously and fiddled with her purse. *"Don't* get up," she said, coming out of her chair. Daggett acted natural, but his eyes wandered the area. Had she seen someone? She was acting that way.

She came across to him, bent to kiss him on the cheek, and forced what felt like a plastic container into his hand. A roll of film? He didn't want to look. "Your boys will work faster than ours," she said. "I need that back. See you to-night." She left.

Daggett opened his hand beneath the table. It was a clear plastic container labeled FAA EVIDENCE.

Inside was a broken glass bulb.

14

THE RECEPTION, HOSTED by the air industry's powerful lobby, began at seven-thirty.

The "private home"—now a commercial building rented specifically for entertaining—had been built in the mid-nineteenth century by a wealthy widow from Missouri. Colonial, it imitated the great southern mansions, since, the story went, this woman had fancied herself a southern belle —not the daughter of a hog farmer as was actually the case.

Carrie, having arrived precisely at eight, waited outside, expecting Cam any moment.

A steady flow of the properly dressed climbed the front steps and passed through the towering front doors, engrossed in petty conversations, mostly concerning the intolerable heat.

At ten past, with the heat and looks of pity getting to her, Carrie queued up with the others, fearing that without an invitation she might be rebuked. The reception line was a bipartisan Who's Who of congressmen, a Democratic congresswoman, and senators.

Carrie passed first through the metal detector, which had become so commonplace at these functions that it nearly went unnoticed, and then on through the reception line, all without incident.

The party was on; it was hot outside, cool in here; time to drink.

The grand ballroom boasted a twenty-five-foot arched ceiling of intricate plasterwork; the walls held large but unremarkable eighteenth-century oil landscapes darkened with age, caged ornately in bright gilded frames. A number of nine-foot-high doors led off to a garden patio on the left, and points unknown—presumably sitting rooms or a kitchen—on the right. She calculated the commission on a place like this before she reached the bar. A trio of electric piano, bass, and drums played a Ray Charles medley from the far end, between two fully staffed and stocked bars. The mood was festive. People were showing off their Nantucket tans. Carrie wished she had one. Hearing snatches of many stories, many laughs, she felt increasingly alone.

Where was Cam?

The drinks went a long way toward making her feel comfortable. An attractive single woman in a lovely dress became the object of much male attention. Gentlemen began to buzz around her, bees to her honey, engaging her in small talk, prying into her marital status, and delivering more drinks than she could juggle with two hands. She lost count after three, sipping more often out of nerves and excitement than a desire to get drunk. Someone who considered a spritzer a stiff order, she was dizzy before thirty minutes had passed.

Who needed Cam?

The compliments kept pace with the drinks and the trays upon trays of international hors d'oeuvres. She understood why single women appreciated Washington so much. On the arm of Cam, the few cocktail parties she had attended had always proved frightfully boring. But now! Now she was having the time of her life. She secretly hoped he'd forgotten about the party, or had a flat tire or a meeting he "simply couldn't get out of." God, had that excuse grown tiresome!

When the band struck up a fairly convincing version of "In the Mood," a few of the older couples began to dance, and as if reading her thoughts, a darkly handsome young man who had mentioned something about being with the National Gallery (what he was doing at this particular party was anybody's guess) invited her to dance, placing her drink down for her and swinging her out onto the floor. As

far as she was concerned, he was the second coming of
Fred Astaire, and in her best Ginger Rogers imitation, she
attempted to follow his graceful footwork. After another
dance she had to take a break.

In the powder room there was a pack of cigarettes on
the counter. Marlboros. Her favorite.

Cam had helped her to quit twice. Their one split had
followed a series of arguments surrounding her "weakness," her inability to kick the habit. But there were the
Marlboros, and she was feeling as good as she could recently remember. As she fixed her hair the pack continued
to stare at her, and finally she opened the hard-box lid,
slipped out a cigarette and put the accompanying butane
lighter to it. She wanted to dislike it, because she knew how
bad it was for her, but with a few drinks in her the smoke
felt absolutely wonderful curling down her throat, tasted
fantastic, and she wasn't sorry at all. She smoked it down,
enjoying herself immensely, stole a few more from the
pack and, placing them in her purse with the disposable
lighter, headed back out to her waiting audience.

A few minutes later, she glanced up and saw Cam entering the room. At first, she felt anger at his being so late.
This was quickly replaced by relief—they had the night in
front of them—and guilt over the cigarettes. She experienced a flutter of happiness within her breast: she was
wearing a new dress, she had a couple of drinks in her, and
her date had finally arrived. But this happiness was quickly
sabotaged as Cam stepped aside, revealing a tan and incredibly fit Lynn Greene. It was all made very much worse
when Cam held up a finger to the woman as if to say *Wait a
minute.* His gesture confirmed that they had arrived together.

Indignation rose within Carrie flushing her face scarlet. She gulped down the remainder of her drink, grabbed
her National Gallery dancing partner by the hand and
steered him out onto the dance floor, immediately in step
with a romantic ballad. She pressed herself close, a slender

hand around his neck, and nestled her head into his comfortable but somewhat unwilling shoulder. The moment was broken as her partner lifted his arm and waved slightly to a tall, extremely handsome dark-haired woman with green eyes, clad in a stunning white dress.

"A friend?" Carrie asked, unavoidably slurring her syllables.

"My wife," the man responded. "Sylvia," as if an introduction were appropriate.

It figured. This man had been the most polite, and while attentive, had in no way come on to her, which was why she felt safe with him. Married! At that instant Cam spotted her, smiled broadly, apparently not the least perturbed. He pushed his way to the bar, where he ordered a drink. He stood by the band watching her dance. Eventually, the song ended. Carrie's partner politely excused himself, caught up to and kissed his wife. Together, they edged through the crowd to the opposite bar, the wife checking one last time to make certain Carrie wasn't following.

"Hello there," Cam said over his glass of cranberry juice. He seldom drank at these occasions, considering them work. He leaned forward for a kiss, but Carrie, suddenly fearing he might smell the cigarette on her, averted him at the last second, offering only her cheek. "Sorry I'm late. Really I am. I could tell you that it was unavoidable, but I know it wouldn't help. Still, it was. I always say that, don't I?"

She nodded, tongue-tied and a little too drunk. It fed her anger but she resisted this with everything she could muster. She would not give in to it. She would not be a victim of behavior patterns as Cam always was. The progression of events seemed apparent enough to her: Lynn Greene worked out of Los Angeles. Cam had gone to Los Angeles; they had reunited; and now, here was Lynn Greene, three thousand miles from home. It could all be explained by work—she was certain of that—but it seemed a little too cozy. Still, she wanted to believe him. It was a new dress. It was a decent enough band. It was early yet. If only she could think of something to say.

"Aren't you talking to me?" he asked.

Fearing the booze might cause her to say something she would regret, she simply said, "Hi," and retreated to her purse, where, against her intentions, she located and lit a cigarette.

The band began to play a poor rendition of a Beatles song.

"What are you drinking?" he asked, making nothing of the cigarette.

This made her feel all the more guilty. "Vodka, in any number of combinations."

"Be right back." He disappeared behind a swirl of dancers. She took a drag and blew the gray smoke high over their heads.

Daggett ordered them *both* vodka and tonics and returned to her as quickly as possible. She continued to smoke, though clearly was uncomfortable about it. He tried his best to ignore it. "Listen," he said intimately, "I really am sorry about being late. I'll make it up to you somehow."

"No need to. You're here. I'm glad for that." She squinted at her cigarette. "I hate being single. I'm so glad I'm not single. Really." Smoke ran into her eyes as she attempted to keep the cigarette away from him. She frowned at it.

He asked gently, "Would you like me to get rid of that?"

"Please."

He pinched it between his fingers as if it were contaminated, and cut his way through the congestion to the far wall where he located a freestanding sandbox ashtray. As he twisted it into the sand, he noticed a gold filter standing butt-up in the sand. A butt identical to the one he had found in Seattle. With some difficulty, he recalled the report that had crossed his desk, naming the brand and style: Sobranie

—Black Russian filters. A rare brand in the United States, it was available throughout Europe, though expensive.

Could it be put down to coincidence that he would find the same cigarettes being smoked here? It *was* a big crowd, an international crowd to be sure. His curiosity won out. He had to know who was smoking these cigarettes. He would think of nothing else until he did, which would only further spoil the evening. He began to justify his need: there weren't that many people smoking; with a brand as uncommon as this, how hard could he or she be to locate? But to allow these thoughts was itself trouble, for suddenly he was filled with pure, hot panic. This was, after all, a party celebrating tougher restrictions on airline security. What if this reception was the target? What if Bernard hadn't built two barometric detonators, as he suspected, but instead, one barometric and one clock?

Could a bomb be smuggled into this party? Doubtful. He had passed through a metal detector and a couple of city cops on his way in. The very nature of the reception would have demanded the toughest security procedures. But what about the cars outside? How thorough *was* the security?

He rudely barged his way back through the hordes and reached Carrie, regretting his words before he even uttered them. "Something's come up," he said as gently as he could. "I'll only be a few minutes. Promise. Not long at all." She rolled her eyes. "Save me room on your dance card?"

Her eyes pleaded with him. He saw hate, love, and confusion.

"Bear with me," he said.

"Go on," she told him. "I'm not going anywhere."

"Only a couple of minutes."

"Sure." He saw the courage and strength it took for her to say this, for her eyes betrayed her, but it was one of those efforts so typical of her. It was times like this that he saw himself through her eyes, and wondered how he deserved her.

"Thanks," he said.

"Go on," she insisted, giving him a gentle but convincing shove. "They're going to play another slow song soon."

He targeted a male smoker and closed in. The important thing was not to panic, not to jump to any conclusions. Part of him *wanted* to believe that the bomber might be here at this party, but the more he thought about it, the more absurd it seemed. Ward's killer was not the only person who smoked Sobranies. And what would an international terrorist be doing at a Washington social affair? Milling with other guests and making small talk. He settled down some with this reasoning, though he didn't abandon his assignment.

The music faded into the background. His attention fixed on the guests. A black and gold cigarette would be fairly easily spotted. He weaved his way through the crowd smoothly. Here, the slate gray fumes rose from a small cluster of talkers . . . A woman . . . A white cigarette with a white filter. There, another. Group by group, face by face, he pursued the smoke.

"Cam!" An arm reached out and snagged him. The voice sounded familiar, but at first there were too many faces with which to associate it. "Right here," the man next to him said. Daggett recognized Richard Tuttle, now a senior vice-president in a security consultant firm. He wanted to break loose, but Tuttle had him firmly by the arm. Tuttle had been a special agent until forced into mandatory retirement at fifty-five. Now he consulted for commercial carriers—for probably five times the pay. His company had been instrumental in the adoption of the recent legislation that this reception was celebrating. He introduced Daggett to his friends. Daggett wanted out. He shook hands all around. He tried to sidestep Tuttle, to quickly move on, but Tuttle, feeling the liquor, retained him firmly in his grip. To tear himself away might create a scene—more trouble than it was worth: Tuttle and Mumford went way back.

Tuttle excused them both and drew Daggett away from the others. He had hard facial features and a youthful laugh. He spoke in a very low register, which sounded un-natural and forced. "You all right?"

"A little distracted is all. I'm in a bit of a hurry. Working," he added.

"I understand."

No you don't, he felt like telling the man. "Well—" Daggett said, giving a little jerk and trying to pull away. Tuttle's grip remained ironclad. "With this one safely in the win column," Tuttle began, "I'm more than likely going to be wearing an executive VP hat any day now, and that's going to leave a hole in the ranks, if you follow me. We could use someone with your experience. Bring you in at the VP level, or damn near it. First year you'd take home maybe forty or fifty—I know, I know," he said, expecting Daggett to protest, "but by year three or four you'd be pulling in *at least twice* that, maybe three times depending on how the rest of the company grows, and we're growing like gangbusters! You'd be at an executive decision level, not one of the flunkies catching a goddamned plane every other day."

"Richard—"

"Hell, this isn't anything close to a formal offer. But I'd like you to let me take you out to lunch one of these days and lay it all out there for you. Make it official and let you think about it. That child of yours, Dirk is it?"

"Duncan—"

"You won't believe the health benefits, retirement plan, and profit-sharing programs we've got. Even some of Dirk's past expenses may be covered here—we'd have to look at that. How about a lunch one of these days?"

Duncan's expenses . . . Here was everything Carrie wanted for them: security, high pay, reasonable hours, benefits. The temptation of a cushy desk job seem only too appropriate when his elevated blood pressure was causing a painful drumming in his ears, and sweat formed on the back of his neck. Was Tuttle sweating? Hell no. Did Tuttle work to midnight only to head back to the office at six in the morning? He was tempted.

"Love to," Daggett said, slapping his damp hand inside Tuttle's huge mitt, freeing his arm. "I'll be in touch." He escaped.

He had lost precious time. He felt both frantic and silly, unsure which to trust.

He scanned the crowd for smoke.

There! Just ahead of him another cloud ascending from a pack of suits and dresses. He wedged his way past a fat woman with broad shoulders, forced against her so that he made full contact with the spongy warm skin of her back, damp at the spine. She threw a practiced elbow, a cow's tail dealing effectively with the annoyance of flies. His hopes rose as he attached the cigarette smoke to a face—an average face of a man of average height. Daggett's view of the cigarette was blocked. But then it came into view: a white cigarette with a brown filter.

He moved on.

Anthony Kort found himself eye to eye with Cam Daggett. He had walked willingly into the hornet's nest and now he felt like a fool for allowing Monique to manipulate him this way. He had wanted to arrive, make contact with the Greek, leave. Monique, on the other hand, believed that for the sake of appearances they should spend at least a few minutes before attempting the contact. She had talked him into it.

He poked her in the back. "How about another drink?" he asked her. His bad temper was due in part to his present brand of cigarette. He had finished his last Sobranie not five minutes earlier and was now smoking a poor substitute, Camel filters. In a city this size, this continental, there had to be Sobranie for sale somewhere. He would put Monique on that.

"I will come with you," she said, excusing them both from the group.

"That was *Daggett*," he whispered only inches from her ear. "Let's get this over with *now*."

Monique's eyes followed Daggett until he disappeared. She took Kort by the hand and led him through a swinging door into the kitchen, the two of them immediately swallowed by the chaos there. She pointed out the door to the cellar. Kort headed down the steps into the dank darkness, where a single unlit bulb hung from a dust-encrusted electrical wire like the bald head of a hanged man. He touched it as he passed beneath it and it swung back and forth like the pendulum to a clock.

In the far corner, to the right of a soapstone sink, was a pair of storm cellar doors with four poured concrete stairs leading up to them. Kort unbolted the doors and, pushing the left door open to the night air, insured himself a means of escape.

The success of the operation relied on the Greek's information. If he couldn't get the exact date of the meeting, then all was lost. Bernard's death meant nothing; Michael's arrest meant nothing.

A pair of heavy feet clumped down the stairs and a thick Greek accent complained in a forced and angry whisper, "I told you in my messages, you and I have nothing to discuss! This is an outrage." Kort pressed back into the shadows as the light came on. The floor became animated with the movement of shadows as the bulb swayed back and forth.

Monique had maneuvered the Greek to the near side of the stairs.

"I will only speak with *him*. That was the arrangement."

"Then it's time we should talk," Kort said from the shadows.

The Greek spun around, nervously. A big man with a swollen chest, thin gray hair and bad teeth, his hands appeared overinflated. He had the shifting eyes of a salesman and the red nose of a competent drinker.

Monique flew weightlessly up the stairs and threw the

door shut behind her. By agreement, she would remain there to signal if necessary.

A wide grin taking his face, the Greek said, "I wondered how this catering job came my way at the last minute—and so well paid. I should have realized . . ."

"What's this about the meeting?" Kort asked.

"I have the *name* for you—the flight mechanic you wanted. His name is David Boote."

"I'll need his address, working schedule, and a recent photograph," Kort said. "We'll set up a dead drop for tomorrow. You'll be notified using the computers. Now what about the meeting?"

"I can't get the date for you. We had it for you—it was to be three days from now—the fourteenth—but they've rescheduled, postponed it at least a week. Both Sandhurst and Goldenbaum are unavailable until the twenty-first of this month. It's the twenty-first at the *earliest*. I'm told the FBI is to blame. We cross-referenced the travel itineraries of these executives in order to identify the date for you. Everything was all set. But then the FBI requested the same itineraries, and a few hours later the meeting was postponed. There's nothing I can do about it now. There's simply no way."

"There *must* be a way," Kort demanded. "You're not thinking this through." He took another step toward the man. "You have been *paid* for this information. You will deliver. You understand?"

"What am I supposed to do? You think I didn't try? I've been throwing money around everywhere trying to get this for you. All I have are a few worthless rumors."

"Such as?"

"They're nothing."

"I want to hear them."

"I have no second source for any of this."

"Even so, I want to hear it."

The big man shrugged. He patted his pockets. Kort offered him a cigarette and they both smoked. "Even the executives themselves don't know when the meeting is to be.

That's what I'm told. They were asked to leave five different days open for travel, beginning the twenty-first. It could be any one of those days. I don't know. Arrangements—*new* itineraries—have been drawn up for each of the executives, but from this end this time."

"I can't wait until the last minute. I need to know in advance. I want those itineraries."

"I understand. I told you—this doesn't help you one bit."

"What else?"

"It's nothing solid."

"Tell me."

"It's nothing."

"Tell me!" Kort demanded, stepping even closer to the man. He smelled like olive oil.

"I've been told that Buzzard Point—you know Buzzard Point?"

"No."

"FBI field office here in Washington."

"WMFO?" Kort said.

"Exactly. Same thing."

"Go on."

"Buzzard Point is going to handle security for the executives. Counterterrorism—an agent named Daggett."

"Daggett? Impossible!"

"You *know* him?"

"I know *of* him. Security? It's not his kind of work. He's already on something else." Kort had to be careful how much he revealed.

"That may be, but I paid good money to learn that someone saw the head of WMFO hand Daggett an Eyes Only file folder, and that the word *itineraries* was mentioned. That same source says that file is the only copy outside the Pentagon. And if Daggett had locked it away in-house, in the tenth-floor safe, as he was evidently supposed to have done, then I would presently be out some serious cash, and you would already have whatever is in this folder."

"But he didn't lock it away," Kort said.

"But he didn't," the Greek confirmed.

"Because of its sensitivity. You don't lock something like that away in a communal safe, even at the FBI." Kort's mind was racing ahead of him. This made some sense to him. "You keep it with you."

"His home? You want me to arrange a break-in of Daggett's home? I could do this for you."

"No," Kort said. He was thinking: Not you. He didn't like this man at all. If the job was bungled, then they would postpone the meeting again and Kort would have to start all over with this.

"Or maybe he carries it with him," the Greek said, thinking too much. "Maybe I could have his briefcase stolen."

"Don't you do *anything*," Kort instructed, his words carrying smoke from his lungs. Kort toyed with the possibilities. The man had a son. Pressure could be brought to bear.

The Greek continued to think aloud. "No, it's no good. To steal the briefcase would alert them. They would simply reschedule the meeting."

"You say you don't trust it. How reliable *is* this information?" Kort liked the sound of his voice down here in the basement. It sounded dangerous. He was thinking: Daggett's briefcase? Daggett a single man. Perhaps Monique could use her womanly charms to waylay the agent briefly while he took a look inside . . .

"Not easy getting one of your people inside WMFO, even in office positions, I wouldn't think. It's hard enough at some of these corporations, I'll tell you that. This person, my contact, is a dear friend. He and I have done business many times before. Even so, I wouldn't trust it. Without a credible second source, some support, you can't trust information like this. You have to have a second source. It could easily be disinformation we're dealing with here. Then again, it's all I have."

It made sense to Kort. Bernard had been Daggett's assignment—his *ticket,* as the FBI called it—for the better part of the last two years. Kort had used a Bernard detonator on AmAirXpress flight 64. Did the FBI already know that? Was that possible? They had caught Bernard here in Washington. Had they made a connection between the two? Exactly how much did they know about his plans? The idea of getting a look inside Daggett's briefcase suddenly seemed a matter of self-preservation. *Know thine enemy.* Monique was a possibility, though a long shot. He would rather do this himself. He didn't trust other people. "How much do you know about Daggett?"

"What do I look like, James Bond? I'm in corporate consulting, not that other stuff. You want to know about Donald Trump, I'll tell you his shorts size. His daily vitamins. An FBI agent? I don't know shit."

Kort blew past him and was half way up the stairs when the Greek called out, "Hey! Is that all? I got baklava in the oven."

Kort stopped. "We'll contact you about the drop. We need that information on this flight mechanic, this David Boote." He started up the stairs again and stopped. "And something else . . . I'll need the cargo manifests for all Quik-Link flights out of National Airport for the next four weeks."

"*That* I can do," he said defensively. "No problem."

"Do it."

"But what about Daggett?" the Greek asked.

Kort didn't answer. The less the man knew, the better.

"Do you have a guest list?" Kort asked Monique as he reached the top of the stairs and the busy kitchen.

"For tonight?"

"Yes."

"There would be one at the front door. I'm sure I could check it."

"Do that."

She clearly didn't like his tone. "Who am I looking for?"

"Daggett."

This confused her. "But we already know he's here. What's the point?"

"Not him. His date. Everyone brings someone to these affairs. Even FBI agents. This is a *social* event. With whom did Daggett come? They would be listed together, wouldn't they? See if you can find a name for me."

"What are you thinking?"

"Do it!" he snapped. "I'll be waiting by the bar."

By the time she returned, Kort had located Daggett in the crowd and had followed him with his eyes until he ended up in discussion with a woman in a peach dress. There is something unique, he realized, in the way two lovers converse, for these two were clearly lovers. He prided himself on his powers of observation. Such powers were essential for his survival. He had no doubt of Daggett's relationship to this woman, nor that that relationship was, at the moment, under a great deal of strain.

"What's her name?" Kort asked Monique, knowing he was right, swelling with the conceit of his success.

"Caroline Stevenson. Is that her?"

"Don't look at her. Use your head!" he scolded.

She grew restless with the reprimand. "So you know her name. We should be leaving. We have been here too long. You said so yourself."

"We're not going anywhere."

"What? But I thought—"

"Fix yourself a drink. Relax. Mingle. We've barely just arrived."

Her confusion arranged itself on her face as anger.

His timing couldn't have been better. Daggett walked away from the woman in the peach dress—Caroline—and she immediately reached into her purse and came out with a cigarette. That purse was likely to contain a set of keys. And one of those keys would admit him to Daggett's house. Kort took his pack of Camels from his pocket and stuffed them into Monique's hand, closing her fist around them. "Hold on to these," he said. "I feel like a cigarette."

She looked down at her hand. "You're not making any sense."

"No, I'm not, am I?" He patted her on the cheek, and cut through the dancers.

"I wonder if you would have an extra one of those?" he asked the woman. She looked up. They met eyes. Hers were fogged with either emotion or booze, or both. She forced a polite smile, searched her purse and came out with one. She struggled with the lighter, finally ignited it, and did her best to steady the flame. Kort interceded, taking her hand gently in his, and directed the flame. He kept her hand a moment longer than necessary before releasing it. She blushed, and he felt the thrill of success.

"I must confess," he lied, "that I have been watching you for some time this evening, wanting to come over and introduce myself."

She looked away uncomfortably. Did he dare push further? His eyes wandered to the purse. If he could only make her drop it, get her to spill it.

"Are you British?" she asked when he didn't go away. "You sound vaguely British to me."

"How perceptive of you," he said. "Schooled in England in my formative years. Living in Belgium now. I'm Carl," he said.

"Caroline," she returned, now looking at him again.

His heart pounded with success—Caroline, the name he had hoped to hear.

"Do you live here in Washington, or are you just visiting?" she asked.

"I'm over here trying to steal as much information as I

can from you Americans on how to run an airline catering company. Food service industry."

"Oh, a *spy* are you?" she said, accompanied by a lilting laugh.

"Yes," he said, joining her laughter, enjoying the irony. "A spy."

She took a drag on the cigarette, closed her eyes, and stumbled backward. It was his first real indication of just how inebriated she was. He glanced at the purse again. In her condition it would be like taking candy from a baby. She had failed to latch it closed. One good bump and he could spill its contents.

He found the same physical chemistry he had experienced with Monique at work here. She's dangerous, he cautioned himself. Get her off to one side, get her to spill her purse, and get it over with. How long would Daggett stay away? He checked the crowd. He didn't see Daggett anywhere.

But there was Monique, looking right back at him. He cautioned her with his eyes and she looked away.

"A friend of yours?" Carrie asked somewhat bitterly.

"A business associate." He leaned in close to her, the purse within reach. "She's an incredible bore."

Carrie erupted in drunken laughter, spilling ashes onto her dress and quickly swatting them away. "I know what you mean," she said. "I know *exactly* what you mean."

Daggett dug through an ashtray looking for any more Sobranie butts. "What the hell are you doing, Michigan?" It was Mumford, the head of WMFO.

An explanation seemed too complicated. "You made it," Daggett said.

Thankfully, Lynn Greene approached at a fast pace. She caught Mumford's eye well before she said, "Could I speak to you a minute, Cam?" Daggett introduced her to Mumford, at which point Lynn explained to both of them in a low voice that the FAA intended to listen to the long-

awaited cockpit voice recorder this evening. She had just
been paged, and was headed downtown.

Mumford cautioned, "I don't want this to get out. Not
here. Not tonight. There's press all over the place. Let's see
what we've got first." To Daggett he said, "Why don't the two
of you disappear quietly. I'll make any necessary excuses.
Let Paul know if and when you have anything."

"Will you humor me?" Daggett asked the man.

"Meaning?"

"If you would lend your authority to something, I could
rest a little easier leaving here." He glanced around. The
party seemed to be thinning. He knew for a fact that most
of the VIPs had made only a brief appearance and had left
by the time Daggett had arrived. "Have the security people
sweep the grounds and vehicles one more time. I'd rest a
little easier."

"Have we got a *problem*?" Mumford demanded.

"A coincidence is all. No hard evidence. Probably nothing. But an ounce of prevention . . ."

Mumford nodded. "I'll pass that along."

A minute later, Daggett found Carrie in the company of
a fellow smoker. They were laughing. At the sound of her
laugh, he felt a twinge of jealousy.

Daggett acknowledged the stranger with a nod and said
to Carrie in a lover's apologetic voice, "Believe it or not, I
have to go. There's a meeting . . ." He searched her eyes
for a glint of understanding. He saw pain.

"Sure," she said with all her strength. "These things
happen, don't they?" She managed to keep the hurt out of
her voice, though her eyes divulged the truth, and he
thought that if he failed to make this up to her, he might
lose her. She stood poised and controlled, an image of dignity and restraint, and he thought himself very lucky to
have such a person.

"What about Duncan?" she asked. "Would you like me
to sit Duncan?"

He hadn't thought about those arrangements. The meeting could run for hours; he wasn't sure how long it might take. "You could call Mrs. Kiyak. That would be a big help. I can do it if—"

"No, I'll do it. It's fine." It wasn't fine. He knew this, but she concealed the truth, an image of strength and endurance. He taxed her. It bordered on psychological abuse, he thought, the way he danced from one failed promise to the next. But this was his expertise, this dancing. It had driven his wife, the mother of his son, into drunken escape. Had driven her away for good. Now he watched as he picked up where he had left off. He watched himself, unable to change—a ship heading straight for the rocks, the currents refusing a different course. "Do you have a ride?" she asked, searching her purse. "You can use my car."

"I couldn't."

"Nonsense. Of course you can. The Crenshaws are still here. I can hitch a ride with them." She handed him the keys. "It's no problem."

He accepted the keys. "Are you sure?"

"Positive."

Daggett felt Lynn waiting, and he glanced over his shoulder to see her at the door. When he looked back at Carrie, he realized the two women were in a staring contest. Without taking her eyes off Lynn, Carrie asked, "Is this meeting with her?" in a subdued voice that had to be boiling somewhere inside her.

"She'll be there." He didn't want to sound guilty, but he heard it in his voice.

She looked at him then, with a sadness so heavy, so burdened by their struggle, that he thought she might cry. He heard the words of a dozen arguments, and wished they never had been. He envisioned their days of happiness and wondered where they had gone. He saw in her face the agony of surrender; she was numb and distant. She had resolved herself to Lynn's presence, he thought, and with it, had closed him out. Possibly forever.

He clutched the keys tightly in his fist, leaned forward, and kissed a warm but unfriendly cheek. "Thank you," he said to her softly. He felt the skin of her face twitch behind an ironic smile.

She still stood there, still held that stoic expression, as he looked back from the door.

Kort, who had steeled his bowels on Daggett's approach, felt impotent and helpless as Daggett took the keys. The man was a menace. In a perfect world, he would have been able to spill her purse, steal her keys, copy them, and then surreptitiously return them to this building so they might be found and eventually returned to her. Now he would have to arrange something else. But Daggett's intrusion reinforced in him the need to get inside the man's briefcase. What poetic justice to have his nemesis deliver to him the final piece of information that would ensure the success of his operation! Yes, it had to be Daggett.

And it had to be soon.

"Your husband?" he asked Caroline, knowing full well they weren't married.

"No . . . No . . ." she said in the anguished voice of a lover struggling for sanity. "Just a friend."

15

"YOU LOOK WORRIED," Lynn said as she tapped on the glass door, summoning the security guard to admit them. The uniformed man came out of his chair and approached them slowly. Despite his big, bulging belly and wide shoulders, he appeared insignificant and tiny in the vast open space of the lobby of the FAA building.

Daggett saw their dull reflection in the glass. They looked good together. A handsome couple. He said, "Nervous, is more like it. If sixty-four is ruled an accident, then I lose the linkage to the other investigations: Bernard and Ward. If sixty-four was sabotage—and I think it was—then I need to know how it was done, now, before Kort has another chance. At this point, this voice recorder *is* my investigation."

The guard reached them. They both held up their identification badges through the glass. She said to him, "I'll do what I can, Cam."

"I know that."

She reached down, found his little finger and gave it a squeeze as the door opened. For a moment their fingers hooked.

When they were well away from the guard, walking across the expansive stone foyer toward the elevators, her heels tapping out a rhythm, she said, "There's something you can't tell me, isn't there?"

He slapped the call button. "There always is, isn't there?" he asked. "Terrific job I've got."

Separating his two worlds—his professional life and his private life—was a barrier of classified information. He had grown to resent it. Initially, the classified information had filled him with a sense of importance, bringing a heady immediacy to his job. But over the years he had come to see it for the hindrance it actually was. He could never fully expose himself to anyone; at home he couldn't share the secrets, at work he couldn't share the fears and concerns. His briefcase, laden with his secrets, weighed him down like an anchor. He felt shackled to it, this material, a prisoner of his own acquired importance. Because of it he had changed from a perfectly normal human being into an enigma. No one fully knew him. Not Carrie. Not Duncan. He wasn't sure he knew himself any longer. His emotions had become classified.

It was at this moment, as the elevator doors closed in the FAA building at nine-thirty on a hot and muggy night in mid-September, that he realized Carrie had been right all along: She needed more of him; Duncan needed more of him; he needed more of himself. He had hoped and prayed for a chance to bring to justice the people responsible for 1023. Now that he had earned such a chance, he felt crushed by the weight of responsibility.

The elevator hummed and belched; the doors growled open like jaws and the two stepped into the quiet brightness of a hallway. The doors gobbled shut behind.

"I meant to apologize for Carrie's behavior," he said.

Lynn said, "What bothers me is that if we're going to be condemned like that, regardless of our actions, well . . . If you're going to be hanged for the offense, then you might as well have committed the crime." She seized his arms, drew him to her, and kissed his mouth. He felt the kiss clear through him, and returned it with no intention of doing so. Down the hall, they heard a door hinge squeak. Lynn slipped away from him, grinning as a sickly-looking short man appeared in the hall and called out, "We're in here." He had almost no hair, and sagging, discolored skin beneath his eyes. His posture was tired. When they reached him, he offered Daggett a limp handshake as Lynn introduced him as George Hammett. "As in Dashiell," he said proudly.

They followed Hammett into a sparely furnished lab room. Electronic equipment dominated the walls. Lynn found her way into an empty chair. Daggett remained standing. One of the chairs was occupied by a middle-aged woman with a stenographer's notebook open in her lap. She was introduced as Mrs. Blake. She had graying hair and a sour expression, and was wearing a blue suit. Mickey Tompkins, the lab engineer, reminded Daggett of a math teacher he had once had: disheveled but energetic. Howard Cole, the Duhning Aerospace representative, wore an expensive suit and new shoes. He was about forty-five with sparse hair and a nervous right foot. The remaining man, Don Smith, bright-eyed with gray-flecked hair, was introduced to both of them as a representative of AmAirXpress. Smith had a southern accent. They all took their seats and Hammett explained, "Don's here to help us identify who's talking, in case we pick up something on the CAM that's not on one of the other channels."

Lynn whispered, "Cockpit area microphone—"

Hammett overheard her and said, "Yes, Mickey, why don't you explain exactly what we'll be listening to."

Mickey Tompkins directed his explanation to Daggett. "The CVR is a thirty-minute loop of Mylar that records four channels simultaneously." He pointed to four different VU meters on his console. "Channel one is the pilot's voice, two is the copilot, three is the CAM—an open microphone in the cockpit—and four is the incoming radio traffic.

"We're going to hear the pilot and copilot running through the usual procedures. We'll hear the pre-start checklist, the engine-start checklist, the after-start checklist. The copilot will then request ground control clearance to taxi. We'll get the taxi checklist. The captain will taxi the plane to position and the copilot will switch to tower control. They'll be cleared and they'll run a lineup checklist. The copilot will call for the captain to execute takeoff roll.

Listen for those words. I'll signal you. Then we'll hear the copilot say the following: 'Paver set? . . . Air speed alive . . . ninety knots cross-check . . . V-1 . . . Rotate.' *Rotate* is what we're waiting for. That's the command to lift the nose ten degrees. When we hear 'Positive rate,' the plane is aloft. After that, we'll see what happens. We all know there's a fire on board. We've all heard the tower tape. The question is whether the CAM or anything on here will give us a better look at exactly what happened on the flight deck *after* they noticed the fire. The tower tape stops right at the moment the co-pilot calls out the cockpit fire. Hopefully this one goes further.

"Over here," Tompkins continued, pointing to another console, "is the DFDR—the flight data recorder. I've set it up so that the two recorders will playback in sync, for the sake of comparison. It's digital, and has a twenty-five-hour repeat interval. It gives us stats on engine performance, acceleration, ground speed, airspeed, heading, altitude, landing gear, rudder—really anything we need." He glanced at Hammett, who gave the nod to begin.

"We'll just listen the first time, if that's all right," Hammett cautioned. "Then we'll have some discussion and take another run with some narration. All right," he said, nodding. Tompkins depressed a button. Daggett marveled at the technology as flight 64 came back to life. The voices were calm and professional. Smith identified the voice of the copilot so they knew who was speaking. Then they listened.

To Daggett, the voices of the pilot and copilot sounded as if they were sitting in the next chairs. He realized that because of the crash, these tapes and this data would be stored permanently by the FAA. For the few, brief final seconds of their lives, these two men were now immortal.

Daggett closed his eyes in an effort to concentrate.

He is the victim again. The man behind the wheel. Not a pilot or a copilot, but a man behind a wheel going about his job. It's hot on the ground and he's anxious to get the bird moving. He says so to the copilot, who ignores the comment and continues running down his lists. The pilot echoes a response. Switches are thrown. Numbers are read. There is boredom in his voice. The haze of Los Angeles spreads out before him across the flat plain of the airfield. He taxis the plane to the line of a dozen or so aircraft waiting to take off. He comments to his partner that it isn't getting any better out here. They'll need to expand the entire airport pretty soon. The copilot switches to tower control and introduces them as 64 Bravo.

Bravo. It hardly seems to suit the performance of the next ninety seconds.

The line of waiting planes shrinks and AmAirXpress 64 Bravo is cleared for takeoff.

The engines race. Daggett can feel the plane accelerate down the runway as it begins to shudder.

COPILOT: *Ninety knots cross-check . . . V-1 . . . Rotate . . . Positive rate.*

CAPTAIN: *Gear up . . . Flaps to ten.*

TOWER: *Contact departure now.*

COPILOT: *Roger. Bill, flap retraction speed. You have speed.*

CAPTAIN: *Flaps up.*

The two men run the takeoff checklist. The sound is good enough to hear the switches being thrown. Each tick of sound is demonstrated by Tompkins, who is pointing to the graph printout from the DFDR.

RADIO: *Sixty-four Bravo, turn left to three–five–two. Climb and maintain to one–six thousand.*

COPILOT: *Roger—three–five–two. One–six thousand.*

A cough. To Daggett it sounds like a quick cough.

CAPTAIN: *We've got a fire on the flight deck. Pete, under your seat.*

COPILOT: *The extinguisher. Fuckin' A!*

CAPTAIN: *Taking evasive action. Request emergency landing . . .*

Silence, except for the whine of the engines and a loud hissing.

The screaming of the engines and the wind continues as the plane roars toward the ground in an uncontrolled fall.

Daggett watched the DFDR's graph paper mapping out the various on-board instruments. Two of the lines changed radically, and he took these to be altitude and air speed. A moment later, as all the graph lines straighten simultaneously, the tape offers a replay of the horrible impact. Followed by silence.

The plane is down, two men dead. The cargo is spread out on the field. There is fire everywhere. Daggett can remember this much: *Hard Fall,* on his pager.

Those in the small laboratory room of the FAA were silent as well. But their faces registered nothing and Daggett was tempted to scream. Both Lynn Greene and Don Smith were clearly affected by the tape. But the others had faces of stone. Mrs. Blake stopped her transcribing. She studied the end of her ballpoint pen and pulled a piece of lint from its tip.

Hammett rose and fingered the graph paper, studying lines. "Well," he said, breaking the hard silence. "Let's hear it again."

Tompkins prepared the equipment and they listened again. After the third time through Hammett said, "Okay, Mickey. Let's hold off a minute." He got himself comfortable in the chair. "Well?" he asked the others.

Don Smith, the man from AmAirXpress Corp., said, "Not much different than what we got from flight control."

Lynn jumped in. "Mickey, would you please replay just the CAM track for a moment? Just the last few seconds is good enough; right as they notice the fire."

Tompkins looked to Hammett for approval, and getting it, rewound the tape and singled out the one track. Daggett heard it differently, with the voices pushed into the background and the engine noise brought more immediately to the foreground. The cough—or was it a pop?—seemed more definite.

"Anybody have an explanation for that sound?" Lynn asked.

Hammett asked, "Familiar to you, Mickey?"

"No, it isn't. I assume it's something in the controls catching fire."

"Agreed."

Tompkins added, "There's nothing to support that, however, on the DFDR. Instruments appear normal."

Lynn said boldly, "If it's not on the DFDR, Mickey, then the possibility exists, doesn't it, that the source of the fire is *external* from the instruments and flight control panels? Something inside the cockpit but not something connected directly to the flight of the aircraft, and therefore the DFDR?"

"I'd say that's *more* than possible," Tompkins replied.

Hammett tensed. He faced the nervous man from Duhning. "And you, Mr. Cole? Is that a familiar cockpit sound to you?"

"No. If I had to make a quick guess, I would say that maybe one of the pieces of cargo blew. Something back in the hold." He sounded asthmatic.

"It's too present for that," Tompkins corrected. "Audibly speaking. A noise from the hold wouldn't sound that clear on the CAM. Whatever the source, it's no more than three to five feet from the CAM."

"Let's listen again," Hammett suggested. "From the start. One line at a time, or whatever you feel appropriate, Mickey. Comments would be appreciated, people." Tompkins worked the machinery. He stopped the playback after each line.

RADIO: *Six-four Bravo, you're cleared for taxi.*
COPILOT: *Roger. Thanks fellas.*

Cole, the Duhning man with the nervous foot, explained, "These first few exchanges are between copilot and pilot. The crew has been cleared to taxi. They run the taxi checklist for the next few minutes as they taxi to the end of the runway."

Smith added in his southern accent, "That voice is Peter's. The copilot."

Hammett asked, "Any need to hear the checklist?"

Cole answered, "No, sir, there is not. We've already listened to the lists three times. There is nothing out of the ordinary there."

Tompkins fast-forwarded the tape through the checklist. No one laughed at the chipmunk sound of the voices.

As the tape began at speed again, Cole said, "Okay, what you just heard at the end there was the crew being switched over from ground to tower control.

COPILOT: *Tower, this is sixty-four Bravo. We're ready for takeoff down here, gentlemen.*

RADIO: *Roger, sixty-four Bravo. Proceed to runway one-six. You are cleared for takeoff.*

COPILOT: *One-six, tower?*

RADIO: *Affirmative. One-six.*

COPILOT: *Roger.*

Cole explained the lineup checklist. The pilot and copilot ran a dozen more checks, repeating each other's words. Distinct clicks were heard as adjustments and settings were cross-checked by the team. "Rewind just that last part, please. Just the last command. What we'll hear now is the copilot call out to execute the takeoff roll. At this point the plane starts to move."

COPILOT: *Execute takeoff roll.*

"And he'll continue to run through the necessary cross-checks."

COPILOT: *Power set . . . Airspeed alive . . . Ninety knots cross-check . . .*

Hammett said, "That's the airspeed indicator. They're ready to go."

Daggett could hear the plane shudder as it roared down the runway. He felt himself pushing back in his seat—the sound was that real.

COPILOT: *V-1 . . . Rotate . . .*

"That's the call for takeoff decision. The captain pulls the nose up at this point."

The sound changed dramatically as Daggett pictured the wheels lifting off the safety of the tarmac. The plane was clearly aloft. He could feel it in the pit of his stomach—like the queasy flutter in an elevator.

COPILOT: *Positive rate . . .*

"They've established a positive rate of climb. Everything is going as planned. The nose is at a ten-degree attitude."

Smith's southern accent contributed, "The next voice will be the pilot, Bill Dunlop. He'll call for the gear to come up."

CAPTAIN: *Gear up . . . Flaps to ten.*

Hammett said, "This should be the tower making the handoff to departure control."

RADIO: *Contact departure now.*

Cole said, "Again, I want to emphasize that this bird is aloft and performing as expected. This is exactly as it should go."

COPILOT: *Roger. Bill, flap retraction speed. You have the speed.*

"Everything is a 'go,'" explained Cole. His jumping foot distracted Daggett, who tried instead to concentrate on the tape.

CAPTAIN: *Flaps up.*

Mickey Tompkins, who had obviously listened to hundreds of such tapes, said, "This checklist isn't worth listening to. They run right through it. Everything is still okay up until the end of the list."

Hammett asked, "Agreed, Mr. Cole? May we skip over this?"

Cole nodded his consent.

RADIO: *Sixty-four Bravo, this is departure control. Turn left to three–five–two. Climb and maintain to one–six thousand.*

Daggett was amazed at the calm, professional nature of all the exchanges. Sixty tons of steel, aluminum, and plastic climbing at two hundred miles an hour. A hundred switches and a pair of steering wheels to keep it aloft. These men sounded like they were reading an owner's manual.

COPILOT: *Roger—three–five–two. One–six thousand.*

Tompkins stopped the tape and said, "It's right here that we get the first sign of trouble. You have to listen carefully." He let the tape roll.

Daggett heard that light pop. And then the same, amazingly calm voice of a man who somewhere in his being must have been experiencing sheer panic. If he did, none showed.

CAPTAIN: *We've got a fire on the flight deck. Pete, under your seat.*

Daggett tried to imagine what was being said. "Was the fire under the seat?" he asked. "Is that what he's saying."

"Doubtful," answered Cole, his right foot going like Gene Krupa's in a fast swing tune. "The cockpit fire extinguisher is kept under the copilot's seat. My interpretation would be that Bill Dunlop is reminding his copilot it's his job to handle the fire." He paused. "Anybody else?"

Tompkins said, "That may be, but the sound of the fire —if that's what we're hearing—is clearly more apparent through the copilot's microphone. I think Mr. Daggett may have something here."

"Let it roll, Mickey," Hammett ordered.

COPILOT: *The extinguisher . . . Fuckin' A!*

CAPTAIN: *Taking evasive action. Request emergency landing . . .*

Again, those in the room said nothing. Even repetition didn't erase the suddenness of it all.

Lynn Greene said, "How do we explain the copilot's tone of voice? Is he saying that the fire extinguisher can't be reached?"

"That's what it sounds like to me," Daggett agreed.

Smith said, "The tone of voice clearly indicates panic.

You normally wouldn't hear Pete talk like that in the copilot's chair."

Daggett didn't need that reminder.

Cole looked over at Lynn. "I think that's unlikely, Ms. Greene. There is nothing beneath the copilot's chair that would be likely to start a fire. The instruments maybe, something in the console, but not beneath the copilot's chair."

If we had stopped Bernard in L.A., Daggett thought, I wouldn't be listening to this.

At the end of the tape he decided to make his stand, before the others began forming what he believed was the wrong conclusion. He spoke up for the first time. "You people are the experts, and I'm nothing more than an observer here tonight, but isn't it possible, given the little cough that can be heard, that the fire was the result of a *small* explosion?"

"Explosion?" Hammett interrupted. "Let's stick with what we're hearing, Mr. Daggett. There is no mention on the CVR of an explosion. The flight crew talks about a *fire*."

"But the fire was caused by *something*," Daggett argued. "That's all I'm saying."

"Which is *exactly* what this investigation will pursue over the next few months. Obviously, our primary concern at this point is the cause of that fire."

'The cause,' Daggett thought, hearing the man's words echo. *Der Grund.* He did not miss the irony. "I haven't got months," Daggett said.

"It's obvious," Cole said while scratching his bald head, "that the crew continues to operate after this fire begins. Equally obvious, is that the fire—or even this alleged explosion—did not cause any serious damage, certainly not enough to bring this bird down so quickly." He pointed an accusatory finger at the graph paper. "The DFDR tells us that the captain's instruments and controls continue to operate properly and, for a few seconds at least, he continues to fly the aircraft." He paused. "So, a more likely explanation is that fumes from the fire overcame the crew. The toxicity of flight deck fires is well documented; the plastics and resins catch fire and can overcome a crew in seconds. *That* is what this tape tells me."

"Agreed," said Hammett. "If we look at this logically, the events seem to be"—he counted out on his stumpy fingers—"rotation, change of course, fire, unconsciousness or death of the crew, impact."

Daggett blurted out: "If the crew had been overcome by fumes, we would have seen it in the blood work-ups. There's *nothing* there to support this. Mr. Cole has a fine theory, but there's simply no evidence to support it."

They were all staring at him, including Lynn. Only then did he realize how loudly he had spoken, and that he had come out of his chair. Embarrassed, he sat back down.

Lynn covered for him. "Mr. Daggett's point is an interesting one. The autopsies evidently do not support the theory of a crew overcome by toxic fumes. At best, it seems to me, this CVR tape is inconclusive. It has to be studied more closely by experts such as Mr. Tompkins so we know *exactly* what is the cause of each and every sound. There's room for further analysis, isn't there?"

Tompkins shook his head violently and said, "Of *course* there is. We'll take this tape apart decibel by decibel. Given enough time," he said, looking cautiously at Daggett, "we should be able to identify and reproduce each and every sound on here—"

"Which means there's a good chance we'll know if the fire began as a result of something mechanical, something endemic to the flight deck, or whether the possibility of sabotage exists."

"I would caution you on that, Ms. Greene," Cole said, cutting off Tompkins's response. "I repeat that the DFDR demonstrates clearly that all instruments and all controls continue to operate correctly until the moment of impact. From what we know so far, sabotage seems highly unlikely, unless you are suggesting that a third party started a fire on board and counted on the toxicity of the ignited materials to overcome the crew. That's stretching it a bit, don't you think? Unless you're suggesting the bomb was a dud, and instead of exploding it only caught fire. But to my knowledge there's been no *evidence* found," he said, addressing Daggett, "to suggest anything like a bomb on board sixty-four Bravo."

"Unless a fire *was* the intended sabotage," Lynn said. "Not all sabotage is meant to kill. It could have been the work of a disgruntled employee. It could have been—"

"*What* could have been?" Cole protested. "That implies there's a device involved."

"He's right," Hammett agreed. "I'd have to agree with Mr. Cole on this. We've seen no evidence whatsoever—"

Lynn interrupted Hammett. "The glass bulb and the possibility of a mercury switch," she reminded.

"That again?" Hammett reminded. "That's hardly conclusive at this point."

The volley of interruptions was followed by an uncomfortable silence. It was broken by the accent of Don Smith, who said slowly, "Two men lost their lives. AmAirXpress and Duhning lost an aircraft. There is no gasping on this tape. No choking. No coughing. No call for help. No sign of struggle. What is there? Mr. Tompkins, what *exactly* do we hear?" he asked rhetorically. "We hear a pop. We hear the call of fire. We hear the copilot's intention to subdue that fire. We hear the fire extinguisher engage. I am not here as an expert, gentlemen—Ms. Greene—in anything other than the sound of my associates' voices. This is a painful experience for me. Those men were my friends. But as far as I can hear, the last thing mentioned on that tape is the fire extinguisher." He looked over at Daggett. Then to Lynn Green and finally at Hammett. "Has anyone studied the fire extinguisher. Have you determined its contents?"

"Let me get this straight," Cole said, jumping in. "You're suggesting that a third party purposely started a fire on the flight deck in order to get the crew to put it out with a fire extinguisher charged with some kind of killer gas or something? Doesn't that strike anyone as just a little absurd? I mean, why bother? If you can get a device on board, why start a fire? Why not make it a bomb and make sure it does the job?"

Daggett answered, "To create the exact confusion we're experiencing right now. 'Absurd' is exactly right, Mr. Cole. That may be what we're expected to believe. I think Mr. Smith may have something. *Has* anyone checked the fire extinguisher? Do we even know where it is?"

Lynn Greene said, "I can't answer that." She looked over to Hammett, who rose, stiff and stubborn, and left the room. Several minutes passed. Tompkins donned a set of headphones and replayed the tape, leaving the others in relative silence. Mrs. Blake appeared to be taking a catnap. Cole read through some papers he withdrew from his briefcase.

Finally the door opened. Hammett had a single piece of paper in his hand. "The fire extinguisher *was* recovered," he announced. Then he lowered a pair of reading glasses and read. "It was catalogued and filed and is presently in the reconstruction hangar. Our 'go team' is still on site." He checked his watch. "With the time difference, I may be able to raise someone out there. I'll ask that it be removed and immediately shipped back here for analysis."

Cole said, "I have a document here that says that fire extinguisher was inspected before that plane left our field."

"A fire extinguisher," Daggett corrected. "Maybe not *that particular* fire extinguisher."

"You still haven't answered my question," Cole objected. "Why bother with such an elaborate plan? Why not just blow up the plane, if that's the point of all of this?"

Daggett hesitated. They were all looking at him. All but Lynn. She was studying the edge of her shoes. He tried to say it strongly, but it came out as more of a forced, dry wind, "Because he doesn't want us figuring it out." And then he added: "In less than a week, he's going to try this again."

16

WEDNESDAY MORNING, DAGGETT awakened alone.

As he made the bed, following his run, he thought about Carrie. She had a white-collar career to build from the ashes of a blue-collar upbringing—she had something to prove. She wanted the suburbs, the barbecues, the new car every two years. Yale or Princeton for their children who weren't yet conceived. Daggett wasn't sure what he wanted. He wanted it all to be different, whatever that meant. He wanted his only son to walk again; he wanted something to laugh about; he wanted his past returned undamaged. The future frightened him.

As he made the coffee he promised himself not to think about it. But promises were made to be broken. Always the same for him—always predictable.

He called out to Duncan.

"Right here, Dad," the young voice came back. "I'm not going anywhere."

"Just checking that you're awake."

"It was a *joke,* Dad. Not going anywhere . . . Get it?"

He got it all right.

He showered and then drew a bath—same routine every day. He walked into Duncan's bedroom. The walls of Duncan's room were not covered with posters of Michael Jordan or Joe Montana, as were the walls of the bedrooms of his friends. Instead, on Duncan's walls hung autographed black-and-white press photos of television and radio sportscasters: Dick Engberg, Al Michaels, John Madden, Pat Summerall. On his bedside table lay the latest issue of *Sports Illustrated* and a hardcover book titled *Roar from the Valley*—a best-selling history of collegiate football. On his crowded shelves was a paperback library of sports biographies. The kid was a reading machine. What else was there to do?

He lifted and carried his son from caged hospital-style bed to steaming water. "You're not getting any lighter," he told him.

"You're not getting any stronger," Duncan replied.

"Meaning?" he asked as he lowered him into the water. There were times to play games with Dunc, to tease him or torture him for saying such things, but this was not one of them.

"If you don't get back to the gym, your arms are going to look like these," he said, prodding one of his atrophied legs. Daggett shaved and brushed his teeth while the boy bathed. The same routine.

"You could use some more bookshelves."

"I could use a Saturday at the library," Duncan said, looking at his dad in the mirror.

"I can do that for you."

"I want to do it *myself.*"

"So we'll do that."

"When?"

"You going to get on my case too?"

"Yes," Duncan replied.

Daggett turned and looked at him. Duncan offered him an impassive expression, and then squeezed and lost the soap. Daggett took a step toward the tub, but his son shot him a look that stopped him; this was something he had to do himself. Daggett watched in the mirror as his son attempted to recover the soap. Whereas a person with use of his legs could drag the bar of soap back with his foot, Duncan could only use his hands. In a moment of quick thinking, he used the back-scratcher as a rake. As he proudly took hold of the soap again, he checked to see if his father was spying on him. Daggett fooled him by quickly averting his eyes, his concentration on the razor and his chin.

Duncan began playing with the bar of soap, squeezing it tightly until it jumped from his hands, catching it, and squeezing it again. Distracted, Daggett nicked himself with the razor. Blood turned the shaving cream pink.

"So when do we go to the library?" Duncan asked, still playing.

"Message received," Daggett said. It was the line he used with Dunc when he didn't want to continue with a discussion. The comment hurt the boy's feelings, and he wondered why he seemed to be hurting everyone around him lately. He felt the need to justify himself. "If I make any promises, Dunc, I may have to break them."

"A broken promise would be better than none at all. It would be nice if I had *something* to look forward to."

He'd been talking to Mrs. Kiyak again. These weren't his words.

"And don't blame it on Mrs. Kiyak," Duncan said.

"You done feeling sorry for yourself?"

"No," Duncan replied angrily.

He could see the boy was finished with the tub. Again he stepped forward. This time, Duncan stopped him. "I'll do it myself," he said.

"Dunc . . ." Daggett begged. He had never done this himself.

A trapeze hung above the tub—complements of the former owner. Daggett stepped back and watched with both amazement and a father's instinctive concern as Duncan reached overhead and struggled with his body weight. Perhaps it was a result of his work on the chin-up bar, perhaps nothing more than determination—a boyish will to prove himself—but Duncan hauled himself up and out of the water, pushed off the wall, and swung his bare bottom onto the edge of the tub. It was a major accomplishment—the first time he had done this completely on his own. Daggett's throat choked with pride. He withheld the applause he had raised his hands to deliver: It wasn't over. Duncan carefully lifted one leg out of the water, over the rim of the tub, and deposited its uncooperative weight onto the floor. Then the other. Facing his father, he began to towel himself dry.

As the wet skin of the useless feet slapped the floor, Daggett cringed. He hated that sound. He resented it. His emotions swelled. He began to clap, though too slowly. A morbid applause. He felt himself coming apart. The window fan revolved listlessly as a light breeze turned the white plastic blades that needed cleaning. The groan of distant traffic mixed with the barking of an angry dog. The neighbor's television was tuned to one of the morning shows. His eyes stung. He felt sick to his stomach. Duncan was smiling, but he looked frightened. Daggett's tears fell. He reached for a towel to hide his face.

Levin entered the bullpen looking tired. On CNN, a good-looking woman with unusually blond hair was quoting figures from Wall Street.

Daggett opened his briefcase and removed some papers. In doing so, he exposed the red file that Mumford had given him. Sight of the file reminded him of this other responsibility, and the fact that he had delegated all of this to Levin. "How are we coming along?"

"Mosner, Sandhurst, and Grady are all arriving by private jet. They are adamant that they alone are responsible for their own planes and that they don't want or need our help. I don't think we're going to change their minds."

"That's a bunch of crap. Their planes are going to be searched and sniffed prior to their departure for here—I don't care what they say. And I mean prior to departure. I mean when the goddamned executives are already on board and the door is ready to close. We're not letting some bozo sneak something on board at the last minute. Kort—if that's who this is—passed himself off as a flight mechanic in L.A., don't forget. Once the cabins are checked for the final time, the door is sealed and the plane rolls. No arguments."

"I told them that already. But all I got back was a lot of shit. All three say they can handle this themselves."

"We better get something in writing."

"Already done. I have letters from the security chiefs of all three companies. We're in the clear there."

"Stupid shits."

"At least it gets them out of our hair."

"Which leaves us the commercial flights."

"Fitzmaurice, Savile, and Goldenbaum all arrive and depart on separate commercial carriers. All three of the airlines I've spoken to have agreed to your suggestion." Daggett's suggestion had been a simple one: Establish tight security for each of these three flights, and then, at the last minute, switch planes. Two minutes prior to boarding, the scheduled plane would be towed to a hangar and thoroughly searched by a bomb squad before being allowed to return to service. Meanwhile, a substitute plane would be taxied to the gate. Luggage would be reloaded, and passengers would board this substitute plane.

"So we're covered?" he asked.

"In principle, yes. The logistics of arranging the various bomb squads and security teams remains a nightmare. All the privates and one of the commercials are coming into National. The two other commercials are coming into Dulles. Sandhurst leaves the night of the meeting. Everyone else stays over."

"Bernard built two identical baro-bombs. The target *must* be a plane."

Levin nodded. "We've been over all this, Michigan. He's not going to sabotage one of these planes. We've got him covered."

"Not one of them is a 959," Daggett said, just to hear himself repeat what he had been thinking for days now. "Damn it, this has *something* to do with a 959." Levin didn't say anything. "Maybe his target isn't this meeting. Maybe that's nothing but another coincidence." He raised his voice angrily. "How can we stop him if we don't know what he's got planned?" He caught Gloria staring at him.

The muscles in Levin's jaw flexed as he bit back any comment he might have had. Daggett felt relieved to be around someone who knew when to keep quiet.

He lowered his voice. "Answer," he said, answering his own question. "We stop him *before* he has a chance to do whatever it is he intends to do. And that leads me to our next point of discussion. I want to run an idea by you." Levin suddenly looked even more tired. Daggett worried he was pushing him too hard. "Listen, even though Mumford assigned me—you and me—to keep these arriving executives safe, he didn't pull me from the Bernard ticket—the detonators. Not exactly. That's important, because it allowed me a lot of leeway I wouldn't normally have. I need to run an idea by Pullman. But if he senses I'm pushing too hard, he may bump me off of what we're still vaguely calling Bernard, which is actually Seattle and the AmAirXpress crash. Some interesting questions were raised last night concerning the voice recorder. With this security stuff pretty much handled, I may be able to get Mumford to put me back on tracking down this guy."

"Why do I get the feeling I'm being set up?"

"I need you to field this for me, to present it as if it's *your* idea."

Levin looked askance. "Exactly *what* are we talking about?"

Daggett said tentatively, testing the water, "The lab was able to work up a blood group using the saliva from the butts I found at the reception." He paused because Levin didn't seem very impressed. "The group matches with the blood from the tooth recovered in Seattle." Again, he looked for enthusiasm but saw none.

Levin's lips puckered. His considerable nose twitched. "That's horseshit, Michigan, and you know it. Saliva? Come on! That's nothing."

"It's the *brand* of the cigarette that interests me, not the goddamned saliva," Daggett said defensively. "It's the *combination* of the two."

"You're saying that Ward's killer was at this reception?" He was humoring him.

"I'm saying, yes, it's at least a possibility. What we're going to do," Daggett continued, now set on a course he refused to alter, "is limit the brand's availability to only a few stores. One or two. I've already done the groundwork. Only four stores in the entire city sell Sobranie Black Russians in the first place. They cost five bucks a *pack*. What we do is put one of our people behind the counter of each of these stores. Then we wait it out. We're good at that. Right? Professionals at waiting around." He was shouting. Bud Togue—Bulldog—who had the desk two desks up from Daggett's, turned his head to complain, but seeing Daggett, apparently thought better of it. Daggett continued, "A customer comes in to buy Sobranie, our man dicks with the cash register—it's fucked up, it won't work. He says the only way to pay is by check or by credit card."

"And we get a way to trace the customer," Levin interrupted.

"You're so smart."

"And we follow them as well? I mean, from the store?"

"Depends how many people Pullman will cut us. Right? That's the point. But if it's a guy fitting the general description, or a woman like *her*," he said, pointing to the grainy enlargement of the woman's face he had taped to the gray burlap baffle, "then, if necessary, our man behind the counter contacts us and then follows on foot. Yes?"

Levin thought about it for some time. "It's a good idea, Michigan, as far as *ideas* go. I mean, it's creative in a weird kind of way, using this guy's habit against him. I like that." He hesitated and concluded, "But you'll never sell it to Pullman."

"That's right," Daggett agreed quickly. He offered Levin a nice, juicy, shit-eating grin. "*You* will."

17

IT WAS CALLED Elite Estates with a slogan beneath the title's Olde English typeface that read: ATTRACTIVE PROPERTIES MANAGED WITH CARE AND PERSONAL ATTENTION. It was a Jeffersonian brick building with oversized true-divided-light windows that reached almost to the floor. Curtains blocked a view of the interior. A brass plaque mounted to the brick above an intercom call box identified the building as a historical site.

He let himself in through the front door and took advantage of a missing receptionist.

"Knock, knock," Kort said.

Carrie glanced up from her desk and smiled mechanically at him. This was replaced immediately by a glint of faint recognition. She was trying to place him.

"The receptionist wasn't at her desk," he explained apologetically. "I saw your name on the door." He tapped the nameplate with a trimmed and filed fingernail. He could practically hear her thinking. He didn't want to make it easy for her; the idea was to challenge her. When she blushed, he knew she had finally remembered. "The party the other night," he said.

"Yes," she acknowledged in a warmer, less professional expression. He savored the moment. She had a beautiful smile. Had she not recognized him, had she not recalled their brief encounter, it would have made things much more difficult for him. "I'm sorry, I don't remember—"

"Carl Anthony."

"How on earth did you find me?"

"I asked around." It was a lie. The night of the party, he

and Monique had followed her home. This morning they had followed her to work.

He studied her. She was a lovely woman in an unusual way. None of the stunning, sexually shocking quality of a Monique. A much more controlled, conservative look. She wore a blue-and-white-striped man-tailored blouse, accentuated by a thin gold chain around her smooth neck. She had used some blush to help define a face seemingly without cheekbones. Lipstick widened her mouth. She had inquisitive bold eyes that forewarned of her intelligence and a posture that made the most of high breasts and sturdy bones. An athlete. A competitor.

The office interior enhanced her femininity—chintz and pastels, Boston ferns and a woven basket of forced tulips of lavender and peach. The room smelled of scented soap, clean and inviting. Or perhaps it was her. The smell relaxed him, like a long, hot bath. Sunlight flooded through the windows behind her, and he thought if he ever built a house, he would want a room like this in which to have his morning coffee while reading the newspapers. And a woman like this would belong in the room with him, humming to herself, flipping the pages of a magazine and giggling privately as she read, distracting and alluring.

"Well," she said, looking perplexed and a bit embarrassed, "please have a seat. Come in. How can I help you?"

"I'm looking for a place," he explained. " 'Why give your business to a stranger?' I asked myself. I decided to combine business with pleasure."

"How kind of you." She delivered this well, but he sensed a reluctance in her. "A rental? A lease?"

"I enjoyed last night," he said, taking a seat now, but not taking his eyes off of her. "I don't get out very often."

"I forget your business. I'm sorry. It's not that . . . It's just that it was a . . . a *spirited* evening for me." She smiled, embarrassed. "My memory is a little fuzzy."

"Food service," he replied. "Those awful snacks you get

on the airplane. Our company is trying to make them more palatable and steal away some of the business."

"Oh, yes, now I remember. You're a spy."

That had a way of sobering him. "Exactly."

"You're over here consulting a Washington-based company, wasn't that it?"

"What a memory! Yes. They're consulting us, actually. Just so."

"And you're from?"

"Europe," he answered vaguely. "That's my 1992 response to that question."

She seemed to find him amusing. "These are exciting times in Europe."

"They certainly are," he agreed, aware of the irony of his reply.

"So, how may I help you?"

She meant real estate, of course. He knew this, but his mind wandered. This room was far too comfortable to think business. He relaxed, his tension drained away. There were several ways she could help him, it occurred to him. The key to Daggett's front door held the top position on his list and now several other possibilities came to mind. She sat patiently waiting for his response.

"A lease. I need a house for six months to a year. Longer perhaps, if things work out." He had decided on this amount of time because he wanted to make sure she saw him as a potentially valuable client. "Somewhere out here in the Virginia suburbs. Not too far from National, but far enough to be quiet and out of the flight patterns." She reached for a loose-leaf notebook as he continued, "And I should warn you that I'm terribly particular. To the point of being finicky, I'm afraid. I have very specific tastes, beginning with the landscaping. I'm something of a green thumb —at least I fancy myself one—and though we're at the end of the season, I would like a place where there's plenty to do in the gardens. Tending the lawn has never been one of my favorites, but I'm *mad* about gardens. Flowers, vegetables, shrubs, it doesn't matter just so long as I can get my hands into the soil and make a mess of myself." He was stretching out the time, still unsure how he would attempt to get into her purse and at those keys. He needed that date of the meeting from inside Daggett's briefcase as soon as possible. There was much to be done. The focus of his attention remained Mosner and EisherWorks—avenging the destruction of his former life.

She laughed in a low contralto. He found the sound soothing, and wished she would do it again. "We have that in common," she said. "A love of gardens. I think I know exactly what you're looking for. But that won't make my job any easier, I'm afraid." She began to turn pages. "That will require some serious hunting." She glanced up from the notebook. "We pride ourselves on satisfied customers."

"Yes, I'm sure you do. I have nothing but time," he said. "No hurry whatsoever." Lies, lies, and more lies. It had become so much a way of life for him, he didn't hear them any longer.

There was that laugh again. He wished he had a tape recorder. She said, "Don't worry. It shouldn't take *that* long."

"Oh, I'm not worried," he assured her. "Not in the least."

She drove a red Ford Taurus with a plush interior and all the extras. It reminded him of Roger Ward. This must have been the car Daggett had borrowed the other night. That reminded him how close he was to enemy territory, how risky this approach. It didn't feel risky. It felt delightful. He glanced over at her. She wore the man-tailored blouse tucked into a khaki skirt. White tights. Leather walking shoes with thick gum rubber soles. He had a fetish about women in cars, he realized. Except for Monique, he had not ridden with a woman in years, and so only discovered this odd lust now, as he longed to reach over and run his hand up her leg, up her thigh and under her skirt. Or perhaps unbutton her blouse and tease her breasts as she drove. Was it her helplessness? Her defenselessness? He considered his fantasy rather tawdry. But he carried it one step further, allowing himself to imagine tying her up in bed, naked and willing, tying her wrists with yarn, or something easily broken, or tying her with bows so that they both knew she could free herself whenever she wished, but tying her down and taking his time with her, exploring, teasing, satisfying. Make her swell, rich with a woman's scent.

"What do you think?" she asked. They had been driving for ten or fifteen minutes through a wooded part of the Virginia suburbs and were now parked in front of a quaint yellow-and-white cottage, its brick chimney thick with ivy, a tarnished copper weather vane mounted to the peak of the roof, shifting slightly with the fluctuating wind. Surrounded by a low wrought-iron fence, with an intricate gate, it reminded him of southern France. Perfect. He felt like walking inside and never coming out. But he needed more time. "I don't mind taking a look," he said, anxious to see the inside, "but right off the mark I would say there's not enough yard to it, not enough lot. Do you see that? It's charming, of course, but hardly the sort of place . . . I'm not sure. Let's have a look. I would hate to be too hasty."

She led the way. He thought that in such a small house there should have been fewer rooms and more emphasis on windows. With an eye on her purse and still no way to get to her keys, he listed its shortcomings and requested they try another.

By the third house, she had relaxed and he had her talking. It was a stucco Tudor with black shutters and leaded windows, large for a bachelor, but with outstanding landscaping including a rock garden and a lovely vine-covered gazebo out back. They were standing in the bedroom, he looking out the window, she wandering the room reciting the house's various features.

Inexplicably, Kort choked up. This home wasn't so different from the one he had lived in as a married man. A feeling of loss surged through him. Without the greed of EisherWorks Chemicals he would have been living in a house like this with a healthy child and a loving wife—it seemed blatantly unfair. He recalled the day Inspector Michael Sharpe had knocked on his door and changed his life.

A home. What would it be like to lock the doors of this house, trapping Caroline inside, and spend the remainder of his life making love to her and tilling the gardens? The thought intoxicated him. Caroline crossed the room and arranged a bouquet of silk flowers. She was speaking, but he didn't hear. She was his adversary's woman. Did that add to his thrill? The palpable quiet of the room absorbed him. He could hear her breathing from across the room. The bed lay like an island between them, inviting his thoughts. Was it so unthinkable? Was this not, after all, the best way to get that key? If he simply took the key, she might mention the loss to Daggett, who would change the lock. But to find a way to legitimately borrow the key?

"What do you think?" she asked.

"It's lovely," he said, referring to her work with the flowers. "Much better than it was. You understand color very well."

"I mean the house."

"Oh. It's very nice, isn't it? But awfully big for *a single man*. Why don't we look at the grounds?"

They strolled the small backyard, she glancing over at him now and then, especially when he stooped to pick a weed or remove dead heads from the flowering plants.

"These beds are being tended to once every other week," he observed. "They would look better if serviced once a week. The flowering plants have obviously taken a beating in this heat," for it was hot again today, and growing more so by the hour, "but everything here needs more water and more attention in general."

"They need you," she said in her best soft-sell voice.

"I'm taking too much of your time," he said, the concern in his voice genuine. He didn't want to do anything but tour these homes with her, walk in gardens and fantasize about making love with her.

"No, you're not. You mustn't think that, Mr. Anthony—"

"Carl."

"It's my job to put you in the home you want. I wasn't kidding about satisfied customers."

They had come to the gazebo and rock garden. It was lovely, by far the prettiest, most well-conceived piece of landscaping on the small grounds. They stood close to each other, neither speaking. In a tender voice Kort said, "I miss the peace of the garden."

Caroline studied him as his eyes stayed on the flower bed. "You were married, weren't you? You said you're single now, but you were married."

He nodded solemnly.

"Children?"

"One," he said.

"Where are they now?"

He stooped, clawed at the earth, collected some dirt in his hand and then released it. He looked up at her and shook his head. He felt his eyes stinging, and it embarrassed him. He was long past crying for them. A heavy silence fell between them, but they maintained their eye contact. "I had no right to ask," she said.

"Of course you did," he replied, absorbed by the beauty of the garden, not wanting her to see any more of his sorrow. "But I don't have any pets," he said, intentionally harshly.

"I wasn't asking as a property manager," she corrected. "I was asking as a fellow human being."

Music to his ears. He played the scene for all he could. "Let's try someplace else. I like this very much, but the house is a little big. Still, it's the nicest of the three."

"Yes. It is big for one person. Shall we go?"

He pointed over to the gazebo and a bench in the shade, produced his pack of Camels nonfilters and offered her one. Monique had promised him a pack of Sobranies;

he could hardly wait. Caroline declined, but she had a pack of her own filtered cigarettes, and a moment later he lighted the cigarettes and they smoked. "It's a terrible habit," he said, later breaking their silence.

"Yes, it is."

"But I love it."

"Me too." She giggled. "I promised myself just this one pack, then I'm going to quit again."

"You're stronger than I," he said.

"No. I doubt that," she said softly. "I don't feel very strong at the moment."

He might have kissed her then, he thought. She seemed to be inviting him to, but he feared if he tried and failed, not only would it spoil his plans, but it would destroy the peacefulness of the moment.

And at this particular spot in time, on a bench in the cool shade, a bevy of colorful flowers saturating the grounds before them, sitting alone with a charming and sensitive woman, the moment was everything.

18

MONIQUE PARKED THREE blocks from the smoke shop on K Street. The first store she had tried had been out of Sobranie and the man behind the counter had recommended this shop. A bright sunny day threw her shadow down in front of her. She chased herself up the sidewalk.

The store—half wineshop, half tobacco shop—smelled wonderful, even though she disliked smoke. It was perfumed with sweet pipe tobaccos, rich cigar tobaccos, and oiled wood.

The man behind the counter seemed out of place for such a shop. He was thirtyish, strong, and very straight-looking. She had expected an old man, balding perhaps, glasses, with a cheery smile and stained teeth. If this salesman smoked, then she was Cleopatra. Probably a graduate student who paid the rent by hawking Turkish nonfilters.

"A carton of Sobranie, please," she said.

"A carton? Sobranie we sell by the *pack*," the salesman asked.

"Ten packs then," she said, annoyed at him. "You *do* have them, don't you? Sobranie Black Russians?"

"Sure. We've got 'em." He bent down behind the counter, slid open a door, and retrieved ten packs.

He scribbled onto a piece of paper and then switched on the calculator. "Fifty-four-fifty. And I can't give change," he said as she produced three twenties. My register's down and it's one of these friggin' electronic kind, self-locking. I gotta have a credit card, if it's all the same to you."

She stuffed the twenties back into her wallet, withdrew her credit card and handed it to him. He ran off the charge and when he returned the receipt said, "Local phone number." She scribbled out the phone number hastily and signed the receipt, mumbling to herself. Everyone made everything so difficult. Intentionally, it seemed. Life was supposed to get tougher and so everyone made sure it did. He disconnected her portion of the receipt, although so clumsily that he tore it, apologized, and handed it over to her. Having placed the cigarettes into a sack, he handed her this as well. *Don't say it*! she willed him silently.

But he did. "Have a nice day."

"You as well," she said, turning and hurrying to the door. At all costs, she had wanted to avoid thanking him.

The light turned red. Daggett honked and ran it. "Are you sure?" he asked Levin, who was busy checking the traffic, fearing for his life.

"He said the credit card was in the name of Maryanne Lyttle. He said that if you put her in dark glasses and a scarf and shot her in grainy black-and-white film, she could be the woman in the photo you passed around. He said she bought a bunch of Sobranie. He was going to follow her. She left on foot."

They drove another two blocks and Levin, eyes searching the pedestrians, said loudly, "There he is! Pull over." Levin jumped from the car.

Daggett watched as the two had a brief exchange of words. The other man pointed while reading aloud from a notebook. Levin jumped back into the car, pulled the door shut and said, "We're two, maybe three minutes behind her. A red BMW, three hundred series. Washington plates. AJ-three-two-something-or-other. He didn't get the full number. Lost her in traffic."

"Shit! Two or three minutes?" Daggett stepped on it. The car lurched into traffic. He drove frantically for several minutes, ran another light, was nearly struck by an ice-cream truck and resigned himself to a lost cause. "I screwed this up," he said. "The plan was ill-conceived in the first place. They should have been two-man teams."

"Then *I'm* to blame, Michigan. Pullman wouldn't give me that."

Stopped at a red light, Daggett closed his eyes in an attempt to calm himself. It didn't work.

Levin said, "We've got a local phone number. We've got a partial on a license plate on a very exclusive and unusual car."

"You think any of that will lead us to her, you're crazy."

"Don't be so sure, Michigan. Remember the earrings? This one may be an amateur."

Peter Drake's well-ordered desk was typical of the counterintelligence boys. CI-3 was mostly Ivy Leaguers. They talked without moving their lips and they wore white button-down shirts and school ties. They wore suspenders and penny loafers. They drank their coffee black and their Scotch neat. On the weekends they played tennis or went sailing in thirty-five-foot boats their parents had once owned. Their wives were pretty and intelligent, with crisp, practical hairdos and clothes like Meryl Streep's. Drake was the tall, dark, and handsome variety. He spoke nine languages and had three degrees, and everything about him reflected this. He rose from his chair, shook hands firmly, and, returning to his chair, said in a soft but clear voice, "Using some of the files confiscated in the bust of *Der Grund,* we think we've ID'd your mystery woman."

"I'm all ears."

"If she is who we think she is, her name at birth was Monique de Margerie."

"Do we have background?"

"We have *everything.* This Michael Sharpe kept dossiers on all his operatives. He was careful not to include anything that would lead to a positive ID. That's why I can't be certain she is who we think she is. But chances are that she is. Bottom line is a less-than-wonderful childhood in a

wealthy French family. Her father was in publishing. She
became a teenage runaway, a prostitute, a drug addict, and
much later, a cash courier for a drug lord. She shows up as
a regular on flights to and from major European markets
and Switzerland.

"De Margerie was 'arrested,'" he continued, drawing
the quotes, "by Sharpe, the leader of *Der Grund,* at that time
a cop—a bad cop. Now, admittedly this is being pieced together on the fly, but Sharpe is believed to have kept the
cash from this bust, a bust he never told his superiors
about. He 'turned' her and began using her as *his* courier.
He had a group of wealthy benefactors spread out over the
continent. Some contributed to *Der Grund* willingly, others
through blackmail. De Margerie carried this cash into Germany or Switzerland. Or both. We're still unclear on that.
There's no telling exactly how much cash, but estimates go
as high as several million dollars.

"De Margerie left Germany two years ago and entered
this country under the name Cheysson," he continued.
"Sharpe evidently planted her as a sleeper in a food service
company based here in Washington, In-Flite Foods, which
caters commercial airlines." His formidable brow knit
tightly as he seemed to consider whether or not to add anything. At the same time he slumped in his chair, as if the air
were being let out of him. He looked back to Daggett.

Daggett said, "What is it?"

"The rest of this is just guesswork, nothing more. There
is much to assimilate from what was recovered in the raid,
but as I understand it you're pressed for time."

"That's an understatement."

"She flew into Frankfurt two days before the downing
of 1023."

Daggett's breathing stopped, and not a muscle
twitched, not a pore opened. He was frozen. If he hadn't
stayed alive, he would have sworn his heart had quit. "Is
she Anthony Kort?"

Drake shook his head slowly. "That's why I call it guesswork. We may be able to piece together a profile of Kort from this same paperwork. But no, she's clearly a flunkie. A driver maybe. A courier mostly."

"She delivered something to Los Angeles."

"It's possible, yes."

"Bernard's detonator."

"Could be."

"But that doesn't seem to interest you," Daggett observed.

"Of course it *interests* me, but the more pertinent connection that I'm trying to make is that she was a flunkie in Frankfurt. She was very likely Kort's driver." He offered a space, and Daggett would have gladly filled it if he could have slowed his thoughts to the point of being able to string a sentence together. But he took too long, and Drake filled it himself. "They're a *team.* An operational team. She's been over here two years waiting to be activated. Now you connect her in all likelihood to the crash of AmAirXpress sixty-four. She's back in action. The Germans round up all of *Der Grund,* but Kort is missed in the sweep. So if you were in Intelligence, what conclusions would you draw from all of this? I'll tell you what I think. I think this bomber you're after is none other than—"

Daggett interrupted, finally able to speak. "Anthony Kort."

Then he was certain his heart had stopped.

He drove the streets for several hours, from one bar to the next, not sure who he was or why he was doing this. Anthony Kort. It filled him with both fear and excitement. Fear that he had but this one chance to get him; fear that Kort would prevail and whatever it was he had planned would be accomplished and he, Daggett, would come away empty-handed; fear that, if given the chance, he would not arrest him but kill him; fear that he might be caught.

He was drunk by the time he headed home, driving all but deserted streets, trying to find his way across to Virginia without his wits about him. It was as he finally spotted a sign to the bridge that he felt his arms, as if disconnected, tug the wheel sharply right at the red light.

A while later, engine running, windows down, the letter jacket in a heap on the seat beside him, he found his car parked outside Carrie's Chevy Chase carriage house. Previously part of an enormous estate, the eighteenth-century stone carriage house was encircled by twenty-foot rhododendrons. The surrounding acreage—which technically did not fall under the parameters of her lease—was, for all practical purposes, hers, since the main house was separated from its former carriage house by a substantial distance. The grounds were shaded by several tall maples, a substantial oak, three extremely old dogwoods, and a small, stone-wall-enclosed orchard of fruit trees: cherry, crabapple, and peach. Moonlight illuminated the moss-covered cedar shake roof and ivy-entwined red brick chimney. The effect was magical. Daggett sat behind the wheel, dazed, even slightly afraid.

She was a woman who had rescued him more times than he could remember. She knew how to listen, how to draw from him the things he feared to face, how to provide a safe environment in which he could unload without judgment or conditions. She was his confessor, his high priest, his therapist. But lately, he now remembered in the midst of his drunken fog, she had become his adversary.

What if she lectured him at this hour? What if she were not in a forgiving mood, but found his unannounced arrival an intrusion? He could almost hear them arguing.

Where, he asked himself, had this relationship gone, that he should find himself having a one-way conversation outside his lover's home, working hard to convince himself *not* to go inside? He *needed* her. From where he sat in his car he could see her amber night light glowing through the bathroom's leaded-glass window. He could smell the sensual perfume of her sleep, could feel the warmth of the spot where she lay in the bed sheets, could hear the peaceful sounds of her breathing as she slept. He wanted these things. But at what price?

He placed the car in gear and drove away, aimless. A car steering itself. Narrow, twisting streets lined with million-dollar colonials. How unfair the world was. The moon beat down so strongly, he didn't need the headlights. He switched them off and drove dangerously through the broken shadows, thrilled by the risk, only switching them on again as he reached a commercial stretch, and the Beltway beyond. He turned the radio on, and for once spun the dial away from WDCN news to a classical station. It was an Italian aria. A woman's indescribably clear voice penetrated the hot night air with emotion so convincing that Cam Daggett wept as he drove.

He knocked on the door several times. The small fish-eye lens winked and he could imagine her eye pressed to the peephole. He finger-combed his disheveled hair and ran a palm over a coarse chin of whisker stubble.

Lynn Greene opened the hotel room door wearing a plain white T-shirt that barely covered her. She greeted him with an infinitely sympathetic look and nodded. He entered, feeling nervous and afraid. Once she had dead-bolted the door, she turned to face him and took him into her arms. Her tears of happiness warming his neck, she whispered softly and tenderly, "I'm glad you came."

19

THE FOLLOWING MONDAY, Kort arrived at Caroline's office anxious to see her. He had spent the weekend alone, resting and reshaping the events of the week to come—monitoring CNN. The Greek had told him that the meeting had been rescheduled, delayed at least a week, which meant it couldn't possibly take place until Friday the twenty-first of September. He needed the information Daggett had—he needed the exact date. Hans Mosner—it had become his mantra.

In the brief two-day period, Monique had become two-dimensional in his eyes, an overgrown child who wanted the damp spot between her legs tickled. She lacked depth. To her, a flower was little more than a means with which a man bought a woman's favors. Caroline, on the other hand, understood balance, symmetry, and dimension, pattern repetition and the resource of texture. She understood the combination of fragrances as well as colors. Her face, which only a few days earlier had failed to impress him, now lingered in his memory, refusing to leave him. Beguiling. Alluring. Beautiful. Irresistible.

He climbed the stairs to her office with a bounce to his step and two-dozen lavender irises clasped behind his back, boyish and bright. He announced himself to the receptionist, intervening before she could ring Caroline. When he turned around and heard the receptionist gasp at the sight of the bouquet, he knew Caroline was going to love them.

She did.

The second house she showed him was one not far from her own, the gatehouse of the former estate. It was terribly small, with a poor kitchen, but she thought it might be interesting to have this man for a neighbor, and it seemed suited for a bachelor. She didn't mention its proximity to her place, but she did try to sell some of its high-tech features in order to compensate for its obvious drawbacks. Accentuate the positive.

"One nice touch," she said, stopping at the small study and pointing to the ceiling, "is that that smoke alarm system is connected by phone line to the fire station in the village. There's also a satellite dish for the television. Over a hundred channels."

He gave the place a good looking over, but in the end declined with a polite "I don't think so."

They reached the third house at half past one. Kort had persuaded her to stop at a Chinese restaurant, and he now produced paper pails of shrimp chow mein, pea pods and broccoli, crispy duck plus a bottle of Acacia Chardonnay. They unfolded the meal in the brick courtyard of a wonderful white colonial. By the second glass of wine Kort had nearly forgotten all about the keys, about shopping for a possible safe house. About Mosner and the meeting.

She cracked her fortune cookie. "Tell me about your wife," she said. "You said there was a child, too, didn't you?"

Where he should have hesitated, should have resisted, should have fabricated a story that could in no way compromise his operation, instead he sat back, poured them each a third and final glass of wine, and began talking, somehow liberated from the complexities and planning of his operation. So narrow had been his vision for so long that as the petals of his thoughts unfolded beneath her light he spread himself open to her. He gave himself to her, willingly and knowingly, all the while sensing the danger of such behavior. This was peace, this moment; he would allow nothing to spoil it.

Carrie wondered how she could feel attracted to a man so quickly. She was experiencing sensations she hadn't felt in years: flushes of heat when he looked at her a certain way, an irregular quickness to her heart, sticky palms and sexual fantasies. Just what Anne had talked about. Was it his extreme self-confidence that did this to her? His accent? His curious glances? Or was it the keen attention with which he studied her every movement, hung on her every word? The flowers? The laughter? Or was it his haunting, inquisitive eyes?

As he spoke of his late wife his voice became throaty and distant. He described a young student, pretty and eager for knowledge. That made Anthony some sort of professor, but she dared not interrupt him. He seemed in a trance. To disturb him might stop him, and she didn't want him to stop. Not for anything. Now it was she who fell into a trance: another of her fantasies. Intimate images of the two of them coiled and entwined, briefly obscured his words. She felt frightened. Was that what she wanted?

When he paused, it was if a bomb had gone off, the silence deafening. "Our child . . ." he had begun. Now he finished, cigarette smoke flooding from his mouth with his words. He glanced at her. She felt him change his words at the last moment; she was certain of it. ". . . was . . . still-born." Again he paused. "It proved too much for my wife . . ."

This was fiction. Why? She accepted it as a challenge. The explanation was hidden within him like paper fortunes hidden inside the cookies that lay on the napkins before them. This was the most stimulating possibility of all: She would help him to express his fears and he would be free of them. At that moment she knew they were to be lovers.

At the fourth house she finally gathered the courage to ask. "It's not that I mind," she began. "In fact, I don't mind *at all*. But do you really intend to lease a house, or is this about something else?"

She studied him. They were in the kitchen. Of all the spots they had visited, this place had affected him the most.

Where he had been talkative and slightly critical of all the other houses and grounds, he had not spoken a word here.

"Will you have dinner with me tonight?" he asked. "Please?" he added, slowly turning to face her. When she hesitated, he said, "We'll discuss the terms of the lease."

She stuttered, "I . . . ah . . . ah . . . whi—which house? The lease, I mean."

"You didn't answer the question."

"No."

"No, you didn't answer the question, or no, you won't have dinner with me?" he asked.

"No, I didn't answer the question."

"Then you will have dinner with me?"

"No. I . . . I mean . . . that is . . ." He was standing too close. Her heart was pounding so hard, she feared he might hear it. She crossed her arms in an attempt to mute the pounding. "I think I'm feeling the wine." She was hoping he might make one of his jokes, or somehow break the silence, but he just stood there staring at her, so close she could hear his shirt rustle as he breathed. He clearly had no intention of speaking until she answered him. "I'm involved with somebody, Anthony." There, she had said it. She immediately regretted having said it, but at least she *had* said it. She was proud of herself.

"The man at the reception," he said. "What was his name? Dog-something."

"Daggett. Yes. That's him."

"And he's involved in your business?"

"No," she said, smirking. He was going to win out, she could feel it.

"I invited you to dinner, Caroline. A business dinner to discuss the terms of the lease. Dinner tonight. We all have to eat, don't we? Does this Daggett not like you to eat?"

She blushed. She wasn't sure what to say. Had she misunderstood him?

He named the restaurant and the time.

"I'll have to check . . ." she said.

"I'll expect you at eight," he said, repeating the time. "Good. That's settled. Now," he added, taking hold of her elbow, looking directly into her eyes, "show me the bedroom, would you please?"

20

IT WAS A French restaurant located on N Street, Chartreuse, two blocks off Connecticut. An unpretentious but definitely romantic setting, low ceiling, candlelight, chamber music turned down soft. Three of the eight small tables were occupied.

She was late. It didn't matter. It didn't bother him. He debated ordering a drink.

A woman cleared her voice. He looked up to see Caroline standing by the table. *His* Caroline, he thought. He jumped to his feet, nearly spilling his water. *"Enchanté,"* he said, taking her cold hand, brushing her cheek with his lips. "You are more beautiful than ever."

She wore a navy blue silk blouse with embroidered stitching in the collar and on the pockets, faux pearls, cream-colored pleated linen pants, a wide leather belt with a delicate gold buckle. Informal but powerful. The silk fell over her full breasts and gathered tightly at her small waist. There was suggestion in the way she had left the blouse unbuttoned well into her cleavage.

He brushed aside the waiter and seated her himself, dipping low to drink in her perfume. She smelled of fresh gardenias.

She blushed. "Good evening, Carl."

"Much better now," he said, finding his seat.

"I interrupted you. You were deep in thought."

He lied, "No, not really." Then he spoke the truth: "Nothing as important as seeing you."

She twitched with the compliment. He couldn't tell if this was good or bad. She said, "You looked quite serious."

"I was worried you wouldn't come," he said. "It *was* serious."

She smiled slowly, but widely. Kort intercepted the waiter's attempt to hand her a menu. Again, he waved the man off. "Is there any particular food you don't like?" He gave her a few seconds to think. "Be honest, or you may not like the dinner."

"You're going to order for us?"

"If you don't mind."

"Mind? Not at all. Please."

"You haven't told me what to avoid."

"Tripe, sweetbread, any of the exotic meats. I love escargots, but I won't eat shrimp because of the way they net everything in sight to catch them, and I won't eat veal because I've heard dreadful stories of how they fatten them and refuse them exercise. If anything, Carl, I'm opinionated. I should have warned you about that."

"So am I," he said. "Especially—as with you, it would seem—when it comes to the environment." He smirked. "Would you care for a cocktail, or wine?"

"Will you be drinking?"

"We're discussing you."

"Wine would be fine."

"Red or white?"

"You're ordering for us. I'll leave that to you."

He ordered her a California wine: a 1985 Silver Oak Cabernet. A bottle. He ordered them escargots, Caesar salad, and rack of lamb.

Halfway through dinner, when she attempted once again to pry into his past, he changed subjects, saying, "I hope to lease the last house you showed me, but I would very much like to take one last look at the yellow-and-white cottage we visited on our first day together. If you don't mind, I'll make my decision based on these last inspections. Does tomorrow work for you?"

She took a minute to search her purse and check her appointment book. He couldn't determine if this mention of business had upset her, but he sensed a definite change of her mood, which he regretted. They agreed on a time.

"You're a hard sell," she told him.

"I warned you: if anything, I'm particular."

A dollop of gravy fell from her fork and ran down her blouse. Kort saw it first. He leaned forward, extended a finger and hesitated, allowing her to stop him if she wanted. She lowered her eyes in self-inspection.

"You spilled," he said as he ran his finger deliberately around the soft curve of her breast. He sat back in his seat, placed the gravy-coated fingertip between his lips, and sucked it clean.

Carrie felt a jolt of heat run from her breast to her toes. Her nipple hardened; she was glad for the bra. She tingled. The small of her back went damp, as did the palms of her hands. What he had just done was outrageous. Rude.

She wanted him to do it again.

She wanted privacy.

The way he smiled, he seemed to be reading her thoughts. It frightened her so much that she banged her way out of her chair.

"Let me apologize," he said.

"Carl . . . I think I should go." She wondered who was speaking for her. This wasn't what she felt. It was as if a script had been placed in front of her and that these lines were expected of her. She couldn't think straight.

"Caroline. There's no need for this. Honestly! Please, sit. Stay."

"Carl . . ."

"Please. Sit back down. I'll be a perfect gentleman."

She tried to stop herself from saying it. Where had such a thought come from? But it surfaced effortlessly and she heard herself say it: "I don't want you to be." She gasped at her own words, and then there was no choice. She turned and hurried from the restaurant, wondering who was controlling her legs. What was happening to her?

She dared not look back. The waiter bowed his head politely as she reached the door. She could feel Carl only steps behind her. Go away! she willed, reeling in embarrassment.

She reached the street. Thankfully, her car was less than a block away. She headed off in its direction, increasing the length of her strides.

His warm hands fell onto her shoulders, and she felt him slow her and spin her around to face him. She heard "What do you think you're doing?" and she felt his lips press against her mouth, and herself willingly accept them. She withered under his strength. As he drew her against him, she opened her mouth and kissed him fully.

It wasn't right, and somewhere deep inside she knew this. But it was very right. It wasn't fair to Cam, but it was just what he deserved.

"We can't," she finally insisted, though weakly. She drew away from him.

"Can't? Look at you," he said, holding her again by the shoulders. "Look at *us*! Is this a business relationship? Is this a friendship? We *need* each other, Caroline. To question that is to—"

"No!" she snapped sharply, now separating from him. He was a client, nothing more. It was absurdity. The first rule! Was he even a client? Had she seen a check yet? Who exactly *was* he? How could she feel so attracted to him so quickly? A few days, a week or so was all . . . She hated herself. "Don't stop me, Carl," she demanded, turning and walking to her car. But as she reached her car she wished he would stop her, wished he would do *something*. She didn't want to leave it like this. "I'll be there tomorrow," she said to him over the roof, knowing he stood immediately behind her.

"I won't apologize, Caroline. If that's what you want—"

"That's *not* what I want," she admitted. You know what I want, she thought. *Damn you.*

He didn't speak; didn't say anything. She felt foolish.

What a thing to say! He controlled her now and this frightened her. It thrilled her.

"Then tomorrow it is," he said, his breath hot on her
neck.

She heard him walk away. "Thank you for dinner," she
said in a choked voice. Said without looking at him. She
was tempted to turn and beg him not to leave her this way.

By the time she had turned around, he was gone.

Rationality had nothing to do with it.

Carl had heated her up and she intended to put out the
fire at any cost. She felt angry with Cam, whether guilt-
driven or not, and she felt like penalizing him somehow,
and she had decided that this was the way.

She knocked on the front door and then let herself in
with her key. Cam was on the couch wearing a set of headphones, a half-empty glass of Scotch on the coffee table, his
eyes open now, but she could picture how he had been only
moments earlier, reclined and deeply into the second movement of Beethoven's Seventh, asleep perhaps, the room
speakers switched off, the headphones up loudly enough
that she could hear the music faintly from across the room.

He seemed shocked to see her. Had it been so long? She
couldn't even remember.

He slipped off the headphones and let them fall to the
couch, the music, though thin, suddenly louder. "Dunc?"
she asked.

"In bed," he answered, reaching out for the Scotch.

"Good," she said, unbuttoning her blouse, unfastening
her belt and walking defiantly toward the bedroom.

"Carrie?" he asked, following her now. Following her as
Carl had. He stepped into the bedroom behind her and she
pushed the door shut and switched off the lights and
dropped the blouse to the floor. She heard him undress. She
didn't want to think of this as Cam. She wanted this to happen quickly, but she wanted to get something out of it.

She worked her way out of her clothes, found him in

the limited light, and pushed him to the bed. She pulled his pants off.

"Carrie?" he asked again, this time bewildered and confused. Good, she liked the sound of that.

No, it's not Carrie, she was thinking. I'm not sure who it is. She stripped him naked, climbed over him, kept him pinned to the bed, and then fell on him fully.

In her mind's eye, she saw Carl beneath her. Much too soon, he swelled and flooded inside of her. But she wouldn't let him go. She wanted satisfaction for herself.

"Carrie?" he attempted cautiously. "My God," he added, "that was incredible!"

Her breathing rapid, her senses heightened but unsatisfied, she felt wild, and unsure of herself. She crawled forward and she lowered herself gently onto his mouth and said in a strange and unfamiliar voice, "Finish it!"

Which he did.

When it was over, she slid off the bed, turned her back, and began to dress in the darkness. Her eyes had adjusted. She didn't want to see him.

"Stay. Please."

"I've got to go," she said.

"Why?" he asked.

"I'm not sure. But I know I've got to."

"This . . . This is all?"

"It wasn't *enough*?" she asked. Where had this new tone of voice of hers come from? She was being purposely cruel to him and she didn't understand it. As she was buttoning the blouse, she felt the wet spot left by the gravy. All that was left of Carl.

"I've never seen you like this."

"No."

"You *used* me," he said in astonishment, in realization. She had turned in an effort to find her other shoe. Even in the dim light they caught eyes, and she knew he could read her face. He could always read her face.

There was no use denying it.

"Yes," she admitted, "I used you."

He said nothing. She reveled in his silence, in her new-found power. She turned and left him lying there.

21

THE RED BMW was registered to a Monique Paine, a name that also appeared on the flight manifest from LAX to Washington, the flight Fragile Ramirez had placed her on using her video skills. This linkage proved enough for a surveillance warrant on the address listed on the registration. Full surveillance, including wiretaps, had begun at midnight the night before, Bradley Levin in charge. Despite the alias, to the FBI she was not Monique Paine but Monique Cheysson. To Paul Pullman and Richard Mumford she was "good, but not enough." Physical evidence linking Bernard's detonators to flight 64 remained the miracle Daggett awaited. Without it, at 5:00 P.M. today his involvement in this investigation came to an end, and his report on the Backman–Bernard bombing began. He had slumped into a deep depression, as much over Carrie's unusual behavior the night before as over his work. Everything seemed to be falling apart.

The miracle came in the form of a phone call.

"It's Chaz," the voice said. "You shouldn't threaten people. Especially when they run the explosives lab. Bad idea."

"I was desperate. You have the one piece of evidence that may save this case for me. Tomorrow won't do, Chaz. It has to be today."

"It *is* today. Why don't you hop the shuttle and get your butt over here? I've got something interesting to show you."

The blue shuttle van appeared in front of the Buzzard Point building at twenty after the hour. Six people got out. A green padlocked chest was removed and transferred over to the security people at the front desk. Daggett and three others loaded and bounced around for the fifteen-minute return ride to headquarters. For Daggett, the ride was interminable.

Chaz Meecham was seated behind his generous desk waiting for him. "We could have done this on the phone," he said, "But I hate phones."

"You and me both."

With a flick of the chin, he indicated the file folder in front of Daggett. "There's your report. Your glass bulb." He rose, shut the office door, and sat down squarely in his high-back leather office chair. He opened a drawer and removed a sealed clear plastic bag containing the remains of the glass bulb. He handed it to Daggett. "If there was mercury in that thing, Michigan, it's long gone. Probably burned up in the fire." After a few seconds he asked, "You all right?"

"Disappointed is all."

"Jesus! Give me a minute to explain. It's not *all* bad. The down side of this report is the lack of any evidence of mercury. Not surprising, incidentally. It's a heavy metal. When the glass bulb broke apart, it was history; and the glass itself was too burned to give us any trace amounts.

"But one man's ceiling is another man's floor," he continued. "The Lord giveth and he taketh away. The fire robbed us of the mercury, but it gave us something better. It adhered to the outside curve of your glass bulb. And we *were* able to identify that as what's left behind when you burn silicon. Silicon, as in what we found in Bernard's hotel room. In fact, the *exact* same chemical composition as the silicon our people lifted from his hotel room carpet. The same stuff. Page three and four, in the file."

Daggett didn't touch the file. "Translation?"

"The way it works is this: When you build a detonator, you create gates between the power source—a battery—and the explosive. Every time a gate opens, the electricity from the battery gets that much closer to the explosive." He raised his hand like a teacher. "Let me show you what one of these babies looks like."

Chaz Meecham left the room. When he returned, he slapped a hard cube into Daggett's hand. "We call them 'ice cubes.' You can see why." Daggett was holding a small brick of hardened epoxy with four wires sticking out. It was small and clear, like an ice cube. Two of the wires were attached to a nine-volt battery clip. The other two were bare-ended and tipped with solder. "The ones Bernard built might not look exactly like this. I have a feeling he packed it all into the altimeter, or why else would he have cut down the plastic? I don't know . . . The point is, he puts all his works inside some kind of ice cube so the operative can't screw it up, can't dink with the electronics. He might leave a way to, say, set the clock, or something like that, but he doesn't want his wiring messed around with. Bernard didn't use epoxy; he used silicon. We know that from the hotel room evidence."

"Is there a reason for that?"

"In bomb-building, there's a reason for everything. Count on it. Silicon dries fast. It's less messy. It flexes easily —might have something to do with the sensitivity of altimeter. Who knows?" Meecham glanced over at Daggett. "He's good, Michigan. Real good." Daggett felt a tension he had previously missed. This was some sort of competition between Meecham and Bernard. Could Meecham, through a few pieces of microscopic evidence found collectively in a hotel room rug, and the mud of an airplane crash, establish exactly what kind of device Bernard had built and what he intended to use it for?

"That's my job," Meecham said. Daggett hadn't realized he had asked this aloud. Meecham lectured, "A simple example of a gated detonator is a clock timer—a single gate. Set the clock to a certain time and, blammo, up she goes. Not so easy on a plane. Not if you want the bird aloft and well away from where it took off. So you use a series of gates: pressure switches, blocks, thermometers, humidistats —you name it; each one responds to a different condition, a different requirement—altitude, time, temperature. It can be any number of things."

"You said he had two altimeters."

Meecham clearly didn't like being interrupted. "Before a plane takes off, the copilot cranks up the air packs—he pressurizes the cabin. Right? He does it wrong, you feel it in your ears. Know what I mean? If you're Bernard, to make sure the plane is aloft, you use an altimeter—present to some given altitude—as your first gate. That way you're insured the other gates aren't activated until the cabin is pressurized. If the bomb goes off in the air, the more damage and the less evidence. Lockerbie was a good example of that; Lockerbie was supposed to blow over water. Anyway, the barometer is your first gate.

"If I were building it," he continued, "I'd use a second gate—a clock timer of some sort—to make sure the bird is well downrange before she blows—"

"Casios? We're pretty sure he bought two Casios."

"I saw that in the report." He shrugged. "I don't know. With Bernard, it's possible I suppose. You have to be into microelectronics—chip circuit design—if you're going to pull the guts out of a Casio and make anything happen. It's certainly possible. So the order is: The air packs crank up the cabin pressure; the first gate, the altimeter, opens, which, by providing electricity, turns on the clock timer. Now that would be a command device we might see. But it's not what Bernard did here. This glass bulb on yours changes all the rules. This bulb means Bernard's detonator contained a third gate. That's the only explanation."

"Meaning?"

Meecham had prepared himself for this meeting. He reached to his right and retrieved a black dial, a glass bulb with two wires, and a small clock. He lined them up in this order. "My guess? Three gates, Michigan: an altimeter switch that opens gate number one after the cabin is pressurized; then a mercury switch as gate number two." He tipped the switch. "The nose goes up and the second gate opens. Bernard has established two rules: the cabin is pressurized, the plane has taken off."

"And the Casio?"

"The Casio is the last gate. After the plane is pressurized and the nose has lifted, the clock starts running down."

"Why the weird face?" Daggett asked.

"I gotta tell you, a guy like Bernard doesn't make a detonator this complicated without damn good reason. So what's the reason?"

"He wants to make sure the plane is airborne before the thing goes off. Isn't that it?"

Meecham shook his head. "It's too complicated for that. The way you do that is set your timer for a good long time. A couple of hours. If the plane is delayed on the ground, then by setting the clock to run late, you cover yourself. No, it's not that.

"Let me demonstrate the problem here, Michigan." Meecham picked up the glass bulb. It contained a shifting blob of mercury. He tilted it so the mercury held in the end of the bulb without the two electrodes. "This is the off position. No contact between these poles. No juice. The detonator is inactive. The timer is not yet hot. But during takeoff, this mercury runs to this end of the bulb and it is hot," he said, duplicating the motion. "There is now juice running from the battery to the timer—the first and second gates are both open. The timer starts to run. But here's the catch . . ." He tilted the bulb back again; the mercury slid away from the twin contacts, breaking the electrical connection. "As soon as the plane levels off, the mercury switch *disconnects* the juice. The timer will stop. No juice means no bomb. The whole fucking thing goes dead."

"So you've got them in the wrong order," Daggett said, after a moment of thought.

"No way. No other order to put them in, Michigan. At least not one that fits with what we know about the way flight sixty-four went down. It made it, what, a mile, two miles downrange? Nothing. What this *tells* us," he said, pointing to his desk, "is that Bernard built this thing to activate at a specific time, during takeoff, while the plane is *still* in a climb. That is the only way to explain this. So you tell me: Now how much fucking sense does *that* make?"

Daggett found himself back with Dr. Barnes from Duhning. The simulator, with Ward at the wheel, had duplicated a dozen takeoffs, all using differing times between takeoff and loss of pilot control. Barnes had wondered the same thing: Why do it?

"Why do it?" Meecham was still talking. Words and faces were mixing around in Daggett's head. "We have *no* evidence of an explosion. No evidence of any explosive material on board. We got squat!"

Daggett said, "You mentioned this mini-detonator last time. You said it burned 'hot.' Does that mean it would be hot enough to start a fire?"

"Start a fire?" His face lit up. "You kidding me? Does the pope shit in the woods? Is a bear Catholic? It'll melt fuckin' metal!"

Finally, the repetition inside the simulator made sense. Finally he had something to take Mumford. He came around the desk, took Meecham's head between his hands, and kissed the man on the mouth.

Chaz Meecham, wiping his lips, shouted, "You're fucking crazy!"

Nodding vigorously, Daggett grabbed the file. "Would you repeat all this for Mumford if I asked?"

"If you promise not to do that again."

"I promise."

22

HE LED HER into the bedroom.

Since he needed a furnished house, he used a complaint about the furnishings as his pretense for getting her upstairs. But she knew better. The sexuality had grown so intense on the drive over that neither had said much. As she climbed the stairs, she felt her knees weaken.

Carl opened the window. Midmorning light streamed in, followed by a slight breeze and the distant, melodious accompaniment of songbirds. In the relative silence, he directed her to the edge of the bed and ran his hands in her hair. She closed her eyes. "That's delicious," she said. He kissed her mouth and she welcomed it.

Carl scooped an arm under her knees, lifted her off her feet and set her down gently on the bed. He opened her blouse and his shirt and he pressed himself against her. Tears fell from her eyes. He asked, in a voice she could hardly hear, if he should stop. She shook her head no.

He gently stole the remainder of her clothes, lost his own onto the floor somewhere, and sat alongside her. Tenderly, carefully, he browsed every inch of her with fingertips that felt like feathers. The breeze ruffled the curtain and the sound of the birds grew even louder. A bold sparrow dared to observe them from the windowsill.

This felt dangerous. Her fears drove her pleasures higher, wind to her fire. Carl refused to have it over with quickly. This stranger milked every sensation he could from her, stretched every experience as if to test her tenacity. To challenge her. Twice she called out for him to enter her. Twice he whispered back, "No." And twice she let herself go.

Perhaps that was the real thrill: the surrender. She turned herself over to him. Her skin, her nerves, her innermost privacies, her *self*. This skillful man owned her for these long minutes. He drew imaginary patterns on her skin, finger-painted her thighs, drew her willingly open until she was fully offered to him. He kissed her there for ages, played with her, toyed with her, drove her to the edge of frenzy, only to retreat and settle her again. "My God," she heard herself cry in a shuddering whimper. He kissed and tongued his way from her navel to her breasts, and back again. There was no end to his patience. He indulged himself with her, drove her clear to the edge and then past it, until she flooded with an intense heat that soothed her and carried her off so far that she neither heard him nor felt him. She reached down and pulled for him, but he would not give her this. He generously refused.

Minutes, hours, weeks later? their mouths suddenly met, hot and wet, and he penetrated her at this instant. She cried out with joy. She felt him swell inside her. Deeper and deeper. Was there no end to him? She felt his rhythms. A connection so full and sweet, so tender and yet so filled with authority. Yes, he owned her.

He pulled back and withdrew. "No," she murmured, wanting him. He teased her entrance. Toyed with her. She opened her eyes and tried to focus on his face, but found it impossible. He was smiling. She knew that much. She could *feel* it from him. Dreamy and distant, she retired to a place so full of joy and pleasure that she wanted to die. "Please," she said, feeling her lips curl into a sleepy smile.

He delivered himself slowly. Smoothly. Further and further. Totally. She arched her back to accommodate him. His hot tongue found her breasts and she felt herself explode. Never anything like this. Never anything close.

She felt a complete and total whole with him. No longer two halves. No names. No faces. No identities. The same. Equals. His pleasure was hers. Her movement was his. Their moment was this.

He went rigid, from toe to head, and erupted inside her. She saw flames. They cried out together. The bird took flight in a soft sputtering of wing. The two lovers convulsed and trembled, cried out and laughed, collapsed in a tangle of sweat and heartbeats.

Naked, he smoked a cigarette by the window. He needed those keys. He needed to clear his head and get back on track. It wasn't easy. She lay peacefully wrapped in the blankets, half asleep. He could feel her staring at him. He studied the backyard. "I would love it here," he said in a distant voice that he hadn't intended. What was happening to him? He felt unable to focus. There was much work to be done and he had no desire to do it. Emotions flooded him, so foreign that before he could prevent it, he became a victim to them. He felt like the juggler who took on one too many items and now found the task before him impossible —watched before his eyes as the circling objects defied his attempts to control them.

"Would?" she asked.

"Will," he corrected, hating himself for his continuing deceit. Could he tell her? Could he possibly risk the truth? The truth? It was nothing but another of the objects in the slowly degenerating circle. "This is the way I will always think of this room," he said. "Us. Now. This moment."

"You seem sad."

"Extremely happy, I assure you. If I could preserve this moment, if I could lock that door over there, the two of us inside . . . forever. Well, that would be my little piece of heaven."

"Can't you?"

"Can I?"

"You don't sound convinced," she said.

"You have another life. I've interfered. Should I sound convinced?"

"I think you should." She threw the covers off. He looked at her. She had a fine body. It had lost its youth, in places, its shape. But there was no body he would have rather seen at this moment. It was perfect. It was her. "Did I show you the two-headed shower?" she asked in a suggestive, humorous tone. "All European tile. Imported. Pressure sensitive controls. May I show you the shower?" she asked, coming off the bed toward him.

She was magnificent, he thought. He tossed the cigarette out the window and watched as it tumbled, end over end, and the sparks scattered on the brick terrace. She headed straight for him and pressed herself against him, wet and warm, and he felt himself begin to swell. "Or should we just stay here in the chair?" she asked, taking him fully in hand and stroking him against her sex.

"Why not both?" he asked.

"Indeed?" she replied, helping him enter her. She closed her eyes and hung her chin on his shoulder.

He listened gratefully to the singing of the birds. He took her firmly beneath the buttocks and carried her to the chest of drawers where he set her down. He drew her ankles high around his back and found her source of pleasure again. He watched her face squirm with his experiments.

Then she bit his shoulder, and they both came at once.

Following a brief nap and a failed shower because of no hot water, they toweled themselves clean, joking about how they would smell. Slowly, reluctantly, they dressed.

Kort did what he felt he had to do. With the steady, sure voice of a cold-blooded professional he said, "Toss me your keys. I'll steal your car and find us some take-out food."

"I'll come with you."

"I wouldn't think of it," he said. "That will spoil any surprises I cook up."

"You're an incorrigible romantic. You know that, Carl?"

"I try," he replied.

"No, you don't try. It's natural. That's what makes you so appealing."

Natural? he wondered. *Call me by my real name,* he willed. *Call my bluff. Whatever you do, don't hand me those keys!*

She fumbled through her purse looking for the keys and, finding them, threw them at him. He caught them effortlessly, a frog's tongue snagging the fly.

He stared at them in the palm of his hands: the keys. A simple little group of keys. A dozen ways he might have obtained them, some easier than others, and yet he had elected this route. Why?

"Carl? Something wrong?"

"Just thinking."

"I'm starved. Ravenous. Stop thinking." She pointed toward the door. "Be off with you!"

"Whatever you say," he said.

Copying the keys was a painless exercise. He pocketed his set, bought them some deli sandwiches and potato salad, and returned to the car. Here, as he was finding a stable location to rest the small bags of hot food, he came across an unexpected bonus: a shopping list written on the back of an envelope addressed to Mr. Cameron Daggett, listing Daggett's street address. This saved him from having to shadow Carrie—or Daggett, God forbid—until being led to the house. It briefly cheered him up. But as he returned to the small cottage, his good spirits waned.

Parked in the driveway, he sat behind the wheel for several long minutes, wondering where life might have taken them if they had found each other under different circumstances. A heavy sadness filled him. Feelings he had suppressed for years bubbled to the surface and spit at him, despite his efforts to contain them. He felt drugged: an unwilling victim of his own conscience. He had violated her, physically, emotionally, and now criminally. He had stolen from her. He had stolen the truth, stolen her trust.

He hated himself.

He slammed the car door hard. He fingered the gate's wrought-iron latch and approached the house solemnly. Angry. Confused.

Oh, yes, he reminded himself sardonically: he had accomplished his goal. *Bravo!* The keys were his.

But what of his soul?

23

MUMFORD'S CORNER OFFICE held them all easily, with room left over for a volleyball game. The pathologist, a Dr. Ben-David; Chaz Meecham from Explosives; and Lynn Greene occupied one of the two leather couches. Ben-David was a small man with pinpoint eyes and dark skin. Meecham looked his usual all-American, and today, a little younger than his forty-odd years. Lynn looked not a penny less than a million bucks.

Daggett took one of the two leather chairs, leaving Pullman isolated on the opposing couch. Mumford appeared comfortable sitting in his leather high-back chair, enthroned behind his expansive walnut desk.

Daggett could no longer act alone. Without Mumford's blessing, he could not raise the manpower necessary to stop Kort from whatever it was he had planned, and so, two years of investigation came down to this one meeting. If Daggett failed to convince Mumford that the crash of flight 64 was not an accident, but sabotage, then he was to begin his lengthy report on the Backman bombing. With three days to go until the Pentagon meeting—which he still believed was directly related to Kort's target—everything came down to his performance over the next twenty minutes.

He felt well prepared for this meeting. He had phoned each person individually so they might know exactly what was expected of them. He was to become a conductor now, and like a conductor he tapped his pencil against the edge of folders piled high on the coffee table in front of him. As with music miraculously coming off the written page, he

hoped that from this ensemble, a wealth of fact and suppo-
sition might develop into a convincing explanation for the
behavior of AmAirXpress flight 64. An *explanation* was all
he hoped for.

He pulled out his list and raised his voice, hoping,
against the odds, he might sound confident. Public speaking
was not his gift. "First off, I'd like to run around the room
with a few questions. I think that will give us a look at some
of the background, some of the groundwork involved." He
looked around for a glass of water. Seeing none, he continued.

"My first question is to Dr. Ben-David. He's both reviewed the autopsy protocols and has had direct discussions with the medical examiners in California who per-
formed the autopsies. Specifically, the topic has been blood
toxicology. What I wanted to ask you, Doctor, is whether or
not you have any way of knowing if a person was unconscious prior to death?"

Ben-David had an unusually high voice, and the annoying habit of pulling at his ear. "What's interesting about
this, is that just such a question came up about four years
ago. In the medical examiner community . . ." he added.
"And then, as now, it involved a plane crash. The concern
was that the pilot may have blacked out only moments before impact. Critical moments, I'm afraid. Leading pathologists were pulled together to research the possibility of
proving or disproving the pilot's consciousness at the moment of death. The speculation was that by measuring the
levels of lactic acid in the blood, we could determine the
level of stress just prior to death. High levels might indicate
the pilot was struggling to control the aircraft. Low levels
might indicate the pilot had died before he was even aware
of a problem. But it never really worked out. The tests were
inconclusive. That's a round-about way of saying, no, we
can't tell—not yet, anyway."

He had Mumford's interest. That was a good sign. Daggett asked, "And the cause of death to the flight crew of

AmAirXpress flight sixty-four? It's listed as a result of impact. 'Body fragmentation,' is the term, I think. Do you go along with that?"

"No. And neither do the authors of that report. Not any longer. The reports are being rewritten."

Mumford barked out, "Is that right?"

"Absolutely," Ben-David answered.

"Well, Jesus Christ! Why didn't *I* hear about this?" Mumford huffed for a few long moments. No one interrupted. No one answered him. The answer was obvious: He was hearing about it right now. "What exactly *was* the cause of death, Dr. Ben-David?"

Ben-David looked to Daggett.

Mumford corrected, "You don't need Daggett's permission to talk. You need mine." He tapped his chest. "This is *my* office. This is my fucking field office!"

"Special Agent Daggett directed my attention to—and I subsequently challenged my colleagues to examine—the level of carbon monoxide in the blood. The toxicology report." He paused, uncomfortable. He seemed to be thinking —looking for layman's terms? "There was a fire on board. We know that." He looked to Lynn Greene, who nodded her agreement. "One good indication of fire is carbon monoxide in the blood. It's often the killer, which is exactly what was believed to be the case here. In fact," he said, tapping the folder in front of him, "the toxicologist believed the two crew members had been overcome by carbon monoxide and had then died upon impact. Body fragmentation, as Mr. Daggett has just said. A plane crash is difficult for pathologists because you have body fragmentation and fire. Special Agent Daggett directed my attention to something in the report that the medical examiners had missed, which was the *high level* of carbon monoxide, and the *lack* of any other chemical toxicant in the blood. Plastic burns to a vapor; it gets into your lungs and into your blood. In a fire, soot gets lodged in your trachea. In the case of flight sixty-four, there is no record of soot in the trachea of either man.

Even given a very few seconds, as was the case here, we should have seen *something* in the trachea. Lung tissue samples from both crew members has since been examined in the California DOJ toxicology lab in Sacramento. They found not only an extremely high concentration of carbon monoxide but the presence of white phosphorus." He paused again. "We checked with the gentlemen now on the other end of that telephone," he said, pointing. "There is no source of white phosphorus on a Duhning 959-600. Not on any Duhning aircraft, for that matter. We then checked the cargo manifest. None there either."

"I'm not sure I follow you," Mumford said. "Where's this leave the actual cause of death?"

"If I may," Daggett said, interrupting. "We're coming right to that."

Mumford didn't like it. Nonetheless, Daggett continued. "Chaz, you and I talked about this detonator. The mini-det."

"Right. Sure thing, Michigan." He faced Mumford. "The long and the short of it, Dick," he said, emphasizing his friendship with Mumford, "is that we have pretty good evidence a *very* sophisticated detonator was aboard sixty-four. Nothing to take to the courts—but fuck the courts. This guy intended to detonate at a specific moment, almost immediately after takeoff. Weird, I know, but it's the only explanation I can come up with. Furthermore, we have *zero* evidence of any explosive on board. Zero. So what the fuck, Chuck? Go to all that trouble and have nothing to detonate?"

Daggett said, "The mini-det, Chaz."

"Yeah, right. Evidence found in Bernard's hotel room suggests the presence of a mini-det. A miniaturized detonator. Pretty high-tech shit, but not impossible for a guy like Bernard to get his hands on. A mini-det flashes hot—real hot. You score the outer casing just right and instead of popping it flares. Flares hot enough to melt some metals. Plenty hot enough to start a cockpit fire. One of the chemi-

cal residues we look for in crash debris, something to indicate the presence of a mini-det, is *white phosphorus.*" He
was nodding to emphasize his point. He pointed at Ben-
David. "Sounds like he found the white phosphorus." He
nodded some more, looked over at Daggett, took his cue
nicely, and sat back.

"Which leads us to Lynn Greene with the FAA," Daggett
said.

Lynn squared her shoulders. It was a case of nerves for
her, but it had a great effect: She had Mumford's attention.
Lynn, who had sided with Daggett all along. Lynn, who had
brought him the glass bulb that—as far as he was concerned—had turned the case. "We hear two distinct sounds
on the Cockpit Voice Recorder just before impact. One is a
soft pop . . . the second is a hissing. Within two seconds,
the bodies *of both men* collapse onto the controls. This is
confirmed by the Flight Data Recorder. Several switches
were thrown that, upon reconstruction, could only be
caused by"—she lifted her arms out—"a body falling forward like this." She collapsed forward to dramatize it. Daggett noted with pleasure that everyone was fully focused on
her. She sat back up. "The hissing continues. Because the
copilot mentions the fire extinguisher, we decided to take a
closer look, wondering if it might be the source of the hissing. This morning we received the results of a lab test conducted on the cockpit fire-extinguisher. Evidence suggests
that the end of the fire extinguisher was subjected to extremely high temperatures. It's possible, even likely, that
the detonator itself was part of the fire extinguisher. Inside
the pressure gauge perhaps. There is further evidence of
white phosphorus, again indicating the detonator to which
Mr. Meecham referred. My guess is that the mini-det not
only started a fire but melted the pressure gauge, releasing
whatever gas was contained inside that cylinder. Examination of the fire extinguisher itself revealed it was not filled
with fire retardants, but instead an extremely high concen-

tration of carbon monoxide. A potentially lethal concentration."

Daggett pointed to Dr. Ben-David, who said, "Pure carbon monoxide, discharged at a close range, would fully coincide with our findings, and would more completely explain the cause of death."

Then he pointed to Chaz Meecham, who said, "And the presence of white phosphorus would explain why we failed to find evidence of explosives. He didn't use any. All this guy wanted was for a mini-det to melt his detonator to nothing. While at the same time opening the fire extinguisher. He burns up what little evidence might have existed, and lets the gas do the rest."

Mumford's mouth was actually hanging open. Daggett thought if he had tried, he could have dropped a paper clip in there.

When he recovered, Mumford said, "So let's say I believe you. Let's say sixty-four *was* sabotaged; let's even go as far to say it was sabotaged by one of Bernard's detonators. And that means *Der Grund,* and quite possibly Anthony Kort. Let's say I buy all that, okay?" He paused while his eyes searched the ceiling in thought. "Why bother with something this elaborate? If all he wanted to do was drop a plane, why the fuck bother with all of this?"

The resulting silence was so intense that Daggett could hear the congestion in Ben-David's lungs.

"What the fuck was the point?" Mumford asked.

In the end, there was only the truth as he knew it. Daggett said tentatively, "Kort didn't want us knowing the plane had been sabotaged. He wanted it to look like an accident. Why? I think it's because he plans to do it again— to drop another 959, here in Washington. That's why Bernard made two identical detonators and why he delivered the second one here."

"We don't *know* that!" Mumford protested. He was a stickler for accuracy.

Daggett pressed on. "Whatever Kort has planned, has

something to do with those tests Ward conducted on the Duhning simulator. You put all of this together and it still doesn't explain what he needed the simulator for. Why repeat the same test—with only slight variations—a half-dozen times?"

"And do you have an answer for *that?*" Mumford asked.

"No, sir. Not yet. But given all of this, I think we're getting closer. I think it's time we had better find out."

Daggett waited while Mumford looked impatiently at everyone in the room. There was a mixture of confusion and expectation on each face. Mumford seemed ready to explode. He finally looked back at Daggett. "Well, don't just sit there. Get on with it!"

24

WHEN KORT ANSWERED the phone, the LED on the small black box he had connected to his room's telephone glowed red, and he knew immediately Monique's line was tapped.

Panic stole over him, unfamiliar and frightening: She *was* compromised. He had to avoid her at all cost.

"It's me," she announced informally.

"I'm sorry?" he said. "I think you have the *wrong number.*"

A long pause occurred as she considered his words. He was dealing with his own sense of panic; he could only imagine hers. There was no time to wait. The FBI—or whoever was on to them—might have trap-and-trace in place. The trap-and-trace would identify his number immediately. As they spoke, cars could be rolling. If she wouldn't acknowledge . . .

"I'm calling *Dallas,*" she said, in a constricted voice.

"No, no." He said. "I'm in Washington. You *do* have the wrong number." He hung up. There. It was done. Over. His operation was coming apart at the seams.

He had to keep them one step behind. He had to keep moving. He had to force all other thoughts from his mind—close all the compartments—and focus on the individual elements essential to his escape. He threw open the Yellow Pages—*Taxi*—while the little black box on his phone line remained the center of his universe. Kort dialed. The dispatcher answered. Assuming his line was also tapped by now but hoping it wasn't, Kort calmly ordered a cab under the name of Anthony—Carl Anthony—for twenty minutes from now. His heartbeat reminded him of horse hooves on cobblestone. Miraculously, the LED on the black box remained dark. He was about to celebrate his anonymity when it lit up brightly. Kort's knees went weak.

Compromised!

The resulting flurry of activity he threw himself into helped overcome his sense of panic. He disconnected and pocketed the small box that warned of telephone surveillance, headed straight to his weapon, checked that it was loaded, and slipped on the holster. He placed an additional two magazines in his left pants pocket: it gave him twenty-seven shots. Not many against an army of FBI agents.

How many would they send? How certain would they be? How much time did he have? He checked his watch. Thirty seconds had passed.

He shoved some clothes into a flight bag and in a single sweeping gesture cleared his toilet articles and cosmetics off the shelf above the sink and into the bag. That would allow him a change of disguise. He pocketed the copies of Caroline's keys. Glanced around.

No time . . . He had been careful in this room. There would be precious few fingerprints found here. Precious little evidence, even for forensic specialists.

He slipped quietly down the back stairs, through the empty kitchen, and out the back door. He walked quickly— but did not run—down the back alley, alongside a neighboring yard. Ten minutes later he arrived at the Farragut North Metro station.

As he descended the escalator, he kept a sharp eye for any possible agents—but it was too difficult to gauge. Any of these people could be agents. All he saw was a transit cop hassling some vagrants. It planted the seed of an idea in his mind.

He boarded the first train available, taking a seat near the overhead button marked *Emergency Stop—$100 fine for illegal use.*

Monique was the biggest problem. How much had he

actually told her? he wondered. Too much. Hell, anything she knew was too much. He had given in to her, revealed more than he should have.

In a perfect world, she would be "made redundant"—as Michael called it—before she brought the operation down around her. Michael had used free-lancers for such jobs on at least two occasions. Kort had worked with them both, though at a distance, acting as bait so the hit men could identify their targets. Kort had committed their impassive faces to memory. They were certainly faces to remember, faces from which to run if he ever saw them again. Michael kept his house in order; no one was ever fully out of his reach.

But what to do about her? Not only did she know *far* too much, she was the key to the operation. Its entire premise revolved around his ability to pass himself off as a guest of In-Flite Foods, to enter the field side of the airport as he had in Los Angeles. To substitute fire extinguishers. It depended on Monique.

He disembarked at the third stop—Judiciary Square, how appropriate!—alert for any tails. He waited, now certain that he wasn't being followed, and rode the Red Line on to Union Station.

Tricks: he knew a hundred. But he felt no safer.

If he killed Monique, what then? Would they think of this? Would they use her as bait?

Monique was beside herself.

She headed straight to her bar and poured herself a deep vodka and tried to sort things out. She poured herself another. *The wrong number!* The ice melted and she didn't bother replacing it. She couldn't feel the liquor, couldn't feel anything but fear. Think! She scolded herself, drinking down another just as fast. Think!

What would Anthony do? Would he desert her? Kill her? Protect her?

Wrong number! It rang in her head. The Greek! The fucking Greek had given her to them. Had to be. Bastard!

She poured herself another.

She felt tempted to look out the window. Were they out there right now? She had no way of knowing what they knew. Were they guessing? Her training dictated that she be the exact woman today and tomorrow as she had been yesterday: flirtatious, sure of herself, a good businesswoman with a nose for vulnerable markets, a provocative woman of the nineties. An actress. Could she do this? Was there any choice?

As she helped herself to three ice cubes, she switched on the television set and tried to be normal. What was normal? Eating a lot of junk food. Drinking vodka. Walking around in only her underwear on the hot nights. Masturbating in the shower . . . Jesus, did they have microphones in place? Did they have cameras? Did they know every little intimacy? Were they listening *right now*? Were they watching her? She coiled more tightly in the chair and hugged the glass.

Was it true that their microphones were strong enough to pick up a heart rate?

If so, then what were they thinking right now?

Kort checked his duffel bag at the baggage counter at Union Station. He rented a Toyota from the Union Station Avis counter using the Carl Anthony credit card for the last time, with no intention of ever returning the vehicle. He knew the FBI would soon question the owners of the bed-and-breakfast, who would give them his alias. The first thing they would then do is conduct a name search with credit card companies, banks, airlines, rent-a-car agencies, other hotels—anything and everything that would give them the next link to him. The credit card could be traced. His one remaining card, under a different name, was necessary to his escape. In a perfect world, it might still serve that purpose.

As with any drive that involved expectation, this one seemed to drag on indefinitely. Thirty minutes passed as slowly as several hours. He got lost twice, despite his attention to the map, but finally drove past the address he had gleaned from the envelope Caroline had used for a shopping list.

The house was singularly unremarkable: common, quite small, and poorly landscaped. It reminded him of several safe houses he had used over the years.

For his needs the property was perfect: A high wooden fence defined the perimeter, making it unlikely, if not impossible, for an adjoining neighbor to see a prowler.

He drove the neighborhood once, alert for any night owls. By the darkness of the houses, most everyone was asleep—a bedroom community living up to its name.

He drove the ten minutes back to the main road and found himself a twenty-four-hour donut shop where he shared a countertop with a reformed alcoholic and a pair of weary traffic cops under the harsh glare of fluorescent lights, and the rambling monologue of a waitress on diet pills. Sipping coffee, with a pair of cops not ten feet away, added to his confidence. He was nobody. Invisible.

He burrowed his way into a *USA Today*, catching up on everything from the Kremlin's monetary policy to Madonna's latest video, ate a jelly-filled donut and switched to decaf for the third cup. At a few minutes past one o'clock the cops returned to their patrol car. By two o'clock, Kort was the only one left, although the occasional motorist stopped for "brain food." Kort made a men's room stop and crammed himself back into the Toyota. He had reviewed his plan internally a dozen times. Now, at two-fifteen in the morning, it was time to carry it out. In a perfect world, he would be in and out of the house in a matter of minutes.

A van, several years old, was parked in the driveway. He had missed this on his first pass. Christ, what else had he missed? He parked the Toyota down the street and waited to see if any neighborhood lights came on.

After several minutes, his copy of Caroline's keys in hand, he left the car, easing the door closed so as to avoid making any noise. He headed directly to the front door. A streetlamp threw a pale blue aura across the front porch. Kort could feel himself disappear in the shadows. There were four possible keys to try. It had to be done quickly and quietly. Alone in his room, he had practiced handling the keys so as to do this efficiently, but nothing fully prepared him for the actual moment. The trick was to do this slowly —to study the matchup of the key and lock before making any contact between the two. But in the darkness, this proved much more difficult than he had expected. The first key didn't fit. He felt his scalp go prickly with sweat. The second key entered, but didn't turn. It made noise coming out: to him a cymbal crash.

The third key turned and the door opened.

He stepped inside.

Thankfully, the door shut as silently as it had opened. He was no cat burglar. This was unfamiliar ground—in every way. Breath short, heart pounding, he withdrew the penlight from his pocket and switched it on. He had taped some gauze over its lens to mute its effects. The woven pattern of the gauze, like a large, white net, spread out ahead of him. He pressed on.

He found himself standing in an uncomfortably small sitting room. Cheap furniture. A television. A shelf of paperback books. If this room was any indication, the floor plan was a rat's maze.

He tried to conceive of the layout, and decided the kitchen would be at the back of the house, the bedrooms and bath to his left.

He moved to his right and through an open doorway.

Another, even smaller, room.

The dull light, with its bizarre pattern caused by the gauze, played over the walls and across the table—a dining table, he realized. It was littered with opened envelopes, stamps, a box of paper clips, and a yellow legal pad.

But no briefcase.

Kort edged past the table toward the end used as a desk. Where was it? Daggett *couldn't* have brought it into the bedroom with him! Was he that careful with it?

He trained the soft light to the floor. He hadn't realized how nervous he would feel. Sweat trickled down his ribs.

Standing on edge, alongside the end chair—exactly as it would be if you had worked with it, closed it, and put it aside—was Daggett's briefcase. It was closed.

Kort had hoped to find it open.

He hoisted it quietly to the table, surprised by its substantial weight, and studied the front latches and lock combination.

The latches were springed. They would make noise as they snapped opened if he wasn't careful.

Was it locked? He was about to try one of the latches when the dim light caught the combination number and froze him:

102003

Ten-twenty-three: A number as significant to Anthony Kort as to Cam Daggett.

He was certain it would open.

He blocked the latches with his thumbs, and opened the briefcase. He stuffed the light into his mouth and began to read.

A gold mine! On top of all the papers, scribbled hastily in pencil, he read the name of his bed-and-breakfast and the address. Although he should have been prepared for this, he wasn't. A drip of his sweat splattered onto a red folder. Kort mopped it up frantically: he had no intention of leaving a calling card behind. It didn't dry very well. It wrinkled the paper. He leafed through the briefcase's contents, one by one, his attention fixed on the sweat-stained folder. Examining the file marked "Rosen" he found three black-and-white police artist's sketches of his face—surprisingly accurate. There was a grainy photograph of Monique in a scarf and glasses. Dozens of reports, notes, memos, and message slips.

He removed the red folder and turned it over. Printed in black block letters around the entire perimeter of the envelope were the words EYES ONLY.

The folder had been last signed off by Richard Mumford. Daggett's name was printed on a cover sheet, his signature alongside.

Kort carefully opened the envelope's string fastener and withdrew the material. The first things he came across were the itineraries! He recognized the names: Mosner, Goldenbaum, Sandhurst, Grady, Fitzmaurice, Savile. He had no interest in flight numbers or carriers, he wanted only the dates of arrival and departure. Four of the itineraries shared a common date: September 21. The thrill of his discovery filled him with an uncanny sense of power. Although arriving on different days, two were departing the evening of the twenty-first. It had to be the twenty-first.

He was going to kill Mosner in two days.

As he quickly scanned the other papers in the briefcase, he suddenly felt ill. The more he read, the more it seemed impossible. He paid no attention to time. The minutes rushed by. Impossible! Daggett knew everything! This memo covered the possibility of explosives on board flight 64. The next addressed the repeated simulator tests at Duhning. There was a photo of Monique. They had a detailed explanation—even a drawing—of Bernard's detonator. What nearly took his breath away was the FAA lab analysis of the fire extinguisher: carbon monoxide. They knew everything! Or did they? Did they know his target? The *actual* target? If they knew his target, he was finished. All his preparation would prove useless. They would be sitting at the airport waiting for him. There would be no way to do what it was he had come to do. He might as well be dead.

The living room light came on. It cast a white rectangle of light into this small dining room. In one clean motion, Kort extinguished the beam of his flashlight and quietly closed the briefcase, leaving it on the table. He crouched, took two steps toward the invading harshness of light, looked quickly into the living room, and, seeing no one, charged through the light and reached the far wall, tucking himself behind the room's open door.

In one quick look at the briefcase, he saw that a section of the red folder protruded from its edge. It appeared hastily closed.

He heard the wheelchair before he saw the boy. The sound of wheels running on carpet was distinctive. He hoped for the sound of the television next. He hoped for a bout of boyish insomnia to be filled with the late, late show so he might be given the cover of noise to escape out the back. But as the boy's mechanical shadow stretched, turned, and filled this room like hand games on a projectionist's screen, Kort realized the boy's destination was the kitchen beyond, a course that would require he pass within a foot or two.

The wheelchair's complex shadow shrank as the boy propelled himself through the doorway and into this room. Kort changed his plan: Once the boy was in the kitchen he would return the briefcase to the carpet and make for the front door.

The boy stopped.

He looked to his right—toward the briefcase—straightened his head, and sniffed the air. "Carrie?" he said softly.

The cigarettes! Kort had smoked half a pack at the donut shop.

The boy's head rotated slowly to his left. Kort tightened his fist, waiting. At the moment they met eyes, Kort slugged him and crushed that nose. The kid's head snapped back and went slack.

He hurried to the briefcase, reopened it, ordered the contents, and was placing it onto the carpet when the idea struck him with a ferocity that he equated with genius. What better way to insure he controlled the operation from here on? He let go of the briefcase and headed over to the boy.

He was heavier than he would have guessed. But then again, dead weight always felt heavier.

25

DAGGETT AWAKENED EARLIER than usual, charged with a renewed energy from his victory with Mumford, and fully aware of the responsibility now placed upon him. He decided a morning run was in order. One or more of the chemical executives was Kort's intended target. Who, and how Kort intended to kill him—them—remained a mystery he had less than seventy-two hours to solve.

He took little notice of the spectacular sunrise, the melodious trumpeting of the songbirds that nested in his neighbor's apple tree, or the pungent fragrance of fresh-cut grass that hung heavily in the air. Dressed for his run, he passed Duncan's room quietly and slipped out the front door, as always, equally quietly. Just after six, there was very little activity, except that of fellow runners, their faces, even their clothing, familiar, their names unknown. He put in an effortless four miles, paying little attention to his route, even less to the color and magnificence of the sharp September day, instead calculating and recalculating where to focus his energies and resources.

His first sign that something might be wrong came when Duncan's alarm rang out and failed to be silenced. Daggett, by this time dressed and in the process of knotting his tie, investigated. Finding his son's room empty, the bed slept in, he stopped the alarm and called out, "Dunc?" The first time he tried this, it was delivered with a father's exploratory uncertainty. There was a half-bath down the hall; he didn't want to intrude on the boy's privacy. But as he stepped back into the hallway, he saw this door standing open, and the second time he called his son's name it carried with it an added degree of concern. One of Daggett's greatest fears was his son striking his head while climbing off the toilet.

The hallway bathroom was empty.

The chin-up bar—that had to be it. "Duncan?" he called out stridently, as his step quickened and the first warm flush of worry crept electrically over his skin. His imagination was running wild by the time he charged around the corner and crashed into the wheelchair. He fell fully over it, rode it into the wall, and collapsed with it. His worry transformed itself into anger—it wasn't the first time Duncan had abandoned his chair with no regard for his father. But the anger gave way to pure terror as his hand went sticky with room-temperature blood. He sat there on the floor, the overturned wheelchair trapping his legs, staring with stunned horror at his open hand. Later, he would not remember anything at all about the next few minutes. Minutes spent frantically searching every conceivable spot his boy might be found.

The cop in him soon took over. Blood in the chair. He checked the kitchen thinking, *The boy comes into the kitchen for a midnight snack, cuts himself . . .* but he found no knife, no sign in the kitchen of Duncan having been there at all. *He's in bed; he awakens to a bloody nose, regular occurrence for him; he heads to the kitchen for some ice. He's in his independent phase and doesn't want to wake me.*

It wasn't until he righted the overturned wheelchair, five? ten? twenty? minutes later, that he found the hand-scrawled note:

I've got him now. Don't DO anything. Nothing at all.
                              —Anthony Kort

He couldn't think. His mind filled too fast with thought and played the devilish trick on him of shutting down completely. Too much water to get down the drain, he overflowed, spilling thought, unable to contain it, unable even to mop it up. His first clear thought was: *The nerve of the man to sign the note.*

Don't DO anything. Nothing at all.

He looked at his watch. He considered calling Mumford immediately, but as quickly ruled it out. He considered calling Carrie, but to what end? He stumbled around the house for the better part of the next hour, unable to sit down, unable to stop walking, unable to pick up the phone. He bumped into furniture and into doors, not seeing clearly through his tears. He ran water, forgetting to turn it off. Twice he stopped before a mirror and contemplated his image, but was too shaken by the face he saw there. One of the mirrors now lay broken in pieces on the floor. He paced the small house endlessly, his mind churning with possible options. Where once existed the shrewd mind of an experienced investigator was now the stomach-knotted panic of a father.

He checked his watch once again. The minutes ticked off relentlessly. Kort was out there planning something. Duncan was . . . Could he afford to stop the investigation? To call in sick? He thought not. People knew him too well. Nothing would stop him at this point. It would draw far more attention to him if he missed work, than if he showed up and looked busy. He felt crushed by the weight of the reality of the situation: If he now stalled the investigation, Kort was likely to succeed with whatever it was he had planned, and Duncan would live. Or would he? If he continued with the investigation, if he made enough headway to actually stop Kort, then someone else—perhaps many, many people—would be spared. He couldn't forget the gymnasium filled with the personal items of 1023's victims. He couldn't ignore the devastation caused by the crash of flight 64. And thinking about it now, he couldn't believe that a man like Kort would spare anyone, even a young boy like Duncan.

His decision made, he reached for the phone and told Mrs. Kiyak to take the day off. The drive to Buzzard Point had never taken so long.

26

HAVING SPENT THE wee morning hours driving circles around the beltway with a paralyzed boy gagged and bound on the floor of the Toyota's backseat, an anxious Anthony Kort headed into the Virginia suburb where Caroline had taken him house-hunting. After much reflection, this seemed the logical answer to his dilemma: He would use one of the houses that she had shown him as a safe house. There simply wasn't time to go through the effort of starting the renting process all over again—especially with the boy in the backseat, especially given the FBI had a pretty good sketch of him, especially given his timetable. Having raided the bed-and-breakfast, the FBI would be expecting him to seek a roof over his head. They could be watching or would have already alerted, hotels, motels, rooming houses, perhaps even property management firms like Caroline's. There wasn't a lot of choice: he had to leave the boy off somewhere and get to the business at hand. He would have to improvise.

Early, early morning, just at sunrise, seemed to him the best time to try it. Any earlier and the darkness itself might raise a person's curiosity. But right at sunrise is when people experience some of their deepest sleep, and with the air gray and grainy in the limited light, the boy in his arms might appear no more than an awkward bundle from a distance.

"We seldom show this one," he recalled Caroline's having told him, though finding the cabin took him the better part of forty minutes. As he pulled down the long twisting drive lined with out-of-bloom dogwood, lilac, and an unbelievably huge hedge of azalea, his recollection of its near complete isolation proved accurate. The drive was potholed. A low stone wall marking the western boundary fronted a dense acreage of wood. Ahead, the road swung right, then turned abruptly left, and the gravel became deeper under the tires. And there it was. A two-room cabin situated on the far end of a former estate that had since been subdivided, the tiny dwelling wasn't large enough for a family, was too remote for most young couples. It was so off the beaten track that someone had installed a satellite dish. Seeing it again for only the second time (she had dropped it from her list of repeat attempts to find him a place), he felt mildly confident the cabin would not be shown in the next day or so—at least this was what he convinced himself of as he sat quietly listening to the car engine cool, getting up his nerve to break in.

Time was everything.

27

HOW TO CONTACT her?

The FBI would have her apartment phone trace-and-trapped, her BMW bugged or under tight surveillance, her office watched. It was a matter of isolating those few moments when she would not be under surveillance, and then deciding if he could find any way safely in and out. A few ideas came to mind.

First, the elevators at her apartment complex. She would ride an elevator from her apartment to the parking garage, and it seemed unlikely that the FBI would have any way of listening in on her once she was inside the elevator. They would know her every move in her apartment; they would follow her car; but in between?

Likewise, in the BMW between her apartment and office building, they could follow—perhaps even listen in—but only from a distance.

Her office would be treated the same way: They would know when she entered and left; they might even have her phone wired; but without an agent lording over her, they could not follow her every move. It was *unthinkable* they would follow her into a restroom.

All windows of opportunity, but none without risk.

Killing her might be easier.

She had the only key to the storage locker that held Bernard's fire extinguisher. He needed her.

He had to think of something.

He arrived at the modeling agency of Bernstein and Wright five minutes before the appointment he had scheduled. He spent these five minutes leafing through dozens of photographs, from which he singled out three candidates who had Monique's general look and body. His first choice turned out to be pregnant. Apologies all around. "She should have been pulled from the book months ago."

His second choice agreed to come right over to discuss the "shoot." For the sake of pretense, Kort was a free-lance fashion photographer.

Cindy Axtell arrived twenty minutes later. The face was perfect, the bust a little flat, the hair too short, but that could be dealt with. At his request, they were shown to a conference room where they could discuss the job "in private."

He closed the door. "Miss Axtell, I selected you in part because your resumé included a few minor acting credits. I'm short on time, so I'm going to be very direct. I am not a photographer. No fear," he said, raising his hand. "I'm not what you're thinking. Nothing like that. What I have in mind will require some acting skills, and I'm prepared to pay for that. I can only hope there is a touch of romance in your heart, for without it, I doubt you will agree to what it is I have to propose."

She crossed her arms *and* her legs, immediately suspicious. She looked like an insect fighting off the cold. "I'm listening, but not for long."

"Nothing sexual *whatsoever*. Furthermore, you get to spend the entire afternoon driving a brand new BMW around town."

Now he had her.

"Before going any further, I have to know *right now* whether or not you are seriously interested in the work. As I said, I have very little time. I can't waste it on you unless you're willing to go forward."

"Interested in *what?*" she insisted.

"Acting. An afternoon of acting is all. Nothing sexual. Completely alone. Twice your going rate. Four hours minimum. Cash, up front." That raised her eyebrows.

"Cash?" He nodded. "You'll double my rate?" He gave another nod. She studied him. "There's something in the car, isn't there? Drugs, something like that? No thanks. I don't think so." She reached out for her tiny purse.

"Drugs?" He laughed. "You don't like the car, you leave it wherever, and whenever you want. You can keep the keys or throw them away. I don't care." He could see he had her good and confused. He decided to push on. "There's a woman I'm very much in love with. She is also in love with me. Her husband is having her every move watched. He's very rich and he hasn't accepted their separation well at all. You may know the type."

She squinted, but he saw sympathy behind the attempt. He exhaled and relaxed.

He had her in the palm of his hand.

Monique braced herself for another wave of panic.

It came as a burning, twisting contraction that nearly buckled her over. She understood the importance of maintaining an appearance of calm, of continuing with her day-to-day activities, of avoiding paranoia. At the same time she saw conspiracy over her shoulder at every turn: the garbage man; the randomly parked car; the repairman fixing the office copier. All suspects.

Three people had asked after her health, so she obviously wasn't hiding it very well.

Five minutes to five. She grabbed her purse and was on her way out when her assistant caught up to her.

"A fax just came in for you. It's marked urgent and private." She handed it to her. Monique accepted it with an unsteady hand. It had no less importance than a stay of execution.

She drew herself into one of the reception room chairs. Hand written, the message was a single paragraph. The return address was Dallas, Texas. Her heart jumped. From *him*. It had been sent by an "Evelyn Macleod." That provided her the two letters—*E* and *M*—which, when at the start of a word, marked where his coded message stopped. It required effort to break it on the fly. She searched the document for the letters *EM* and found them in employees. *Employees* was in the second sentence. She mentally extracted the second letter of every word up to the word *employees.*

> re: Employee problems.
> Monique:
> Ugly confrontations at loading attempts for night flights. We've attached only nonunion, away-base employees to the night work, and it's causing problems. Suggest a price increase to match unions before it becomes more organized. Please advise by morning.
>
> —Eve

She couldn't do it in her head. She stole a pencil from a Snoopy cup on the front desk and wrote it out:

g-o-t-o-t-o-i-l-e-t-n-o-w

She broke it out backward, and then she saw it: *go to toilet now.*

She crumpled up the message and was about to throw it out when she thought better of it. "Good night," she said to the receptionist.

"See you tomorrow," the receptionist said. This stopped her. She knew better. She took one last look around the office. She had built a pretty good life here, she thought. God willing, she would never see it again.

The walk to the bathroom dragged on. The clicking of her pumps was like the ticking of a clock. She felt her pulse at her temples.

She turned the handle and stepped inside.

A blond woman stood at the sink, her head down. She was wearing a short red leather skirt and a black leather jacket. Another bolt of panic slapped her. FBI? If he couldn't make contact with her . . .

"Take the center stall and lock the door," the blond woman said once the hall door had shut. "We're alone." When Monique hesitated, the woman added, "Hurry! Strip down to your underwear and pass your clothes to me in the end stall. There's a shopping bag there. Put that stuff on." The model dried her hands and then entered and locked the toilet stall next to the wall, the one immediately adjacent to Monique. "If someone comes in, sit down. Make it look like you're on the john."

Monique obeyed her. She shed her clothes in seconds and passed them through. In the shopping bag she found a duplicate red miniskirt, the same sheer blouse, and a black leather jacket. All her size. At the very bottom of the bag was a blond wig, a pair of oversized eyeglasses, and, beneath these, a pair of scissors. She stared at the scissors, but only briefly. She knew what had to be done. She clipped off great locks of her hair and dropped them into the toilet. For the wig to fit she had to have shorter hair.

He had thought of everything.

"Thank you so much," she blurted out. She was crying again. She hated herself for it.

"You must love him very much," came the voice from the stall.

Cutting off most of her hair was the final blow. Her life was over. She could feel it.

"Give me your keys, and tell me where you parked."

That was when Monique understood Kort's plan.

"It's in the reserved spaces," she said. There was too much to do. She was all thumbs.

The door to the hall opened.

Monique froze and dropped to the toilet. She saw the other woman's hands seize the discarded clothing, and then she, too, sat down on the toilet. The woman who had entered took the only remaining stall. She urinated, flushed the toilet, and washed her hands. She left.

A tube of lipstick and a compact slid under the panel. Monique picked it up. With two more snips, most of her hair was gone. It floated in large clumps on the surface of the water. She flushed it away, and with it, the last several years. The short-haired blond wig felt horrible. She checked the compact's mirror and seated the wig properly. The bright red lipstick was awful, but it changed her looks dramatically. The gray-tint glasses polished it off.

Another person. Cheap, sexy—easy.

The woman next to her passed a ball of clothes to her. She whispered, "Put them in the shopping bag. *You* will carry it. I carried it in." She heard the other woman leave her stall then. Monique put the compact and the clothes in the empty shopping bag and opened the stall door.

She gasped. This woman, dressed in her clothes (the skirt pinned in the back, she noticed), wearing her makeup similarly, and a wig that imitated the hair that had just been flushed down the toilet, looked amazingly like her real self. "It'll work," she said.

Cindy Axtell nodded and smiled. "Yes, I think it will. Give me two minutes." As she spoke, she snatched Monique's purse and dumped its contents into the empty purse she had brought with her. They then switched purses. Monique handed her the keys to the BMW. Axtell said, "Take the *stairs* to the lobby—that way you won't run into someone from your office and have to explain yourself. Once downstairs, walk right out the front doors. Put some hip into your walk. Make it sexy. The idea—his idea—is that the more you stick out the less you'll be seen. Is that a man's way of thinking, or what? Once outside, turn left and keep walking. Go into the hotel bar in the next block. Sit alone and order a drink. Don't drink alcohol, and don't talk to *anyone.* He'll meet you there. But it may take him quite a while. Be patient. He said to make sure to tell you that."

Monique checked herself once in the mirror.

Axtell said, "You two are real lucky to have each other. He seems like a great guy."

Monique played along. "He is." She meant every word.

"He told me to park the car anywhere and just leave it. I know you're eloping and all, but even so . . . can't I call you or something, tell you where it is?"

"Don't worry about it," Monique said, trying to sound confident, not knowing what kind of story Kort had built, but now beginning to guess. "Whatever he said . . . You know how it is."

The other woman shrugged.

Monique loved that car. She hated to be without it. Her world continued to come apart before her eyes.

Cindy Axtell dropped the keys into Monique's empty purse, opened the door and left.

Monique looked at her watch and started counting off the two minutes.

28

KORT THOUGHT OF his ideas as flowers, germinating from seed, tenderly breaking through the stubborn surface to the life-giving light beyond, from which they absorbed energy, converted it, and continued to grow until bursting with color and scent that would set up the proper conditions to form the seeds so the process could begin again. No thought simply arrived, fully conceived and developed. There was a period of fertilization, germination, of adolescence and of maturity, each important to the construction of the next, the structure as important as the end point. So it was that by seeing the transit cop hassling the bums in the Metro station the night before, and feeling the unbearable weight of Daggett's knowledge of his operation and the likelihood of failure, his formidable imagination had given birth to a series of ideas that had ended in the purchase of a pair of gray canvas trousers with a stretch waist, a white golf shirt, a brown windbreaker, and a pair of rubber-soled canvas shoes from a chain store that had a sister outlet not twenty blocks away in trendy Georgetown. He paid cash for it all, having stopped at a cash machine only minutes earlier. His major enemy now was not only Daggett, not only Lynn Greene and the FAA, not only all of the agents of the FAA, FBI, NTSB combined, but his own body. Fatigue drilled through him from his temples as if someone were screwing a vise shut on his head. It bulged his eyes, dried his throat, tortured his stomach, and caused a massive, unforgiving headache at the top of his spine. The muscles in his shoulders felt welded tight. Exhaustion had poured sand in his eyes.

And there remained much to do. The flowers of his fertile imagination were reaching harvest. Having seen the contents of Daggett's briefcase, in desperation he had reached a single, inescapable conclusion: He had to die. As long as he remained alive, the FBI would continue to pursue him.

He liberated the new clothes of their tags and stapled advertisements and regrouped them into a single bag.

The trick had been to locate a fire escape exit door from the Red Line tunnel somewhere between Dupont Circle and Farragut North, a task made easier by studying engineering plans available to the public at the Library of Congress, which Kort had entered promptly at one o'clock that afternoon, following his hiring of Cynthia Axtell at the modeling agency. It was one thing to identify the hieroglyphic markings on the library's microfilm, and another thing entirely to actually locate the door itself down a back alley off the spiderwebbed streets of this city. But every such plan had its logistical setbacks, and Kort would not be deterred. At long last, it was the very street person he sought who unknowingly led him to the anonymous steel door marked in five-inch stenciled white letters:

NO PARKING ANYTIME
DO NOT BLOCK DOORWAY
EMERGENCY EXIT

He followed the man through the door, which was blocked open appropriately enough with a crushed beer can, after waiting several minutes so he wouldn't frighten him.

Never frighten a man you intend to kill.

The steel door led down an impossibly long flight of steel steps, dimly lit by the glow of red exit signs and arrows pointing up, and suggested that the street people who used these subway tunnels as their shelter were among the most physically fit people in the city. He didn't count them,

but he guessed them at about six hundred steps, perhaps
two hundred vertical feet—twenty stories—of descent, and
he wondered about his ability to climb them at a full run
later that night. With each landing, the intensity of the heat
grew markedly, forcing Kort to understand the desperation
of those who elected to dwell here. It was stiflingly hot,
suffocating air, reeking unnaturally of burning electricity,
steel, and rubber, and did nothing to improve his already
deteriorating condition.

The tunnel was black as night, as dark as hell itself,
relieved only occasionally by a low-watt bulb in a steel
safety cage, mounted high above the trunk lines and plumb-
ing pipes that ran endlessly along the poured-cement walls.
An unseen gravel complained underfoot and contributed
no doubt to the dry, caustic dust that quickly lined his nos-
trils and flared a bitter taste at the back of his raspy throat.
He stopped intermittently, listening for and identifying the
dragging footsteps of the man who had preceded him.
When at last he paused and heard nothing, he put himself
on guard, for either a train was coming, and the stranger
ahead knew well enough to take shelter from being seen in
its single headlight, or he had taken roost in a spot where
he intended to consume the better portion of the spirits he
carried in the brown paper bag at his side. Either way, Kort
knew enough to be on full alert, for his moment was at
hand. His fingers stroked the cool shaft of the small penlight he had used the night before in Daggett's home, and he
readied himself to use it.

He smelled the man before he reached him. And then
he stopped, perhaps as close as ten feet away, close enough
to hear the ragged breathing and the crisp sound of ripping
aluminum as the cap of the unseen bottle was twisted open.
He heard the eager lips smack with the drink, and the
throat choke down the sweetness of the fortified wine, the
tropical fruity smell of which now overpowered the man's
vile body odors.

The rumbling of the approaching train grew in the distance like the first hint of a summer storm whose magnitude was foreshadowed even from the horizon. The power clawed its way toward them, a dragon from its lair.

Only now did Kort step forward and shine his light on the poor soul whose first instinct was to protect his rights to his bottle by cradling it tightly in his elbow. Only now did he study the man's size, and approving of what he saw, remove his gun, unseen behind the blinding glare of his flashlight. "Get away," the stranger croaked weakly in his wet rheumy voice, clutching his comfort even more tightly and rotating away from Kort, who drew closer with each step.

The thunder of the approaching train bore down on them, made louder by the unforgiving qualities of strict confinement and hard cement. Kort went deaf as he stuck the light against his leg to hide its beam, leaned behind a strut to avoid the dragon's sole eye, which arrived and passed with unusual speed. With the dragon's body and tail carried behind it, the lights of the train cars casting a strobed, flickering brilliance on the sagging pipes above them, Kort addressed his victim with the stabbing glare of the flashlight, and lowered the butt of his weapon squarely into the center of the man's head with all the strength he had ever found inside himself. The bubbling scream was sweet music, buried by the grinding whine of the departing train, buried by the dull pop of breaking glass as the bottle fell and broke inside its bag.

Buried, but not forgotten. For this man would live yet again.

His work soon completed, Kort left the stench and heat without his bag and made the arduous climb up what proved to be four hundred and eighty-six steps to the relative coolness of an oppressive September afternoon.

In Georgetown, at the twin sister of the very store he had shopped earlier in the day, he purchased an identical pair of gray canvas jeans with elastic waist, a white golf shirt, a brown windbreaker, and a pair of canvas shoes. This done, his head splitting open with pain, he headed off to make his phone call, for with one flower now blooming nicely, he had an entire garden to attend to.

29

"THERE'S A BANK of pay phones in the Old Post Office Building. Ground floor. Be there in ten minutes." Daggett heard the line go dead, and only then did he reflect on the harsh severity of the man's slightly accented voice, only then did he know that after two years of searching he had found Anthony Kort.

The Old Post Office had been converted into a restaurant mall and offered a variety of ethnic food shops with Formica tables, plastic forks, and paper napkins. At three o'clock in the afternoon the concourses were nearly deserted, though an ice-cream parlor and a woman selling colorful helium balloons were doing brisk business with the tourists. Daggett found the bank of three pay phones and waited impatiently for one to ring, ignoring the obscene graffiti scrawled in pen on any surface that would hold ink. He blamed Clint Eastwood and *Dirty Harry* for this pay phone scheme—run a cop from pay phone to pay phone until you've got him on a clean line, or until you're confident he's all alone. Daggett wondered which it was to be, how long it was to last. He hoped Kort wouldn't keep it up too long; he had no patience for games. He was reviewing the words he would say when the middle phone rang.

"Me for him," Daggett said answering, "at the place and time of your choosing."

"Impossible. More phones upstairs. One minute." The line went dead.

"Shit," Daggett said, slamming the receiver down and drawing attention to himself. He galloped up the stairs two at a time and stopped a hunchbacked old man sweeping up cigarette butts and asked him where the phones were. He found them pushed back in behind a video arcade that had gone bust. As he moved his shirt cuff to check his watch, the pay phone to his left rang loudly.

"No more of this," he said into the receiver. "This is bullshit. I'm not trapping the phones."

"You will be on the northbound side of the Dupont Circle Metro platform at nine o'clock tonight. It goes without saying that you will be alone. I want all the itineraries. You understand."

"I'm offering you a trade," Daggett said, "me for the boy."

"Northbound side. Nine o'clock tonight. Alone. That's all there is between your son's life and death."

"How do I know he's still alive?"

"You don't." Kort hung up.

Remorse, as he had never experienced, overcame him with such ferocity that he ran to the public toilet and vomited. His face crimson with blood, he collected himself at the sink, the man in the mirror older by years than the man who had jogged that morning. It was as if his father's words to him, and his to his own son—*the only way there is through*—were coming back to haunt him, as perhaps they had haunted the men of every generation in his family. For there was indeed only one way out of this now, and he had to wonder how much of this was a self-fulfilling prophecy. In some secret, dark corner of his heart, he had wanted the chance to take on, one-on-one, the man responsible for the death of his parents and the paralysis of his son. No warrants, no papers of extradition, no courts, no jail cells. No rules.

And now, it appeared that time had come.

30

"CHEYSSON IS MISSING!" Levin whispered, craning over Daggett's desk. Daggett felt a knot block his throat and no words would come out. It had begun. Daggett refused to roll over and play dead, but he had yet to formulate a plan of his own. Perhaps this was the purpose behind Kort's request—he had wanted Daggett's attention focused elsewhere.

Levin continued, "She left her office at five. Nothing unusual. Our people followed her out to a department store off the Beltway."

"A department store? They should have stopped her."

"I know . . . I know . . ."

"That's the oldest trick in the book."

"Listen, they watched all the exits, they watched faces not clothing. She never came out of there. She's still *in* there. We got caught shorthanded. They're requesting backup."

"She's *not* still in there. Count on it." Daggett couldn't think clearly. He found guilt a suffocating emotion. Each hour he traveled farther down the path of deception, the more congested his brain became and the more difficult and tentative he found his position. He had come too far to abandon this investigation, to abandon his son without a fight. "Call a meeting," he said.

"A meeting? What the fuck do I do about Cheysson?"

"We *lost* her, right?" he asked angrily. "Forget about Cheysson. We don't need her. Call a meeting. Tell Gloria to do it. Pullman, Surveillance, Tech. Services. I want them all at the meeting."

"Don't need her?" Levin shouted.

Daggett said calmly, "Keep your voice down, Bradley. This isn't for public broadcast."

"You've lost your fucking marbles."

"Maybe. But I've *found* Anthony Kort. Now call the fucking meeting before I change my mind."

31

MONIQUE WAS FREE.

Kort's plan worked flawlessly: she walked out of the office building with no one the wiser. An hour later she had received his message in the hotel bar. For the next two hours she moved from one location to the next, Kort probably watching her, and everything around her, at each and every stop. She was walking with wings on her feet, not only because of her newfound freedom but because of her feelings for him, and her realization that the two of them would now be together. He had saved her life—literally. He was her white knight; there was nothing she would not give him, nothing she would not do for him.

At a few minutes past eight she was riding in the passenger seat of the Toyota.

"You saved my life," she said. "How can I ever thank you?"

"Take off your clothes." He pulled a gray plastic bag from the backseat.

"Right here?" she asked, misunderstanding him.

"Change into these. Immediately. There's no time!"

She didn't argue. She unzipped the red leather skirt, raised her hips, and slipped it off. She continued to change as they talked.

"I need the key to the storage locker," he said coldly. He was in no mood for sloppy sentimentality.

She nodded as desperation and fear replaced her ebullience. "You're angry with me?" she asked incredulously. "You think I did something to cause this?"

"I don't want to go into it."

He was completely emotionless. A wave of intense cold swept through her. "It must have been the Greek. It wasn't *my* fault." She located the keys in her handbag and handed them to him. She asked, "How can you wear gloves when it's this hot?"

"I live in these things."

"It's a private mailbox," she said, referring to the key. "Do you want me to write down the address?"

"I *know* the address. This," he said, pocketing the key, "is all I need."

"Why did you do this? Why did you help me?" she asked, not wanting the answer.

"I need you."

"That's not why."

"It is." The light changed and he started off again.

"You're going through with it?" She was stunned.

"Of course. We came to do a job. We're going to do it."

"You're insane." She felt tempted to tug the door open and run away.

He felt himself smile. He nodded in agreement. "It's true."

"Need me for what?"

"To baby-sit. You know how to cook, don't you?"

32

HE HAD COME here to tell her about Duncan. About his decision. He had come here because he had no idea what the next few hours had in store for him, and yet Carrie deserved to be a part of it. Carrie had been the stabilizing force in his life these past two years and he needed her now, regardless of their present problems. He had come here out of selfishness. But when he opened his mouth to speak, he didn't mention Duncan. He couldn't bring himself to, for he knew through her eyes his decision had been the wrong one. But it was over now, and there was no going back. "I went to her the other night."

She obviously didn't need any names. She searched her purse for a cigarette and lit it.

"I came here. I parked out in the drive and I couldn't bring myself to come inside." When she failed to say anything he wondered if this was going to end up a lover's monologue, and he feared if it was, then these few minutes might be their last together. "I thought we would argue. All we ever do anymore is argue."

"What was she like?" Carrie asked spitefully. "Was she everything you dreamed?" She added bitterly, "You *do* dream about her, you know. You talk about her in your sleep."

"It wasn't like that. I wanted to sleep with her," he confessed, "but she refused."

"She really knows how to play you, doesn't she?"

"Maybe she does."

"I've been seeing someone," she admitted, glancing up

and blowing smoke over his head. It was an act of defiance; she knew how he hated the cigarettes.

He felt a stab of blinding pain shoot right through his lover's heart, and he wondered with self-pity what else the world had in store for him today. And where he might have expected of himself intense anger and jealous fury, he felt only a weeping disappointment. He was too taxed to deal with this properly. He felt the air go out of him. "I wondered what that was about the other night."

She nodded. "Yes. That was part of it."

"Do I know him?"

She raised her eyebrows and coughed out a laugh. Smoke escaped with the laugh. "Do *I* know him? He's a stranger. Someone I met recently, that's all."

"Is it everything you dreamed?"

That caused her some pain and he felt good about it. He had had his chance with Lynn and he hadn't taken it. Regret overcame him. He didn't want to lose Carrie. He didn't want to stay. He didn't want to lose Lynn, but he didn't even have her yet. He had stepped out onto an emotional floating log and now, the faster he ran, trying to stay on, the more precarious his position. Several. minutes passed. Some of the longest minutes of his life.

"I thought I had fallen in love with him," she said.

"Past tense?"

"Just plain old tense right now."

"Word games? You're going to play word games at a time like this?"

"We play all sorts of games, don't we? That's the stage we're in, isn't it? We play games with each other's emotions. We play games with ourselves."

His heart wanted to hate her, but it lacked any punch. All the strength had gone out of him during the meeting. There was nothing left for his hate to feed on. "Why bother telling me?"

"No bother." She forced an evil smile and took another drag. "I wasn't going to. I'm not sure why I did. Probably because of what you said about *her.* I'm afraid of her. She's everything I'm not."

"She's a friend. That's all."

"Bullshit."

"So it's bullshit."

"So it is."

"This isn't why I came here."

"Why then? You haven't been here in *months.* It's always your place. Always your terms. Always you, you, you. You know what that's like for me?"

"Duncan's been kidnapped." There. He had said it. It was the only possible defense against the truth, and it had just the effect he was hoping for. "Sometime last night," he added. Her anger and spite vanished magically, replaced by a wave of shock that swept through her, charging her eyes with sympathy and stealing her voice in fear. Just seeing her reaction tightened his throat. He remembered the term they had used: *body fragmentation.* It was how he felt. "I have to meet him tonight."

"*Who?* What are you talking about?" Tears came to her frightened eyes and she placed down the cigarette and reached for his hand. Hers was cold. He felt relief at having told her. He felt tired all of a sudden and he welcomed the feeling. Anything, but what he had been feeling.

He found himself drawn to tell her what it was that had been going through his mind for the better part of the last few hours. To confess. This was why he had come: to make his confession. "It's funny . . . You stand on high moral ground for most of your life, and then someone adjusts the scales like this and you find you're no different than the people you've spent your life pursuing. Given the right set of circumstances there's nothing we won't do. *Nothing.* And if we're no different, then we're all the same. And if we're all the same, then what does it matter who you lock up and who you let go free?"

"What are you talking about?"

"He thought he could blackmail me. Duncan's life for some itineraries."

She appeared nervous then. Her voice warbled. "What are you saying?"

"I couldn't do it."

"Cam?"

"Am I wrong?"

"Do *what*?"

"Was I wrong?"

"Wrong about *what*?"

"We'll have a man at every station. Two, on the southbound platform, but only just me on the northbound. Just as he asked."

"Who?"

"I've told you. The man who kidnapped him."

"You've double-crossed him?"

"I love that boy. I knew that you, more than anyone, would understand that. You *do* understand, don't you? I can't play by his rules. They kill the hostage. They *always* kill the hostage."

She was weeping, for now she understood. Her shoulders began to shake and her nose began to run and she made a sound like a dying animal. Alone, and distant. His face convulsed and his tears ran along with hers. Tears of betrayal. He had betrayed his only son. His vision blurred and he lost sight of her. He hated himself for what he had done. There was no forgiveness to be found. Not from this woman. Not from God. Not from anyone. Not ever. It was his decision and now he lived with it, while others were bound to die because of it.

They went on crying for a long time, and it occurred to him that they were in a premature mourning, and this terrified him. Her cigarette burned down to a long tube of gray ash, and was broken as the filter fell from the ashtray. "Thank you," he said softly. He squeezed her hand and it collapsed under his grip.

She looked at him through a face made ugly by grief.

Her fear was palpable, her hate tangible. It was out in the open then: She thought he had done wrong.

He stood, tempted to kiss her on the cheek, but simultaneously repulsed by the idea. "I'll call you," he said, but he doubted it.

He was halfway to the door when she called out in confusion, "But *how* did it happen?"

"I'm not sure." He grabbed hold of the doorknob and its familiarity did something to him, sparked something inside him that tore at his heartstrings. He found himself staring at it, wondering if he'd ever be back here again. "No idea. No sign whatsoever of forced entry. Maybe Duncan let him in or something. I can't believe he would have. Not in the middle of the night. Somehow he got into the house. Who knows?"

She started to come out of her chair, but changed her mind and sat back down heavily. He was grateful for that; he wanted out of here. "I'll pray for you," she said, her throat catching. "I'll pray for you both."

33

PARKED FIVE BLOCKS away from Dupont Circle, Daggett waited nervously in the front seat of his car for the go-ahead. The face of the man in the backseat of the car parked directly across the street was hard to see, but as Daggett answered his car phone, hearing Pullman's voice reminded him of the size and importance of this operation. In less than three hours, Pullman and Mumford had placed over sixty agents into the field. Each platform of every stop on the Red Line was now covered, as was the Metro Center, where it joined up with the Orange and Blue lines. Tech. Services had equipped every one of these agents with communication so they formed an instant network across the city, and in some cases, into the suburbs. Fears persisted that the radio network might fail in certain areas, given the depth of the tunnels and the great distances involved. But as the minutes ticked down toward nine o'clock, communication vans with relay amplifiers were whisking across the streets of Washington to destination points established in four key areas. This city was WMFO's sole territory. The special agents, squad chiefs, and executive officers took great pride in their ability to throw a net across it in a matter of hours.

"We've got a green light," Pullman said.

"We wait to see if he's going to produce the boy. We're agreed on that," Daggett reminded. The FBI was world-renowned for its handling of kidnappings. For every one case the public heard about, there were twenty other successes that went unmentioned. Even so, Daggett suddenly wondered about putting his trust in the Bureau. He prayed to God it wasn't something he would regret the rest of his life.

"We're all of us—down to a man—with you on this, Michigan. It took great courage to do what you've done."

"Or great stupidity," Daggett said before hanging up the phone and starting the car. Pullman said the most idiotic things. He glanced one last time to his right, and this time he could see Pullman, face pressed near the glass, his right hand shaking a thumbs-up signal. Jesus, the guy was all John Wayne. The hand of fear reached inside Daggett, took hold of his guts, and twisted. He might have vomited if there had been anything left.

He travels down the gray intestine that is the elevator, the itineraries folded inside the pocket of his letter jacket. The smells tell him he is deeper; he has left the fresh air for the stench of machinery and man. He is repulsed by it. He turns his head and looks back up at what is now a tiny, ever-shrinking black hole at the top of the tunnel. The increasing heat makes him think of hell. This is punishment for all his failure. Failure: he wears it like a waterlogged coat three sizes too big.

Nine o'clock on the dot. He tries to focus on the faces in the crowd. What crowd? It's pretty thin down here now that the rush is over. People are out eating dinner, home watching television, gone for an evening swim at the club. Families in the safety and security of their homes. The very people that he and the others are sworn to protect. But they aren't doing a very good job of it. For all the secrets, all the meetings, all the hardware and software, the expense accounts, the ciphers and fibers and fingerprints and videos, they have failed. Cheysson is at large. Kort is at large.

Kort is standing at the far end of the platform not forty feet away, staring at him. Smiling.

At first, Daggett can't believe his eyes. He thinks like a cop. Can't help it. The composite sketch isn't exactly right: the chin isn't quite as pointed, the ears stick out a little farther. He clears his throat for the sake of the microphone he's wearing. The signal he's made contact. He can picture the flurry of the resulting activity above on the street. Efficient bastards, the Techies. He's glad for that.

He takes a few steps toward Kort, who raises his hand to stop him. It's a smart move. From here, a kill shot would be unlikely. On a moving target, next to impossible.

The string of round lights embedded in the concrete of the platform begin to blink in unison announcing the arrival of a train.

A train!

Kort's face twitches with recognition. He does the unexpected. With the simple motion of his index finger, he waves Daggett forward.

His eyes dart to the empty platform and Daggett can feel him calculating his timing.

They don't have agents on any of the trains; that was agreed upon by all. Too many innocent lives at stake, too much left to chance. That was why at this moment they were so carefully guarding the stations themselves.

Daggett prays Duncan will be on the train, his face purposely shown in a window.

They are within ten feet of each other now. Neither will survive a gunfight at this distance.

"The itineraries," Kort says.

Daggett produces them but does not relinquish them.

"Duncan," he says back to the man, holding on to his bait.

The train pulls in. Kort's eyes dance nervously between the itineraries and the train. The train slows.

"The itineraries," he repeats.

Daggett shakes his head. "My boy."

Only then do Kort's eyes alert Daggett to trouble. It's a middle-aged man in blue jeans and old, beat-up running shoes. His windbreaker is unzipped and his hand is going inside, and Daggett can see it coming. He's either a plainclothes or off-duty cop with a nose for trouble.

"We got a problem here, fellows?" He flashes his badge proudly.

Neither Daggett or Kort so much as flinch.

The train doors slide open.

"Hey! I'm talking to you!" The other hand goes deeper into the jacket.

"Nice try," Kort says to Daggett.

"FBI!" Daggett shouts at the other man, reaching for his ID.

But the itchy cop mistakes the move and comes out with his gun. Daggett dives, reaching for his own weapon.

Kort kills the cop with two shots to the chest, the second of which lifts the man off his feet. The screams echo eerily in the cement tomb.

Daggett remembers later that as he comes to his feet all the train cars appear empty because every single passenger is now on the floor. For it's the train car where Daggett looks first. Only a split second later does he see Kort hopping off the platform into the darkness of the tunnel.

The tunnel? That's suicide. That wasn't in the plan! He shouts, "The tunnel!" Knows the microphone will pick it up.

He leaves the relative safety of the platform and follows into the encroaching darkness.

The footing is bad. It's hotter than hell in here. He can't see a thing. He has to slow down, it's so dark. The grayness of image is dying, sucked dry by the ever-increasing black. A few more yards and he stops to listen. He can hear the fast footfalls up ahead. He continues on, around a long, graceful curve of tunnel. When he is finally swallowed by near pitch-black, a match fires off at his knees. He screams and falls to the tracks, finger on the trigger.

It's a bum. A fucking half-naked street bum holding a match out as lighting.

The footfalls continue deeper into the darkness.

Daggett stuffs the gun away and hurries off. He had come within a split second of killing that bum. His nerves are raw. He picks up his speed. He's losing Kort.

He passes an area that smells of urine and excrement. He doesn't stop because he can still hear Kort running in the distance.

The next time he stops, the footfalls are gone.

It is not exactly silence. He can hear a train. Ahead of him? Behind? He's not sure. But no footfalls. He creeps forward cautiously, his gun back out and held in both hands. The grayness of image has returned: his eyes have adjusted. But it is no form of light. It is more a mosaic of hard shapes and vague edges. It is the crunching of dirt under his feet and the whine of that train, which is clearly growing closer.

The face shoots out from behind a black rectangle, and he is knocked entirely off his feet. His gun fires as he falls. He sees a bright yellow flash and realizes it was not his gun, but a gun being fired at him. He rolls inside the tracks, well aware of the existence of a third rail carrying enough electricity to turn him to dust. He rolls and he rolls. He hears two more rounds.

The earth begins to shake beneath him. The train is coming. *The train!* He explodes to his feet and charges off into the darkness, which, thanks to the approaching train, is growing ever more light. The tunnel continues its curve to the left. At a full run now, he catches up to the ever elusive image of Kort's back as he continues to fade around the huge curve. Like a sterile sunrise, a brightness fills the tunnel until Daggett is nearly blind with white light. He's lost him. One moment seen, the next, gone. He stops. Chest heaving. Hand held to block the approaching light, his face retained in shadow. He's terrified. The sound is overpowering. He wants to scream. The train barrels down on him.

At the last possible second, only yards in front of him, Kort breaks from the shadows and dives to clear the train. It is meant to be perfect timing. But he catches a foot . . . something wrong . . . he falls . . . An image—that is all. A black blur in silhouette met by the stark white light and charging roar of several tons of train.

Daggett screams, "No-o-o-o-o-o!" But it is too late. The

impact is instant, and he's showered in a spray of blood and flesh that soaks him through.

When he awakens by the side of the tracks, he is overcome by the sticky goo and the stench. He pulls himself out of his blood-soaked clothes as quickly as they will come off. Stripped down to shorts and shoes, his eyes wiped clear, he staggers, feeble-legged, down the tracks, toward the ever-increasing sound of the army of approaching footfalls. Kort is dead; he feels victorious. But he has not won. Where is Duncan? How will they ever find Duncan without Kort alive?

His tears run red with another man's blood.

34

CARRIE STEVENSON SLEPT poorly. Not only did she worry for Cam, but she hated him, hated herself, hated everything. She had been tempted by the apple and now found its juices poison. Her tryst with Carl, which had brought her so much immediate happiness, had delivered a devastating aftershock of sorrow and regret. She reverberated from that aftershock, her entire body trembling as she wept openly for hours on end, lying naked in a bedroom too hot to permit sleep. Her blood was tainted with remorse so tangible that her own body odor disgusted her: she smelled of *him.*

Worming around inside her was the humiliation of his silence. She had given herself fully to him—the things they had done!—and then she had paid with the heart-wrenching impatience of sitting by a phone that brought nothing but silence all day. He had vanished from her life, replaced by a despondent Cam whom she realized she loved with all her heart. She had ruined everything.

Adding to her confusion was the discovery, not five minutes earlier, that someone had rearranged her keys. She kept all the teeth to her keys facing the same direction, *except* Cam's, which made it easy to spot in the bunch. Now its teeth were facing the same way as all the others. That was wrong. That was *impossible,* unless that key had been removed and later replaced. By someone else. Someone other than her. A single memory played repeatedly in her mind: She saw herself lying in bed, warm and feeling delicious, as she handed Carl her keys so he could buy them some take-out.

■

One of the major fallacies of this campaign for truth was that she forced herself to relive memories so vital and fresh, so stimulating, that she caused herself an enormous amount of sorrow and grief. She also reminded herself just how wonderful those few days with Carl had been. Each house at which she arrived sparked a memory of a moment, or a turn of phrase, or a certain look of his, and by the third house he completely dominated her thoughts again. Twice she had to pull the car off the road to complete her crying without risking a traffic accident.

The list of properties remained at her side, the names checked off one by one as she returned to them. If she was anything, she was efficient. Memory by memory she traveled back in time, smiling to herself, then frowning, then lighting a cigarette and attempting to smoke herself to death.

She wandered the gardens, sat in the same chairs in which they had sat, recalled their discussions. She missed him. He had brought diversion to her life; he had taken her away without her going anywhere. A marvelous gift. And what she had thought might require two hours at most, stretched on into the afternoon as she unknowingly delayed herself with these detours into sentimentality.

A few minutes before five, having come away empty-handed, depressed and alone, she checked back in at the office finding only phone messages of no substance. The hollowness of her defeat turned her strong voice to a whisper and her rigid posture to that of an old woman. Sheila told her to go home, and so she did.

It was only as she returned to her home on the subdivided estate that she remembered having shown Carl the gatehouse. It wasn't much of a place, which is why she didn't list it with her company, and rarely showed it, unless the owners, who lived in one of the master house's segmented condominiums, asked her to. But when things had

begun warming up with Carl, driven by a girlish impulse to
have him living close by, she had shown him the property,
entering from the southern entrance and making no reference to its relative proximity to her own residence.

She parked her car in the garage, walked to the door of
her carriage house, and then, changing her mind, set off
through the dense copse of trees along a path that once had
been the main road into the estate. Lined with towering
maples, the road itself was now overgrown with bramble
and other wild shrubs, the only way through it an aimlessly
twisting game path cut by the few deer who also made their
home here. Miraculously, for the sake of good footing, this
game path followed the estate's former driveway. Carrie
plunged herself into the insects and the sudden darkness of
the forest, and made her way as quickly as she could.

A new section of driveway had been established at a
right angle to the short stretch of the old road that remained in use. Because of this obstruction, the deer had
steered clear of the new road, and so their path weaved
toward the back of the former gatehouse. And so, too, did
Carrie. Forced off the trail in order to reach the small clearing that held the cabin, she forged a path of her own, steering clear of the bramble with its razor-sharp teeth, and
avoiding the dead fallen limbs as best as possible.

It was a beautiful place, really, when you considered
the privacy and quiet that resulted from its isolation. Had
they invested a little more into the remodel, increasing the
size or improving the one bathroom and tiny kitchenette,
she might have unloaded it in a minute. As it was, it just
didn't have a market.

But it had a broken window.

That was new. Panic overcame her. Someone had broken in! She had been here not five days ago with Carl, and
there had been no broken window at that time. Should she
run back and call Cam and try to explain that a window
was broken in one of her rentals and that he had better
come quick? She was being childish. Vandalism was the

likely explanation. This fit the exact description of what was believed to be local teenager activity—kids breaking into homes hoping to find a bottle of booze, or a bed in which to screw. The village weekly had been full of such reports this summer, with the recently past Labor Day weekend being the worst. As property manager, she had an obligation to report any damage to the owners. She would therefore have to assess the damage.

She stayed out of sight, debating her options. Call Cam, or just go take a look? She stirred with anger, disgusted that anyone would violate private property in this way. She stirred with fear that it might not be teenagers at all.

She slipped quickly into the backyard and sneaked up to the back door, where she paused, ears alert for the slightest of sounds. She couldn't hear anything above the drumming of her heart. Her emotions swung alternately between childish terror and adult anger. She didn't know which to trust. It seemed so silly, this broken window. It seemed so terrifying.

She turned the doorknob and pushed.

She stepped inside the closet-sized kitchen and paused, because as she attempted to step over the window's broken glass, she found, to her surprise, that it had been swept up. She had never known her heart to beat this strongly. There was the faint smell of cooked food where there should be none. Squatters? she thought. Or Carl? Fear overcame her. She understood nothing of her own actions. Rather than flee, she found herself drawn into this place, drawn into its mystery. Compelled to continue. She found herself well into the small house and continuing, step by quiet step.

And then she froze. A brand-new shiny padlock and latch were crudely affixed to the study door. It was the cabin's only room besides the small bedroom and the bath, which communicated with both. A maternal instinct, to which she had no biological claim, seized her nonetheless and, looking left and then right, she placed her hand gently on the door as might a psychic trying to draw energy from it. "Duncan?" she whispered into the crack.

The excited but terrified voice that answered her, wordless and vague, as heard through the thickness of the door, high-pitched and frantic, cut through to the very core of her being. It was him.

Wildly uncontrolled, she instinctively grabbed hold of the door's handle and pushed it ferociously. The door banged open, stopped by the padlock, revealing a space of less than an inch, and beyond it, propped up on the floor with his dead legs dragging behind him, was Duncan, coming at her as quickly as those arms would carry him.

It was only at the last possible second that she saw the woman to her right, and in that fraction of time managed to spin quickly and push shut the bedroom door, through which this woman was coming. The woman jumped back, but the door caught her forearm in its vise, and bounced back as if it had hit a rubber stop. The woman shrieked in pain.

"Carrie! Carrie! Carrie!" Duncan screamed from his jail. But Carrie barely heard him, frantic with fear, her full attention on the hand that protruded from the door against which both women were now applying their full strength. The damaged arm forced itself farther into the door like a lever, and Carrie found herself losing ground. Without thinking about it, for having thought about it she never could have done it, she reached up, took hold of this woman's smallest finger and pulled it sideways, applying enough pain to drive the arm back the other way through the crack in the door, and provoking another outburst of suffering from whom it belonged. Finally, her pressure on the door proved painful enough to cause this limb a farther retreat. Then, with the other's arm caught at the wrist, Carrie placed both her hands against the door and walked her feet back, angling her body increasingly more steeply, inflicting even more weight against that wrist while, at the same time, moving the toe of her right shoe within inches of a cane chair that sat in the hallway beneath a set of coat pegs. It wouldn't do to allow that hand to escape. This building had a front door as well, and all that kept her and Duncan's keeper from each other, was the fact that this woman's arm was pinned by this door. Stretch as she did, her foot tended to push the chair away from her, not bring it closer. Lower and lower she drew herself to the ground, the bumping from the other side, the shrieks of horror and Duncan's plaintive wailing, all conspiring against her. As if by a miracle, her toe finally caught the leg of the cane chair and slowly, inch by inch, she dragged it toward her.

Her heart hammered wildly in her chest; she was shaking with fear. She walked her weight up the door again, rotated her back to it and body-blocked it with such determination, such authority, that she actually heard bones break. In that instant of what had to be inexplicable pain, she withdrew her weight, wedged the chair beneath the handle and banged it convincingly into place, trapping the wrist there.

Tears blurred her vision, and doubt haunted her. Would it hold? "Carrie!" Duncan pleaded, his small fingers having hooked through the open crack.

"Get back," she said, continuing to support the chair's leverage on the door with her weight. The fingers on the end of the woman's hand, as red as any she had ever seen, twitched behind the owner's attempts at freedom. Testing the chair's wedged ability to contain the hand, Carrie slowly removed her weight until left completely alone. "Get back," she repeated, screaming it loudly. "Hurry!" she scolded, as she saw the chair buckling behind the repeated bumps of the woman on the other side, and that hand began to move in the crack in the door. Duncan scrambled back, his twisted feet dragged lifeless behind him.

She threw her shoulder into the door and heard the distinct sound of tearing wood as the screws pulled loose. Again and again she delivered her shoulder into it, her back to the kitchen, her eyes on that chair and the hand that gained movement with every bump of the adjacent door. She could actually feel Duncan's door giving behind her efforts—the door was coming open! A piece of the door-jamb splintered and what had been an inch of space became two. The progress elated her, and briefly her tears ran clear of her eyes, restoring her vision.

Her shoulder bruised by the pounding she delivered, Carrie risked ignoring the woman's hand and the chair, and switched to her unused shoulder, spinning fully around. And then she gasped, and stopped altogether, her voice useless, her head reeling.

There, blocking the doorway to the kitchen, hands clenched into fists, his eyes wide with disbelief, stood Carl.

35

DAGGETT WOKE UP at one o'clock in the afternoon, in his own bed, with no recollection of how he had gotten there. The sun outside his window was that intense September auburn light that was faithful to the approach of autumn. The dry throat and sluggish headache refreshed his memory—he'd been driven here in Pullman's car, another agent driving his, where a Bureau doctor had prescribed a pair of sedatives intended to help him through what at the time was being described alternately as trauma and shock. After everyone had left him, he had chased down one of the sedatives with a stiff Scotch, and that, no doubt, had proved his downfall.

He remembered having showered to wash off the blood and then having bathed in incredibly hot water, hoping unreasonably he might sterilize his skin. With a few refills from the hot-water spigot, that bath had taken the better part of an hour. His combined medications were getting the best of him by the time he hoisted himself out of the tub using Duncan's trapeze, and lowered his head to the pillow at 3:00 A.M.

He started coffee, showered again, and dressed in clean clothes, welcoming their fresh scent—indeed, worshiping it, as corny as a television ad. When two cups of coffee failed to jump-start him, he tried scrambled eggs, but only managed to eat half of them. Weary, feeling toxic and hung over, he climbed into his car and headed into work.

He was greeted by those at Buzzard Point with a sailor's reception. People he had not spoken with in ages appeared out of their office cubicles and shook his hand or slapped him on the back. "We're gonna find the kid," they all said in one form or another, and it became clear that the huge machinery of WMFO and all it represented had aligned itself to this single cause. "Michigan—this," and "Michigan—that," he half expected to find himself at the head of a banquet table when he rounded the corner into the counterterrorism bullpen. Instead he found a room completely abandoned, except for Gloria, who burst into tears, and could not be understood as she attempted what amounted to condolences. In a vain attempt to quiet her, he embraced her for the first time in his life, a gesture that only served to push her farther over the edge.

This was how Pullman found them, entwined in each other's arms, Gloria sobbing hysterically. "They want you down in debriefing," he said to Daggett with a captain's ungraciousness. "And I want you back at your desk," he said to Gloria.

"Where is everybody?" Daggett asked with a sweeping gesture of his hand.

"Every free agent in this field office with a good set of legs is out there on the street trying to scare up information on your boy or Cheysson. The general consensus here is that Cheysson is too secondary to attempt to carry this thing off without Kort, and with their infrastructure broken down because of the German raid, we assume whatever he had planned is dead in the water. All she can do now is run. We're turning the heat up to blue flame. All of Cheysson's co-workers at In-Flite are being subjected to the third degree: where she liked to vacation, where she might go if she was in trouble. We're gonna find the kid, Daggett."

"How about my clothes? How about my letter jacket?"

"Taken care of. *Everything* is taken care of. Now get down to debriefing and get ready to do your imitation of a broken record. You're in for a long one."

"What about the initial reports? I'd like to read whatever we have on last night."

Pullman glanced at Gloria and then back at Daggett. "It isn't going to work like that."

Gloria's eyes said more than Pullman ever would. Daggett was being shut out.

"What's going on?"

"Personal involvement like this is technically conflict of interest."

"Conflict of interest? This is *completely* in my interest!"

"First things first. We need you debriefed and we need your full report."

"That could take days! You're railroading me?" he asked.

"We're trying to find Cheysson and your boy. Now do your fucking bit and get down there to debriefing. Now!"

The two men, chests swollen and standing only a few feet apart, both held their ground. Pullman, in as private a voice as he could muster, said, "Don't do this."

And with that, Daggett turned around and headed for the elevator.

It was only through the repeated telling of his story, required of him in the debriefing, that the first seeds of doubt were secretly planted. Whispered voices at the back of his mind provoked and challenged a wealth of possibilities. Upon review, the ordinary seemed fantastic, not to those to whom he detailed the events of the previous evening, but to himself, to the investigator who regularly studied the transcripts of such debriefings as these. By the time four hours had passed, he held in his heart the terror of uncertainty, despite his full awareness that he had witnessed it all with the very eyes that looked out at the men who now questioned him. Distracted by his own conflicting thoughts, his explanations tended to wander offtrack, and soon they had him starting all over, the sand in his hourglass turning to water and running freely from top to bottom, the hours racing by.

At ten o'clock that evening, seeing his exhaustion, his inquisitors pardoned him, but warned of renewing the session upon his arrival the next morning. Hours were agreed upon. Hands were shaken, smiles exchanged. No one doubted Daggett, but two men had died, and there was much to explain.

As he passed through the hallways, considerations now chewing holes in his reason, he heard the patter of quick feet approach from behind and turned to greet an anxious Gloria, in whose hand some papers fluttered like broken wings. She stopped abruptly, and in her face he saw his own, for she looked terrified. "I got you what I could," she explained, handing the papers to him. "There isn't much yet."

He looked down at the papers, now transferred to his own hand, folded them into his pocket, and thanked her with his eyes.

"I'll keep you posted," she said.

"I have the strangest feeling," he confessed.

"You need sleep," she instructed. "Hot soup and sleep."

36

WITH A SWOLLEN wrist and broken finger that Kort had splinted for her, Monique drove the Toyota to David Boote's home at eight-thirty on the morning of September twenty-first. Kort smoked a cigarette in the seat beside her. Boote's shift didn't start until ten. He lived only a few minutes from National Airport, outside of Alexandria in a predominantly black area.

Kort screwed the heavy silencer onto the end of the gun and then placed the gun in the nylon holster that carried it under his arm.

"You are not going to use that?" she asked.

"In L.A. we had to protect our methods, in case we failed. We had to take certain precautions to throw them offtrack. Dougherty was perfect for that. He was a known drunk and we injected him with enough booze to knock him out. Who is going to put too much faith in such a man's statements? We need no such precautions here. This is the end of the line. For us. For Boote. For everyone involved."

"But he is just a mechanic. He has nothing to do with this."

"Drive," he instructed.

The brick apartment complex was in a litter-strewn neighborhood where rusty chain link fences protected lawns with no grass. The air smelled of dog shit and sour beer. "Same thing as last time," Kort said.

He felt the whites of her eyes.

They approached the door. Kort checked the number one last time and knocked. The man who answered might have been Dougherty's brother. He needed a shave and a fresh undershirt. He looked hung over. The Greek did good work.

"Airport security, sir," Kort said, beginning his familiar line. "We've had a breach of security and need to check all IDs. You mind getting yours for us?"

Unlike Dougherty, this man needed no convincing. He wanted to get back to the coffee Kort could smell. He wanted this over with.

So did Kort. "You mind if we come in for a moment?"

"Not a bit," the man responded.

"We can wait here," Monique objected, interrupting quickly, trying to stop what to Kort was the inevitable.

He stared her down. "We'd like to come in, if you don't mind."

But David Boote, which was his name, paid them no mind. He was gone in search of his identification tag. Kort stepped inside. "Wait in the car," he told her sharply.

She retreated down the path. Her shoe tangled in a plastic grocery bag driven by the considerable wind, and she bent to be rid of it.

Kort pushed the door shut.

Boote rounded the corner, his ID in hand, and Kort's withdrawn weapon put two holes through the center of his chest and a third in the middle of his forehead once he was down. He knelt, while the body was still twitching, and tugged on the ID from the man's persistent grip. He felt heady from the kill. Next were Mosner and the others; next he eliminated their manufactured death and destruction while directing the world's attention to their lies and conspiracies. He smelled victory and it smelled sweet. He slipped the ID into his pocket, put the gun away, and hid the body in the coat closet. He dragged a small throw rug and covered the bloodstains. He left the house and walked to the car, where he found her clutching the wheel with her one good hand, pale and trembling, and he saw the ravages of tears staining her eyes red. "We do what we have to," he said. He needed her strong.

She said nothing. She started the car and drove off.

"Stop," he instructed as they passed the huge hangars that were part of Brown's Aviation. "Pull over."

She steered the car into the breakdown lane, allowing a van to pass. "What is it?" she asked.

"The wind," he said, pointing up to the Day-Glo orange wind sock that billowed atop the third hangar.

It took a moment to get his bearings. He spun himself in the seat until he figured he was looking due east. "It's the wrong wind," he said, checking his watch.

"What do you mean?"

"The *wrong direction!* We need them to use runway thirty-six—three-six. This wind will put them on eighteen. It's no good." He consulted a cryptic timetable he kept in his shirt pocket, rechecked his watch, and said, "We'll just have to wait."

"Wait?"

"We'll go back and wait. We'll have to hope the wind will change by this afternoon. There's another 959 this afternoon. It doesn't have a chemical cargo, but it's the only thing we can do. There's a radio band for the weather."

"Wait?" she repeated. "No chemical cargo? I thought that was the whole *point* of this!"

"We have no choice. Turn it around. Take us back."

"I do not understand. I thought that was the point of the operation—the chemical cargo."

"Who cares if you understand. Drive the car!"

"You should not have killed him. Do you see? You should not have killed him."

"No one cares about Boote. He's but one of many. Believe me, no one cares."

"I do not believe you," she said, negotiating the turn. "We all have someone who cares," she snapped, wishing she did. "Or what is there left to live for?"

37

"I SUPPOSE YOU think I'm a beast," Kort said from his perch on the edge of the bathtub.

Her hands were bound in front of her with a long white plastic tie, a variation on the kind used to seal trash bags. It held her wrists together so tightly that her hands had swollen. Her left ankle was bound in a similar manner, but with a nylon rope hooked through it. This rope connected at its other end to an unforgiving pipe. Kort had tied both knots in the nylon rope strongly, and then had taken the added precaution of lighting the knots on fire and melting them into a molten mass so that they could not be untied under any circumstance. Her improvised handcuff didn't stop her from smoking the Sobranie he offered her. But she didn't answer him, even though her lips were free to speak. She had no words that could express what she thought of him, and only in the last few minutes had she contained her rage so that now, shackled and sitting on the floor of the bathroom with her legs tucked up into a ball, she was wet with the perspiration of anger.

"None of this was planned. None of it. Least of all that I should fall in love with you." He studied her unforgiving eyes and nodded. "Oh, yes, Caroline. Do you think that you, or the boy for that matter, would be alive right now if that were not the case? I have no desire to hurt you. There's hurt enough in this world."

"You're mad."

"I'm not going to argue the right or wrong of what it is I do for I need answer only to myself on that score. Only to myself and to Him," he said, looking at the ceiling, "and I've made my peace with Him."

"I wouldn't be so sure."

She had never witnessed his temper before, but it flared, red hot, and he dropped to one knee and pressed his face to hers. "What the fuck do you know about it?" Her face, wet with the spit of his rage, turned away, and behind trembling hands the cigarette found her lips and she sucked hard and cowered as Kort returned to his perch.

He continued nodding, wouldn't take his eyes off her. He *was* mad. His hand found his wallet, and his fingers found the photograph tucked inside the leather slot and he leaned forward, frightening her, and slapped it down onto the top of the toilet seat. "This is *their* work. This was my child," he said viciously. He withdrew his hand. She could feel him staring at her, willing her to look.

She was afraid to look, but knew it wouldn't be over until she granted him this. And when she did look, her stomach buckled and bile burned her throat. She turned away, and though trying to contain herself, heard the plaintive cry that escaped her. He had won and he knew it. He continued that strange nodding, as if convincing himself, and without looking at the photo, returned it to the wallet. "We all have our reasons for what we do," he said.

"You used me," she managed to say, for this fire had been burning inside her ever since Cam had mentioned the keys.

"I could have taken your keys at any time. I didn't use you. Not in the way you mean."

"Then it was the keys."

"Yes."

"And now?"

He snubbed his cigarette out in the sink and stood towering over her, looking down at her. He held out another cigarette for her. He waited until she looked up and accepted it. Their eyes met and she wondered how anyone so gentle could do the things this man did. She recalled their lovemaking as if it had been years ago, and she couldn't stop her tears from falling. She hated him more than any person on earth, and yet her tears were the tears of love.

"There are two kinds of fools in this world. Fools who are fools because they do nothing. And fools who are fools for what they do. But I'm no fool."

He walked to the door.

"Don't do it, Carl—or whoever you are. There are other ways . . . *Don't do it!*"

This turned his head, for even she was surprised at the concern in her voice. Slowly a smile took his face. Her tone had clearly impressed him. He stared at her for a very long time, but she felt nothing. Only ice cold. "Not Carl," he said, widening his grin. "It's Anthony Kort." He shut the door.

She knew the name because of Cam. Reality sank in: Anthony Kort. She understood Cam's relentless determination much better then, and she felt horrible for the things she had said to him. She folded up as once again her insides stung with poison. He had been *inside* her, this monster. Did it not make sense that a monster should be born to a monster?

"You bas . . . tard!" she screamed as loudly as she could, until all the air went out of her. Though as she heard the door to the other room shut and their low voices there, she knew her words meant nothing. A man like this only understood actions.

It sounded as if they were leaving. She heard the word *airport* and she knew something had to be done. Now!

The unlit cigarette, remained on the floor at her knees where she had left it. She stuffed it into her lips and frantically drew on it, pressing against it the smoldering butt of her last. She puffed and puffed, desperately trying to get the new one to catch, and finally it did ignite and she swallowed the smoke victoriously.

It wasn't that she wanted a cigarette. It was that she had a plan. And now that she knew who this man really was

—now that she understood—there was nothing she wouldn't do to stop him.

Less than a minute later the car pulled out and she went to work.

38

"DO YOU HAVE them?" Daggett asked Lynn before she was even inside the house.

"Yes, but—" she answered, immediately interrupted.

"Put them over there. I'm on the phone. I'll be right with you." He returned to the phone and said quickly, "Sorry about that. Yes. Mechanics, that's right." He glanced up at her. She stared at him, wondering where all this energy came from. He motioned for her to put the papers she had brought on the dining room table. "Anyone who doesn't show up for work this morning . . . I know that . . . It's important . . . Yes . . . I'll give you two numbers. If I don't answer at the first, try the second. It's extremely important. It may involve one of your planes . . . That's right."

She hadn't expected to find him this animated. She thought she would find a man, drinking perhaps, tucked into a corner and cold.

"They won't let me be part of it," he explained as he headed straight to her papers, energy exploding from his every movement. "I've been put on the sidelines because of my personal involvement. If I go into work they're going to lock me in a room and interrogate me for the hundredth time. And today's the day," he said in a troubled voice. "The meeting. There's no time for any of that."

"I think you lost me," she admitted, putting down her purse.

"I had it in front of me all along," he explained, running his hand through his hair. He checked his watch for the third time since she had arrived. His nervousness rubbed off on her and she found herself anxious and hot. "Take a look at this." He slapped down the note Kort had left him on the day of Duncan's abduction.

"What about it?" she asked, wishing she didn't have to, but she saw nothing.

"It's written on my memo pad." He pointed to the small piece of paper. "That's my name there at the top. Duncan gave me that pad for Christmas last year."

"You lost me."

"I keep that memo pad in my briefcase."

"So?"

"So Kort fucked up."

"Cam . . ."

"Kort asked me to deliver the itineraries. The meeting in the subway station—he wanted the itineraries."

"Yeah . . . So?"

"This memo pad was in my briefcase. He got it from my *briefcase.* He had already seen the itineraries. Get it?"

"No."

"If he had *already seen* the itineraries, then why did he ask me to deliver them to him?" He only waited a second before answering himself. She had never seen him like this; she felt afraid of him. "Because he needed a reason—a really good reason—for me to believe he would risk a face-to-face meeting. It's all double-think. It's all outthinking the other guy—putting yourself inside his head. Get it?"

"Then why *did* he ask for the itineraries? No, I don't get it!"

"Because he needed a witness. It had nothing to do with itineraries. He needed me—the head of the investigation—to witness his death. But he wrote his note on the wrong fucking memo pad, and it's going to hang him."

"He's alive?" She reached for the edge of table in order to balance herself.

"Damn right he's alive." He scattered a bunch of his own papers and thumbed through the ones she had brought for him. He removed the runway map of LAX. "The scale is too big, so we can't even see Hollywood Park, but take my word for it." He fished through the debris for a ruler, measured the scale of miles, and then measured off the end of the open map. He signaled her to hand him the salt and pepper. She did so. "Hollywood Park is right here," he said, placing down the salt shaker.

"I don't have the slightest idea where you're going with this."

He leaned forward and slammed the salt shaker down once again. She jumped back. "*This* is where sixty-four hit. Right here. Exactly here." He took the ruler in hand and measured off the distance. "You see the size of Hollywood Park—it's huge. Barnes was the one who told me," he said, confusing her. "Barnes told me the simulation at Duhning and the crash of sixty-four confirmed the same flight pattern. The real plane and the simulator flew the same distance; and in both cases landed in the same place. If you transpose the simulation to a real map, then the plane crashes in Hollywood Park. He told me that," Daggett said, "and it went right over my head."

"You're frightening me."

"Good," he said, nodded wildly. "The truth is frightening, isn't it? 'Physics,' Barnes said. I wasn't listening to him. Physics! You remove pilot control and the plane falls. In effect, the 959 pilots were all trained by Ward—they would all perform these first few minutes of flight in the same manner: Kort could count on that. He *is* counting on that."

She felt her eyes go hot and scratchy, and she knew she was about to cry. She stepped toward him wanting to comfort him, wanting to give him some peace. He stopped her by taking hold of both her shoulders and waiting for her eyes.

He stepped back, held up a finger, and returned to the maps she had brought. "Bear with me." He began tossing papers everywhere, and in doing so, added to the image of insanity. The huge sheets of white snow fell and covered the carpet. Only then did she notice the wheelchair, folded

and leaning against the wall. There was no stopping her
tears. She let them fall and watched her favorite man slip
over the edge. "The question," he said, resettled, "is what's
his target? And which airport will he use, Dulles or National? The plane has to leave from one of the two airports,
right? And *that*," he added, "is why I needed you to bring
this." He turned to make sure she was with him and seeing
her, he set the map down slowly, a comic who realizes he's
no longer funny. "Don't give up on me. Don't do this."

"It's over."

"It's not over."

"Kort is dead, Cam. They'll find Duncan. You have to
believe they'll find him."

"If you don't pay attention, you'll never convince the
others."

"Don't do this!" she shouted, crossing her arms to fend
off the cold, backing away from him.

"I'm not off my rocker, damn it all. I've figured it out!
Jesus!" he said, pounding the table so hard, he broke the
leaf and all the papers spilled out onto the floor, covering
his feet. He watched the papers settle and sadness drained
into his face. "You don't believe me? The memo note isn't
all." He dropped through the floor and dug his pile of snow
until he located a particular piece of paper. "Gloria, bless
her heart, got me the early reports, including one from the
hospital where they took what remained of him—whoever
he was." He tried to make the table leaf work again, and
when he failed, walked around to the other side. "The thing
about being the lead investigator is that you hold dozens—
maybe hundreds—of different pieces of data in your head.
One department knows this; they tell you. Another finds out
that; they write you a memo. But you're the only one with
all the pieces."

"What do you mean, 'convince the others'?" she asked.

"See? You *are* paying attention. That's good."

She stepped closer to him, still afraid, though he had
calmed and she found herself drawn to him.

"They would have spotted this eventually. Today, maybe. Tomorrow. Next week. Probably next week, because we don't like outside reports. We like to generate our own reports. If it's FBI, then we trust it. If it isn't . . . We'd rather wait until one of our own comes in. My bet? No one's read this report very carefully. And even if they had, they would think it's a mistake. Why? Because despite all our pissing and moaning about evidence, we trust the agent over all the evidence combined. The lead agent? No one's going to question what I saw down there. They see something wrong in a report, they'll order another report. They find that report comes back wrong, they might even order it done again. That's the way we work—take it or leave it."

"Spotted what?"

"And I'll tell you something else: You repeat the same story enough times and you start to look at it real carefully, and I just plain didn't like the way it sounded. A guy like Kort fires off a couple rounds point-blank at me and misses. Kort? No way. Not from that distance. So why did he miss? Because he needed me as a witness."

"Spotted what?" she shouted, shaking the paper he handed her.

"Blood alcohol. The hospital didn't work up a blood type, but when someone does, it won't match either. But by then it'll be way too late. The guy who hit the train was six sheets to the wind. Two-point-one-oh blood alcohol level. Smashed. Blotto. Shitfaced. And believe me—the Anthony Kort I was chasing in that tunnel was stone-cold sober."

She scanned the hospital report and her eyes found the tiny little box: *2.1*, it read. Now she did believe, though she didn't want to. He was back with the maps, tossing things everywhere.

"Okay . . . Okay . . . Let's have a look here. The scale is different . . . Damn it . . . Damn it . . ." He checked the runway map of LAX and that for Dulles and did some math calculations right onto the wood of the table. Then he grabbed the ruler and a pencil and drew a line six inches off the end of a runway, checked his numbers, stopped, measured an angle with Duncan's protractor, and drew another line. His fingers searched the end of this line. She could feel his disappointment. He leaned closer to read the map. "There's nothing out here. Nothing at all. Suburbs. Nothing but suburbs. That *can't* be it."

"Nothing *where?*" she hollered, her confusion overwhelming her.

As Cam threw the Dulles map onto the floor and unrolled the map of National Airport that she had brought for him, he explained impatiently, "The target isn't the plane. I mean it is, but it isn't. Not really. The target is on the *ground.* The plane is the bomb. He's going to drop a plane, and he knows exactly where it's going to fall."

She looked over his shoulder as he did some more math and began drawing lines—this time from a runway at National Airport. "Who would believe it, right? He's counting on that." He smelled as if he hadn't showered, and his whiskers were long. His plotted course ended in the Tidal Basin of West Potomac Park, near the Jefferson Memorial. He checked it twice. "It's not working," he said. "It's not possible. I *know* I'm right about this. I know the *evidence* is right."

She leaned over him. He moved aside, his eyes glazed. He had grown suddenly distant. "Runway thirty-six is the more common," she said, pointing. He didn't move. "Depends on the winds." She took the ruler from him and duplicated the first leg of the 7 he had drawn. She measured the angle off this new stem, and drew the final short leg of the projected flight—where the plane would slip left as it fell. The pen stopped before it reached its destination, before she completed the work, because she had raised her head in disbelief. Cam stared at the point of the pen too. He looked as terrified as she felt. The tip of the pen rested on the Pentagon.

"The meeting," Daggett said in a forced whisper that

revealed his fear. "That must be where they're holding the meeting!"

The phone rang. He turned and stared at it. "He's going to crash a plane into the Pentagon."

"Cam?" she said, drawn by the ringing phone.

He was frozen. "My God. He's going to kill them *all.*"

She hurried to the phone and answered it. "Just a minute please," she added as she reached it out to him. "Quik-Link Courier, or something like that."

"Daggett," he said, accepting the phone's receiver from her. He listened, searched for a pen and, finding one, said, "This Boote, you tried calling him? . . . Nothing? . . . Can you give me his home address, please?" He scribbled out an Alexandria address. "You have a Duhning 959 in your fleet," he stated emphatically. "I'm psychic," he said, obviously answering the man. "Ground it . . . What are you talking about: 'in person'?" He checked his watch. "There's no time for that. Ground the fucking plane . . . I'm telling you, I'm FBI! No . . . No . . . You can't call me at the FBI. I'm not at the FBI, I'm home . . . Okay . . . Okay . . . I'm on my way. How long until that plane goes? How long? Shit! You better stall it, mister, or you'll be looking for work . . . Damn!" He slammed the receiver down. To Lynn he said, "The guy hung up on me. He wanted to call me back at the office to make sure I'm for real. He thinks I'm a hoax."

"They have a 959?"

"It goes in half an hour." He pointed into the dining room. "Take all this stuff to Buzzard Point. To Pullman. Mumford, if you can get to him. Tell him you know the meeting is at the Pentagon. That ought to do it. Explain it as best you can, but whatever you do, get someone to ground that plane."

She checked her watch. "You'll make it before I will."

"Put your foot into it." He had the front door open. He pointed to the phone. "And have someone check that address for a David Boote. Kort's doing this one the same way he did L.A. Tell them that. L.A. was nothing but a rehearsal. This is the real show. Tell him I gotta have some backup."

He said something else, but she didn't hear. He was still shouting at her as his van knocked over the mailbox, raced ahead tires screaming, and disappeared down the quiet suburban street.

39

CARRIE STEVENSON KNEW what had to be done. She couldn't be sure they had left together, and so rather than bang on the door that communicated with the room in which Duncan was kept, she stood and searched the medicine cabinet, remembering this Frenchwoman had put on some fresh makeup that morning. She found a dark brown eye-lining pencil, and with this she wrote SMOKE ALARM on a piece of bathroom tissue.

She stretched out fully then, her ankle bound by the rope to the pipe, and was just able to reach the crack beneath the communicating door. It was a substantial gap, the door having been cut to accommodate the carpet on the other side. She took a drag on the Sobranie and then scratched lightly on the door until she heard the distinct sound of Duncan dragging himself across the carpet. She pushed the tissue through first, relieved as it vanished. Next, she carefully stuffed the cigarette under, butt first. She scratched again. It disappeared.

She sat back and prayed. One of the selling points of this cabin was that the smoke alarm system was tied in directly to the fire station. There was no such alarm in the bathroom, and even if there had been, with her leg bound to the pipe she never could have reached it. But Duncan, because of his disability, had not been tied down, and having been here only days ago with Kort, she remembered the layout of the room well enough to recall the substantial floor-to-ceiling bookshelves. So now, it all came down to Duncan.

■

Having extracted the toilet paper from the crack in the door, Duncan unfolded it and read the message. From his perspective on the floor, as he rocked his head to look, the white smoke alarm mounted in the ceiling seemed about as far away as the moon on a clear night. It wasn't until he heard her scratching again that he saw the cigarette, and it wasn't until he took the cigarette from her and saw it burning that he realized what was expected of him. The moon, hell—it looked more like Pluto.

As he lay there thinking about it, feeling the impossible was being asked of him, the cigarette's ember spit fire and some ash floated to the carpet like fresh snow. Then he understood: He only had a few minutes in which to accomplish this. The cigarette was half burned.

He tried to carry it by pinching it between his knuckles, but with his hands his only means of propulsion, he resorted to sticking it into his lips, squinting away the smoke and hurrying to the bookshelf. By the time he had dragged himself to the bottom of the bookshelf, his eyes stung and he was coughing. He hauled himself up to a sitting position using the first few shelves. Now, the face of the bookshelf appeared to him a multicolored sheer granite wall stretching impossibly into a sky of white Sheetrock clouds far, far overhead.

Initially, he didn't think about the task before him as a series of pull-ups, which in fact was exactly what it was. Instead, he thought about the task in terms of the goal: to reach the smoke alarm before the cigarette burned out. With his mind focused on this end, he stuffed the smoking cigarette back between his lips, having taken a moment for fresh air, and began his journey, the dead weight of his legs following behind him like an old dog on a long leash. To him, the shelves were merely rungs to a ladder, and it didn't occur to him that by the time he reached Hemingway he had the equivalent of two complete pull-ups behind him. Fully airborne, and with two shelves to go, the smoke alarm suddenly seemed no closer, and it was then, as he placed his hands next to each other and began to grunt and heave, that it occurred to him that he couldn't do this. This was a pull-up and he couldn't do a pull-up. This consideration, which had the impact of a startling discovery, served to weaken not only the strength in his trembling arms but his resolve. Impossibility had no shades of gray, and for weeks he had proven this impossible.

But then again, he thought, if this was impossible, how had he climbed this far already? A quick glance down confirmed his substantial elevation as well as delivered another stream of stinging smoke into his eyes, which he huffed and blinked away and corrected by looking up again. If he could do two pull-ups, why not four? His father's voice spoke to him as clearly as if he were standing right there in the room with him: *The only way there is through.* Now Duncan understood. His attention had been on the smoke alarm, not on his own strength, his own weakness, not on his journey but his destination. Hot ash glancing his chin and falling like stones from the face of the mountain, he refocused his attention on that alarm, and drew himself up. His arms burned and shook like rubber, but he paid no attention. He pulled and strained and lifted himself another shelf higher. Victory was but a single shelf away. His fingers found it and he grunted loudly. Nothing could stop him now. His eyes crept past the final shelf and he snagged his belt on a shelf below. He had reached the summit.

With one hand craning him out toward the center of the room, the other waving the cigarette immediately beneath the vented grate of the plastic smoke alarm, Duncan took his first and last drag of a cigarette in his life, kissing the end as he had watch Carrie do, and drawing the smoke into his cheeks and down into his virgin lungs. He exploded into a ferocious cough, spraying out smoke and spit until the alarm disappeared in his cloud.

His fingers lost purchase and he fell.

Those few seconds of his descent seemed to him like long hours. He had no legs with which to brake his fall. In fact, his legs seemed more like anchors that only served to accelerate him. He had no chance to defend himself. His attention fixed not on the floor below him but on the smoke alarm overhead, where the results of his cough still swirled.

Then, like the buzzer sounding the end of the game, the shrieking electronic cry of the alarm split the air, signaling victory. This stole all of his attention. He hit the floor hard —too hard—headfirst.

It was only as he came to that he realized he must have blacked out, for above the shriek of the alarm he heard sirens in the distance. But he savored this moment of singular victory as no other. His neck hurt like hell, but the scream of the overhead alarm was sweet music to his ears.

No one charged through the door to silence it. No one came in to kill him. "Duncan! Duncan!" he faintly heard Carrie hollering from her side of the door. "You've done it!"

40

AS DAGGETT TURNED onto the George Washington Memorial Parkway it became immediately clear to him not only that Lynn Greene would be delayed by unexpected bridge construction but that he, too, was about to slow to a crawl. Having left the congestion at the bridge behind, he focused instead on the snarl of vehicles up ahead and was reminded of the recent August afternoon when Bob Backman had lost his life. He wasn't driving a company car, so he lacked any form of communication, as well as a police bubble, both of which might have served him well, though he wasn't sure how. In a progression of events all too familiar to any urban driver, distances between vehicles shortened, as did tempers. A chorus of discordant car horns, like white-plumed steam whistles, vented some of this anger. Windows rolled down; heads leaned out. Brake lights flared, blinking in matching pairs, bleeding toward Daggett like a string of Christmas lights, as he, too, found his foot tapping the brake, continuing the chain reaction.

Traffic stopped.

The multicolored necklace, of which his van was but a single bead, lay dormant on the hot pavement, alive, impatient and anxious, restlessly surging forward but without any measurable progress. And whereas the last time he had found himself in this same predicament and had taken several minutes to make his move, this time he hesitated only long enough to force his van through gaps left by unwilling neighbors and onto the freshly mowed grass, where he subsequently abandoned it.

Of the thirty minutes he had given himself at the start

of this journey, he now counted only twelve remaining. He had not gone for a run since the morning of discovering Duncan's abduction two days ago, and this painful reminder of his son's perilous condition served to lengthen his strides and increase his pace. He ran faster than he had in ages, even fully clothed as he was. Within minutes, he was jumping dividers and crossing lanes, precariously dodging the hazards of moving traffic, the industrialized section of the airport just ahead. He saw the sign for Federal Express. He saw AVIS and HERTZ. He high-jumped a low steel fence on the run, slapped a car on the hood as it nearly hit him, and ran against traffic. He could just make out the sign for Quik-Link Courier, a hundred yards away.

41

THIS TIME, WHEN Kort examined the wind sock, high above the hangars, he noted with satisfaction that it, too, reflected the change in direction he had first observed out at the gatehouse. Monique, with her position as a vice-president of In-Flite, was to have escorted him onto the field through one of the four vehicle entrances to National's tarmac. Knowing that she had been a subject of the FBI's investigation, he could only assume that those at In-Flite would be well aware of the chaos she had caused, and would more than likely detain her for authorities were she to show herself there. However, as she had been quick to point out, at National she was something of a fixture with the gate guards, coming and going as many as several times a day. The possibility that the FBI would have contacted the subcontracting security companies at both airports seemed slim, especially given Kort's "death" the night before. Nonetheless, the possibility remained, and so, as she drove up to National's remote east gate, Kort's hand remained fixed to the butt of his weapon.

"Hi, Charlie," she said, rolling down her window. Kort unfastened his seat belt and prepared to use the weapon. Monique stopped him with a casual touch.

"New car, Miss Cheysson," he said.

"Mine is in the shop."

"Even so, you don't have a sticker."

She handed the guard Kort's guest identification tag and he looked it over, handing it back. "He's okay. But I don't know about the car," he said. "You're supposed to have a sticker."

"What should I do? Do you have the authority to look it over, or do I have to check with Airport Police?"

Kort delighted in her choice of tactics. Resentments and jealousies ran high between the various subcontracted security agencies and the ubiquitous Airport Police, who oversaw, but did not directly manage, all security subcontractors. By challenging this man's authority, she forced him into a decision.

"Let me have the keys to the trunk," he said.

She turned toward Kort and smirked. The guard popped open the trunk. As he did, Monique slipped out of the shoulder restraint, leaned forward, and grabbed Kort's flight bag. She quickly unzipped the bag and placed the fire extinguisher between the bucket seats, in plain view. Charlie slammed the trunk shut and came around the car, peering into the back. When he reached the front and looked past Kort, he said, "What about that?"

She replied, "For one of our trucks."

Apparently satisfied, he came around the front of the car and leaned down on one knee. Kort was thinking how simple it would be to run him over. A moment later he entered the guard booth and lifted the phone.

"What now?" Kort asked.

"He probably has to get permission from his people, but at least we kept Airport Police out of it," she said in a self-congratulatory tone.

It was only then that Kort realized the guard was all alone in the booth. He pointed this out to Monique.

"That happens now and then. They must take turns going to the bathroom or something."

"I don't like this phone call," Kort said.

"Be patient."

"He's not even talking. What if he's stalling?"

"He's not stalling. He's getting permission."

"There's nobody out here. I can take him out."

"Have some patience."

"I don't like the way he's looking at us."

"Please!" she scolded.

Kort looked around quickly. They were at the far end of the field, a good quarter-mile from the center of activity. The nearest building had something to do with maintenance for one of the shuttle companies and it was at least fifty yards away. He didn't like this phone call. He had plenty of patience, but this was taking too long. "Something's not right," he said. "He's stalling." He climbed out of the car. She leaned across the seat and grabbed for him, but missed. He checked the immediate area one last time. All clear. "Excuse me, sir," he said. Charlie the guard was just hanging up the phone.

"You see," Monique said conspiratorially, still leaning toward Kort but seeing for herself that Charlie was off the phone. "Get back in here."

"Miss Cheysson," the guard said, viewing Kort somewhat suspiciously. "If you'd just back it up and pull it over there, please. The line's still busy. I can't get through, and I've got to get an authorization number before admitting your car onto the field."

Kort put the first and only bullet necessary into the man's nose, taking a piece out of the back of his head and knocking him down as if he were made of cardboard. Monique barked with horror but quickly controlled herself. Kort hurried to the guard booth. He hit the switch that opened the red-and-white-striped boom and waved Monique through. He stuffed the body inside, tripped the switch again, lowering the boom, and slid the booth's metal door closed. He took one step toward the Toyota, reconsidered, and tried the plastic sign that was framed on the front of the booth. PLEASE HAVE IDENTIFICATION READY FOR GUARD, it read in big bold print. It moved. He slipped it out of its frame and flipped it over. GATE CLOSED. He returned it to the frame, ducked under the boom, and joined her.

She drove away at an incredible speed.

"Slow down," he said. "No need to attract attention."

Her lower jaw was trembling. "They'll find him."

"Maybe not for a while. These are the chances we take."

"And how do *I* get back out, please? *You* have the mechanic's identification. You can slip out without any problem—"

"Anyone can slip *out* without a problem. It's getting in that's the problem." He placed the fire extinguisher back in the bag, and removing the coveralls from it, slipped them on. He clipped Boote's ID crudely to his pocket, though he faced the man's photograph against his chest so that only the backside of the ID showed. Identification tags, especially on baggage handlers and mechanics, often ended up clipped on this way, hastily returned to clothing after falling off. "Park it over by the terminal somewhere. You've got your ID. You can get out any door you want."

"You shouldn't have done it."

"We're fine. Five minutes is all I need. We're going to lose the car, so we'll meet at the Pentagon Metro stop in one hour."

That turned her head. "What, are you kidding?"

"I want to see my work," he said, motioning for her to pull over. The tailfin of the huge 959 with red-white-and-blue letters spelling QUIK-LINK, lay waiting for him, twenty yards to their left. It was scheduled for takeoff in a matter of minutes.

42

DAGGETT ARRIVED AT the entrance to Quik-Link Couriers out of breath and in a full sweat, his watch showing less than five minutes of his estimated thirty remaining. To his frustration, he found himself in the midst of a shift change, at the back of a long line of fresh employees stretching from the company's self-provided security check-in. He quickly broke out of the line and reached the bottleneck, where employees were individually showing their ID tags to either one of the two guards who manned the station. Daggett removed his ID and allowed it to hang open.

"FBI," he said loudly enough to gain the attention of the man closest to him. "It's an emergency. I have to see whoever's in charge."

"You carrying a piece?"

Daggett removed his weapon and showed it to the man.

"You gotta leave it with me."

"That's absurd. I'm here on business. I'm FBI!"

"I don't care if you're J. Edgar Hoover, pal. The piece stays with me."

"You know a guy named Henderson?" Daggett asked, recalling the name of the shorter of the two men with whom he had escaped the Bernard explosion. "Airport Police?" The guard's brow furrowed. "Henderson, I think. Call him up. Now. I want that piece with me. Tell him Special Agent Daggett. He'll okay it." The guard put the gun out of sight, pointed to where Daggett could come through, and turned his attention to a waiting employee. Daggett grabbed the phone's receiver, forced it into the guard's hand, and repeated, "Henderson. Now."

"Yeah, yeah," the guard said, slightly intimidated and beginning to dial. "Check back in a minute."

Thanks to a receptionist who seemed either frightened or impressed by his considerable lather, Daggett was led to a back warehouse filled with sorting equipment, bright blue mailbags, and a level of activity one expected to see only in television ads. The manager, a lanky man in his late fifties with an Air Force haircut and a drill sergeant's charm, after hearing Daggett's opening salvo, pulled him out of the way of a tug towing three trailers and said, "You got to be shitting me. First I've heard of it."

"All I'm asking is that you stall that plane long enough to speak with my superiors."

"Maybe I can do that."

"Maybe?"

"I gotta check with *my* superiors first, right? Listen, I'm not trying to be a pain in the ass here, but I gotta check you out and I gotta check with St. Louis before I hold up the afternoon flight. You know how many bomb threats this company gets? You have any idea?"

"This isn't a threat. I'm FBI. I'm working on *information*. I'm telling you that your 959 isn't leaving the ground, if I've got to see to it myself."

"Now let's not get like that. Okay? You want to play fucking tough, friend? *I* can play fucking tough. Believe you me." He tapped Daggett on the chest with a metal finger. "You come with me. We'll make some fucking calls." He walked away, his face a bright red.

Daggett saw the hole he had dug for himself. He'd been too pumped up by the run, too hot to act cool. "What about the plane? Can't you at least *hold* the plane while we make the calls?"

"One thing at a time, friend. One thing at a fucking time."

43

KORT HADN'T REALIZED how close he had cut it. Having planned to sabotage the morning plane, he realized now that the afternoon information he had was off by at least half an hour. Holes in information troubled him. He took them as bad omens. In a perfect world, there were never any holes.

Unlike the AmAirXpress flight 64, which he had so easily boarded during preflight maintenance, when he had experienced no cockpit activity and had gone about his task completely alone, this time he stepped into a hornet's nest. At the plane's starboard midsection, large mail sacks, some stuffed to the limit, others limp and mostly empty, were being unloaded from towed trailers and tossed onto an active conveyor assembly that shuttled them up into the fuselage, where they were presumably stowed and secured for flight. On the left side of the plane, as Kort climbed the steep stairway to the flight deck, another maintenance engineer hurried past him carrying a stainless steel coffeepot. "Fucking coffee machine's down," he said angrily. "See if you can do something."

I can do something, all right, Kort was thinking. What he did, once inside the plane, was place the flight bag down, remove the fire extinguisher, and step into the flight deck, where he unexpectedly encountered the two men he had come to kill. They were running through a checklist, each echoing the other with cryptic terms and busy fingers. Kort, whose unusual calm was rattled by finding the seats occupied, suddenly realized he was all but invisible to these two. They paid him no mind whatsoever. He dropped to one

knee, fire extinguisher in hand, at which point the copilot
said, "You got the coffee fixed yet?"

"Working on it," Kort answered.

"What gives?" the man asked as Kort went about working in the cramped quarters beneath his seat, reaching in
from behind. But the pilot demanded his attention as he
threw another switch, and Kort avoided an answer.

He unfastened the clamp holding the existing extinguisher, removed it, and replaced it with the one he had
brought. Having earlier set the detonator's timer to the exact time specified by Ward's simulation of this flight—forty-
seven seconds—he had nothing more to do. The beauty, as
far as he was concerned, of Bernard's detonator was that it
didn't require being turned on or activated. The pilots did
that for him, first by pressurizing the airplane, and second
by pointing the nose into the sky. At that point the clock
would run, the gas would be released, and, at long last, it
would all be over.

Tasting success and victory, Kort slipped out of the
flight deck and debated whether to place the extinguisher in
his bag or not. He knew well enough that hesitation was an
operative's biggest enemy. The appearance of confidence
was everything. He stuffed the extinguisher away and was
just zipping the bag shut when the other mechanic came
bounding up the stairs and stepped right past him. This
man headed directly to the onboard coffee maker. As Kort
stood the man asked, "You new?"

It caught Kort off guard. Should he just leave? Did he
dare? "Yeah," he said, attempting to sound as American as
possible. He turned to face the man.

"Thought so." He stuck his hand out. "Russ Kane. Good
to meet you."

Kort shook his hand firmly, his mind going blank. He
needed a name . . . His eyes found the airport identification tag riveted to the fuselage. "David Duhning," he
said.

"Like the plane!" the other said. "I can remember that."

"Nice meeting you," Kort said. He hurried down the steep steps, his feet driven by fear, the sweat under his arms beginning to run.

44

"YOU GOT ANY kind of paperwork about this?" the manager asked, leaning his hard mouth with its broken teeth away from the phone's receiver.

"Paperwork? Are you listening to me? That plane has been sabotaged!"

"Call you right back," the man said into the phone, and hung up.

Daggett had been in enough similar situations to know when to give up. He could argue himself red in the face, but John Wayne here wasn't buying. "You're never going to forgive yourself for this, you know that?"

"So why don't we talk to *your* superiors, Mr. Hot-fucking-shit Eliot Ness? Answer me that?" He picked up the phone. "You tell me who to call. You give me a number and a name."

Daggett knew that even if Lynn had reached Buzzard Point, even if she was meeting with Pullman at this very moment—which, given the traffic, seemed doubtful—Pullman was unlikely to support him on this without a hell of a lot more than intuition. The truth of the matter was that Kort's plan had accomplished exactly what he had hoped it would. The machine of the FBI was moving in one direction, and you didn't reverse it by simply throwing a switch.

Daggett reached the door to the small office, which he swung open.

"Listen," John Wayne said earnestly, turning to Daggett so that he failed to see the man just entering the building, a man in coveralls carrying a flight bag. And out on the tarmac, beyond the huge plate glass windows, beyond the flurry of activity, the stairs were wheeled away from the plane as the TUG began the pushback. "We insure every one of those packages at full refund. 'Positively, absolutely,' and all that shit—that's what we're up against here. That's our competition. I delay that plane, then every single one of those packages is going to be late tomorrow and that means something on the order of fifty grand out the window. You see my problem here?"

"Your problem is, you're not listening."

His pager sounded.

He reached down inside his coat, to where it was clipped to his belt, so he could read its message. Maybe Lynn had made better time than he had thought. Maybe he now had the authority to stop that plane.

The LED read: DUNCSAFE. He silenced the beeping, a sense of relief overcoming him unlike any he had ever felt. Tears welled in his eyes. He made a single, irrevocable promise to God and whoever else was listening, that from this moment forward his priorities would change. From this moment on, it was all to be different.

"You all right?" John Wayne asked.

"Never better," Daggett answered.

Then he glanced to his right and saw that the plane was no longer there.

45

INEXPLICABLY, AND YET automatically, as Anthony Kort heard the sound of a pager he jerked his head to find its origin. Perhaps it could be attributed to a keen sense of survival. As with a large cat on patrol in the jungle, the slightest unnatural sound caused an immediate state of alert. Whatever the reason, he glanced quickly and then just as quickly away, his bowels going to water and his headache returning as if someone had clipped him. Daggett!

The first thought that occurred to him, since he was in a killing mood, was simply to pull out his weapon and gun the man down. But the two security guards only a few feet away would have to follow Daggett, and then who? It would get messy. Given such a bloodbath, it would be a miracle to make it out of here alive.

His second thought, which came to him late and revealed to him just how personal this had become—since his first thought had concerned Daggett, not the success of the operation—was how the hell Daggett had known to come here. Panic stole into him. Daggett knew he wasn't dead. Daggett knew about David Boote. There was no other explanation. And Daggett was knowingly risking his son's life.

These discoveries filled Kort with such a sense of dread and failure that he nearly gave himself away by failing to watch where he was going. He nearly crossed the security line at the wrong location, a mistake that would have certainly caused him added scrutiny, and might possibly have revealed his fraud.

But if Daggett was here, then Daggett knew. And if Daggett knew, then he would stop the plane, and everything

Kort had worked for was over. An impossible consideration. He pulled himself out of the way of the others and
watched as Daggett continued arguing with the man who
looked like John Wayne, and the TUG cleared out of the
way of the 959 and it began to taxi. Maybe not, he thought,
taking another step toward his freedom. Maybe it was a
perfect world after all.

Then he watched as Daggett looked up and he, too, noticed the plane had begun its taxiing; he watched as Daggett
sprinted to the large plate glass windows and stared out at
the departing plane. Strangely, he could hear the man
thinking; he could hear him trying to figure out how to stop
the plane, and at that very moment Kort found himself
faced with an instinct that had ruled the animal kingdom
since time began: fight or flight. He could stay and attempt
to stop whatever it was Daggett had planned, or he could
take fifteen more steps toward the door and be gone from
here forever.

Another place, another time, his decision would have
been simple, for he would have fled, resolved to return another day, for another operation. But given the unusual circumstances of the collapse of *Der Grund,* the limited nature
of his cash reserves—enough for a year, two at the most—
and, more importantly, the pain in his heart for what his
few short days with Caroline had taught him about what it
was he really wanted from life, he found his feet firmly
planted. This operation had consumed him for the better
part of eighteen months. Everything he had worked for—
the end of EisherWorks, the death of Mosner—came down
to the plane that was now taxiing toward takeoff. The defor-
mity of his child, the loss of his wife and child, would finally be avenged. Five minutes? Ten? And the single largest
act of terrorism on American soil would be burning on the
television sets of a billion people worldwide. For days, even
weeks, the newspapers, radio and television news broad-
casts would speculate on the nature of the once secret meeting, would speculate on the government's funding of chemi-

cal weapons programs. A few more precious minutes before the sweetness of victory.

He couldn't allow anyone, certainly not Daggett, to take that away from him.

46

DAGGETT PULLED OPEN the door. Hot fumes engulfed him.

"You can't go out there," John Wayne hollered. "You need field clearance."

He spotted a car, a discolored and scratched Quik-Link logo on its door panel, just pulling up to his left. It occurred to him there was still a chance to stop this plane. If he could damage the landing gear . . .

He walked at first, because he didn't want to alert the manager too quickly to his intentions. But as he heard "Hey!" barked from behind him, and recalled the two security guards, he realized there was no room for subtlety, and broke into a run.

The keys were in the ignition, which confirmed there was a God, as far as he was concerned, and also confirmed that he was meant to stop this plane at any cost. It was only a matter of removing the fire extinguisher. Such a simple task, and one now so far from possibility. He should have acted sooner, he realized. He should have ignored protocol and headed straight to the plane. This realization flooded him with guilt. If that plane went down, it was his fault.

On the far end of the fuselage, just before the tail and the huge company logo, he could make out *Duhning 959-600*. He could recall from his trip to Seattle and his visit to the Duhning simulators, exactly what it looked like inside the flight deck; he could recall from his late night in the FAA lab, from the voices recorded there, exactly what conversation was now taking place in the plane that lumbered along a hundred yards in front of him. Recollections so vivid, he found it hard to concentrate on his driving.

The car was not exactly long on acceleration. He put his foot into it, and rather than surging ahead, the engine sputtered, flooded, and nearly died. He backed off, allowing it to cough its way back to life and then tried a more gradual approach, to which the car responded quite well. The speedometer marked the increase in speed as the distance to the taxiing plane inexorably shortened. He heard a confusion of car horns dropping down the musical scales as he left them behind him, only to realize too late that these were warnings of his straying off course. The asphalt field was laid out in a complexity of corridors, marked with road paint, delineating traffic lanes for planes, support vehicles, and automobiles. Daggett had stayed from the predesignations, and the wolflike cries of warning came as he found himself a fly beneath the foot of an elephant. The front wheels of a 747 bore down him, fat black rubber so large that they might have flattened him had the pilot not veered at the last possible second, avoiding the collision. Now, added to his confusion, for he had briefly lost sight of the 959, he heard the familiar wailing of a police siren far in the distance, and knew damn well where it was headed.

Suddenly, he found himself surrounded by huge aircraft. Everywhere he swerved, there was another plane in line. This one heading away from him, that one quickly approaching. Their sheer size instilled such a sense of vulnerability that despite the huge amounts of open tarmac, it seemed instead there was nowhere to go. He negotiated himself a position and a path in a narrow no-man's-land created between the wingtips of the crisscrossing traffic, and increased his speed once again. Up ahead, its image distorted by the blurred heat waves escaping the tarmac like a giant plastic curtain, the 959 pivoted on its right tires and crossed an active runway where a commuter plane was just landing. The resulting image, foreshortened by the great distances involved, briefly made it appear the planes would collide, and he wondered if he could be so lucky to have this plane stopped by some unrelated force completely out of his power. But as they cleared each other easily he began to comprehend the enormity of the field, and to realize not only how deceptive it was but how far he had yet to go to reach the 959.

With the sound of the siren still a good distance off, but growing closer, he had to plot a route across not only the taxiing aircraft to his right but also the active runway beyond. He peered beneath the fuselage of a taxiing Boeing, and caught sight of another plane landing, and realized with a good degree of trepidation that the planes were coming one right after another, in intervals of only five or ten seconds. The thought of maneuvering this sluggish car through that gauntlet, gave him pause. Perhaps the answer lay just ahead—he could follow in the path of a jumbo jet as it was cleared to cross.

He accelerated in an attempt to join a crossing already in progress. He saw the other car far too late, his attention to his right, on the taxiing planes, not his left. In that brief, flickering moment of panic when one senses imminent danger, Daggett understood he was about to be hit broadside. He raised his arm defensively to shield his face on impact, and leaned away from the wheel, faintly reminded he had forgotten his seat belt. The blow came with enough force to shatter all the windows in one blinding fraction of a second. His car slid fully sideways a good fifteen yards, right into the path of the taxiing planes. He was thrown, headfirst, against the far door panel, which he literally bounced off of, and after spinning through space, he found himself in the backseat as the car slid to a stop, the frightening smell of fresh gas surrounding him, mixing with the caustic odor of burning tire rubber. The cubed pellets of the broken windows enveloped him like foaming bath water.

Dazed and disoriented, he shook his head in an effort to clear it. Glass flew off him like water from a wet dog. His right arm was numb, as if he'd slept on it. Only then was he capable of accessing what had happened to him. Only then did he look through the open windows of his car, through the open windshield of the other, and find himself face-to-face with Anthony Kort.

47

KORT TOOK THE collision much harder than he had expected. His forehead had glanced off the steering wheel and was bleeding into his left eye. He had hit Daggett's car dead center, and the two had slid, pretty much together, for quite a distance.

The first thing he saw, as the orbs of blue light settled from his vision, was Daggett, in a similarly dazed condition, staring back at him from the rear seat. He reached for his holstered weapon, inside the coveralls, but it wasn't there. He spotted it then, where it had been thrown, on the floor of the passenger seat, and stretched to retrieve it, prevented by his seat belt. Clumsily, he freed himself, took hold of the gun, sat up quickly and aimed.

The second thing he saw, a vision delayed by his murky left eye, was the huge front wheels of a jet as they swerved away from Daggett's car and connected fully with the back fender of his, spinning him around furiously, a full hundred and eighty degrees. His shot rang out vaguely in the direction of the terminal, as the gun once again flew out of his possession and out of sight. The massive underbelly of the jet streamed overhead, his car passing between the twin set of midships landing gear, and miraculously avoiding further contact.

He scrambled out of the car, rolled onto the tarmac as he collapsed from weakened knees, and came to his feet as he saw Daggett crawl over the front seat and slip behind the wheel, and the car begin to roll. At first, it failed to register that a car so badly damaged could possibly run, but run it did. It ran away from him. And he ran after it.

He reached for the back strut of the missing rear window just as the engine caught and the car leapt ahead. His fingers firmly fastened, the acceleration threw him up onto the trunk of the car. He pulled himself up to and through the space of the missing window and tumbled into the backseat. Briefly, he caught the fearful whites of Daggett's eyes as the driver saw he had company. In one swift movement, Kort sat up and locked his right arm around Daggett's throat and drew his arm tightly into a choke hold. Only seconds now, and it would all be over.

48

DAGGETT FELT THE arm clamp around his Adam's apple like a vise, and the voice of some nameless instructor from a dozen years earlier spoke as clearly to him as if he were sitting in the seat next to him. *Within five to seven seconds, the victim loses consciousness.* He slammed on the brakes. The grip continued. He felt the energy drain from him as his brain was denied blood. Darkness loomed at the edges of his vision, a tunnel narrowing, and the entire tarmac, with its endless lines of planes and glowing jet engines, with its puffs of smoke as tires bit the asphalt, and sirens crying like frightened gulls, seemed suddenly caught in a lovely rosy twilight.

His fingers groped for the release lever that controlled the front seat. He knew it was there, just out of reach perhaps, but definitely there. They brushed it once, but did not light. The vise tightened its grip. He leaned forward for the lever, and as he did, increased the pressure on his neck. Unconsciousness beckoned. He touched the lever. As his foot squeezed down on the accelerator, lurching the car forward, he jerked the lever, released the seat, and shoved it back as quickly and as far as it would travel. He heard the man scream as his feet caught beneath the seat, and felt the arm's strength briefly weaken. He reached up, took hold of the man's hand and pulled hard, diminishing the pressure, gasping for air as he tugged once more and spun to break the hold.

Kort released him completely then, as the car drifted out of control, driverless, slowing and wandering out into a lane of incoming aircraft. Daggett made no rational decision; logic or training played no part in his actions. He dove over the seat at the man and went after him like a wild animal. In the limited space of the car, the ability to fight effectively was reduced to a few painless blows, at which point each man responded by going for the other's neck. Daggett was at a complete disadvantage here, his throat already weakened considerably by Kort's choke hold. And it was only as he realized that Kort was strangling him with one hand, while he choked him with two, that an array of tools—wrenches and screwdrivers—was strewn about the floor of the backseat, and that Kort had taken a screwdriver in hand.

He realized this fully as Kort stabbed him between the ribs.

He knocked the man's hand from the tool, leaving it stuck in him, the pain momentarily blocked by some survival switch thrown inside the brain, pinned the man's arm beneath his knee, and found a wrench in his hand. Where that wrench had come from was anybody's guess. It was as if God Himself had handed it to him. As he raised his arm high to deliver the blow of a lifetime—or a *death*time, he was hoping—the intensity of the pain from his wound then found him, both electrifying and numbing. Rather than coming down strongly, as he had intended, the wrench was delivered effectively but not fatally to the front of Anthony Kort's skull.

Breathless, bleeding, and stark raving mad, Daggett looked up to see the 959 at the end of the runway just releasing its brakes for takeoff.

49

DAGGETT REACHED BACK, located the source of his pain, and removed the screwdriver with a single agonizing pull. A scream, born as much of rage as of pain, resounded out across the open expanse of tarmac and, despite the roar of a dozen jets, was heard by two baggage handlers traveling on a TUG outside Terminal A. With the screwdriver removed, the wound bled badly. He started to crawl back over the car seat before realizing the limitation of movement imposed by his injury, and ended up sliding, face first, down into the seat that itself was broken, stuck in its track, nearly in the backseat. A huge jet passed directly over him in a deafening roar as it landed. He glanced to his right in time to see the tires of the 959 begin to roll, confirming his greatest fear: He wasn't going to stop it from taking off.

His reaction was immediate. Sitting forward on the edge of the broken seat, the radiator now steaming, he nursed the car up to its maximum speed, abandoning any pretext for safety, cutting a straight line toward the control tower. He drove directly beneath the planes where necessary, cut others off in their paths, and narrowly missed a direct collision with a single-engine Cessna he hadn't seen until it lifted off the runway, one tire actually bouncing off his roof. As he traveled at over sixty miles an hour toward the tower, the 959 traveled faster toward its takeoff. Again he found himself haunted with the memory of the dry, professional voices as the two pilots negotiated a hundred tons of airplane down a runway and into the skies. Most critical of all was that he note the exact moment the plane's wheels left the tarmac. He racked the rearview mirror (the only surviving piece of glass in the car) to afford him a view of the plane, his shirt sleeve tugged back, the seconds counting off.

With Daggett still thirty yards away from the tower, the plane took off.

He had his driver's door open before he applied the brake. It was only now, as he skidded to a noisy stop by the base door to the tower, that he realized the sirens and the activity he had believed directed at himself were in fact clustered around one of the distant gate entrances to the field. Then, as if to prove him wrong, he heard another siren and saw two flashing lights approaching him at high speed.

He checked his watch: ten seconds gone; thirty-seven remained. He could picture Chaz Meecham's description of the detonator. With the cabin pressure in effect, and the nose pointed up, the timer had begun to count down the flight's final seconds.

The guard, at the bottom of the tower, his weapon drawn, stepped in front of the only door blocking it. "Hold it right there, buddy. Hands out where I can see 'em."

"FBI!" Daggett called out, still limping at a painful run toward the man. Not slowing. His hand fished for his ID and he realized it wasn't where it belonged. Somewhere in the backseat of the car perhaps; misplaced but not lost. The authority in his voice caused the guard a moment's hesitation, allowing Daggett to come another two steps closer. He had no time to debate that authority, or to rummage the car in search of a plastic laminated piece of paper with a color photograph. He *was* FBI. That was all that mattered. He had something less than thirty-seven seconds and only a vague idea of how he might yet prevail.

He pulled up just short of the man and kicked him in the groin with his full momentum behind the blow, simultaneously ducking and blocking the weapon out of harm's way. He pushed the guard aside, jerked the door open, and started climbing stairs. Each time he lifted his left leg, the hole in his ribs felt exactly like Kort had stabbed him there again. He hobbled up the stairs at an amazing pace, hollering out in agony with every other step. As he reached the first landing, his watch telling him twenty-seven seconds, shots rang out from behind him. Whoever had been driving that patrol car was now pursuing him.

One of the bullets hit him.

There was no explaining it. Instead of concentrating on what now seemed like endless steps ascending to the tower, instead of seeing his life pass before his eyes, or hearing his mother's voice, or seeing a vast white room where ghostly white figures welcomed him, he charged up the stairs.

The bullet hadn't slowed him at all. It passed through the flesh of his arm, just below his left armpit. Seventeen seconds. One last flight of stairs. Footsteps nearly on top of him now. They're going to shoot me dead, he was thinking. I've come all this way to be shot dead by my own kind.

And there was Hairless—Agent Henderson—the stump of a gumshoe who had been part of the Bernard arrest signaling for the two guards behind Daggett to hold off their fire. "What the fuck?" he shouted at Daggett, his eyes on the two bloody wounds on his left side.

But Daggett blew past him shouting, "The Quik-Link 959, the Quik-Link 959, who's got it?"

Twelve seconds, his watch pleaded.

"Flight control's got that one . . ." a woman shouted out.

"There's a bomb on board! Patch through to them!" Daggett yelled at the top of his lungs, thinking in terms of police radios, sprinting toward her. He hadn't known exactly what he would do once he reached here, but at the time it had seemed his only chance of getting through to them, the only possibility of communicating, was from this tower. What had Meecham said? A three-way switch, each phase of which had to be working in order for the detonator to blow. Daggett could stop the timer only by closing one of the earlier gates. Think! Think! Not enough time for the plane to level out. "Tell them to decompress the cabin! Decompress the cabin, right now!"

Seven seconds.

How could they remain so calm, these people? In a voice that might have been mistaken for a priest's, the young woman called out in a southern drawl, "Mayday, Alpha-one-five-niner, this is National ground control on an emergency intercept. Explosives on board. Please decompress aircraft immediately. Repeat, blow air packs immediately. Mayday. Mayday."

"Five seconds!" Daggett screamed.

The room had gone as silent as a library, Daggett's breathing and the hum of electronic gear and cooling fans the only sounds. The woman said calmly into her headset microphone, "Emergency intercept, Alpha-one-five-niner . . . confirm loss of cabin pressure. Confirm loss of cabin pressure . . ." She placed a hand firmly to her earset. "Alpha-one-five-niner . . ."

Daggett, watching the seconds expire on his watch said, "Now!" his eyes then straining out the window to see an aircraft that was too far away to be seen.

"Confirm   please,   Alpha-one-five-niner.   Confirm please . . ." Her hand still on the earphone. Every head in the room was turned. It seemed every breath was held. She looked to Daggett and nodded without a hint of expression. "That's affirmative," she said to him. "We've got callback."

It was as if he were a beach ball that had been over-filled with air to the point of bursting. His tremendous sigh of relief washed away the anxiety with a huge expulsion of air that was soon echoed by everyone in the seats around him. "Tell them to level out—they've got to get out of the climb—and get them back here as fast as possible."

She went about the communication in that same flat-toned, monosyllabic southern drawl. Daggett turned around. Henderson's face had gone ash white.

"We found the other detonator," Daggett said.

Henderson nodded. "I kinda guessed that."

50

THEY MET ON that same beach on the Maryland shore where he had first spoken to her. It was early October, and the autumn winds had whipped the green sea into white-caps, winds that warned of a storm from the south, and caused Lynn Greene to raise her collar in defense. She was scheduled to leave the following day, returning to Los Angeles, and this had seemed an appropriate place to both of them.

As they walked, arm in arm, working the very edge of the water, their shoe prints were occasionally swallowed and erased from the sand. Sandpipers, like the Secret Service, hurried ahead of them, staying just beyond reach. There was some freighter traffic in the big shipping lanes far out to sea, and Daggett couldn't help but wonder where each ship was headed and what adventures lay in store. There had been a time in his life when he had wanted to be a sea captain. There had been times in his life when he had wanted to be many different things, but he was what he was; and this was what he had come to tell her.

"Is it okay to say that I don't like it, but I understand?" she asked him.

"It ain't over till it's over," he said.

"Then this will never be over," she replied. "Will it?"

"No, I don't think so."

"We should have made love that night. I've been kicking myself over that."

"I think we did. I've never loved you as much. I know that. We gained new ground that night. You listened. It's a marvelous gift to be able to listen. Something I'm working on."

"I *do* love you, you know."

"Yes, I think I do know."

She broke loose from him and chased the birds, and when she returned to stuff her arm into his, she had glassy eyes, and he wondered if it was the wind. "It gets so damned complicated."

"It does."

"But it seems so simple."

"It is: I have to see this through to the end. It may come tomorrow, it may come in a year's time. It may be that she and I find a way through together, and I owe that to her to try. If it was you . . ."

"I know. I would want the same thing. You're right. I know you're right, but it hurts."

"Yes, it does."

She stopped him. There they were, standing in the exact spot he had been standing when she had so boldly challenged him to come inside.

She withdrew her hand from the pocket of her coat slowly, cautiously, until she had his attention. She spun her hand over, opened up her fingers, and there lay a key. "Just once," she said, looking over at the cabin.

They made a mound of warmth on the bed out of all the blankets, their coats, and two large bath towels she found in the closet. They ended up tangled in the darkness of that cocoon, magically entwined in a perfume of their excitement, hearts pounding through their skin, fingers clenched into a single fist. The explosion of their contained love, was, as Daggett put it, "Something only an explosives expert could understand." But she encouraged further investigation on his part, and so, in the language of their professions, they teased each other until her suggestion of "only once" was long past, and the orange autumnal sun lit the sky a shocking pink.

They were silent on their walk back to the car, although she giggled several times and followed this by squeezing his arm tightly. She finally said, "I suppose that may have to hold us a lifetime."

"It had better," he answered her. "I'm not sure I could live through that again."

51

SIX WEEKS LATER, Anthony Kort sat waiting in a chair at Dulles International Airport. Across from him sat Monique Cheysson. His hands, like hers, were handcuffed; a chain linked his wrists to his shackled ankles. It was first time he had seen her since that day at the airport. She looked worse for wear. They had had separate hearings. He had been told by a guard that she had been caught several days after the bombing, while trying to board a train bound for New York. He had no way of knowing if this was accurate.

His attorney had won him the right to wear civilian clothes instead of the humiliating orange jumpsuit that the federal prosecutor had requested. Monique was dressed in a blue denim dress. He'd seen enough of orange jumpsuits for a long, long time.

The extradition was to Germany, where he was to stand trial for the downing of 1023. His attorney believed that this had come about from a failure by the prosecutor to build a "winnable" case that might get Kort the death penalty. The Feds very badly wanted the death penalty. Now their hopes hung on Germany.

He was surrounded by FBI protection. He recognized one of them, a guy named Levin, who had acted as an assistant to Daggett through many of the interrogations. Today, Levin seemed to be running the show without Daggett. He appreciated the irony of FBI protection.

The reason for all the concern was that Michael Sharpe had escaped prison. A total of four members of *Der Grund* had been freed in a daring helicopter raid on a prison, leaving the European press to speculate that Sharpe and his organization were exceptionally well funded and well connected. There were rumors of a secret "Green Fund" operating out of the Swiss banks, and a cartel of former industrialists who had "gone green." Only two weeks before the break, *60 Minutes* had run a segment on Sharpe's recruiting of criminals and his "crusade of terror." Now his well-organized escape led the press to speculate that Sharpe knew the identity of some or all of the industrialists funding the organization and its operations, and that it had been these people who had freed him.

Recent headlines had focused on Kort, and hopes had been raised that his trial in Germany might bring out some of the missing facts, might widen the already growing international investigation. America loved a good headline.

This was why he wasn't surprised when, looking out at the plane being readied, he recognized the face of one of the food service personnel. His whole body twitched when he saw that face—it was one of Michael's henchmen. Michael had no intention of Kort telling them anything, that much was obvious. He looked over at Monique and he smiled thinly. She stared back at him without expression. He hoped they would sit them next to each other on the flight. He wanted to die alongside of her. With all he had been through, nothing should have surprised him. And yet sight of this man did.

"You all right?" one of his guards asked him.

Kort smiled widely. It had been months since he had felt such a thrill. "Couldn't be better," he said.

52

DAGGETT SAT NERVOUSLY in the hospital waiting room.

Right about now, Kort's plane would be taking off.

He had his priorities set. He had told Pullman a flat no. Levin was handling this for him.

Just beyond a series of sealed doors, doctors were conducting the first exploratory surgery since Duncan had felt warmth in both his feet only ten days before. X rays confirmed that something—perhaps the fall from the bookshelf, two months earlier—had radically moved his third vertebra, and though the resulting progress could not be medically explained, there was a desire on the part of specialists to wire that vertebra in place before it slipped back again. If things looked okay in there, they would be doing that just about now.

She came down the hall toward him, and he stood to greet her. First they kissed, and then they hugged tightly. She had brought them Chinese take-out and she claimed she had not rigged the cookies, although he recognized the print of her typewriter and he doubted there ever had been a fortune that read *Your son will play baseball with you within the year.* It brought tears to his eyes and caused him to spill his coffee, which brought a moment of panic, but both were quickly mopped up.

His pager sounded at his belt. Daggett reached for it. But then he caught himself. Rather than read it, he switched it off and ignored it. Today was not a day for pagers, he reminded himself. That had been the whole point of telling Pullman no. He had not known such happiness in ages. He looked back upon the past few months, the past few years, and thought: I wouldn't do it any other way, even if given the chance. Where previously he had lived under the cloud of despair, now he felt the warm rays of hope. All was not perfect—it was not a perfect world—but given time . . .

GLOSSARY

ATM	Automatic Teller Machine, banking
CAM	Cockpit Area Microphone
CNN	Cable News Network
CVR	Cockpit Voice Recorder
DFDR	Digital Flight Data Recorder
DOJ	Department Of Justice, Sacramento, California
FAA	Federal Aviation Administration
LAFO	Los Angeles Field Office, FBI
LAX	Los Angeles International Airport
O.O.	Office of Origin, FBI—the field office that instigates an investigation
SA	Special Agent, FBI
SAC	Special Agent in Charge—departmental head of an FBI field office
WMFO	Washington Metropolitan Field Office, FBI

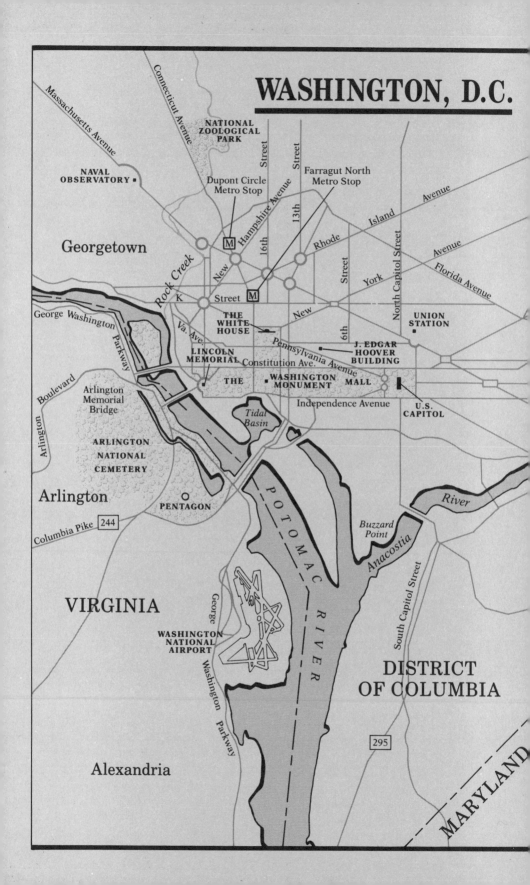

WASHINGTON, D.C.

Massachusetts Avenue

Connecticut Avenue

NATIONAL ZOOLOGICAL PARK

NAVAL OBSERVATORY ▪

Street

Street

13th

Dupont Circle Metro Stop

Farragut North Metro Stop

Avenue

Georgetown

New Hampshire Avenue

16th

Rhode

Island

Avenue

Rock Creek

New

Street

York

Florida Avenue

North Capitol Street

Ⓜ

K

Street

Ⓜ

New

6th

UNION STATION

George Washington Parkway

Va. Ave.

THE WHITE HOUSE

Pennsylvania Avenue

J. EDGAR HOOVER BUILDING

LINCOLN MEMORIAL

Constitution Ave.

Parkway

THE

WASHINGTON MONUMENT

MALL

Boulevard

Arlington Memorial Bridge

Independence Avenue

U.S. CAPITOL

Tidal Basin

Arlington

ARLINGTON NATIONAL CEMETERY

River

Arlington

○ **PENTAGON**

P O T O M A C

Buzzard Point

Anacostia

Columbia Pike 〔244〕

R

South Capitol Street

George

WASHINGTON NATIONAL AIRPORT

I

VIRGINIA

V

E

R

DISTRICT OF COLUMBIA

Washington Parkway

〔295〕

Alexandria

MARYLAND